STORM OF DECEPTION

STORM OF DECEPTION

John T. Lancaster

To order additional copies of this book, contact:
Xlibris Corporation
1-888-795-4274
www.Xlibris.com
Orders@Xlibris.com
82755

CHAPTER 1

Bzzz.

Seth reached over and hit the snooze button to grab another ten minutes of sleep. The night-light shining through from the bathroom hit him in the eyes. "Shit!" Seth rolled over in bed to avoid the night-light from disturbing his precious few extra minutes of sleep. His face came to rest next to the pillow where his now-deceased wife of almost eight months once slept. He couldn't help but remember the smell of her perfume that would linger on her pillow. "Shit," commented an irritated Seth. He was too distracted now to return to sleep. He sat on the edge of the bed and this time turned off the alarm clock. Seth rubbed his face with both of his hands to fully wake up. He had had a restless night of sleep. It was just after five in the morning. He could hear raindrops tapping at the windows and hear small waves breaking on the beach a few hundred yards from his bedroom window. It was a sound he could listen to all day. The house was Seth and Maribeth's dream home. They scrimped for a year until they could find enough money to put a down payment on their dream beach house. They had been in the house only a few years when Maribeth died. The life insurance on Maribeth paid off the mortgage on the house, but Seth had said on numerous occasions to their friends and family that he would gladly give the money back if he could have her back.

As Seth Jarret sat on the edge of his bed, he pondered on the day ahead. He knew he had a long day ahead preparing the house for the imminent storm and the additional work as a result of the storm. Seth was the local chief of police of Surf City, North Carolina. In the past, Maribeth was there to take care of a good deal of the household items in preparation of storms; now he would have to do it alone. Isabelle, a forecasted category 4 hurricane whose width was approximately two hundred miles across and moving at about fifteen miles an hour, was approaching his home and the small island of Topsail, North Carolina, a small barrier island approximately thirty miles north of Wilmington. Isabelle had weighed heavy on Seth's mind, causing him to have a sleepless night.

Once Seth and Maribeth developed roots in Surf City, they became familiar with the National Oceanic and Atmospheric Administration (NOAA) out of necessity because of the periodic hurricanes that would pass their way. They learned how experts categorized hurricanes: first by their wind speed and second by the damage they could expect the hurricane to wreck as it passes through a given area. Isabelle, being a category 4 hurricane, meant "sustained winds of between 131 to 155 miles per hour and damage to be *extensive*." Seth remembered the devastation hurricane Andrew inflicted in South Florida, also a category 4, when it came through. Seth reflected also on the residents of the Gulf Coast who were victims of hurricane Katrina, a category 3 hurricane, when it came ashore. He couldn't help but wonder how many people were still trying to rebuild their lives after hurricane Katrina.

NOAA was predicting hurricane Isabelle to come ashore at approximately midnight. The tropical storms, which sometimes turn into hurricanes, are given alternating male and female names starting with the letter *A*. Each hurricane season runs from June 1 to November 30. Isabelle was to be the ninth tropical storm of the year. North Carolina had been spared during the months of June, July, and August, but now in late September, hurricane Isabelle was looming large on the front lines as the year's worst storm. Isabelle spawned off the coast of Africa and built her strength from the warm waters of the Atlantic Ocean. Residents throughout the southeast keep a watchful eye on storms developing off the west coast of Africa. As these storms make their way across the Atlantic, the residents of the southeast hope the storms never fully develop or are pushed off into the cooler waters of the north Atlantic where they go to die.

Seth, despite the daunting task of preparing his town for the possible landing of Isabelle, reminded himself that at least it was happening in September versus over the late spring and summer. In late spring and summer, the population swells to approximately 7,500 to 10,000 as a result of the beach comers and tourists. Now that is was officially fall, the population of Surf City had shrunk back to its population of 1,500 local residents. He also had to be on the alert for the typical thrill seekers trying to get onto the island to ride out the hurricane and surfers looking to catch the "ultimate ride" on waves provided compliments by hurricane Isabelle.

Seth appraised himself in the mirror before he started to shave. He was forty-two years of age. Exercise throughout his life kept him in better shape than many of his peers. As he began to shave, his thoughts drifted back over his life and focused on his wife as they often did. In college, he played rugby for Plymouth State College, a small college in New Hampshire. After college, he continued to play rugby while he was in the marine corps. He quit playing after he got out of the service and joined the Charlotte Police Department.

Maribeth's true passion was art. She grew up in the Cleveland area painting city scenes and Lake Eire. When Maribeth turned eighteen, she and a fellow artist moved to Asheville, North Carolina, to pursue their art careers. They took jobs waiting tables at night and painted mountain vistas, old homes in Asheville, or some of the nearby small farms during the day. After several years living in Asheville, Maribeth and her friend went to Charlotte to meet some old friends that also moved down from the Cleveland area. While the two were in Charlotte, they went to a small party where Maribeth met Seth. Less than a year later, they got married in Asheville, but Maribeth agreed to move to Charlotte where Seth worked as a police officer.

Some years after Seth and Maribeth were married, Seth was in a shoot-out. The shoot-out was the result of a failed armed robbery of a Charlotte bank while he was on duty. After the shoot-out in Charlotte, Maribeth begged Seth to find a less life-threatening job despite surviving the event without a scratch. A friend heard that Surf City was looking for a new chief of police and recommended Seth to apply for the job. Seth applied for the job. A couple of the Surf City deputies also applied for the job as well, but the board thought that Seth's experience on the larger Charlotte Police Department and his military background would add some experience the department sorely lacked.

Living in Surf City was quiet and relaxing. In the off-season, the town was dramatically reduced in size, and as a result, the year-round locals knew one another if nothing else but by sight. Crime was almost nonexistent during the fall and winter. In the spring and summer, police calls were usually the result of too much alcohol combined with too much sun. Although Maribeth enjoyed life in Charlotte, she reacclimated herself to a more subdued lifestyle in Surf City. Although she worked part-time as an office manager in a real estate office, her primary enjoyment was painting beach scenes. They enjoyed the beach and the friends they made on the island.

Most of their friends were in law enforcement or the fire department in Surf City, Holly Ridge, and Pender County. In January, they went to some friend's house in Holly Ridge, a small town about ten miles inland from Surf City, for a Super Bowl party. On their way home from the party, a young man ran a stop sign and broadsided them on Maribeth's side of the car. She survived the accident for nearly three days before passing away early one morning at a hospital in Wilmington, North Carolina. Seth was devastated about losing his wife of some eight years. He spent the next couple of months rediscovering himself before returning to his duties as chief of police. He was periodically tearing up at anything that reminded him of Maribeth, like the smell of her perfume on her pillow.

Seth let Argo, the black-and-white springer spaniel, out to do her mornings chores. Seth and Maribeth had gotten Argo to keep Maribeth company while Seth did his evening patrols. Though Argo was Maribeth's dog, Seth was delegated on the morning rituals of taking the dog out and feeding her every morning. Seth found that he enjoyed getting up early to take Argo out for her early-morning chores. He found it peaceful and often used the time to collect his thoughts or just let life pass as he cleared his mind. Often he would end up sitting on the deck of the house overlooking the ocean with a cup of coffee and watch beach comers pass by while he read the morning newspaper. On his way in from taking Argo out, he made sure to leave the drapes open so he could watch as the morning sun came up over the horizon. Argo was right on Seth's heels as they entered the house. Seth grabbed a breakfast bar from the cupboard and started the coffee machine on his way to the shower.

Seth needed to pack the van he rented the day before with some of his and Maribeth's personal effects and drive inland to Burgaw. The drive would take him at least a half hour each way. Seth packed up much of their belongings the night before. While he had packed, he had reevaluated the importance of each item. Things that he and Maribeth once felt were precious or had sentimental value seemed to lose some of their luster while other things found new meaning for him since her passing. When Seth and Maribeth first moved to the island, they packed up almost all their belongings when they heard a hurricane threatened the island. Since that time, they decided to concentrate only on those items that had the most sentimental value or were valuable, everything else they figured insurance could replace. Seth looked over the boxes he packed the night before and realized he packed more than he and Maribeth had packed in years. Seth laughed at himself for getting so sentimental. He decided this time he would go ahead and pack everything, and after the storm, he would reassess what he had done. He would need to limit the amount of things he packed in the future. He continued about his business preparing for the impending hurricane. Burgaw, the county seat of Pender County where Surf City is located, is approximately twenty miles inland. Seth was going to leave the precious belongings with Burt and Jeanine Warner. They were some friends that Seth and Maribeth became close to through Seth's job as the chief of the Surf City Police Department. Burt is a deputy with the Pender County Sheriff's Department. He was at the party the night Maribeth was killed. Burt is a burly man close to Seth's age. Jeanine, like Maribeth, was a couple of years younger than her husband. Neither couple had had any children, which was another thing the two couples felt they had in common.

The rain stopped while Seth was in the shower. As Seth finished dressing, he could see the sun rising from the windows of his bedroom. The sky was giving way to a beautiful sunny day. Once hurricane Isabelle began her final ominous move toward Surf City, the rain would reappear in mass, along with powerful winds, including tornados, and an uncontrollable ocean demanding to invade the small barrier island.

Seth began the painstaking process of "boarding up the house" that is a common practice for the islanders. This involves placing plywood over the windows and doors to protect the house from the high winds and flying debris. The previous homeowners had cut all the boards Seth used to cover the windows and doors, making his task somewhat easier. He made a mental note to consider buying more modern hurricane shutters after the storm. It would be even easier to have the type that simply rolled down over the windows and doors. As Seth boarded up the house, he remembered fondly their move to the quiet town of Surf City. They lived in a small one-bedroom house just off the island. They lived as cheaply as they could until they accumulated enough money as a down payment on their dream home, an ocean-front beach house. The house was not ornate. It was simple, but it was on the ocean, and it was theirs, now Seth's.

After Seth boarded up the windows, he loaded the boxes he packed the night before into a rented van. He had taken his police Ford Bronco over to some friends' house the previous day since he planned on storing his precious belongings at their house. This was the third time that Seth had packed for a hurricane since he and Maribeth moved to the island. The previous two times, Maribeth did the packing of their precious household possessions while Seth was relegated to taking care of the outside preparation. Once inland and out of harm's way, Maribeth would spend the rest of the time worrying about Seth who always had to stay behind because of his position as chief of police and the added worry of waiting to find out if she would even have a house to return to. This was the first time Seth had to manage everything on his own.

Seth put the ladder and outdoor furniture in the storage room under the house. He looked up at the pilings of his home. Seth hoped that the storm water would indeed go under his home, versus through his home, as designed to do. Most of the homes on the island are built on pilings that too many visitors reminded them of homes on stilts.

As Seth finished preparing the house for the approaching hurricane, he could see his neighbors doing many of the same things. The mood among the homeowners was solemn instead of the usual lighthearted cajoling. Neighbors were helping neighbors, but the air seemed tense. Maybe it was the size of the hurricane that was hindering the camaraderie among the neighbors. Other homeowners that Seth typically saw only in the summer months were there too to protect their investments. He also noticed many of the local handymen hired by people too far away to make the journey back to the island, boarding up homes and moving outdoor furniture safely indoors.

It was almost noon when Seth looked down at his watch. "Damn," Seth said aloud. He still needed to stop by the bank and pick up some money before heading onto Burgaw. He knew he had to stop by the bank; there was no telling how long the banks would be closed if the hurricane hit the tiny island. Federal regulators mandated that banks would be closed no more than three days, but after a hurricane, especially the size of a category 4, all bets were off as to when they could reopen locally. If the island were closed to the general public, it would not matter if they were open or closed, but Seth never wanted to be without cash, especially after a hurricane. With the power out, cash is king in a hurricane-stricken area. He also wanted to fill up the van and his Surf City police car and also several five-gallon containers for police-emergency use only for fear that the gas stations could be closed for some time after the hurricane. In the past, once power was lost, the pumps at the service stations would not work. Sometimes it took several days before the power could be restored. Seth paused with his thoughts. It hadn't been all that long ago when he was telling Maribeth to go to the bank and fill up with gas when they prepared for the last hurricane they last went through together. Seth always looked out for Maribeth after they were married, much like her father once did before they got married.

When Seth finished loading everything into the van, he made one last walk-through the house before securing it as best he could. He knelt down to Argo and promised to return before the storm arrived. Seth ran to the bank to get some money and then to the service station to get gas. He started his short drive to Burgaw. As he left the island, he noticed much of the traffic heading to the beach. Several of the people headed down were driving trucks, vans, or SUVs loaded with boards to protect the homes. Some pulled utility trailers behind their cars and trucks; Seth assumed it was to bring back as much as possible from their homes. Seth noticed each little town that he passed through grew congested with the unusually higher volume of traffic as people prepared for the worst. Many of the locals learned from previous experiences that you could never plan enough.

Eventually Seth arrived at Burt and Jeanine Warner's home. It was just before Seth got into Burgaw on the outskirts of town. The house was a small two-bedroom house next to some farmland. Jeanine's parents owned the adjacent farmland. When Jeanine was growing up, she used to work on the small farm. They grew tobacco, soybean, and corn. This time of year, the land was plowed under for the winter. After Jeanine and Burt were married, Jeanine's father gave them the house and some land adjacent to the farm. The land wasn't much, just enough that she could have a garden with a little patch left over. Jeanine often would joke with her friends that it was her dowry.

Seth drove the van down the short gravel driveway. As Seth came to a stop, he saw Jeanine coming out of the house with her dog Barney, a mixed breed of unknown origins. "Where's Burt?" called Seth from the window as he pulled the van around behind an old wooden shed.

"I can't believe you're asking me a question like that," responded Jeanine. "Just like you, he has police shit he's gotta get done. I'm sure he's directing traffic or something police related to get ready for this damn storm that's coming."

Seth liked the way Jeanine got directly to the heart of the matter. She never minced words. He also knew she was never short on the expletives. He gave her the customary hug. "Yeh . . . I've gotta to get back to town to do the same police shit." He gave her a big grin as he said "police shit."

Jeanine knew Seth was giving her a hard time. It was a teasing that went on regularly between the four of them, Jeanine, Maribeth, Burt, and Seth. It was something that she missed since Maribeth died. Jeanine started to tear up when she saw Seth staring at her. She was remembering the fond times they shared together.

"Now we can't have any of that now," commented Seth. "Next thing ya know and we'll both be sobbing."

Jeanine noticed Seth wiping the tear from his eye. She ignored the opportunity to tease him. Even though it had been several months, it had been hard on the both of them. "I know, I know. I just can't help it." Jeanine wiped the tears from her eyes. "You want to come in for a glass of tea or anything?"

"Thanks, but I've gotta get back to town," replied Seth. "The traffic is getting backed up, and if I don't leave now, I may never get back." Jeanine followed Seth over to his Surf City police car, a Ford Bronco, that Burt helped him bring over the previous day. "Tell Burt to give me a call tonight and let me know how things are going. You take care of yourself too." Seth gave Jeanine another long hung, and then he held back and gave her a stern look in the face as if he were her big brother making a point. "You and Barney need to stay at your parents' house tonight if Burt doesn't make it back before dark. Hell . . . even if Burt makes it back, all of you need to stay with your parents. They need you as much as you need them during this kind of a hurricane."

Jeanine threw her arms around Seth's neck and gave him a big kiss on the cheek. She let go and stood in front of him. She wiped tears that were streaming down her face. "You take care of yourself too and give Argo a hug for me." Jeanine reached up and wiped her lipstick off Seth's cheek.

"You know it," replied a confident Seth. Seth climbed into his Bronco and rolled down the window. "I'll give you a call tomorrow. Don't worry . . . I'll be all right." Seth backed out of the driveway and started heading back to Surf City. He noticed Jeanine still in the driveway waving and wiping tears from her eyes. Seth reached over and turned on the radio. He wanted to listen to some music for the drive back and try and take his mind off seeing Jeanine. Just seeing her brought back too many memories of Maribeth and the good times they all shared. Seth was trying to move forward with his life, and now he was feeling the hurt all over again. He began to look forward to a few busy days compliments of hurricane Isabelle just to take his mind off what he was feeling.

Seth's mind drifted from the good times he and Maribeth had to the more immediate police matters. He barely noticed people heading in the opposite direction with their trucks, vans, and trailers loaded down with their personal effects. There was a steady stream of traffic on the narrow two-lane road leading away from the coast. Seth noticed the leaves on the trees starting to change colors complemented by the dark green pine trees. Just as Seth reached the edge of town, he noticed that the bridge was closed to allow boaters traveling north and south along the Intracoastal Waterway to pass. He assumed they were looking for a safe place to store their boats during the hurricane. Seth sat in his car and took a moment to watch the boaters making their way along the Intracoastal Waterway. Off in the distance, Seth noticed some waterfowl in some of the saltwater marsh. He couldn't help but sense their vulnerability with the approaching hurricane. Seth's mind came back into focus when he noticed the cars start to move ahead of him. He put the car into gear and headed onto the island.

Once Seth arrived in Surf City, he felt his strength rejuvenated from the drive. The time he spent on the drive home helped him regenerate his batteries for the long evening ahead. As the local sheriff, Seth was bound to the town for the duration of the hurricane and into the next morning or possibly the next several days. All five of the town's deputies were also to report indefinitely once their families were evacuated and their homes were prepared for the worst. Seth had an uneasy feeling in the pit of his stomach about hurricane Isabelle, which seemed to mirror the sentiment of many of the town's people once they heard Isabelle was headed in their direction. Though he was living in Charlotte at the time, he had heard about hurricane Fran from the islanders. It was one of the worst hurricanes to hit the island, and it was still fresh on the mind of many of the island residents. Fran hit the island in 1996. The ocean came across the narrow island in various places. Several homes on the island had been reduced to little more than piles of timber at a beach party. The island was closed to everyone, including the evacuated residents, until the National Guard could help secure the island to prevent looting and hazards could be neutralized.

When Seth arrived at the police station, he was happy to see four of his five deputies already there. Ned Willard, his somewhat-of-a-maverick assistant sheriff who always ran late, was nowhere to be seen. Seth parked his patrol car and entered the station house. "All right, gentlemen, we've gotta start making our rounds. I want you to have your lights flashing and sirens blaring. Get on the bullhorn and start making the announcement that everyone is to evacuate the island by 2100 hours—no exceptions!" When Seth was through, three of the deputies made their way to their respective patrol cars. The last deputy got on the telephone with the state police to monitor inland traffic. The plan was to help direct the last of the islanders leaving the island to avoid traffic jams while making their way to safety inland. Ned pulled up as the last patrol car pulled away.

"Ned, glad to see you could make it," commented Seth.

"Sorry, Chief, couldn't get the wife out the door." Ned's wife, Sarah, was a rather large woman who was not particularly motivated. Often Ned ended up running errands and straightening up around the house due to Sarah's slovenly nature. When Sarah did work, she worked as a part-time dispatcher and the town's tourist coordinator. Ned, however, was very conscientious despite chronically running late. "What do you need me to do?"

"We need to go over our plans to make sure everyone is evacuated and that traffic keeps moving off the island. It's getting late in the day, and traffic seems to be a little bogged down. We also need to coordinate our plans with Topsail Beach and North Onslow police departments to secure the island if this thing hits us." The only other townships on the small island were Topsail Beach, about five miles south of Surf City, and North Onslow that was about ten miles north. "Ned . . . I need for you to monitor the traffic around the bridge to make sure it keeps moving and no one is coming on the island without a damn good reason. I also need for you to follow up with the deputies making their round with the local businesses and make sure they're closed. Have someone run by the local bars and make sure they're closing down. You know there are those who keep holding out for that one more drink at the bar. Also, have someone take a drive along the beach and run off any stragglers, especially the surfers."

Ned responded, "You got it, Chief." Ned called to the lone deputy who was hanging up the telephone, "Come on, Jack, we've got work to do." He also called to one of the other deputies over the police station's base radio, "After your rounds, Sam, check on our supplies. Make sure we have plenty of water, food, flashlights, and batteries. If you see we're low on anything, go by the store before it closes and pick up whatever you think we're gonna need. We're gonna be here tonight, and I don't want to run short on anything!"

Seth smiled to himself as he listened to Ned direct the other deputy about checking on the supplies. Seth had been in a few mild hurricanes but realized he could not remember everything. He was glad to have Ned follow up behind him when it came to hurricane preparedness. Ned had been in several hurricanes. For him, preparing for the hurricane had become almost an afterthought. Ned was one of the Surf City deputies that applied for the chief of police position when Seth did. When Seth took over as the chief of police, he thought that there might have been some conflict between them. It wasn't long after Seth arrived when Ned came to Seth and said how glad he was that Seth got the job as chief and that he had learned a lot from Seth in the short time he had been there. After that, Seth found he was more relaxed and felt he could rely on Ned without repercussions.

Seth went into his office and closed the door behind him. He made a conference call to Topsail Beach and North Onslow police departments to coordinate their respective efforts should Isabelle come ashore. Plans included preventing access to the island until all hazards were neutralized, protecting against looting, and bouncing ideas off one another, trying to cover anything the others may have forgotten. Each of the police departments created their own checklist for hurricane preparation. Each year the lists got longer as a result of local changes and the experience the police departments gained with each passing storm. There were only two bridges onto the island, one at North Onslow and one in Surf City. Determined looters, through their own experience, found it convenient to bring their boats up to the local docks along the Intracoastal Waterway where they couldn't be seen and loot the nearby homes. All three police departments acquired boats after hurricane Fran to help prevent future looting and help the Coast Guard by policing the local waterways year-round on the island. The police departments stored the boats during the hurricane, but once the storm passed, they could easily access them for patrol purposes. The police departments found that having the boats was also a way to help stranded boaters around the island, rescue swimmers, and police for boaters who were under the influence. With the local police having their own boats, the demands on the nearby United States Coast Guard was dramatically reduced, allowing them to address higher-priority concerns.

As the day wore on, more and more of the islanders packed their cars, vans, or trucks and began leaving the island. Many had already left while Seth was returning from Burgaw. Several of the property owners that did not live on the island year-round had also already come and gone after they secured their vacation homes for Isabelle. With the homes and businesses slowly being evacuated and the windows being boarded up, Surf City began to take on the look of an abandoned fishing village. The only signs of life were the traffic crossing the town's lone bridge leading to the mainland. An eerie feeling came over Seth as he drove around the nearly deserted town. The local weathermen on the radio painted doom for everything in Isabelle's path, which added to the eerie feeling. Seth saw Ned directing the deputies, and occasionally he listened to him over the police radio. He had them directing traffic and occasionally going door-to-door to make sure everyone was leaving if he happened to see a light still on in a home or business. The police officers started at the south end of the town and made their way to the north end of the town.

Seth ran into Hugh Dugen when he went back by his house to pick up Argo. Hugh is a young lieutenant stationed at Camp LeJeune, the nearby marine corps base. Camp LeJeune's claim is that it is "the largest amphibious training base in the world." Seth climbed out of his Ford Bronco and called out to Hugh, who was on the deck of his house, "Hugh, better get a move on."

"I'm going as fast as I can. Just about ready to send the little lady on her way," Hugh shouted back. The "little lady" was Mary Dugen, Hugh's now-three-months-pregnant wife. They had gotten married once they found out Mary was pregnant. They lived together for three years on the island before getting married. They were neighbors of Seth and Maribeth. When Maribeth died, Mary would periodically invite Seth over for dinner or bake him something that he could warm up in the microwave to eat for a couple of days at a time. She didn't stop until Seth begged her to do so. He appreciated her kindness, but felt he needed to start moving on with his life. Seth felt that by starting to make his own meals, he had crossed one of the many hurdles he needed to cross as part of the process of getting over Maribeth. Hugh and Mary moved to Topsail Island a couple of months before Seth became chief of police. The four of them had gone out a few times into Wilmington, the largest city in the area, for dinner and sometimes a movie. Hugh was six feet four inches and weighed two hundred and forty-five pounds. It was not uncommon to see Hugh out running in the mornings or in the evenings. He would run about five miles a day and then lift weights in one of the rooms of his house, which he had converted into a weight room. Mary was a petite five-foot-tall woman who weighed a little over one hundred pounds prior to her pregnancy.

"Aren't you going with her?" "No . . . I've got duty tonight." For Hugh, duty meant working with the military police at Camp LeJeune. For Hugh and Seth, the police work and their military background was a common link. Often the two would share a beer with each other and exchange a police or military story while taking in the ocean vistas from either of the decks of their home that overlooked the ocean, with one always trying to outdo the other with one of their police or military stories. "I've got reservations for Mary in Clinton." Clinton is another small town about an hour inland from Topsail Island. "She should be safe there."

"Sounds like you've got things under control."

"I tried to find her a place in Burgaw, but all the hotels and motels were already booked. Clinton was the closest thing I could find inland."

Both men had heard stories from the locals of how hurricane Fran came ashore on Topsail Island and then moved inland as far as Raleigh, which is about two hours inland from Topsail Island, before burning out. Along the way Fran caused flooding, uprooted trees, and destroyed homes.

Seth made some more idle conversation and then said his good-byes. He went into the house and picked up Argo. He took her down to the Ford Bronco where he placed her on his seat and then patted her on the bottom to move over to the passenger's seat. He loved to take Argo along on his police rounds if the weather wasn't too hot. He enjoyed the company, and Argo enjoyed the local townsfolk's attention. Seth continued to make his rounds hurrying people along and helping wherever he felt he was needed.

As Seth made his rounds, he found himself occasionally loading boxes into trucks and vans for many of the local residents. He felt that the small-town persona should not be missed especially in times of trouble. He frequently encouraged his deputies to do the same. As the day wore on, the sky gave way to dark threatening clouds, and the rain from earlier in the day returned. The winds began to pick up. The rain whipped across Seth's windshield, and the wind rocked the Ford Bronco as Seth drove around the small town. Seth got the distinct feeling that they were going to feel nature's wrath over the long-anticipated night ahead of them.

Seth listened to one of the local Wilmington radio stations so he could monitor the progress of hurricane Isabelle. The reports indicated that Topsail Island stood one of the highest probabilities for a direct hit by this category 4 hurricane. Seth had heard all this before. He knew that predictions were just that—predictions. He also knew that though the prediction indicated that Topsail Island stood one of the highest probabilities, one hundred miles in either direction was equally possible. With a category 4 hurricane approaching, it was best to be prepared for anything no matter what the probability. He was not going to take any chances. Everyone, except emergency personnel, would be off the island if he had anything to say about it!

As nine o'clock in the evening approached, the once small beach and fishing town had become the long-awaited ghost town Seth hoped for. Seth and his deputies made their final rounds in search of the determined souls who were refusing to leave. The deputies went door-to-door for the final round. Each time the deputies discovered someone in their home, a deputy would escort them to the town's lone bridge leading off the small island. A deputy was posted at the bridge to keep anyone from coming on to the island. Just after ten o'clock, Seth had the bridge tender adjust the swinging bridge to prevent further access to the island. He knew that closer to the time that Isabelle was to hit Topsail Island, he would need to adjust the bridge back to its normal position to allow entry and exiting for emergency purposes. He also knew that he would have to leave the bridge unattended during the hurricane but felt that he had created the deterrent he needed in the meantime. By temporarily adjusting the bridge to make it impassable, Seth no longer needed to station a deputy at the bridge. Seth had learned through his short tenure as police chief how to get the most out of a police department with limited resources.

Seth called Jeanine at her parents when he realized that Burt never called him. Jeanine answered the telephone on the first ring. Seth sensed something wasn't right when he heard the concern in her voice. "Jeanine, is Burt there? He hasn't called."

"No, he hasn't, and I'm worried."

Seth could hear the tension mounting in Jeanine's voice. He could tell she was fighting back tears. "Calm down, Jeanine. Let me see if I can track him down. I'll call you back or have him give you a call." Seth contacted the Pender County Sheriff's Department. He talked to several acquaintances he made through Burt. Before long he had Burt on the phone.

"What's up, Seth," asked Burt?

"I've been talking with your wife. She's upset that you're not home and haven't called," answered Seth.

Burt looked down at his watch. "Shit! I've been so busy I didn't realize what time it is. I was supposed to be home a couple hours ago." He was upset with himself for not calling Jeanine.

"I guess I can count on you to call and/or go home," Seth sarcastically commented.

"Yeh. Let me give you a call tomorrow," responded Burt.

"Thanks. I'll talk with you tomorrow. Good luck!"

"Good luck to you to!" answered Burt.

No sooner had Seth said good-bye to Burt and he was out the door. Seth got on the radio to his deputies. The weather was deteriorating quickly. It was just after eleven at night. The sky was darker than usual with the added cloud cover from the hurricane blocking out the stars and moon. "Once you make your final rounds, I want everyone back to the station in thirty minutes or less!" Seth rode around looking for signs of anyone lingering. He left Argo at the station hiding under his desk. Argo's canine instincts were in high gear. She wanted no part of what was in store for the island. He saw his deputies making their final rounds. They were fending off the wind and the rain as they knocked on doors and looked in windows wherever they saw lights from inside the homes. Seth's thoughts drifted back to the last hurricane he and Maribeth went through. She was in Burgaw then with Jeanine and Burt; he was stuck in Surf City bound by his police duties. He wished she was there now waiting for him to call her. An angry conversation with Maribeth because of a late call from him would have been welcomed right now. Instead, Maribeth was dead, and he was waiting for Isabelle to seek her wrath on Surf City and Topsail Island with all her might. He felt alone in the world. Just then rain whipped across his windshield and sent a stop sign careening into the side of his Ford Bronco, bringing him back from his distant thoughts. "Shit!" exclaimed Seth. The wind was shaking the town's few stoplights, and the other traffic signs were swaying back and forth with each gust of wind. Debris was being swept sporadically in all directions. He noticed many of the local business structures barely withstanding the early winds from hurricane Isabelle's outer bands. Seth thought to himself, *God, I hope this thing misses us!*

By eleven thirty, Seth and the deputies had completed last-minute items and settled in at the police station for the long night ahead of them. They were huddled around a television located in the police station's small break room. The windows were covered, adding an unusual darkness to the station house. They were watching the hurricane developments from WECT. They placed a few battery-powered radios, flashlights, and lanterns at the ready for when the power went out. The power always went out when a hurricane came through. WECT, the nearby Wilmington television station, was announcing that the National Weather Center was predicting that the eye of the hurricane was to come ashore at about 2:00 a.m. near Cape Fear, a small town just south of Wilmington. Everyone knew that most often the greatest storm surge was north of the hurricane's eye. The storm was already beating at the police station's roof. To the men inside, it sounded as if the roof was going to peel off at any minute. They could already hear debris hitting the sides of the building with a tremendous amount of force. Metal hurricane shutters covered the windows, so the men couldn't see out, but more importantly, so that nothing could get blown through the glass windows. Periodically, the men would be startled when a loud thud would hit the metal shutters or the side of the building. The men would give one another a fearful look and then try to act disinterested. It was almost one thirty when the power finally died. The telephones had been out for a couple of hours already. Cell telephones were the only source of communication with the exception of the station's police radio, but that was reserved for emergency purposes. The men would be in the dark for the rest of the night. Cots were set up in the main area of the police station, but no one was interested in sleeping. For some, it was fear, and for others, it was a sense that they needed to be prepared for the worst. The coffee in the coffeepot was cold and without power there was no way to warm it. The men snacked on sandwiches supplied by a local delicatessen and some cold sodas from a cooler Ned packed when he went home for dinner. There were also some apples and stale donuts to snack on as they waited for the worst of the hurricane to pass.

Argo sought Seth out and lay at his feet. Seth regularly petted the frightened dog, trying to offer some comfort.

Hurricane Isabelle came ashore at Cape Fear as the National Weather Center predicted. Sustained winds were reported in various locations in the 150-miles-per-hour range. The damage inflicted from Isabelle was mounting from the powerful winds, and the fact was that she was moving painfully slow, at about 15 miles per hour. Reports were coming in that rooftops were being peeled off and tossed aside as if someone was peeling a ripe orange. Several beach houses that were once on pilings were now piles of lumber awaiting a match for a bonfire while other beach houses were washed out to sea. There were reports that the ocean had cut swaths across Carolina Beach, Wrightsville Beach, and Figure Eight Island, all points north of the eye of hurricane Isabelle and just south of Topsail Island. Rain was covering points from Charleston, South Carolina, to Nags Head, North Carolina. Tornados as a result of hurricane Isabelle were reported in Brunswick, New Hanover, Pender, and Onslow counties. The National Weather Center's prediction of a category 4 hurricane had painfully become a reality.

Seth and the police officers sat by the radio listening to a Wilmington radio station providing constant updates. People were calling into the radio station from their cell phones to give individual accounts of their experiences as a result of hurricane Isabelle. Often as they spoke, they would end up screaming aloud as a gust of wind tore through their homes, startling them further. A lone propane lantern provided the only light in the station house. Seth could see the concern on each of his deputy's faces. He hoped that his own face had not given the men any hints of his own fear. He felt he needed to be strong for them. Though most of the men had been in at least one hurricane, they could never overcome the fear within them. What would happen to them there on the tiny island? Were their families safe? Would they have a home to return to? Would the police station survive the storm?

When the winds began to die down, Seth decided to take action. He sent his police officers out in teams of two for fifteen-minute trips to survey the situation. They watched for anyone that somehow remained on the island and was now caught in the hurricane's perilous elements. There were stories on the island from past hurricanes where people broke into neighboring homes seeking refuge after their own home had collapsed due to the ocean's storm surge or their home was peeled apart from a tornado spawned from a hurricane. Others had had their home washed out to sea from the storm surge, and often the residents themselves were gone, never to be found. One team would go north and the other team to the south. They were to stay in continuous contact with the station on the patrol car's radio. Seth claimed he wanted to hear every detail, but he knew it was his way of making sure they were all right. He often held his breath as the deputies occasionally screamed over the radio followed by a temporary silence when flying debris nearly hit their patrol cars, or they caught sight of a home collapsing from the high winds or storm surge. Though Topsail Island was not directly in the hurricane's path, it still was receiving a significant portion of rain and wind from the feeder bands that comprised much of the hurricane's outlying parameter. They also heard reports of tornados touching down in nearby Holly Ridge and Hampstead from the local police departments or residents calling in their own accounts of the storm. The men would look at one another in grave fear since many of the Holly Ridge and Hampstead police deputies were friends or relatives of Seth's deputies.

CHAPTER 2

As midnight approached, Juan Mendoza gathered his men together in the house to give them final instructions for the evening. The instructions related to their pilfering weapons from Camp LeJeune, a marine corps installation. The installation was chosen from the remaining military installations because the men considered it to have the most exit points once they acquired their armaments.

Juan also brought the men together to determine if they individually or collectively had reservations about going forward with the mission. His only fear was that there would be a stampede of the men electing to back out. It was a risk he was willing to take. He did not want his men moving forward into a night filled with so much risk without the same enthusiasm with which they began the mission in Miami. Juan was surprised to receive a unanimous consent to go forward. Several of the men expressed their anxiety about returning to their families in Miami without being able to complete their mission. They were not about to let any kind of a hurricane stand in their way on completing their mission as scheduled. Some in Juan's company actually felt that the hurricane provided the necessary distraction to make their mission a success. Antonio Mendoza was the last to express himself, "I could not live with myself if I allowed a hurricane to stand in the way of helping my brethren who have given their lives in Castro's prisons or perished in the Florida Straits in order to break free of his iron hand."

After Antonio spoke, a chilling silence hung in the air. Each man looked at one another, one man gaining strength from the next on what they were about to do. Juan let Antonio's powerful words sink in before he spoke. "Those are powerful words, Antonio." Juan paused again, "All right, men, let's make it happen!"

The house Juan and his men had chosen was based on its remote location. Juan and some sympathizers in North Carolina found the house on one of Juan's many reconnaissance trips to the area. After they found the house, they did a great deal of research on who owned the home and determined the owner's habits. Other homes were chosen as a backup plan, but Juan wanted the house that they ultimately decided to use because it met all their needs. Once it became apparent that the house was a weekend retreat for the owners, arrangements were put into action. Juan had some sympathizers tap the homeowner's telephones and had someone move in near the owner's principal residence to keep track of their every movement. They didn't want any surprises!

When their mission was complete, they would return to the house to spend the night before returning to Miami. Juan Mendoza was a Cuban American and the designated leader of the seven men in his company. They were on a special mission for an organization known as the Cubans for a Free Cuba. Juan joined the Cubans for a Free Cuba after graduating from high school in Miami. Cubans for a Free Cuba was an organization organized initially to liberate Cuba from Fidel Castro. Since its inception, the organization found itself providing needed assistance to the Cuban American population in Miami and throughout the United States and Latin America by finding jobs, offering financial assistance, etc., for Cuban refugees or displaced Cuban Americans. The organization lobbies frequently on Capitol Hill to promote legislation to foster its interests as well as seeking financial assistance for Cubans arriving in the United States via the Florida Straits, the barrier separating Key West from Cuba.

Juan's father, Miguel, had hoped Juan would go on to college, something he was never allowed to do in Cuba as a Cuban national. Miguel had grown increasingly proud of his son as he moved up rapidly in the Cubans for a Free Cuba organization. Juan's father left Cuba shortly after Juan was born. The only memories of Cuba for Juan were the stories told to him by his father. Miguel had been moderately successful in Cuba as a landlord of some commercial property. He rented office space to local family-owned businesses in downtown Havana. He owned six buildings that he rented to small entrepreneurships. Miguel often reminisced about the decadent years when Fulgencio Batista was president of Cuba. Movie stars and mafia bosses would come to Cuba and spend bundles of money. Cuba was known back then as the "Disneyland of the decadent" and the offshore banking center for the wealthy. When Fidel Castro took control, Miguel saw the free-trade economy deteriorating rapidly and gathered whatever money he could scrape together and left with his family for Miami. Before taking the perilous journey through the Florida Straits, Miguel turned his rental property over to a cousin. It was Miguel's hope that his cousin could continue to make a living from the property as it did for Miguel and his family. It wasn't long before the Cuban government took control of the property, and Miguel's cousin ended up farming sugar near Santa Clara in Cuba.

Once in Miami, Miguel took the little bit of money he brought with him and opened a small supermarket in Little Havana that catered to Cuban Americans.

The small supermarket proved to be relatively successful. Miguel hoped that once Juan graduated from college, he would take over the supermarket, maybe even open up more supermarket locations throughout South Florida. Instead, Juan insisted he wanted to join the Cubans for a Free Cuba. Juan later told his father that his determination to help free Cuba from Fidel Castro was because of his father's stories of what a wonderful place Cuba was prior to Castro. Ever since Juan told Miguel his reasons for wanting to free Cuba, Miguel would tear up with pride at the thought. It no longer mattered to Miguel that Juan wasn't interested in taking over the supermarket. Miguel subsequently turned his attention to his daughter, Margerite, to take over the supermarket, a bright young woman who was in the business school at the University of South Florida in Tampa. Margerite worked in the supermarket on her school breaks. Miguel was impressed with how quickly she caught onto the business. Miguel was proud of his children and their successes. Ever since they arrived in Miami, he made sure his children never forgot their Cuban background. It was equally important to him that he; his wife, Adriana; and his children learn English. At home and around the dinner table, they would speak Spanish, but once they left home, they were to speak only English. Miguel felt that without learning the language of their new homeland, it would limit the family's successes.

Juan's second in command was Antonio Mendoza. Antonio was a second cousin to Juan and only a year younger than Juan. Antonio's father, Tito, sent Antonio to live with his relatives in Miami when he was six years old. Miguel received a call one day from the Immigration and Naturalization Service when Antonio first arrived in Florida. He brought Antonio home from the INS office, and after that Juan and Antonio became inseparable. They played together and went to the same schools in Miami. Tito was considered a threat to the Cuban government because of his known anti-Castro sentiment. Tito was listed on the Cuban interior ministry's most wanted list and as a result spent most of his life moving from location to location to avoid being arrested or more likely killed. Tito made a point of never spending too many days and nights in the same place. Tito's travels took him to the highest point in Cuba, the Sierra Maestra to the sugarcane fields near Santa Clara or near Havana. Ironically Tito's movements were much like Fidel Castro's prior to coming to power. For this reason, Tito sent his son to the United States. Tito knew he could not raise a son spending every night in a different place to avoid being arrested. He knew Antonio needed a stable environment to grow up and get an education if he was going to be successful. He also feared that if he were ever caught, Antonio would surely suffer the same fate as him, death. One summer night, Tito arranged Antonio's passage with some other Cuban dissidents headed for Miami through the Florida Straits. When word reached to several Cuban businessmen in Miami that Tito's son was en route, they put pressure on Washington, the Miami Division of the

Immigration and Naturalization Service, and the Coast Guard to ensure his safe arrival. Antonio and those in his company were eventually found in the Florida Straits and received direct passage to Miami and were promptly granted asylum. Those that dare the Florida Straits and make it to U.S. soil are granted permission to stay in the United States, but most are found while in the Florida Straits and returned to Cuba via Guantánamo Bay.

Antonio almost never made it to the United States. Not only had word of Antonio's passage made it to several friendly Cuban Americans sympathetic to his successful passage to the United States, but word also made its way to the Cuban interior ministry. The Cuban Marina de Guerra Revolucionaria, a coastal defense force, had been on alert searching the Florida Straits for Antonio. A reward was also offered to anyone capturing Antonio and turning him over to the Cuban Interior Ministry. As Antonio and those in his company were being helped onto a U.S. Coast Guard cruiser, the Cuban Marina de Guerra Revolucionaria arrived, resulting in what almost turned into an international incident. The Coast Guard cruiser rescued Antonio and the others in international waters. The Cuban government argued that the rescue took place in Cuban waters and demanded the U.S. Coast Guard turn Antonio and the others in his company over to the Cuban Marina de Guerra Revolucionaria. Local news stations in Miami heard the incident unfolding over their communication satellites and dispatched news crew helicopters to the sight of the rescue. The news crews began filming the incident and televised it internationally. After several hours of the standoff, the Cuban Marina de Guerra Revolucionaria acquiesced and withdrew. The Cuban Americans in Miami celebrated the rescue with a full-scale celebration on Calle Ocho, a part of Little Havana in Miami. However, the Cuban government was furious. The Cuban interior minister went on a rampage arresting twenty-five people in Cuba that were believed to have been accomplices and had them thrown in prison for undetermined prison terms.

Others in Juan's group were Roberto and Miguel Benitez. The Benitez brothers had a small lawn-care business in the greater Miami area. Hector Henriquez was the manager of a supermarket owned by Juan's father. Jorge Ramirez was a branch manager of a bank owned and operated by Cuban Americans on the Brickell in Miami. The bank itself was the second largest in Miami-Dade County. Tony Ermandez and Gerardo Zapata owned and operated a number of commercial fishing boats based on Biscayne Bay in Miami.

The plan was for Tony Ermandez and Gerardo Zapata, the fishermen, to take a stripped-down cabin cruiser north along the Intracoastal Waterway and meet the others at the house they staked out in North Carolina. The house was located on a narrow river that connected to the Intracoastal Waterway. The waterway then flowed into the New River that ran adjacent to Camp LeJeune, a marine corps base. The boat had been stripped down to the bare minimum for their mission and sailed to North Carolina from Miami via the Intracoastal Waterway. The others in Juan's company made their way to North Carolina by bus or airplane. They met in an innocuous location in Wilmington, North Carolina, where they eventually procured a rental truck for their mission. The procurement called for Roberto and Miguel to steal a U-Haul from a leasing office in Wilmington and pick up the others en route to the hideout. They had thought about renting a truck but felt it may leave too much of a trail to follow, even with fake IDs and credit cards. An organization member sympathetic to Juan and his men living in Los Angeles sent Juan some license plates off an abandoned U-Haul he spotted in a junkyard. The license plates were valid for a few more months, so Juan brought them with him from Miami. They made fake registration documents to go with the tags in case they were stopped by the police. The others that made their way up from Miami rode in the cargo portion of the truck to the hideout. The hideout was ideal for parking the truck overnight because of its isolated location. The house was located on the mainland. It was a short distance from the town of Surf City, located on Topsail Island, and a little farther away was their target, Camp LeJeune. There was the easy access by boat to the Intracoastal Waterway from the hideout. There was about a half-mile drive down a gravel road, after leaving the main road that led to the house. The house itself was surrounded by trees with the exception of one side bordered by a small river that was rarely used during the fall and winter. The small river was only used by the ten homeowners that owned property along its banks. All the homes along the small river were used as vacation homes and sat on large tree-lined lots. Seth and his men could dock the boat next to the house before and after their mission as well as prior to their return to Miami without drawing too much attention to themselves because of the remoteness of the house.

Before they left on the mission, Juan turned to Tony. "Are you sure you're okay with this? I mean in this weather?" Juan asked Tony in private, out of earshot how he felt about navigating the boat during the hurricane.

Tony almost laughed, "No problem, boss. I'm okay. It's just another day on the water. However, if this thing turns much more, I'm gonna find a safe dock or eddy, and we're gonna have to ride it out from there."

Juan appreciated Tony's honesty. "I know you're experienced in rough seas, but you must have the final word before we proceed. There is too much on the line for any fuckups."

Tony recognized Juan's concern. "We'll be all right."

"Well, let's get going then," commanded Juan. As they turned and headed out in their respective directions, Juan patted Tony on his back in an approving gesture. Tony glanced back over his shoulder to give Juan a confident wink that everything would work out.

Tony and Gerardo headed for the stripped-down cabin cruiser while the rest of the men joined Juan in the recently "procured" U-Haul. Tony jumped onto the boat and started the engines. The motors came to a muffled roar, and the diesel fumes permeated the damp air. Gerardo waited in the rain for Tony to give him the okay to untie the ropes securing the boat to the dock. Gerardo had a fishing baseball cap on that he bought in Surf City earlier in the day. They wanted everything they wore to appear local to the Surf City area residents. The men were instructed before leaving Miami that they were wear nothing that indicated they were from Miami.

Freshly fallen rainwater mixed with the Intracoastal Waterway saltwater air was soon pouring from the bill of the cap Gerardo was wearing. Periodically a sting of the salt would irritate Tony, and he would blink to remove the sting, a trick he learned captaining his fishing boats in Miami. Finally, Tony gave Gerardo the okay to release the boat from the dock so they could begin their part of the mission. Gerardo leaped on board, taking care to land safely on the wet deck and rocking boat. Tony put the boat into gear, and as he did, another cloud of diesel fumes hung in the night air. Gerardo took the spotlight Tony handed him and moved to the bow of the boat. With the cloud cover from the rain darkening the evening sky and Isabelle's hurricane-force winds knocking out the local power, the surrounding area was black as ink. The only lights they could see were off in the distance from homeowners' who had their own personal generators to light their homes or light generated by some kind of independent battery source. The remoteness of the house was now their enemy in that there were no channel markers to guide them through the narrow waterway. Tony needed Gerardo to help guide him through the unfamiliar narrow waterway by kneeling on the bow with the spotlight looking for homemade channel markers created by the local residents. Once in the Intracoastal Waterway, Tony would use the familiar lit channel markers to help guide him. The men slowly made their way forward toward the Intracoastal Waterway that would take them on to Camp LeJeune. Periodically, Tony could hear familiar sounds of the boat making contact with the bottom of the waterway. The boat was light, having been stripped to the bare minimum in anticipation of the load they would be returning with, but for now, it helped keep Tony from running aground on the waterway's bottom. Tony wondered how problematic it would be to negotiate the shallow river once they returned with the additional weight of the arms. For Tony, maneuvering the cabin cruiser through the narrow waterway was relatively easy considering he was used to maneuvering one of his many fishing trawlers through the waterways around Miami.

Eventually Tony and Gerardo reached the wider Intracoastal Waterway. At first Tony had a difficult time steering the light boat through the Intracoastal Waterway no longer protected by land. It took Tony a few minutes to gain control of the boat now that it was in the open water where the heavy winds and dramatically turbulent waters tossed the light boat about. After several near-tragic mistakes, Tony had a better feel for the boat. Tony thought about his comments to Juan before they left. He was thinking he might have been too cavalier for his own good as he wrestled with the boat against the wind, waves, and currents. However, he was starting to feel better now. His next challenge would be to find the meeting point on Camp LeJeune in the darkness and in the storm. Gerardo helped Tony by occasionally taking the helm while Tony reviewed the charts to determine their location and their appointed destination. After what seemed like an eternity to the two men, Tony spotted the familiar landmarks that he needed to guide him to where he was to dock the boat. He hoped that they wouldn't have to wait too long in the driving storm for the others to arrive with the load so they could return to the warm and dry cabin.

CHAPTER 3

It was just after 1:00 a.m. when the men reached Camp LeJeune. The U-Haul truck slowly approached the Sneads Ferry gate that provided one of the accesses to Camp LeJeune. Sneads Ferry, a town adjacent to the marine corps base, is a small fishing village located on the New River. The New River is one of North Carolina's rivers that have access to the Atlantic Ocean and the Intracoastal Waterway. The Sneads Ferry gate is not as frequently used as the other gates that access Camp LeJeune. It is usually quiet and solitary compared to the other entrances to the base. There were six men in the fourteen-foot U-Haul, two in the front and four in the back, usually reserved for boxes and other cargo. The men remained quiet and still as the truck approached the gate that provided their needed access to Camp LeJeune.

Privates Jack Matthew and Toby Clark were stationed at the Sneads Ferry gate on this lonely hurricane-swept evening. Jack was from a small town in Idaho. He had joined the marines to get out of his small town. Like Jack, Toby was from a small town but from Michigan. He was sold on an advertisement that if he joined the marines, "he would see the world," so he joined up at a recruitment center in the next town over from where he lived. They both independently volunteered to take the midnight-to-six-in-the-morning shift. It wasn't long before the two bonded with each other. They figured that if they took the graveyard shift, they wouldn't have to get up early in the mornings. Rarely did any officers show up at their post, and when they did, they were gone as fast as they came. They also liked it because not much went on, and they could listen to the radio and play cards. Toby was into Jack for about a hundred dollars and was planning on getting his money back from "this potato-eating Idaho redneck."

Jack heard the truck as it approach the gate and came to a stop, waiting for authorization to enter the military post as instructed by many of the signs leading up to the gate's entrance. Jack put his cards down and went to the window to see who dared brave this weather.

"What is it?" inquired Toby.

"A couple of guys in a U-Haul. I better go out and see what the fuck they're doin' out here on a night like this."

"Fuck it. They're probably just passin' through." People often used the Sneads Ferry gate as a bypass around the town of Jacksonville when heading north or south when travelling the Seaboard Highway, Highway 17. If you did not cut through the base, you had to go around Camp LeJeune, which was a longer route. There tended to be less traffic cutting through the base as well. "You don't want to get out in this shit. Just wave 'em through and let's get on with this game. I got some money to win back from you."

The two men could hear the wind whistle and the rain hitting the small guard shack where they were stationed. "Naw, I better go, what if it's some fuckin' officer? He'll ream us later for abandoning our post if we don't go out."

"Yeh, right! On a night like tonight, some fuckin' officer has nothin' better to do than ride around in a U-Haul to test us? Yeh, right!" Toby was sarcastic in his remarks as he often was to Jack.

Jack thought for a minute about just waving the U-Haul through. "Naw, I'm gonna at least take a look." Jack threw on a poncho and slung his M-16 over his shoulder and proceeded into the night. Since post-9/11, the military has stepped up their efforts to scrutinize access to military installations, looking at identification and full inspections of vehicle, often including looking under the hood and in the trunk.

Juan planned for the guards to check for identification and inquire what they were doing. Juan brought bogus identification that he picked up in Miami. The plan was to tell the guards he and a few friends were moving his mother to Wilmington to live with him. She was currently living in Swansboro. They had gotten a later start than they had hoped. His identification included a bogus Wilmington address and telephone number. He needed to get everything moved that night because his mother was to be released from a nursing home, and she needed a place to live once she was discharged.

Jack walked cautiously toward the passenger's side of the car. He then walked around the back of the truck as he made his way to the driver's side of the truck. Wind and rain whipped across his face and caused his poncho to fly back and forth, allowing the rain to drench his once-dry clothes. When he got to the driver's window, he tapped on the glass for the driver to roll down his window.

Juan reluctantly rolled his window down.

"May I see some identification?" asked Jack as he fought off the wind and rain.

Juan produced his bogus driver's license and handed it to Jack.

Jack took a cursory look at the picture on the driver's license and then the face of the man driving the truck. He used his flashlight so he could look at the other man in the truck. Jack took another deliberate look at the driver's license. He stood in the wind and rain trying to decide how much more he was willing to do in this intolerable weather. He handed the man back his driver's license. "Have a good evening." Jack stepped back and waved the man through. He watched as the U-Haul slowly disappeared into the night as he made his way back into the comforts of the guardhouse.

Jack stepped inside the guardhouse removing the poncho and shaking it off on the guardhouse floor. Water sprayed across the small room.

"Watch it," exclaimed Toby.

Jack started to return to his seat when Toby gave him a smug look. "You know I was right," commented Toby. "Now deal!"

Juan was relieved with the perfunctory examination by the guard. He was relieved not have to go through some long diatribe that lacked even the smallest amount of truth. Juan shifted the truck into first gear and proceeded to the predetermined ammunitions depot, one of the many located throughout the base. The ammunition depot had been specifically selected from "someone on the inside." Juan had never met or even spoken with the Insider, but Julio Chavez was confident in the man, and that was good enough for Juan. Juan answered only to Julio. Juan found the truck more and more difficult to drive because of the frequent gusts of wind that rocked the truck from side to side. The men had been listening to a radio they brought along in the cargo portion of the truck to keep up with hurricane Isabelle's developments. Since the men were from Miami, they were more than familiar with hurricanes and the damage they can cause. All the men with Juan, including Juan, knew someone that lost their home or a loved one as a result of hurricane Andrew. The men thought about postponing the mission but knew how unpredictable hurricanes could be. They felt that if they postponed their mission, it would prolong their time away from their families and work. They also felt that the hurricane would provide excellent cover for what they were about to do. They knew most people, including the military personnel, would be in some kind of shelter protecting themselves from the hurricane, not expecting anyone out doing what they were about to do.

The windshield wipers were going as fast as they could go, but they couldn't keep pace with rain making visibility nearly impossible. Juan sat with his face almost pressed against the windshield trying to see the road in order to drive. Debris covered the road, and flying debris struck the sides of the truck, causing a reverberating sound that echoed inside the truck. The men in the cargo portion of the truck held tight to keep from being tossed around as the gusts of wind rocked the truck. As the truck neared the ammunition depot that the men planned on breaking into, Juan checked his rearview mirror to see if anyone was behind him. He almost laughed at the thought of anyone being behind him as he looked into the rearview mirror. Even if some were behind him, they couldn't see each other except for maybe the taillights of the truck and the headlights of the car behind him. He thought how foolish he was for daring the storm. The weather, with its high winds and rain, had been a deterrent thus far to anyone interfering with them, and this was no exception. They were very much alone. Juan turned out the headlights of the truck as he pulled off the main road onto a gravel road that led into some nearby woods. Roberto and Miguel Benitez jumped out of the cargo hold of the truck on cue from Antonio Mendoza. An innocuous sign indicated that the gravel road led to the ammunition depot no. 8 that they were looking for. Once again, the Insider was the responsible party for the information on what sign to look for. They entered the nearby woods and made their way until they came along the fence with barbed wire poised along the top protecting the ammunitions depot from intruders. It was difficult to see and walk as the wind and rain pounded the two men. They noted that the rain almost seemed to come at them horizontally and sometimes bottom up when the wind gusted. As the men made their way along the fence, they could hear the electricity pulsing through the fence. The humming from the electricity in the fence offered an ominous feeling to the two men. Roberto and Miguel noticed that the rain that came in contact with the fence seemed to sizzle, giving them an eerie feeling as they made their way. Signs were sporadically posted at numerous points along the fence, indicating "Danger High Voltage."

The men proceeded slowly along the fence line looking for any sentries. They had been forewarned that there were sentries posted throughout the ammunitions depot with the sentries' instructions to shoot anyone attempting to break in on sight. Roberto and Miguel in due course spotted two lone sentries huddled next to some large trees using the canopy of the leaves and branches in an attempt to shelter them from the storm. Roberto and Miguel watched the sentries try and brace themselves from the gusts of wind without much success. Roberto and Miguel crept toward the sentries in an effort to keep from being heard. The two men felt certain the sentries could hear them. They could not help themselves from stepping on fallen limbs, causing loud cracks, or the sound they made while slipping on the mud caused by the rain, leaves, and pine-needles-soaked ground. However, the howling wind and branches breaking from the surrounding trees masked the sounds Roberto and Miguel made as they crept toward the sentries. Once they were within twenty feet of the sentries, the men drew the tranquilizer dart guns from their jacket pockets. They took aim, but the wind kept the men from holding their guns steady. Rain fell into their eyes further, hindering their efforts to tranquilize the sentries. They moved in closer on the sentries in order to fire their tranquilizer dart guns with more accuracy. As the men approached, Miguel slipped on a wet log, as he did one of the sentries turned to determine the commotion. The sentry spotted

Miguel and Roberto. He turned to take aim with his M-16 rifle when Roberto fired his dart gun. The dart made its way to the chest of the sentry with a quiet thud, causing him to lose his balance, falling backward and subduing him. The second sentry was attempting to seek cover from Miguel and Roberto when Miguel regained his balance and fired his dart gun. His dart struck the second sentry in the throat, also subduing him. Miguel and Roberto felt some relief that they were able to subdue the sentries without any bloodshed. Miguel felt a pain in his stomach that the dart struck the man so ruthlessly in his throat. He could see in the man's eyes the pain of the dart striking him, but Miguel knew the alternative of having to kill the man would have been far worse. The men proceeded toward the sentries and checked to see if they were okay. They removed the tranquilizer darts from the sentries as instructed by Juan. Roberto placed his hand on each man's chest to see if they were breathing. Both sentries appeared all right aside from being rendered unconscious. They tied the two unconscious sentries to a nearby tree, making sure that the men were protected as much as possible from the elements. Roberto and Miguel continued to search for any other possible sentries. They continued their search along the parameter of the fence. Once they felt there were no other sentries, they radioed to the truck and told Juan to proceed onto the gate. As the truck pulled up in front of the gate, Roberto and Miguel started to join the others still covered by the dense trees surrounding the ammunitions depot until Juan motioned for them to wait in the woods from the cab of the truck.

Juan made a call from the disposable cell phone that he bought since arriving in North Carolina as he stopped the truck just out of view of the surveillance cameras guarding the entrance, once again based on security information provided by their Insider. Every detail of their mission had been rehearsed over and over in Miami. The call was to a local telephone number Juan was given in Miami. Juan assumed the number was most likely a local pay phone on Camp LeJeune or to another disposable cell phone.

CHAPTER 4

A man answered the telephone on its first ring near Camp LeJeune's main electronic surveillance building. It was a disposable cell phone that the man purchased at a mall in Jacksonville, North Carolina. "Yeh, it's me." The voice lacked any emotion.

"We're here," responded Juan. Juan was feeling anxious and worked to restrain himself.

"Okay, I'll take care of it." The man hung up the telephone and proceeded into Camp LeJeune's main electronic surveillance building. The door to the electronic surveillance room slowly opened. A desk just inside the door sat vacant. On the other side of the room was another desk that conspicuously sat vacant as well. The sentries assigned to the respective desks had been temporarily called away. They were to be temporarily sent on a military rouse, but with hurricane Isabelle an excuse, it became readily available. They were sent to tie down some tarps covering military equipment. The operation was so carefully orchestrated that many of the operatives did not know one another. The only thing that one operative knew about another was possibly a voice. The man gradually opened the door to an adjoining room with a typical marine corps sign in red-and-gold. The sign read, "Surveillance Personnel Only, Authorized Personnel Only, Do Not Enter." Once the man had the door ajar, he removed two tranquilizer dart guns, one from each pocket of his trench coat. Holding the tranquilizer dart guns in each hand, he used his elbow and foot to push the door open. Once in the surveillance room, he took aim at the two men attending to the surveillance monitors in front of them and fired tranquilizer darts into the neck of each of the men. The dart guns were fired by the man without any emotion; it was very deliberate as if taking aim at a target on a firing range. The two surveillance operators slumped forward in their chairs and fell unconscious. The man checked each of the men for a pulse and then turned off the surveillance monitors, tape recorder, and the electronic fence, making Juan and his men enter the ammunitions depot undetected. The surveillance monitors were not foreign to him. He turned off the monitors where he knew Juan and his men were. He made sure to leave the other surveillance monitors running to avoid anyone else at the other locations from noticing that their surveillance had been turned off. He ripped several cords from the computer equipment and from the power source to make the investigators believe that whoever broke in did not know what they were doing. He waited long enough to watch as the monitors' lights flickered out once the power was removed. He calmly closed the door behind himself as he exited the surveillance room. He pulled the cell phone from his coat pocket and dialed Juan's number as he exited the building.

Juan heard the dull humming from the electronic fence subside as he waited in the cab of the truck. A few moments later, Juan's cell phone rang. "Hello."

The stranger's voice was once again on the phone. In a stoic voice, Juan heard, "It's off." The man hung up without waiting for Juan to reply.

CHAPTER 5

Juan moved the truck in front of the locked gate to ammunition depot no. 8. Juan motioned to Roberto and Miguel to come over to the truck. Juan handed Roberto some bolt cutters. Roberto walked over to the gate and clipped the lock. The two men opened the gate, and the truck entered the ammunitions depot. Juan waited for Miguel and Roberto to jump on the rear tailgate before the truck proceeded into the compound. Juan followed the directions he was given to a building numbered 2501 located inside ammunition depot no. 8. Roberto jumped off the back of the truck with the bolt cutters as Juan backed the truck up to the loading dock. Roberto clipped the lock on the door of the building numbered 2501. Miguel jimmied the door with a crowbar, and seconds later the door sprang open. As the six men entered the building, they automatically formed three teams of two. No one said a word. The teams worked efficiently grabbing wooden and metal crates that contained the weapons that they needed. They were looking for weapons that would be useful in urban assaults and, when necessary, guerilla warfare. They loaded Sterling and M3 submachine guns. They loaded M-16 assault rifles some equipped with 40-mm grenade launchers. The men also located the M60 general-purpose machine guns. As Juan and his men pilfered through the ammunition depot, they located MP5 silenced machine guns and grenades. They located and loaded the M47 Dragon, known for its ability to take out tanks and the shoulder-launched, surface-to-air missile FIM-92 Stingers that have the ability to shoot down helicopters and maneuver targets. The men loaded the crates into the truck waiting outside. After twenty-five minutes, one of the men signaled to the others that they had five more minutes. Juan decided earlier that to spend more than thirty minutes inside the ammunitions depot would be ill-fated. Thirty minutes was more than what Julio Chavez, Juan's superior in Miami, had recommended, but Juan felt that to do anything less would not be enough time to accomplish the things they needed because of the weight of the crates.

—

CHAPTER 6

Hugh got to the provost marshal's office (the military police station) at Camp LeJeune early since Mary left for Clinton along with the rest of the coastal residents. Since Hugh was forced to evacuate Topsail Island, he elected to report early for work. He had gathered a few more items from the house that Mary did not have room for in her car and took them with him to work. He figured that the items would be safer in his car than at the house, potentially in harm's way. When he arrived at work, he hung out with the guys who were finishing up the earlier shift. Then Hugh decided to use the time to complete some reports he had been putting off. He decided to make use of a vacant interrogation room to complete the reports and catch up on some reading in a police journal he had set aside a few days earlier.

"Looks like you're in for one hell of an evening," commented one of the military patrolmen who popped his head in the interrogation room. The fellow MP also had an appetite for the police journals, and often the two men would exchange stories they read.

Hugh glanced out of the corner of his eye and gave the patrolman a grin as he responded, "You may be right about that."

"Catch you later," commented the MP as he disappeared down the hall.

It was common practice among the more veteran MPs to hang out with the men coming off one shift before starting their own shift. Much of the interaction was just ribbing one another, but often the interaction included some insights into things for the next shift to be on the alert for. Hugh had finished several reports from the previous night's patrol when Private Larry Shays arrived. Larry was Hugh's most recent partner. Hugh's other partners were either discharged from service on their own accord or became ranking MPs with their own rookies. A colonel teamed Hugh and Larry up as partners a couple of months ago. Larry loved to tell everyone he was from the mean streets of Miami, but Hugh knew he was from just outside of Miami proper, a place called Kendall,

Florida. When Larry acted tough around the other MPs about how he had grown up on the tough streets of Miami, Hugh would always ask, "Aren't you from Kendall, Florida?" Hugh did not think much of Larry. To Hugh, Larry was a punk. Larry had had a few minor scrapes on base with the military police when a colonel thought it might help straighten Larry out if he spent some time riding around with MPs. He began riding along with MPs during the evening shifts when he was off duty from his job in the motor pool, where he worked as a mechanic. As it turned out, when the Colonel came around one day some weeks later and asked Larry how he was doing, he told the colonel that he would like to become an MP on a full-time basis. Before Hugh knew what hit him, Larry was his regular partner. A number of MPs voiced their disapproval among themselves, but no one dared do more than that. It was not wise to question a ranking officer's decision no matter how ridiculous it appeared to be.

"How's it hangin', Larry?" asked Hugh.

"Fine, sir, how you doin'?" inquired an upbeat Larry.

"Can't say I'm lookin' forward to tonight."

"Me neither." Larry logged in with the duty officer, and the two left shortly thereafter for their patrol. Hugh always drove. He told Larry that he did not like anybody else's driving but his own. It was mostly the truth; Hugh also felt driving helped make the time pass more quickly.

The patrol car slowly made its rounds. The base was void of anything but wind, rain, and flying debris. "Looks like the biggest thing to look out for tonight is getting hit by some of this flying debris," commented Hugh.

"I think you're right," replied Larry. About that time, a large piece of metal flew by, just missing their patrol car and startling the men.

Since Larry and Hugh had been riding together, the worst trouble they had encountered was a barroom brawl at the Noncommissioned Officers' Club. It was just after a Super Bowl game that came down to a close finish. Several of the opposing enlisted men got into a pushing and shoving match that deteriorated quickly into a melee with just about the entire club. Larry was getting the raw end of a sergeant's fist during the melee when Hugh saved him. Larry, on numerous occasions, professed his undying gratitude to Hugh ever since that time.

Hugh could feel the car jerking with each gust of wind. The car running over fallen debris made the evening's ride even rockier. The rain pounded the windshield, making visibility near impossible. Hugh was not going to be detoured by the storm and continued to make his rounds as usual. They toured past the numerous ammunitions depots on their patrol. Each time they passed, they received a nod from the sentries, indicating everything was all right. Hugh felt bad for the guards left in the wind and rain to guard their respective posts. Larry was less sympathetic, making callous remarks at their expense to Hugh, who disregarded the comments.

Hugh and Larry passed by the Sneads Ferry gate as part of their patrol. When Private Toby Clark heard Hugh's patrol car, he ran to the window to indicate everything was okay and to let Hugh see that he was hard at work. Toby and Private Jack Matthew found that going to the window typically prevented anyone from entering the guardhouse. Hugh periodically would enter the guardhouse regardless just to shake things up. As a result of entering the guardhouse, he would often disturb them from what was normally a quiet evening of cards. Hugh would always threaten to turn them in, but Toby and Jack knew it was only a threat. Hugh would usually comment as he left that if any other officer caught them, they could plan on spending some time in the local brig. Hugh knew that their post was generally quiet and that passing the evening playing cards was harmless entertainment for them. Hugh was more concerned that the men would meet cars entering and leaving the post. When Toby saw Hugh's patrol car drive away, he returned to the card game he and Jack were playing. Hugh drove the patrol car to the other gate on yet another side of the large marine corps base. When he received the same signal that everything was okay, he continued on with his rounds. They proceeded to another one of the many ammunition depots on their patrol and found the guards at their post despite the weather. Most of the guards were huddled under some sort of shelter until they saw Hugh's patrol car. As soon as they caught a glimpse of Hugh's patrol car headlights, the sentries would scramble to put up a facade that they were standing at their post. Hugh could see from his patrol car what was taking place, but he could hardly blame the men. Who in their right mind would attempt to illegally enter a military installation during a category 4 hurricane, much less try to steal weapons?

Hugh and Larry proceeded back toward the Sneads Ferry gate to make their second round before they took a break. They moved toward ammunition depot no. 8, which they had previously patrolled earlier in the evening. It was to be the start of their second round of patrolling the ammunition depots. "Hey, Larry, flash the searchlight over that way," Hugh pointed in the direction he wanted Larry to direct the light. Each patrol car was equipped with a searchlight mounted on the roof that the passenger would operate while the driver made the patrols. The driver could operate the searchlight if needed, but whenever there was a passenger, military regulations required the passenger to operate the searchlight. From Hugh's inquiry of the regulation, he discovered much to his amusement that the United States government spent a few million dollars investigating the hazards of the driver operating the searchlight while driving. Hugh caught a glimpse of a U-Haul as their patrol car made its way toward ammunition depot no. 8.

"Where?" asked Larry

Hugh gave Larry a more empathic indication by jabbing his finger in the direction he wanted the light. "Over there!" The spotlight caught the side of the

U-Haul up near the building. Hugh turned the patrol car toward the front gate of the ammunition depot. He stopped the patrol car in front of the gate. He could see from the patrol car headlights that the locks had been cut. The gates had been pushed back together to avoid the casual glance by a less-than-competent patrolman noticing the impropriety. Hugh also noticed there was no sign of the sentries he and Larry saw earlier in the evening.

"Larry, get out and open up the gates. We're gonna check this out!" Hugh waited in the patrol car while Larry sauntered over to open one side of the gate and then the other.

Larry jumped back in the patrol car, shaking as much rain off as he could as he entered. "Jesus Christ! Is it coming down!" shouted Larry.

Hugh ignored Larry's comment. He had heard Larry complain too many times before to care. Larry complained about everything, especially if he had to do anything more than was minimally required. Hugh was far more concerned about a U-Haul parked next to an ammunitions depot in the middle of the night. Hugh turned off the headlights of the patrol car. "Larry, turn off that spotlight!" Hugh slowly directed the patrol car toward where the U-Haul was parked. He stopped, facing the front of the truck just far enough to make out the license plates on the front of the truck when he turned the headlights on again. Hugh made a mental note that the rear of the truck was backed up to the warehouse for loading. "Run a make on the plates. Also ask the dispatcher if an alarm was triggered at this location." Hugh didn't expect much. He knew if the truck had been rented that day, it would take at least a day or two before U-Haul could enter the information into their computer system. He felt that if it was a robbery, the truck had most likely been stolen anyhow. He was particularly concerned that an alarm had not been reported at the location. As Hugh and Larry sat in the car waiting for a response from the dispatcher, Hugh's mind began to wonder. If it was a break-in, why hadn't the alarm gone off? What would possess anyone to break in to a military ammunitions depot during a hurricane? A chill consumed Hugh. Whoever it was must be a desperate individual or individuals. Hugh's mind drifted to Mary, his pregnant wife, and the thought of how much he loved her.

Finally the voice of the dispatcher came over the radio, "There is no information available on the vehicle. There is no indication of an alarm triggered at ammunition depot no. 8."

Hugh's mind snapped back to the matters at hand. Hugh's assumptions proved correct. Hugh took the radio from Larry. He called back to the dispatcher, "Send backup to ammunition depot no. 8, building 2501. Also, have someone run by the surveillance center. Now!"

"Roger that!" responded the dispatcher.

CHAPTER 7

Miguel caught a glimpse of Hugh's patrol car spotlight as it briefly lit up the U-Haul. Miguel turned toward the ammunitions depot and softly called to Juan and the others, "Spotlight!"

Juan heard Miguel's low but urgent call. "Everyone, get down. No one moves! Whatever happens, let me initiate it!" Juan had made contingency plans for just about everything. This was the only part of the plan that Juan could not be prepared for, the random patrol car. Juan knew someone on the inside was getting paid to detour the MPs, but the random patrol car was always a possibility. Juan also knew that an MP would certainly investigate a U-Haul parked at an ammunitions depot, especially in the middle of the night. He was aware that the MP would call for backup. Juan's mind raced for an answer trying to figure the next plan of action. He and the others would just have to respond the best they could and hope they could get away without anyone getting hurt or inflicting too much damage.

Juan watched as several of the men pulled out their tranquilizer dart guns that they had been carrying. Antonio Mendoza and Jorge Ramirez each pulled out Colt .45 pistols. Juan could see the shine of Antonio's and Jorge's pistols from a security light in the distance. Juan looked at the men with contempt, but they could not see Juan's face because of the poor light. Juan had told the men not to bring firearms. He had ordered them to only bring tranquilizer dart guns.

The men knelt behind whatever they could find and remained motionless. Juan could feel his heart pounding in his throat. He sat quietly trying to hear the MPs approach, but the rain striking the tin roof, the wind howling, and the rustling of the trees disguised their movements.

CHAPTER 8

Hugh left the lights on and parked the patrol car next to the rear of the truck. "Radio back to the station that we're going to take a look around. Tell them again we need backup—now!" Larry called back to the station as Hugh got out of the patrol car and made his way slowly along the side of the truck. Hugh could hear Larry's call and then the dispatcher's reply. Hugh had his flashlight in one hand and his Smith & Wesson 9mm semiautomatic pistol in the other. Hugh crept forward cautiously, stalking his quarry. Larry got out of the car and closed the door behind him. *Bam.* Hugh gave Larry a cross look as if to say, "Why not just announce that we're here?" Larry closed the gap quickly behind Hugh as they made their way to the entrance of the warehouse. Hugh noticed that a convenient rock was placed at the base of the door, forcing it to stay open. Using the jammed door as a shield, Hugh took his flashlight and slowly panned across the room.

Unexpectedly, a shot rang out. Juan was startled. The gunfire broke the once-still darkness. Juan tried to think that this was not the way they had planned the operation. There was to be no gunfire, and no one was to be hurt or killed. If they were caught, there was a contingency plan.

"Get down, Larry!" shouted Hugh. Hugh stepped into the doorway to return fire in the direction he saw the gun flash. He heard someone collapse back and the air rush out of his lungs. He had shot Antonio Mendoza squarely in the stomach. He felt sick with disgust. It reminded him of his experience in Desert Storm as a soldier. An eerie silence ensued. Without looking in Larry's direction, Hugh called out again, "Larry, call for backup—now! Tell them shots are being fired." Hugh felt someone press firmly against his back. He writhed as he felt a sharp instrument slide into his lower back. The person then twisted the object and thrust it upward into his torso. Hugh felt a warm dampness run down his lower back and legs. His body slowly began to turn cold as his blood flowed out of his body. The person relaxed his grip. Hugh fell to the ground, rolling to his side. Hugh caught a glimpse of the person who had stabbed him. He saw Larry standing over him with a knife covered in his blood. Hugh looked incredulously at Larry as if to ask why. Hugh grasped for air, and silently his life ebbed away. His thoughts rested with Mary and his unborn child as life slipped away. Larry stood over Hugh looking down at him as a conquering hero. He called to the men in the warehouse, "I've got things under control—come on out!"

CHAPTER 9

When Juan heard Larry's voice, he recognized it from a couple telephone conversations he had during the planning stages in Miami. He had never actually met him. Juan peered out from behind the crates he had taken refuge prior to the two MPs' arrival and during the brief but fatal shooting. He slowly stepped toward the voice he had heard. He could see the silhouettes of one man standing in the doorway looking down at another lying motionless on the ground.

Larry knelt down next to Hugh's lifeless body. He wiped his knife clean against Hugh's rain-soaked jacket. He closed the blade and put the knife back in his pants pocket. "No more kissing up to you, asshole!" Larry looked up and saw Juan Mendoza standing in front of him. Larry stood up and smiled smugly at Juan. Juan looked coldly back at Larry. Juan raised his gun, took aim, and shot Larry in the shoulder. Larry felt the hot metal pierce his skin. He fell backward over some crates that Juan and his men had lain in the doorway of the warehouse that they were about to load in the truck when they were interrupted. He glanced at Juan for a second before losing consciousness. Juan felt no remorse for having shot Larry. Based on their brief encounter, Juan viewed Larry as a "taker," someone out solely for himself and never to be trusted.

Juan's men quickly threw what they had been carrying, including the crate lying in the doorway into the back of the truck. As the men loaded the crates onto the truck, they couldn't help but notice the bloody and unresponsive Hugh lying on the platform of the ammunition depot. They each felt remorseful for their part in his death. Roberto found a blanket lying just inside the door to the warehouse and placed it over Hugh's face and body. Hector called to Juan, "What should we do about him?" referring to Larry.

"Leave him!" Juan shouted to the men. "Let's get the hell out of here. They're going to have backup here any minute!" Miguel went over to Antonio Mendoza. "How is it?"

"It's bad. Get me up, we've got to get the hell outta here." Juan ran over and helped lift Antonio into the back of the truck. Juan ran to the passenger's side and jumped in. The others jumped into the back of the truck, and Miguel pulled the door shut behind them. Roberto Benitez, Miguel's brother, was already behind the wheel with the engine running.

"Move it!" shouted Juan to Roberto. "Once you hit the main road, slow down. I don't want to draw any more attention to ourselves if we can help it." The truck lurched forward slowly from the additional weight of the newly acquired arms. The truck's wheels slipped on the wet soil mixed with leaves and pine needles before gaining traction. Although the rain continued to fall, the constant wind had mildly let up some now that the hurricane had begun to pass them. Roberto sat as close to the wheel as possible trying to keep his eyes on the road with the windshield wipers trying to keep pace with the rain. The periodic wind gusts still rocked the truck from side to side, making steering the truck difficult, but with the added weight, the truck held to the road more than before. The truck made its way slowly through the darkness. They soon found the road that would take them to their next destination and pulled off onto yet another dirt road leading to a small hunting lodge for Camp LeJeune's military personnel. The truck made its way past the small hunting lodge and stopped near a dock on the New River. The dock was provided to military personnel living on Camp LeJeune for recreational boating, one of the many benefits provided to the base residents. Although not yet visible to the group in the truck, Tony Ermandez and Gerardo Zapata were waiting huddled under a shelter adjacent to the dock. They were trying to shelter themselves from the wind and rain. They used a flashlight to signal the approaching truck to their specific location.

Juan looked toward the dock and was alarmed not to see the boat. As the truck slowed almost to a stop, Juan leapt out and raced toward the two waiting men. "Where the fuck is the boat?"

Tony and Gerardo grinned at each other and pointed to the boat. The men had found a small inlet near the dock that provided some solace to the boat. The inlet provided relief from the constant pounding of the waves that the boat would have otherwise received alongside the dock. "We found that inlet to keep the boat from crashing into the dock. We figured it would be easier to load the boat there," commented Gerardo.

"How'd it go?" asked Tony.

"They got Antonio," replied Juan.

"What!" commented a shocked Tony. Tony's eye panned toward the truck where he noticed Hector and Jorge helping Antonio from the rear of the truck. "Put him on the boat!" cried Tony. Tony approached the men carrying Antonio. Once Tony was close enough to the men, he could see the blood—and rain-soaked clothes Antonio was wearing from a distant light coming from the dock. He looked over at Juan. "Any other casualties?"

"Yeah, some MP." Juan started to mention his encounter with Larry Shays but thought better of it. Larry was only known as a participant in the whole affair to Juan and a few others. Tony was not one of those few who needed to know any more than what he already knew.

"Shit, no one was supposed to get hurt," commented Tony.

"Hey, no shit. They just happened upon us," Juan sarcastically replied. Juan paused for a brief moment and regained control of himself. "I'm sorry. Let's get this stuff loaded and get the hell outta here. We can talk about the details later," commented Juan.

"Forget about it. We're all feeling the pressure," replied Tony. Tony knew Juan was right. "Okay, let's get it loaded on the boat and get out of here," shouted Tony to the men. Tony and Gerardo moved onto the boat so they could stow the crates on the boat. They needed to make the most of the limited space while distributing the weight evenly.

Hector and Jorge carried Antonio into the cabin of the boat. He was drenched in his own blood and rain. No one could tell how much blood he had actually lost because his clothes were so wet. Antonio was shivering from the loss of blood and the dampness of his clothes. Jorge grabbed some blankets from a cupboard and covered Antonio before returning to assist the others. Hector and Jorge returned to help unload the truck. The wooden and metal crates were a challenge to load during the storm. The ground was wet, mixed with the autumn leaves and pines needles, causing the men to continuously lose their footing as they carried the crates from the truck to the boat. The men's hands and legs were bruised and bloody from each fall with the crates careening into them. The boat was rocking despite being docked in the quieter inlet.

"This is it," announced Miguel as he and his brother brought the last crate over to the boat to be loaded.

CHAPTER 10

"Everyone, on board!" commanded an anxious Juan. The men climbed aboard. Miguel and Roberto raced back to the truck to wipe it clean of any fingerprints. Once they were satisfied of their efforts, they quickly made their way back to the boat. Gerardo was untying the bowline and Jorge the stern line.

After Miguel and Roberto were on board, Tony glanced around, as captain of the boat, to make sure all were on board as well as everything was safely secured. Tony put the boat in reverse, but it did not move. The weight of the arms encased in the heavy metal and wooden crates caused the boat to rest on the river's muddy bottom of the eddy. Roberto and Miguel, without hesitation, jumped into the cold fall river water without a second thought. The two men began to push with as much strength against the murky bottom as they could muster after having loaded and unloaded the crates filled with military arms. Tony put the boat in reverse again with as much power as the diesel engines could generate. The fumes from the diesel exhaust hung in the evening air. The boat gave and started to back into the deeper river water. Miguel and Roberto swam toward the boat as best they could in the choppy cool water, reaching opposite sides of the boat. The others reached over to help the men aboard. The men kept losing their grip of one another. Everyone's hands were covered in rain and mud from the dock area. Trying to grab hold of the men in the rough water was compounded with the boat tossing from side to side as the waves pounded the boat. After repeated efforts, the men got Miguel into the boat, pulling him in by whatever they could grab hold of. Roberto was eventually able to grab hold of the boat's railing and pulled himself onto the boat. Once Tony saw that the two men were on board, he put the boat into forward gear for the return trip to the hideout. The boat made its way slowly at first in the choppy water before gaining momentum. Everyone held tight to keep from being tossed overboard as the boat and the waves fought one another.

Roberto entered the cabin to attend to Antonio. He knew the trip back would take some time and wanted to help make Antonio as comfortable as he could. He found a few more blankets in another cupboard. He took the blankets he found and began tearing them into strips to try and make bandages to slow the bleeding.

Juan could hear whimpers from inside the cabin as the bow of the boat pounded into the oncoming waves. He stuck his head into the cabin and asked Antonio, "How are you doing?" He waited a few seconds, but there was no response.

Roberto gave Juan a sad look to indicate things were not going well. Roberto held his hand firm against the wound. He took his other hand and put it against Antonio's neck to feel for a pulse. "He's lost consciousness, but I can still feel a weak pulse," answered Roberto to Juan's call to Antonio. "He needs a doctor!"

"I know," responded Juan. Juan could see the concern in Roberto's face. "Do what you can for him," requested the saddened Juan.

Tony kept wiping the brackish water from his eyes. It burned, but to a sea captain, it was nothing more than a slight nuisance. The windshield wipers on the boat were no match for the rain and river water constantly covering the boat's windshield as the waves broke over the bow. Tony used the channel markers along the river fore and aft to help steer the boat. He could barely see the channel markers at times due to the rain and the burning from the salt in his eyes. He steered the boat into the direction of the whitecaps to keep from capsizing the boat. The men took turns helping to spot for the oncoming waves and helped to keep track of the channel markers. The men also did their best to spot debris in the water caused by the hurricane. They dared not to use the boat's spotlight to help guide their way for fear of alerting the Coast Guard or anyone else of their presence. The boat's running lights were off as well adding to the perils of steering the boat.

The New River is about a two miles wide at its widest point, is relatively shallow, and is used primarily for recreation. Intermittent lights from some of the homes with generators along the river offered some comfort to the men. This night, the river was turbulent from the hurricane winds. Isabelle was now past them, but strong winds and rain continued to linger. The boat made its way along the New River for over an hour until it met the Intracoastal Waterway. On a normal evening, the same distance should have taken about only half the time. They knew they had the water to themselves. Who else would be foolish enough to brave the river or the Intracoastal Waterway during a storm like this? The only person they feared seeing or hearing them was the bridge tender at Surf City. They slowly made their way under the cover of darkness and the constant rain. They could see in the distance what appeared to be a lantern coming from the bridge tender's house, the only source of light due to the power outage, compliments of hurricane Isabelle. They hoped that the wind and rain would mask the boat's engines. On their way to Camp LeJeune, the hurricane was more intense, but now that the storm had mostly passed, the engines disturbed the early hours of the new day.

CHAPTER 11

They continued down the Intracoastal Waterway past the Surf City Bridge for about another ten minutes. They were not making as much headway as they had hoped as a result of the hurricane's lingering elements. Eventually, they reached the narrow waterway to their final destination for the night. It was a small river that Gerardo and Tony had taken earlier in the evening. Tony slowed the boat so he could guide the boat into the narrow waterway. Gerardo moved out onto the bow of the boat and knelt down. He would need to spot for the homemade water markers that guided them out. He would need to be extra careful on the way in because of the additional weight of the boat. He hoped with the additional rain that the narrow channel would be higher for their return trip. The trees and elevated shoreline helped to calm the turbulent waters from the lingering storm. Although the rain and the wind had subsided, it remained a nuisance. The winds howled into the darkened night. Gerardo called out to Tony on which direction to steer the boat. He was happy with himself for committing to memory where the deep water ran in the waterway. The rest of the men sat in silence. They followed the dark river, eventually finding the dock next to a small house guarded by more trees. It was the same house that the men started from before the evening's horrid adventure. Gerardo leapt out onto the dock, almost losing his footing from the rain-soaked dock, to help guide the boat in as it made its way alongside the dock. Roberto threw Gerardo the bowline that he tied to a cleat on the dock. Jorge threw him the stern line to tie to another cleat. The men disembarked the boat with the newly claimed weapons. All the men helped to carry Antonio from the boat and into the house.

"You take the first watch," commanded Juan to Hector. "We'll take one-hour shifts." He looked over to Miguel. "You'll take the second." He proceeded to bark out the order of shifts to each of the men. The men did not argue. They accepted their assignments. It was dark, and the windswept rain hindered the men's walk as they made their way from the dock to the house. It was not far, but in the remaining hurricane elements with branches and other debris being carried by the winds, it seemed to take forever. As each man entered the house, they shed their wet, muddy clothes. They each dried themselves with the supply of towels from a linen closet across the hall from the cabin's only bathroom. Tony and Gerardo helped Antonio remove his bloody and rain-drenched clothes in the master bedroom. They placed him on the bed and got him some towels. Seeing Antonio without his shirt was the first time the men had had a chance to see the extent of Antonio's wound. The bullet had struck him squarely in the stomach. Antonio was white from the amount of blood he had lost. He was shivering. Tony and Gerardo took turns putting pressure on the wound to try and stop the bleeding. Juan searched the house for some clean bandages and alcohol to clean the wound. He found what he was looking for in a cupboard in the kitchen.

"He needs a doctor," Miguel shouted. Juan could see the distress in Miguel's eyes.

Juan returned, "Where the hell do you think we're going to find a doctor tonight?" Juan knew his response was cold, but he felt that no matter how bad things were, he had to maintain control. He was the *leader*.

"Well, we can't just let him die," countered Roberto.

"I know," exclaimed Juan. They could have looked in a phone book, but the men were unfamiliar with the area. "If we start knocking on doors in the middle of the night asking for a doctor, we'll only draw attention to ourselves. Besides, what are we going to do with the doctor after he's through?" continued Juan.

"We could take him with us and let him go later," answered Jorge. One man was already dead, and that was one more than they had planned. "Or we could leave him here tied up, and eventually he'll work himself free. By that time, we'll be long gone."

Juan tried to think. Everything would only leave clues as to who they were and where they may be headed. "We'll have to just wait until morning," Juan commented. The men looked grimly at Juan. They felt that by morning, it would surely be too late for Antonio. The men grudgingly left Antonio's bedside and climbed into waiting beds, some into sleeping bags, and went to sleep. They were all physically and emotionally drained. They dropped off to sleep immediately.

Before Juan went to sleep, he looked at Antonio lying on the bed covered in his own blood. Childhood memories flashed in his mind, including the day Antonio first came to live with Juan and his family. Juan also remembered the days in Miami when cocaine became the social drug and crime escalated. Drug dealers murdered their rivals without a second thought. Juan remembered seeing others he knew shot much like Antonio, in the stomach. They were dead within the hour. How could Antonio survive this long? It was sheer will. Juan knew by morning Antonio would be dead. He would have to go to bed planning on what to do with Antonio's body come daybreak.

CHAPTER 12

The first MPs to arrive at ammunitions depot were Corporal Robert Hastings and his partner, Private Joshua Walters. Their patrol car pulled up to the gates of ammunitions depot no. 8. They first noticed that the gates were ajar, and there was no sign of the sentries. Private Walters used the spotlight to pan the darkened ammunitions depot as Corporal Hastings slowly drove into the compound, keeping his eyes open for potential combatants. There was no sign of the U-Haul that had been previously reported. They made their way to building 2501. The spotlight caught sight of Lieutenant Dugen and Private Shays's patrol car. The spotlight then found the two men lying in front of the doorway to building 2501. Corporal Hastings stopped the patrol car and put it in park. He quietly sat in the car, looking cautiously. Private Walters grabbed for the door handle to get out. "Wait," demanded Corporal Hastings. "We need to make sure it's safe before we go any farther." Both men paused to scan the area once more before getting out of the patrol car. Wind and rain compliments of hurricane Isabelle swept across the car. The men did not want to find themselves in the same predicament that they found the men that lay before them.

Once Corporal Hastings felt it was safe, he called over the patrol car's radio for the dispatcher to send an ambulance on the double and that they were proceeding to the fallen men. "Private, get your sidearm out," ordered Corporal Hastings. The private did as he was ordered and kept watch. Corporal Hastings moved to the closest man, Private Shays. He knelt down to feel for a pulse. He found a strong pulse. He then moved on to Lieutenant Dugen. The rain pounded on the men as they attended to the two fallen MPs. The corporal felt for a pulse but found none. He stood and used his flashlight to scan the area when he noticed he was standing in a pool of blood, Lieutenant Dugen's. Corporal Hastings rolled Hugh onto his side looking for a wound. He found the knife wound in Hugh's lower back. The corporal moved Hugh back to the position he found him. He stepped back out of the blood, and a cold chill ran over him. Corporal Hastings used his flashlight to pan around the area when he notice blood mixed with rain on the loading dock and coming from building 2501. Corporal Hastings made a mental note of the blood and the wound in Hugh's back. He knew that the rain and wind would deteriorate the crime scene, and he wanted to be sure he had a mental picture to relay to the crime scene investigators when they arrived. Lieutenant Dugen was a friend, and he wanted to do everything in his power to make sure that whoever did this was caught. The young corporal noticed Lieutenant Dugen's Beretta lying on the ground just out of the fallen lieutenant's grasp. He would need to remember this too.

"Private, spread out and see if we can find what happened to the sentries. They have to be somewhere around here," ordered the corporal. "I'll wait here for the ambulance. Keep your eyes open. If you run into any problems, get down and call me. Don't try and take 'em by yourself."

"Yes, sir!" responded the young private. The private held his flashlight in one hand and his sidearm in the other. He made his way along the side of the building. Off in the distance on the other side of the fence, his flashlight caught sight of the two sentries bound to a tree. They were struggling to untie themselves when they caught sight of the private approaching them. They were groggy waking up from a drug-induced sleep. "Hey, Corporal, I found the sentries," called the private over his police radio.

"How are they?" asked the corporal.

"They look all right. They're on the other side of the fence. I'll have to go around," replied the private.

"Get to it then, Private." While the private was searching for the sentries, the corporal was attending to Private Shays. The corporal noticed that Private Shays's sidearm was still in his holster unlike the lieutenant's. The corporal was checking the private's wounds when he found Private Shays's knife. The corporal remembered that Lieutenant Dugen had a knife wound and put Private Shays's knife in his pocket to turn over to the investigating officers. While the corporal attended to Private Shays, the ambulance and several more MP patrol cars arrived.

CHAPTER 13

Larry regained consciousness when he felt the EMTs attending to his wounds. He was lying on a stretcher in the back of a military ambulance. From the sounds outside of the ambulance, the wind and rain had somewhat subsided from where it was when he had lost consciousness. He looked out the back of the ambulance and saw the area covered with MPs. He also saw numerous men in suits covered in trench coats that he assumed to be Naval Criminal Investigative Service (NCIS) agents. Larry saw a couple of men in trench coats talking with two soldiers that Larry assumed were the sentries subdued by Juan's men. He noticed that each sentry was being questioned independent of the other. Larry's attention was distracted by the sound of the rain hitting a heavy plastic object. He noticed a stretcher just outside the ambulance in front of him. On the stretcher was a plastic body bag with someone enclosed. Larry assumed the body bag contained that of Lieutenant Hugh Dugen. "Hey, Major, the private's awake," shouted one of the attending EMTs to another man some fifty yards away.

Major John Lawrence heard the EMT's call. He promptly excused himself from the person with whom he was engaged in conversation and made his way to the ambulance. He climbed into the rear of the ambulance where Private Larry Shays was resting. Major Lawrence brushed as much rainwater off himself as he could as he entered the ambulance. He removed his military hat that had been carefully covered with plastic to protect it from the evening's rain. Larry could see the major was truly "government issue." Major John Lawrence was a few years shy of a thirty-year career in the marine corps. By all accounts, he should have been discharged from the marine corps in yesteryear. To many that he served with at NCIS, he was a relic of a bygone era in the marine corps. His abilities did not lie in his physical attributes; it was his exceptional analytical abilities that served the marine corps and him well prior to the advent of the personal computer. His tenure in the marine corps was purely a reward for his past years of service by those that carried political clout in Washington. He knew he would never receive any further promotions. He elected to stay in the marine corps simply because he did not have anyone or anything else. He often wowed the politicians on Capitol Hill with his polite charm that made him indispensable to those with political clout. His face was aged by time and his assignments in warm weather ports. He had an award-winning smile. Now with advanced technology, the marine corps had to find a position that would allow Major Lawrence to get his thirty years of service provide the marine corps with some value and allow him to wow the politicians on Capitol Hill. Hence, he was reluctantly assigned to the NCIS Washington DC post.

"Private Shays, Major Lawrence." Major John Lawrence introduced himself to the very smug Private Larry Shays. Major John Lawrence had served in Desert Storm on an aircraft carrier in the Persian Gulf. The assignment had been temporary. During Desert Storm, he gathered data and relayed it to the ground troops in the field. Since Desert Storm, he was reassigned back to the NCIS in Washington DC. Most of his work entailed pushing paper from one governmental office to another with an occasional wiping the nose of a congressman here and there. It was the wiping of the congressman's nose that required his rank. Major Lawrence arrived earlier in the day despite the approaching hurricane on a routine investigative mission to assess base security. John knew it was a token assignment, but that seemed all the marine corps relegated him to as he waited his retirement. He was to focus most of his attention determining how secure the ammunitions depots were maintained and the quality of the electronic surveillance surrounding the ammunition depots at Camp LeJeune, North Carolina. Major Lawrence was not trained in this arena. He received coaching from several of those assigned to his office. Those more qualified for such an investigation were assigned to other higher-priority tasks, working on the upcoming budget or testifying before someone.

Several military installations throughout the southeastern part of the United States had had submachine guns, assault rifles, and heavy weapons stolen under very similar circumstances. John was sent to assess base security weaknesses at various naval and marine corps installations. His plans were delayed that day since all base personnel were preparing for hurricane Isabelle. John was a man of average height and build. He was fit from a self-induced regimen of exercise and diet. John sat on a small bench inside the ambulance normally reserved for emergency personnel attending to patients. "You and Lieutenant Hugh Dugen had one hell of a bad night here! Can you tell me what happened, Private?"

Larry paused for a moment to collect his thoughts. He had rehearsed this moment in his mind over and over again. Though there was no award for his pending performance, what was at stake was several years in Leavenworth Federal Prison. "I'll do my best, Major." Larry asked one of the EMTs to adjust the back of the stretcher so he could sit up and talk.

John felt that he was getting ready for a Broadway performance. He could tell that Private Shays was building for a crescendo. John wasn't sure how Private Shays was mixed up in the break-in, but there was an air to Private Shays that John knew felt wrong.

After a bit of melodrama about his wound, Larry finally spoke. "The lieu and me saw this U-Haul parked in front of the 'munitions depot warehouse so we went to check it out. He had me call the dispatcher to request backup. The dispatcher can back that up. As we entered the warehouse, they started shootin' at us. I guess I fell unconscious when I got hit after the shootin' started."

"Did you see any of the people?" asked Major Lawrence.

"I didn't see anybody's face 'cause it was too dark, but I think I did see 'em wearin' fatigues."

"What kind of fatigues?"

"Ya know . . . army type."

"Did you hear anything or recognize anyone's voice? Maybe an accent?"

"Can't remember." There was a brief pause. "Oh yeah, I remember hearin' something. They sounded country. They were talkin' about gettin' back to some compound and how the stuff was goin' to be great to train with. I think they might be part of one of those militias," responded Larry.

John looked over at one of the EMTs. "How's Private Shays?" inquired John.

"He'll be all right, Major. He's got a gunshot wound to his shoulder. He should be okay in a couple of days. I'm going to have to leave it to the doctors to tell you more," answered one of the attending EMTs.

"Okay, get him out of here." John looked over at Larry. "I'll see you later!"

As John exited the ambulance, he whispered to an MP. The MP got in the ambulance with Larry. Once the MP was seated, John turned to the MP as almost an afterthought. "Stick close to him. We don't want anything to happen to Private Shays."

John looked at Larry with a casual smile. "We'd hate for anyone to come after our star witness."

Larry tried to make himself comfortable on the stretcher. He thought to himself, *Round 1 goes to Private Larry Shays.*

The EMT attending to Larry gave John a salute that he returned in kind. The EMT reached forward to close the doors to the ambulance. John heard the EMT inside call to the driver, and then the ambulance pulled away.

CHAPTER 14

John began to mull over his brief conversation with Private Shays. He also mulled over the entire crime scene in his head. He reached into his pocket and removed a plastic bag containing Private Larry Shays's knife. Corporal Hastings, who was first on the scene, found Private Shays lying on the ground. When the MP helped to attend to Private Shays's wounds, he discovered the knife. The MP commented that when attending to Lieutenant Dugen's wound, the wound appeared to have been caused by a knife. The MP took the knife as potential evidence and gave it to John. John made a point of asking the corporal where Lieutenant Dugen's sidearm was and Private Shays's sidearm when he found the men lying on the ground. John was impressed with the way Corporal Hastings had made a point of noticing so many intricate details often overlooked by a novice. He also thought about his conversation with the NCIS officers after their interrogation of the sentries. Only one of the sentries caught any kind of a glimpse of the perpetrators, and he claimed they wore black clothing, and their faces were covered in neoprene ski masks. Yet Shays claimed the men wore military fatigues. John wondered that maybe because of the size of the operation, certain perps wore military uniforms and others wore black clothes to blend into the night. John also wondered if maybe the perps were marines looking to make a fast buck.

John noticed several footprints in the mud in front of the landing to the ammunitions depot warehouse and tracks from where a truck once stood. Were they mostly from the perps, or was the crime scene trampled with overzealous EMTs and MPs? He also noticed large tire tracks next to the footprints. Larry's comment about a U-Haul made sense. How else would you steal the amount of weapons that was missing unless you had some kind of moving truck? John noted the heavy indentions in the mud from the weight of the truck. John noted that the electronic security had somehow failed. He did not see any signs that the electronic security had been disabled at the ammunitions depot. He also took a mental note that the fence to the ammunitions depot and the doors to the warehouse had been cut, most likely with some heavy-duty metal clippers. He thought about the two sentries that had been subdued by tranquilizer darts, yet Lieutenant Hugh Dugen had been brutally stabbed in his lower back. Lieutenant Dugen's death seemed almost personal. Was there more than one group of perpetrators? It looked like whoever was trying to wound him wanted him dead, possibly his own partner. But who shot Private Shays? By the way Lieutenant Dugen's body was positioned, there was no way he could have shot Private Shays. John made a mental note to check the bullet from Private Shays's shoulder to Lieutenant Dugen's gun.

As John thought through the scenario, Colonel Charles Radford appeared. He was in charge of Camp LeJeune's military police, the provost marshal.

As far as Colonel Charles Radford was concerned, he only reported to the base chief of staff or the commanding general himself. He was not happy about one military relic, Major John Lawrence, reviewing his security. He had chalked it up to typical military bureaucracy. "Good morning, Colonel."

"'Morning, Major." The two men exchanged salutes as almost an afterthought.

"Officer of the day called you, Colonel?" inquired John.

"Yeah. Major, you have any idea who did this, or what the hell this is all about? I don't like any of my men getting sent to the morgue or the hospital. Hugh was a damn fine MP, can't say as much for Private Shays, but he was still a part of my command." Colonel Charles Radford was stern in his approach toward John. He had been that way once he heard Washington was sending someone to investigate the security under his command.

"Colonel, I don't have a whole lot of ideas right now, but with a fresh trail and your permission, I would like to start the investigation." John didn't believe he really needed the colonel's permission since he was on assignment from Washington. John's years of experience in the military told him though that if he wanted the colonel's support, he should follow military protocol. In the end, John knew it would pay off if he wanted the colonel's cooperation. He fibbed to the colonel about "not having a whole lot of ideas." John certainly felt that Private Shays was *dirty*, but his experience taught him to keep his mouth shut until he had something he could hang his hat on.

"Get on with it, Major. You have my permission, but I want you to update me regularly, this means before you notify Washington. I don't want you doing some fuckin' end around horseshit on me! You talk to me before anyone in Washington. Got it, Major?" spoke a sharp and forceful Colonel Radford. Colonel Radford stared directly at John with a determined expression waiting for John's response.

"Yes, sir," replied John with a loud affirmation. John hated when a superior officer felt he had to play the tough-guy role, but John accepted it frequently and would move on.

As Colonel Radford started to leave, he turned to John, "One more thing, Major, I had my office notify the Jacksonville Police Department that we would need the services of their forensic team. They should be here any minute now."

"Thank you, sir. Sergeant?" John addressed the next ranking soldier other than the colonel on the scene.

"Yes sir, Major," answered the sergeant.

"First, I want you to instruct all sentries at the gates to forbid any U-Hauls from leaving the base. If they find any U-Hauls, they are to be searched for anything suspicious. Have the men use gloves. If they find anything remotely out of the ordinary, they are to report directly to me. I also want you to send MPs to all the gates to the base. They are to relieve the sentries there. Call up the next watch early if you have to. I want an MP to drive the sentries from the gatehouses to the provost marshal's office where I have been working. I don't want them to talk with any of their fellow sentries. I want to interview them at my office individually. Put the sentries in separate interrogation rooms. I do not want them to go anywhere prior to my interview, got it?" John was trying to remember as much about interrogation procedures as he could as he barked out his orders. John's analytical mind was hard at work.

"Yes sir, Major. Anything else?" continued the sergeant.

"Yeah, I need a driver to take me over to LeJeune's central electronic surveillance building." The sergeant started rounding up his squad and barking out the major's orders. He enlisted the services of a young private to take Major Lawrence to the central electronic surveillance building.

As John waited in the patrol car to be chauffeured to the central electronic surveillance building, he noticed the Jacksonville Police Department's forensic team arrive. He started to give them Private Shays's knife but decided to wait. The raindrops on the window obscured his view of the forensic team hard at work—the tedious task of gathering the most minute piece of evidence. He knew the rain would hinder their efforts. John felt certain that much of the evidence was probably already washed away or of no forensic value. He felt they would be able to obtain DNA from the blood found in the ammunitions depot warehouse, but would there be anything to match the sample to? John believed that as organized as these perpetrators were, finding any fingerprints was a remote possibility.

CHAPTER 15

The private got in to the patrol car, startling John from his thoughts when he slammed the car door shut. The private started up the engine and put the car in gear headed for the central electronic surveillance building. As the men made their way to the central electronic surveillance building, John got on the patrol car's radio to start rounding up the much-needed additional MPs. He knew he was going to need all the support available to him. Every criminal journal he ever read and his training as an NCIS officer advised that the first few hours in any investigation were often the most critical. John wanted to make the first few hours work for him, and he wanted the manpower to make it happen. "Corporal?" John knew Corporal Bruce McDermott was manning the evening, now early morning, command radio shift at the provost marshal's office. The Corporal had called him at two in the morning at Camp LeJeune's only Officers Hotel to inform him about the break-in at the ammunitions depot. John had gotten directions from the corporal to the ammunitions depot. Now he felt it would be more efficient if somebody chauffeured him around since he was unfamiliar with Camp LeJeune.

"This is Corporal McDermott," responded the weary radio operator.

"Corporal, this is Major Lawrence. I need for you to round up about fifty more MPs to start searching this base."

"Right now, sir?" inquired the corporal.

"Yes, now!" John knew rounding up fifty men in the early hours on a raining morning was going to be a challenge enough without the help of a category 4 hurricane that just passed through.

"But, sir, we've never even had fifty MPs here at LeJeune."

"Very well then, get me the chief of staff on the radio," demanded John.

"Sir?" responded the corporal.

"Get me the chief of staff!" barked the determined John.

"Yes, sir." John could hear the reluctance in the corporal's voice.

—

As John waited, he knew the chief of staff would be pissed off at being awoken in what was now the very early morning hours. But he knew he would be more pissed off if this happened, and he was not informed first. John knew nothing happened on any base without the chief of staff's knowledge, and if anything did, "God help those responsible." Next thing John heard was, "Colonel Marks here, what can I do for you, Maaajooor?" John could tell by the annoyed tone of voice and the long "major" that the colonel was none too happy. John quickly updated the colonel on what he knew so far. "So what do you need, Major?"

"I need fifty men to assist me with the start of my investigation," answered John.

"I'll see what I can do. Let me make a few calls, and I'll see if I can't get you some help. I'll have the men meet you at . . . the provost marshal's office," replied Colonel Marks.

"Thank you, sir. That would be great." John realized that the colonel had already hung the phone up as he was thanking him. John knew that "make a few calls" meant one call to the chief of staff's aide and that there would be no further telephone calls made. He knew that they would meet him at the provost marshal's office pronto.

As the patrol car arrived at the central electronic surveillance building, he noticed there were no sentries present. John entered the building where he found the two men who had been attending to the surveillance monitors lying on the floor. The missing sentries were attending to one of the men. Major Lawrence flashed his NCIS badge and turned to one of the sentries. "What happened here, Private?"

The sentries looked at each other uneasily wondering if whatever their reply would find them in trouble. After a long uncomfortable silence, one of the sentries responded, "We were called away to assist in tying down some tarps covering equipment a couple of blocks down the way. When we returned, we found these two lying on the floor . . . out cold."

John continued his inquiry, "Have you called an ambulance, Private?"

"Yes, sir! One's on the way."

"The equipment that needed to be tied down, wasn't it tied down before the storm?" inquired John.

The sentry that had been doing most of the talking continued, "I guess so. It looked as though some of the ropes had been torn loose by the wind."

John listened and then asked, "Torn loose or cut?"

The sentry thought for a moment. "I guess it could have been cut." He was not sure where John was going with his questions, but he did not want to be put into a situation where he would have to retract anything later. Retracting a statement was something no one in military service ever wanted to do.

John looked at the sentry who had been doing most of the talking. "When I'm done here, I want you to take me to where those ropes came loose."

"Yes sir, Major."

John made a mental note to follow up further on who called the sentries away from their post. He turned to the two men who were still groggy, "Can you tell me what happened?"

Both men started to talk before one of the men took the initiative. "We were monitoring the central security surveillance system as usual when we were shot in the neck by these darts." The private who had been talking handed John one of the darts, and then the other private handed John his dart. "We didn't hear nothin'. Just *bam*, and the next thing we were wakin' up on the floor."

John was careful in handling the darts. He was hoping not to smudge any potential fingerprints remaining after the sentries had already handled them. He looked around and found an empty envelope on a nearby desk and placed the darts in the envelope. He put the envelope in his pocket along with Private Shays's knife that he retrieved earlier. John looked back at the sentries. "Who told you to go tie down the equipment?"

Both sentries looked uneasy, and then the one who had been doing all the talking responded, "It came from the dispatcher." John made a note to talk with Corporal McDermott on who instructed him to call the sentries away to tie down the tarps covering the equipment.

As John looked around a little more, he noticed that several cables had been torn out of the wall and some from the back of the monitoring devices. John turned his attention back to the men who were monitoring the surveillance equipment. "Did you notice those wires were disconnected?"

The men were caught off guard. They had been intent on attending to their own injuries. "No, sir," responded one of the men. "I believe we can fix it. Once we do, we'll send you whatever we have." He was referring to the videos.

John appreciated the vigilance of the young soldiers. "Private, I appreciate your enthusiasm, but let's have forensics check for fingerprints before we disturb the crime scene any more than it has already been disturbed." John could tell his remarks had cut deep into their enthusiasm, but concern for the men's feelings was not paramount to John. Solving the break-in was!

John remembered it was not all that long ago when each military base had its own criminal investigative service, some smaller than others depending on the size of the military base, to handle military criminal investigations for the navy and marine corps. Due to budget cuts within the department of defense, "luxury" was quickly becoming defunct for many of the military installations. Washington came up with a cost-cutting idea of subcontracting forensic investigations out to the local authorities that had the resources in lieu of budgeting the military a criminal forensic team at each base along with the necessary equipment. When an investigation needed to be performed within the military framework for confidential purposes, the NCIS would send in a team from Washington to do the investigation. The downside was that sometimes leads would go cold while a team of investigators could be dispatched to the crime scene.

John looked at the two sentries that had been called away to help tie down the tarps covering the equipment. "Take me to where you tied down the tarps." The soldiers promptly complied. They walked to the location in what was now just an annoying rain shower. John noticed that the distance was not far enough to drive but far enough to detour the sentries for someone to get in and out of the surveillance room without being seen. The sentries showed John the ropes. To John, the ropes had clearly been cut. He pulled out a knife from his pants pocket and cut the ropes once again and marked where he had cut the ropes. He placed the rope samples in a plastic bag that he confiscated from the patrol car that took him to the surveillance building. He planned to give to the forensic team the ropes to ascertain if the ropes were in fact cut. John instructed the sentries to find some rope to resecure the tarp.

John walked back to the surveillance building. When he arrived, he noticed an ambulance had arrived. A couple EMTs were tending to the men from the surveillance monitoring station.

"How are the men?" inquired John of one of the EMTs.

"They should be all right. Once we get a couple of men in here to take over for them, we're gonna take them in for x-rays and some routine follow-through procedures just to be on the safe side." The EMT was not speaking from his own assessment, but protocol from similar situations.

"Very well then." John found his driver. "Take me back to the provost marshal's office." When John returned to the provost marshal's office, some of the fifty men he requested from the chief of staff were beginning to arrive. Within the hour, the soldiers were on hand, and John began to brief them. John gave each one of them a list of items to look for to assist in his investigation. On the top of each list was the U-Haul followed by wire cutters. They were to touch nothing, but report directly to him day or night if they found anything.

CHAPTER 16

As the morning wore on, the rain continued to subside. The clouds quietly gave way to a blue sky. The air was still heavy with lingering moisture from the evening's storm. Seth and the deputies resumed their patrols to assess the damage Isabelle had inflicted on the small island. Seth directed the deputies, "Ned, take one of the deputies and a patrol car. Close access to the island from the bridge. No one, and I mean no one, is permitted access to the island, not homeowners—no one." Seth knew the bridge tender would be back at the bridge first thing in the morning to allow emergency vehicles onto the island and boats passing north and south access to the Intracoastal Waterway. They had his home telephone number, so he could be contacted at any time. Seth also knew that the bridge tender could not prevent other vehicles from accessing the island. Usually a bridge tender manned the bridge twenty-four hours a day, allowing cars to cross and opening the bridge for boats heading north and south. "We've got to see how things stand before we can start letting people onto the island. There could be loose power lines, sinkholes, and who knows what other hazards. We also need to watch for looting." Seth had been in contact with the North Onslow Police Department throughout the night and at first light. They had closed the northern access to the island. The north bridge was the only other bridge leading onto the island. That bridge was under the jurisdiction of the North Onslow Police Department. "The rest of you, split up, and let's check everything out. Watch for downed power lines and other hazards. Be careful!" Seth felt like their mothers repeating everything over and over but wanted to be sure nothing was left to chance. He left one deputy behind to attend to the station and answer incoming calls. Seth went out to patrol the town on his own and look for hazards and victims as a result of hurricane Isabelle. Argo was on Seth's heels as he headed for his patrol car. "If anyone calls, tell them we are assessing the damage and to listen to their local news. Let them know the island is closed to everyone. And I mean *everyone*! Reassure them that we are doing everything in our power to protect their investments."

Luckily, Topsail Island had been spared most of Isabelle's rage. Isabelle came ashore with sustained winds better than 150 miles an hour at Cape Fear, a small town south of Wilmington, North Carolina, making it a category 4 hurricane as predicted by the National Hurricane Center in Miami, Florida. The hardest hit areas were Oak Island and Bald Head Island. According to the radio, Wrightsville Beach, Carolina Beach, and Figure Eight Island, several points north of the eye, had suffered considerable storm surge. Wrightsville Beach and Figure Eight Island are located slightly north of Wilmington. Carolina Beach is located south of Wilmington. Isabelle was about one hundred and seventy-five miles across and traveled at about fifteen miles an hour. The hurricane continued moving northwest, causing extensive damage and flooding inland. The local news stations reported the storm surge had crossed the respective islands in various places. Several homes had been swept into the Atlantic Ocean and left only pilings on where people's vacation homes once stood. The governor ordered the National Guard to be dispatched to Wrightsville Beach, Carolina Beach, Figure Eight Island, and surrounding areas. He had also declared the area to be a disaster area. It was reported that the president of the United States was to make a visit within the week. The National Guard would start arriving the next day; until then the state police and the local police would have to guard against looting, direct traffic, and help wherever necessary. The Red Cross was already en route to the area along with FEMA (Federal Emergency Management Agency). The governor had contacted the general at Camp LeJeune to request the general to dispatch troops to fill in during the interim. State police and marine corps helicopters were flying over the islands to assist and radioing the location of potential looters. They also were radioing trouble spots such as where the ocean had cut swaths across the islands and where roads had been washed away. The fact that much of the areas that were hit the hardest were islands helped prevent some looting, but not all. There were still those repugnant individuals that chose to use their boats to take advantage of island homeowners to loot.

Seth was amazed at how Isabelle had inflicted such fury during the night. Now the day after was sunny as if nature was somehow reconciling for Isabelle's torment. He could see places where the ocean had burst through sand dunes. The locals had always been protective of the dunes since they help protect the island. Often tourists wander through the dunes not realizing that the dunes are nature's way of protecting the islands. Seth noted the damage on a clipboard he brought along. He stopped by his home for a quick look and to let Argo out to do her chores. Seth got out of his Bronco to walk through his house to assess the damage. He flipped on the light switch as he entered, remembering the island was still without power. He had been spared! He took a private moment thinking of Maribeth and the place they once called home. Seth noticed a few shingles missing from the roof. Sand was everywhere, but there was nothing that could not be easily repaired or cleaned up. He returned to his patrol car and resumed his patrols with Argo at his side. While on patrol, as Seth reached any of his deputy's homes, he would call them over the radio and assess the damage for them, if any. Most were already aware since they had made their own detours to assess their own homes, but they all appreciated Seth looking out for them. The small office police station was made for almost a family-type atmosphere. Those who had not been to their home listened eagerly for the damage report and gave a sigh of relief that they too had been spared collateral damage. All in all, Surf City was lucky for only receiving relatively minor damage. The major damage to the island had been in North Topsail and points on the extreme south end of Topsail Island.

Chapter 17

Seth returned to the station so he could contact the other island police departments to once again coordinate plans for safeguarding the island and for the islanders' eventual return. He also was eager to hear their assessment of damage to the island and any other developments he may have missed while on patrol. As Seth entered the police station, "Chief," called the lone deputy who had been left to answer the phones, "A Major Lawrence over at LeJeune called."

"Did he say what he wanted?" It was not unusual for Camp LeJeune to call. They usually called to see if one of their soldiers was in the local jail from a night of too much drinking or to check on one of their soldiers living on the island that was a no-show at work. "They know we evacuated the island."

"All he said was that you needed to call him ASAP. Said it was real important. Here's his number." The deputy handed Seth the note with the telephone number scribbled at the top.

Seth took the message and went into his office, closing the door behind him as he entered. He dialed the number. "Provost marshal's office, Private Rodriguez," shouted the voice on the other end. The spit-polish voice that snapped to on the other end of the line reminded Seth of his days in the marine corps.

"I need to speak with a Major Lawrence," requested Seth.

"Yes, sir."

There was a brief pause. "Major Lawrence here."

"This is Chief Jarret with the Surf City Police Department. I'm returning your call."

"Yes, Chief, thanks for getting back to me." John shuffled several pieces of paper on his desk trying to remember who Chief Jarret might be and where the hell Surf City was.

"What can I do for you, Major?"

"Chief, we had a little problem over here. It appears during the storm last night someone had the balls to break into one of our 'munitions depots and took a fair amount of weapons. They also killed one of our MPs in the process."

"Major, you can't be serious. Who the hell would have the balls to brave that storm?"

John paused for a moment to listen to Seth's inquiry. "We're not sure who it was, but we're looking for cooperation from the local authorities." John paused for a moment and then offered, "We know they were incredibly brave or incredibly stupid and lucky."

Seth heard the sarcasm in John's voice but let the comment drop. "What did they take?" Seth was concerned that firearms in the wrong hands locally could be disastrous. The shoot-out in Charlotte would pale in comparison to what someone could do with a stockpile of military weapons.

"Sorry, Chief, I'm not at liberty to discuss all the particulars with you at this time. What we need is for you to be on the lookout for what should I say . . . suspicious behavior or strangers in your area. I know this time of year, the beach communities are a little slow, so newcomers should stand out. We know they used a U-Haul, but we don't have the license plate number, size, or any other details at this time. We would also like for you to check with some of the local gun dealers that you may know about and find out if anyone has recently acquired any military arms and now has them for sale. We're contacting all the police departments in the area to ask for assistance. We feel they may still be in the area since the storm most likely would have slowed them down."

"I should say. That storm was a bitch. Do you have any leads, or can you tell me what I should be looking for?" Seth knew that the major was not going to give him details of the weapons, but he was hoping for more than just "suspicious behavior" or "strangers and a U-Haul."

"We're working on that right now. We'll update you as soon as we know something or have something more we can sink our teeth into. The only thing we have right now is a guard who believes the perps may be some Southern boys. He said they were wearing fatigues last night. Who knows what they may be wearing now?" John felt Private Shays knew more than he had let onto earlier and was planning on a return interrogation with Private Shays, but for now he did not want to disclose supposition to the locals, only facts! "We also have reason to believe that our MP may have shot one of the perps during the robbery, so you may want to contact any doctors, veterinarians, or anyone with medical training."

Seth loved the term "perps," good old police talk for perpetrators. "I'll alert my deputies right away."

"Hey, Chief, let's keep as much of this under our hat as possible . . . it makes us look bad."

"I understand, Major. I'm an ex myself."

"What branch?"

"Marine corps, same as you." Seth assumed the major was with the marine corps since he was calling from Camp LeJeune, a marine corps installation. "Spent some time in Desert Storm."

"Yeah, me too."

"Where?"

"On a ship in the gulf."

"You had a cush job. Like Saddam had a navy?"

"They weren't big, just a pain in the ass. My job was in intelligence. We gathered data and relayed it to you boys in the field. I'm a jarhead like you".

Seth could talk one marine to another with ease. "Yeah, that was some good intel." Seth was anxious to end his conversation so he could get to the more pressing issues associated the posthurricane situation. "Okay. Look, I've gotta run, but I'll pass the word to look for anything out of the ordinary and for 'suspicious behavior' or 'strangers.'"

John could hear the irony in Seth's tone but elected to let it pass. He needed assistance from the local law enforcement and was smart enough to know that you don't mess with the good ole boy network by picking a fight over the little things.

"We'll keep an eye out for a U-Haul, and we'll contact people around here with medical training." Seth continued, "Keep us posted on any developments you make so we can update our profile on the perps. By the way, if you make it my way, I'll buy ya a beer and tell you what a hero I was."

"Look forward to it, Chief," replied John.

Seth hung up the phone. He went out to his deputy at the front desk. "Look, LeJeune had some problems last night with a break-in. I want you to let all the deputies know that they need to be on the lookout for anything out of the ordinary. They need to keep their eyes out for a U-Haul. Also, have them contact anyone they know or can think of with any kind of medical training—doctors, nurses, veterinarians, EMTs, etc. Ask them to network with some of the local gun dealers, pawnshops, etc. We're looking for anyone trying to unload military arms. Tell them—do not announce it over the radio!" Seth's fear was that people with police scanners may hear the broadcast, and then he would have everyone all over his back along with a mass panic.

"You got it, Chief."

CHAPTER 18

Seth went back into his office and closed the door. He started making the phone calls he originally returned to his office to make before he was sidetracked with the Camp LeJeune incident. Most of the day slipped away talking with the governor's office; the Pender County sheriff's office; other local, county, and state law enforcement; and various news agencies.

Seth called Burt and Jeanine Warner. He wanted to find out how they fared during the hurricane. Since Maribeth's death, they were the closest things Seth had to family or close friends in the area. After about the twentieth ring, Seth heard a voice. It was Jeanine. "Jeanine . . . it's Seth." Seth could hear Jeanine trying to catch her breath. "How did you make out during the hurricane? We heard there were tornados all around your area."

Jeanine was glad to hear Seth's voice. "We made out all right."

"How 'bout your folks?" asked Seth. He knew Jeanine lived next door to her parents.

"They're all right. A tornado did rip through nearby, tearing down some neighbors' homes, a small Baptist church, and an elementary school. About twenty-five people are in temporary housing or staying with friends or family, but no one was killed or needed major medical treatment. All in all we were lucky. How about things down your way?" inquired Jeanine.

Seth quickly updated Jeanine on things in Surf City but intentionally left out what happened at Camp LeJeune. "Look, is Burt there?" asked Seth.

"No. He left early this mornin' after he saw that we were all right around here. Like I'm sure you've been doin', he had to do more police shit to do today. He left me here to work in the yard piling up tree limbs and other debris. He stayed here long enough to at least remove the boards from the windows."

Seth laughed listening to Jeanine's comments about Burt. He knew Burt was all cop, and Jeanine was comfortable with his dedication to the sheriff's department. Seth also knew that when Jeanine put her foot down, that was it.

"So what else have you been doin'?" Seth felt he would make a little small talk before returning to his police duties. He needed the break.

"Hell . . . like most of the people in the state of North Carolina, I've been hanging on any news aired by the television stations. I've been watching any information regarding Pender County, Topsail Island, and more specifically Surf City. I've been worried about you boys down in Surf City. Most of the news has been covering Wrightsville Beach and Wilmington since they are the larger towns in the area. It makes sense that they would be covering mostly Wilmington and Wrightsville Beach since the television stations for our area are based in Wilmington. Besides, it sounds like they were hardest hit anyhow." Jeanine was direct, but she cared about Seth. She also knew all the men that worked with him, including Ned's wife, Sarah. Since Maribeth's death, she felt almost like a surrogate mother to Seth.

Seth quickly chimed in when she caught her breath. He knew if he didn't, she would go on forever. "We're all right down here. My house survived the storm. The house lost a few shingles, and there's some beach erosion, but nothing that can't be easily fixed or replaced." Well, the beach erosion wasn't good, but with some posthurricane bulldozing, his life would return to some state of normalcy.

Jeanine sensed that Seth was trying to end the conversation, so she quickly asked how the rest of the deputies' homes were and some of their friends.

Seth gave Jeanine a quick summary of everyone's home that he could remember.

Jeanine then replied, "So when am I going to see you again?"

"I believe it will be a couple more days, the National Guard is on its way, and we have several power lines down. Some of the roads are still impassable. Besides, I need to pick up that van with my priceless possessions."

Jeanine loved Seth's sarcasm and complimented him by offering a chuckle. "Let me know so I can fix up something nice for you to eat when you come by. You and Burt need a reward for all your hard work."

"I look forward to it," responded a modest Seth. "I'll give you a call in a day or two."

After a little more joking around, they said their good-byes. "You take care of yourself," demanded Jeanine.

"You take good care of yourself and say hello to Burt for me."

As Seth hung up, some of the deputies returning from their rounds overheard Seth. In the past, they would have thought it was Maribeth, but they had all been around Jeanine and knew it had to be her. They were all well aware of how Jeanine had taken over as surrogate mother to Seth. "Be good and brush your teeth," shouted the deputies.

Seth laughed off the jibes. He often teased the men and knew their jibes were a return of fair play. "Why aren't you guarding the bridges?" asked Seth.

Ned replied, "Relax, Chief, the North Onslow police are guarding the bridge up next to them, and the Pender County sheriff's office is guarding the bridge near us."

"Did they give you permission to leave?" asked Seth.

"No!" replied an exhausted Ned. Ned was tired. All the men were exhausted. They stayed up most of the night patrolling and listening to news updates to find out if they were going to wash into the ocean. He was at the point of turning on Seth.

"Then why are you here?" Seth hated when the men would act without consulting him first.

"Well, it didn't make any sense for all of us to guard one small bridge. Besides, we haven't eaten or slept in hours." Ned was trying to be as tactful as he could with Seth. He knew Seth hadn't slept either. He also knew that no matter how hard he and the deputies worked, Seth would always do more.

Seth realized how petty he was getting. The deputies had not had any relief for more than twenty-four hours. It was a small department, and Seth could see the fatigue and concern for their own well-being in their faces. "Okay, I want you guys to go home and get something to eat and a few hours' rest. I realize it's not much, but we are here to look out for the residents that aren't here to look out for themselves. Come back at eight tonight."

The men were happy to hear Seth give them some time off. They knew a few hours were not much, but the fact still remained that their department was small. They also knew that even though Seth was sending them home, he would stay and keep the office running.

CHAPTER 19

John began interrogating the sentries that were on duty at the gates providing access to Camp LeJeune during the hours when the break-in occurred. There are three entrances to the base. Two of the gates had only two sentries each on duty. The other one, the main gate had five sentries during the evening shift. John felt that if anyone were going to sneak on and off the base, it would be at one of the gates that were less traveled. John reviewed the logs from all the gates. John dispatched the NCIS agents that accompanied him from Washington DC to check the gate's log for nonmilitary personnel vehicles accessing Camp LeJeune. The main gate reported two U-Hauls entering the base. The NCIS agents went to the addresses on the base listed in the log and found the trucks still there along with the lessees. None of the gates reported any U-Hauls leaving the base. John was satisfied with the NCIS investigation relating to the activity at the main gate. Two enlisted men guarded the gate that permitted access from Hubert, North Carolina, onto the base. Both were enlisted men getting out of the service and planning to move back home once they were discharged. Their military records, though short, had been exemplary. John met with the sentries and was satisfied with their answers. He was further satisfied to find out that a motorist trying to flee from Isabelle had his vehicle die near their gate around eleven o'clock at night and was forced to spend the duration of hurricane Isabelle with the sentries. The three men stayed locked in a small gatehouse. John telephoned the motorist at his home earlier and was satisfied with his answers corroborating the sentries' stories.

The remaining sentries John had yet to interrogate were Privates Jack Matthew and Toby Clark. John sat down with Jack to begin his examination. Jack pretty much had nothing to say and kept inquiring if he needed to have an attorney present. John kept asking, "Do you think you need one?" John sensed uneasiness in Jack. He couldn't quite put his finger on the problem but figured maybe if he spent some time with Private Toby Clark and returned later to further his examination of Private Jack Matthew, he may crack, possibly with the help of fabricating the truth. After some time questioning Jack, John left the room. He wanted Jack to wrestle with his thoughts. John strolled down to the break room and made himself a cup of coffee. He figured he would take a breather to regroup before his examination of Private Toby Clark. John entered an adjacent interrogation room where he found Private Toby Clark nervously pacing the floor.

"Private Toby Clark?" inquired John as he entered the interrogation room. John knew whom he was talking to and used the trite question as an icebreaker. John sat down in a metal chair closest to the door, one of two in the room, and waited for Private Clark to take the seat opposite from him.

Toby was startled when he heard John's voice. He snapped a salute. "Yes sir, Major" barked Toby.

John gave a matter-of-fact salute back to Private Clark.

Toby saw the major take a seat at the table. He hesitated before taking a seat across the table from John.

John watched carefully as the private fumbled around before taking the seat opposite from him. Once the private was seated, John began his examination. "Private, I understand that you and Private Matthew were at the Sneads Ferry Gate all alone last night."

"Yes sir, Major." Toby's voice quivered a little as he spoke. What could be wrong for him and Jack to be interrogated? "Well, except for the usual patrol that stopped by to check up on us." He was referring to Lieutenant Hugh Dugan and Private Larry Shays's patrol.

"That must have been pretty scary with that hurricane coming through? Nowhere to go and trapped in that old brick building. Whatta think, that building is maybe, say, fifty years old?" John was trying to soften Private Clark up before he decided to get tough with his interrogation.

"No, sir. That building wasn't goin' anywhere."

"Were you aware of any U-Hauls entering the Snead Ferry Gate last night?" asked John.

"Yes sir, Major. There was one that came through kinda late." Toby remembered that he and Jack were playing cards when the truck came through. It was his idea to ignore the truck during the storm, but he remembered Jack went out and checked it anyway. Toby remembered watching from the window of the guardhouse that Jack halfheartedly checked the truck out because the wind and rain were relentless. Toby figured this was a good time to cover his ass. "Jack went out in that storm and checked the truck through."

John listened intently to Toby's account. "I see according to your log that Private Matthew did check out at U-Haul. Were you watching him when he checked the truck through?" Often civilian motorists would obtain a pass to go through Camp LeJeune to avoid going around the base when heading north or south. The pass was good only for Highway 172 and was to be returned to a sentry at the opposite end when the civilian motorist exited the base.

"Yes sir, Major."

"What kind of job did he do?" inquired John.

"He was thorough."

"How thorough? What did he do?" probed John.

"I mean, he checked the truck out!" Toby was nervous. He wasn't sure how much Jack had told John about the truck.

"Did he look at driver's licenses? Did he open up the hood and cargo bin of the truck?"

"I don't remember," replied Toby.

"I thought you said you were watching. It was only last night. How is it you don't remember?" John's voice began to become agitated. He had not had any sleep, and he realized that Toby or Jack or most likely both were holding something back. He was just flat out of patience with this cat-and-mouse game. Toby began to squirm in his chair as he realized John was beginning to lose his patience. After a few moments, John shouted, "Private Matthew said that he did go and check the truck out, but because it was storming, you refused to go out and help log the truck in!"

Toby jumped to his feet and shouted back, "That fucking asshole."

John allowed a quiet pause to encompass the sparse room and calmly asked, "What kind of truck was it?"

"Fuck!" Toby knew he had been played. "It was a U-Haul." What did he care? So what, a truck came on the base. How much trouble could they be in? He had spent a few nights in the brig for drunk and disorderly in the past; he could handle a couple more. Big deal, he thought.

"Did you see how many people were in the truck?"

"Yes." Toby dropped the military formalities. "I saw two men."

"Can you describe them?"

"Naw, it was dark and raining. You couldn't really see much through the windows." Toby was thinking what was it with the truck.

"What time was it?" asked John.

"I dunno maybe midnight, one a.m."

After further interrogation, John realized that he had gotten all he was going to get from Toby. "Sergeant," commanded John.

"Yes sir, Major." A burly man stepped inside the small interrogation room. He came to attention as he entered.

"Keep an eye on this man." John left the room. He walked down the hall and entered the room where Jack was seated at a barren steel desk.

"Private!" John commanded Jack's full attention. "Private Clark stated that the U-Haul I was asking you about came though around midnight or one a.m. last night. Which is it?"

Jack could not believe what he was hearing. Had Toby told them the truth about not doing a proper investigation of the truck?

"Private," shouted John, "I am through being nice. I want to know the time and how many people you saw." John wanted Jack to be thinking about the time more than a sloppy examination of the truck so when he asked his more probing question, Jack would not be as concerned with his answer.

Jack paused and then responded. "It was midnight, and I only saw two men."

"I understand from Private Clark that you barely went out to investigate the U-Haul. You didn't even look at a driver's license much less look in the back of the U-Haul."

"No, I did check the driver's license of the driver," replied Jack. He got quiet. "I didn't check in the back. I know I should've, but it was hell in that storm. I got drenched for the couple of minutes I was out there."

John opened the door to the interrogation room and found the sergeant standing post outside the interrogation room where Toby was being held. "Sergeant, I want this man and Private Clark put under arrest for abandoning their post." The sergeant put his hand radio next to his mouth and called for assistance.

Jack looked at Major John Lawrence incredulously. "For not looking in the back of a truck?"

John knew neither Jack nor Toby had any idea what had happened. John looked intently at Jack. "Because you two didn't do your job, Lieutenant Hugh Dugen is dead."

Jack couldn't believe what he was hearing. He had always liked the lieutenant. Jack had worked with the lieutenant for a couple of years.

Four MPs arrived within minutes with handcuffs and shackles. They attached them to the wrists and ankles of Privates Jack Matthew and Toby Clark. The two men were read their rights and were immediately escorted over to the judge advocate for booking. From there, they would be taken to the brig. There the two men would await trial in a military court.

John got one of the MPs on duty to take him over to the base hospital where Private Shays was being treated. It was a relatively short drive. As John rode along, he noticed the clouds giving way to the persistent sun, and he started to feel a warm sense of relief. He noticed the road covered in debris. Trees were lying across several of the roads, and men with chainsaws were severing the limbs into manageable pieces. Tree limbs, garbage, and other items covered lawns and were nestled next to buildings. Camp LeJeune's public works was comprised principally of enlisted personnel to attend to the fallen debris. Progress Energy, the local power company, had trucks dispatched to the area to restoring power to the homes throughout the base. Occasionally they, too, were removing fallen tree limbs draped across the power lines.

It occurred to John as he rode along that he had never been in a hurricane. In fact, he had never been near a natural-disaster area. He grew up in the Washington DC area but had never been so close to a natural disaster. He had never felt the fear or the anguish or the torment that he found the locals experiencing. He felt saddened but also saw a sense of pride as the local residents immediately started cleaning up and rebuilding their lives.

He entered the hospital and inquired with the duty nurse where he could find Private Lawrence Shays's room. The nurse looked in a register and gave John the room number. He quickly found the room and entered. He found the private lying in a hospital bed reading the local newspaper, a sight that to John seemed odd. To John, Private Shays appeared far removed from the emotional arena of his recent experience. He felt that Private Shays was more suited for some kind of low-end reality television show complete with tawdry sidebars.

"Private Shays?" asked the major as a form of introduction in entering the hospital room.

Private Larry Shays sat up in his hospital bed, placing the newspaper across his lap to greet the familiar face. He had been lying in bed having nurses attend to his every whim, including fetching him the local newspaper. He felt a little uncomfortable since having his uniform removed and put into the hospital gown. "Yes sir, Major. What can I do for you?" He knew this time would be coming ever since he left the ammunitions depot. He dreaded the moment, but he had etched Major John Lawrence's personality in his mind. He had prepared himself for this moment, and he was going to put Major Lawrence in his place once and for all.

"I'm here to follow up on our conversation from last night. Are you up for a few more questions?" Not that John really cared, but he felt it might make the private a little bit more willing to answer questions if he was polite. John noticed Private Shays adjust himself in the bed. He wondered if the private was being courteous or preparing himself for the interrogation. It wouldn't be long before he knew which.

"Yes sir, Major, fire away." Larry thought that he had deflected most of the questions but knew there would be the standard follow-up questions, especially the one to see if his story changed. He was ready to play the game with Major Lawrence.

"Think, is there anything you may have left out?" John hoped that this lowlife bastard would come clean and tell him everything, but he knew that was a remote possibility. If this guy was the type to knife his partner in the back, he was not going to give up easily.

"No, sir. I remember some Southern accents and then *pow*! Next thing I remember is being treated by the medics." Larry grinned to himself. He then remembered the burning sensation from the bullet passing through his skin. Larry rubbed his shoulder as he thought to himself about Juan firing point-blank at his shoulder. Even though he knew Juan was following through with the plan by injuring him, he was going to get Juan back!

"Did you hear any names, or maybe they said something out of the ordinary? Maybe some expressions?"

"Naw, oh yeah, they said something about the 'cause.'"

"The 'cause'? Think, what did they say?" *Just maybe, just maybe*, thought John, *this guy could be telling the truth.*

Larry sat back and chuckled to himself. The "cause," that was a good one. This had gone better than he could have hoped. He didn't like getting shot, but he had killed Hugh, that sanctimonious son of a bitch, and now he was playing this major for the fool that he was.

Larry had grown up in Kendall, Florida, a town just west of Miami. His father was arrested when he was in junior high school for armed robbery of a convenience store. Prior to his arrest, he worked as an electrician for a local contractor. His mother worked evenings as a nurse. Larry remembered they never had much money. His parents used to fight when his mother came home from work and his father would be leaving for work. Periodically the neighbors would call the police because his father would smack his mother around, and her screams would alert the neighbors. In middle school and high school, he hung out with mostly the Cuban children from his neighborhood. Larry was known to his friends as "Anglo." It wasn't meant as derogatory; he was the only white kid in a neighborhood comprised of Cuban Americans. Just before Larry's father came up for parole when Larry was in high school, his father was killed. It was alleged that the killers were some African American men in a rival prison gang. The prison guards dismissed the incident as racially motivated. Eventually an African American man was charged, but he was already serving a life sentence for another murder conviction. Larry hated the African American kids at school after his father's death. Larry identified only with the Cuban American kids after the incident. His loyalty was further meshed when some of the Cuban American kids from his neighborhood and he drove over to Liberty City. They bought a gun and planned to kill some African American kids over in Liberty City. Once they got to Liberty City, no one in the car had the nerve to carry out the shooting, but Larry's loyalty was theirs.

After about an hour into the interrogation, a doctor came into the room. "Major, I'm going to have to ask that you discontinue this interrogation. This man needs his rest."

"Doctor, I didn't mean to overstay my welcome," replied John. For John, the timing could not have been better. He needed an excuse to break off the interrogation. He felt that something was missing and didn't want to come across as eager to leave. "Well, I guess that will have to be all for now, Private. We'll pick this up later, Private!" John wanted to revisit Larry's comment about "the cause" during his next session.

John gave an intentional pause and then turned toward the doctor. "Could you give us a minute, and I will be out of here."

The doctor nodded. "All right, Major, but I will be back to examine Private Shays in a few minutes, and I'll expect you to be gone." The doctor left John and Larry in the sanitary hospital room.

John directed his attention back toward Larry. "Private can you explain to me how your knife had Lieutenant Dugen's blood on it?" John had not even turned the knife over to the forensics to test for Lieutenant Dugen's DNA, but he decided to roll the dice to test Private Shays's reaction.

"Sir?" Larry had not expected the question. Why had Juan shot him? If he hadn't shot him, he would have had time to hide the knife. Larry was spinning, precious seconds were ticking away, and he had to give the major an answer. "I'm not sure what you mean, Major." Larry thought this would buy some time to come up with an answer. Any answer that would make the major just go away.

"Your knife, the one you carry. All the MPs on your shift recognized it. We found Lieutenant Dugen's blood on it. How do you explain that?" John thought he recognized a squirm come from Private Shays.

"I guess those country boys that broke in used it on the lieu once they took me out of the picture. I guess they wanted to make it look like I was the perp." Larry was reaching; he couldn't come up with anything else. This would have to do.

"You guess?" asked John. He stood staring at the confused Private Shays, letting him know his answer was not acceptable.

The doctor reappeared. "Major, you're out of here. I need to examine the private, and then he needs his rest."

"Private," countered John in a stern reply, "we'll pick this up later." John stepped into the hall and held a radio to his mouth. He contacted the dispatcher at the provost marshal's office and requested two MPs be dispatched immediately to stand guard on Private Larry Shays. John wanted to hear his order be confirmed by the dispatcher. John found a small bench in the hallway in visible sight of Private Shays's hospital room and took a seat to wait for the MPs to arrive. He made several notes to himself regarding his conversation with Private Shays. John also made several notes to himself regarding the surveillance room and other relevant items associated with the investigation. He knew he would eventually need to write a report for the JAG Corps for the prosecution of the perpetrators once his investigation was concluded.

CHAPTER 20

From the hallway, Larry heard the major request the guards. He thought to himself as the doctor attended to his gunshot wound and a nurse took his vitals, *I've got to get the hell out of here.*

After a while, two MPs entered Larry's room. They both stood facing Larry. One stood next to the doorway to the room, and the other sat next to a window. The men did not interact except to alternate, leaving the room for restroom breaks and something to eat. Two other MPs were dispatched later in the day to relieve the day shift.

Once the MPs arrived, John returned to his temporary office at the provost marshal's office. He wanted to find out if the fifty additional men and MPs he requested had found anything new in the investigation.

Larry began to ponder what he would do next as he lay in the hospital bed watching the MPs watch him. He felt that his story was weak, and Major Lawrence was piecing together information that would certainly lead to his arrest. He was not about to go to Leavenworth Federal Prison for anyone! His father died in prison, and he was not about to let the same fate happen to him. He had to escape!

CHAPTER 21

Once John returned to his temporary office, he looked through a stack of messages on his desk. Most of the messages were minor items. There was a message from his superior in Washington DC, Colonel Martin Armstrong. He knew what the message was about without even calling. Colonel Armstrong would want an update, something John was not ready to provide. Calling in an update without anything substantial would not make for a pleasant conversation. He was on a fact-finding mission, and now there was a theft of some significant arms and murder of a soldier all while he was present. He could not help but wonder if they would send someone else to take over the investigation, especially since a homicide was not his forte. John had attended the University of Maryland. He often felt that though he had been successful, if he had gone to the Naval Academy in Annapolis, maybe his marine corps career would have been that much more successful. Most of John's peers in Washington DC had gone to the Naval Academy. They were younger and had moved up through the ranks faster. When he went to the University of Maryland, he had not thought of joining the marine corps. Once he graduated, he thought of political aspirations and felt that a few years of decorated military service would look good on his political resume, but that had been seventeen years ago.

"Major!"

John was startled from his thoughts. It was Lieutenant Colonel Radford. "Yes sir, Colonel?"

"What have you got so far?"

John quickly updated Lieutenant Colonel Radford on what he had, which was not much more than what the Lt. Colonel already knew. John held back on who called the electronic surveillance sentries away from their post to help tie down the equipment during the hurricane. He felt confident that the lieutenant colonel had given the order but did not want to start a confrontation this early in his investigation. He also did not tell Lieutenant Colonel Radford about Private

Shays's bloody knife. He knew Private Shays was under Lieutenant Colonel Radford's command and felt that if he told the Lieutenant Colonel about Private Shays's knife, the lieutenant colonel may confront the private or defend him as his subordinate. If the lieutenant colonel confronted the private about the knife, John would lose his edge in the investigation. He wanted Private Shays thinking about him. He hoped that with the private thinking about him, he would make a mistake. John wanted the private to think he would be back any minute with the evidence that would take the private to Leavenworth Federal Prison. Would the private make a mistake? Would he make a run for it with the MPs standing guard? John hoped he would. Possibly run with John on his heels to lead him to the weapons and his accomplices.

"Major, I've been in touch with your CO [commanding officer] in Washington, and he tells me he wants you to continue the investigation against my best judgment."

John couldn't believe what he was hearing. "Me, sir?" It slipped out; John wished he could bring the words back, but it was too late.

"You sound surprised?"

John did not want the lieutenant colonel to think he was not capable of handling the task. "Well, I figured they needed me back in Washington. I have a stack of paperwork a mile high on my desk that I thought they wanted me to take care of."

"I guess not. Your boss told me that since you were already down here, he wanted you to follow through with the investigation. I guess he figured you already had a leg up on anyone else he would send down." The lieutenant colonel continued. "This doesn't mean that you're off the hook reporting to me. Now you'll report to Washington and me—regularly. Your CO also informed me to provide any additional staff that you needed."

John replied, "Thank you, Colonel. For now, I'm fine, but I'll be sure to let you know if I do."

Lieutenant Colonel Radford left John to resume his thoughts. John sat there a moment and digested what had just happened. Why was his commanding officer letting him continue the investigation? He had virtually no experience in a homicide investigation. In fact, he was learning as he went along. He thought, *Thank God for those police shows on television.* Or he would have no idea as to what to do. His thoughts then returned to the investigation. Why would a group of thieves stealing weapons from a military post use tranquilizer darts and then stab someone in the back? Was Private Shays the killer? If Private Shays was the killer, how was he connected?

CHAPTER 22

Seth and his deputies were inundated with calls from out-of-towners and the evacuees inquiring about their property. Some of the locals that were displaced as a result of hurricane Isabelle were calling to find out about their property and when they could return. Because of the news media's coverage, many thought their homes were washed away or reduced to timbers. Seth asked Ned if Sarah would mind earning a few dollars answering the calls as well as acting as police dispatcher while the rest of the police department attended to the posthurricane problems outside the office. Sarah had done it in the past, and for her, it was a chance to make a few extra dollars, something she and Ned desperately needed.

The deputies at the local bridge in Surf City were turning away irate motorists who had traveled from outlying areas in hopes of checking on their property, only to be turned away until the National Guard could be dispatched to prevent looting and assist in allaying hazards. Other deputies were increasing their patrols looking for looters that were using their personal boats to access the small island. The state police had dispatched helicopters to the area to assist in the search for looters. They were also filming the respective islands throughout the area hit by Isabelle to be broadcast on news stations in the Carolina's and Virginia in hopes that homeowners seeing their property on television may relax somewhat.

While Seth was on patrol, Ned called, "Hey, Chief, Mary Dugen is here and wants to go to her house."

Seth hated it when his deputies put him on the spot. He hoped that his deputies would handle the special requests by simply explaining that there were *no exceptions.* Now Mary had known that Ned had contacted him. "Did you tell her that the island was closed to everyone for safety reasons?"

"Yeah, but she said you would be willing to let her go home."

Seth liked Mary, and they were neighbors, but he felt this was a sneaky tactic on her part. Reluctantly Seth replied, "Tell her I'm on the way." This meant that he would have to stop his already-increased duties due to Isabelle. "Ned?"

"Yeah, Chief."

"Make sure you tell everyone that there are no exceptions!"

Seth was on the northern end of Surf City; after about ten minutes of negotiating potholes, debris, and downed power and telephone lines, he arrived to greet Mary. "How was your drive back from Clinton?"

"It was a little slow. There are a lot of people heading this way. Also a lot of the roads are flooded from all the rain they got inland. The rivers and creeks are well past their banks. Did we have much damage here?"

"Yeah . . . there was quite a bit. We were lucky in that it was less than we could have had. There are several downed power and telephone lines causing safety problems. A few roads buckled from water pushing its way past the dunes. There is also a lot of the usual stuff that we get when one of these things pass our way, but nothing that can't be repaired or replaced with some hard work." The *usual stuff* meant beach erosion, shingles torn from rooftops, sand spread everywhere, etc. Seth was eager to get back to work, so he kept the conversation short. "Mary . . . the island is closed to all nonemergency personnel. We also don't even have power, and I don't expect any for the next couple of days."

Mary gave Seth a sad look. "Please, can I go home?"

This was what Seth was trying to avoid. He could not resist this in any woman. "Mary, if I let you go home, you have got to promise me that you will stay there. You can't go out. I don't want anyone to see you. Got it! You do realize there is no power."

"Agreed," replied Mary.

"Okay, why don't we get you on home. Follow me because there is some flooding and some of the roads are a little dangerous due to all the downed power lines."

After a short drive, they arrived at Mary's house.

"Excuse me one minute while I drop Argo off at the house. I'll be right over," announced Seth.

Mary's house, like Seth's, had some visible signs of shingles missing from the roof, and sand covered almost everything. Mary was relieved to see things were in good shape considering Isabelle had passed so close. She had had visions of returning to nothing when she left. The fear of a category 4 hurricane coming ashore finally subsided as she made a quick assessment of things that needed to be done. As Mary entered the house, she reached to flip on the light switch, remembering Seth's comment that there was no power.

Although Seth was happy to see Mary and that there was little damage to the Dugens house, he was seething underneath that Mary had manipulated their friendship to gain access to her house. Seth's mind returned to his other compounded duties: electrical hazards, looters, and that mess at Camp LeJeune—guns in the hands of the wrong people! Seth started to excuse himself.

"Chief, would you mind helping me with a few items from the car?"

Though Seth had his mind on other matters, he was a pushover when it came to helping out a woman in distress. The small-town atmosphere had worn off on Seth since he and Maribeth moved to Surf City. "Sure, Mary, but I need to get back to my patrols."

As he was helping unload Mary's car, Ned called Seth from the bridge again. "What is it, Ned?" Seth was gruff as he responded over the radio he carried on his hip.

"A couple of MPs from LeJeune need to see Mary."

Seth didn't see any harm in the MPs coming onto the island, but why did they need to see Mary now? A chill ran down Seth's spine. He remembered his conversation earlier with Major John Lawrence over at Camp LeJeune about the marine that was killed during a break-in. He tried to dismiss the thought, but it kept him feeling uneasy. "Is there anyone over there that can lead them over here?"

"Sure, Steve is here with me." Steve was another of Seth's young officers. Steve was a single young guy from the area that had always wanted to remain in the area. When he graduated from Topsail Senior High School, he started working construction. When the job with the police department became available, he applied. Seth decided to take a chance on him. Seth figured that since he was from the area, he may have a good rapport with the locals as well as a good knowledge of the area. Seth sent him for police training where he excelled among his peers. He was pleased with the way he developed as a police officer. Thus far, Seth's impressions of Steve were correct. Steve was reliable, and he took orders well.

"Have him lead them over here ASAP."

Mary could not help but hear Seth speaking with his police officers. She looked at Seth with concern.

Seth and Mary sat in the kitchen exchanging small talk while waiting for the MPs to make their way through the island melee. Mary started to make a pot of coffee before she remembered there was no power. After a few minutes, Seth and Mary watched the MPs arrive from a kitchen window. Mary became uneasy as the two men got out of their car and deliberately walked up to the front porch.

Seth and Mary stepped out on the porch to greet the MPs. Seth introduced himself and Mary, Hugh's pregnant wife. The ranking marine corps MP was Captain Ross. "Mrs. Dugen, could we step inside?"

Mary made her way in the front door with Seth and the MPs close behind. They followed her into the kitchen that was just inside the small house.

"Mrs. Dugen, would you please sit down. I have some bad news?" Captain Ross was a burly man. His size indicated lengthy hours in a gym followed by a solid diet of carbohydrates. His personality lacked the requisite for delivering bad news. He was more suited as the narrator of a nature study, direct and without the slightest inkling of emotion.

Mary's knees crumbled as she braced herself on a nearby wooden kitchen chair. Her eyes immediately fill with tears. She would have sat down as requested had her body not crumbled involuntarily in the chair. She couldn't take her eyes off the young captain even if she wanted to. Mary sat waiting for the dire words to come forth from the young captain.

The captain continued, "I'm sorry to have to inform you that your husband was killed while on duty last night."

Mary cried out, "No!" The tears that had started when she heard there was bad news poured down her cheeks. She began to shake as she looked at Seth and the two MPs that had come to bring her the news of Hugh's death.

Seth knelt down beside Mary as he took her in his arms. She responded by wrapping her delicate arms around Seth's waist, squeezing him firmly. She needed his strength. Her tears ran from her cheek and were absorbed into Seth's police uniform shirt.

Seth jumped in, "How did it happen?" Seth could see the captain was a bit reluctant to reveal too much about what had happened, but he pressed on. "Did it have anything to do with the break-in last night over at LeJeune?"

The young captain was startled to hear that Seth knew about the break-in.

The captain directed his attention toward Seth. "I'm sorry, sir, but I'm not at liberty to discuss anything more with you right now."

Seth could see Mary was emotionally drained. He looked up to the captain. He stood to make his point heard. "I believe she has a right to know. Don't you?"

The captain looked at the sobbing pregnant widow. Reluctantly, the captain gave an obsequious nod and continued, "Hugh was the soldier killed during the break-in." The other soldier, a private, looked at the captain, stunned that the captain would reveal such confidential information. The captain looked at his subordinate. "It won't hurt anything. Besides, she has a right to know what happened to her husband."

Seth watched as the MPs feebly tried to console the recent widow. They were messengers of tragedy without much sensitivity. They asked if Seth knew of someone nearby that could help comfort the despondent woman. Seth explained that they were neighbors as well as friends, and finding someone to help console Mary would not be a difficult task. The MPs were eager to excuse themselves and to return to Camp LeJeune. Consoling a grieving widow was not in any military training manual.

Seth knelt down to console Mary once again. She threw her arms around him again. Seth pulled himself free to look Mary eye to eye and ask, "Is there anyone you want me to call?"

Mary summoned all the strength she could muster. She nodded and went into the bedroom. A few moments later, she returned with a box of tissues in one hand and an address book in the other. Mary returned to the chair she was sitting in when she received the tragic news. She thumbed through a few pages of the tattered address book before she came to the two names she wanted to give to Seth. She gave Seth the name of Hugh's mother and sister, as they both lived in Ohio.

"Mary, why don't you lie down, and I'll call your in-laws." Seth knew that Mary was an only child, and there was an estranged relationship with her parents. At first Mary thanked Seth for his concern and said she'd make the calls, but then realized it was for the best if Seth made the calls. Mary returned to the bedroom to lie down, leaving Seth to make the dreaded phone calls. Before she left, she found some aspirin in the kitchen cupboard and washed them down with a glass of water. Seth sat down at the kitchen table with the address book and the cordless house phone. Seth's first call, which he knew by heart, was to Sarah, Ned's wife. He wanted Sarah to come over and take care of Mary, despite the islands restrictions, until a family member could arrive to help Mary. Seth figured it was a good idea to bend a few rules for Mary and her relatives than to force her to leave the familiar surroundings of her home in her present condition. Sarah knew Mary from some of the local gatherings where they became friends. Seth then called Hugh's mother in Ohio. He tried to keep the conversation short, but she hounded Seth with question after question. After almost an hour, her questions ceased, and she agreed to call other family members, including Ned's sister. She informed Seth that she would be on the first flight she could find to Wilmington and planned on being with Mary the next day if she had to drive there herself.

As Seth concluded his conversation with Hugh's mother, Sarah arrived with a propane lantern, a thermos of hot coffee, a portable gas stove, cans of various soups, and chips. God, Seth loved how the locals could improvise under the most adverse conditions.

Once Seth saw Sarah had everything under control, he excused himself. Seth walked home to find Argo anxious for a long-overdue trip outdoors. "Come, girl," called Seth. He picked up the receiver from the cordless home phone, recharging it in its cradle in the living room, and walked out onto the deck overlooking the ocean. From here he could watch Argo, call his office for a routine update since his absence, and try to remember why he and Maribeth moved to the coast.

CHAPTER 23

Juan and the others awoke before dawn to find Antonio Mendoza dead. Antonio was lying cold, a pasty white hue to his complexion, and soaked in his own blood. The mattress where Antonio lay was soaked in his blood. The men were not sure when the owners would be returning. Once they decided to use the house as their hideout, they found out who the owners were. After not too much effort, they found out that the owners were Dave and Jill Murphy from Durham, North Carolina. Both were retired professors from Duke University and used the house for weekend getaways. Julio Chavez had sent one of his people to stake out the Murphys to ensure they did not surprise the men while they were using their house as a staging area for their mission. The man Julio sent tapped their telephones and set up listening bugs in various places throughout their house in Durham to try and determine when they would be making their next trip to their house near the shore.

Jorge went over to where Antonio was lying and knelt down beside him. He said a short prayer. He looked coldly back at Juan, who was standing in the bedroom doorway. "We should have taken him to a doctor." Each man took his turn beside Antonio saying a prayer softly with a personal gesture. As each man left Antonio's side, they gave a disapproving stare toward Juan.

Juan could feel the men's contempt for him with each passing glare. He looked sadly back toward the men gathered around the small room. "It would have ended our mission." Juan hated having to defend himself with the men. Sadly he also knew that because of the type of wound Antonio suffered, he was lucky to have lived as long as he did. Most would have never have made the trip from Camp LeJeune back to the house with such a wound.

Miguel responded, "What are we going to do with him now? We can't leave him here!"

Juan countered, "We're going to have to bury him here."

Jorge spoke sharply at Juan, "We can't, it's not right."

"We have no choice. I want you to take him out into the woods and bury him."

The men looked at Juan in disbelief at what they just heard. Antonio was like a brother to Juan. Yet Juan was now willing to bury Antonio in some distant place that Juan nor would anyone else he knew ever be able to return.

Juan looked back at the angry men; his patience had run out. "We need to do this now!"

Jorge stood up and called Roberto Benitez and his brother Miguel to assist him to take Antonio into the woods. Hector looked coldly at Juan as he left the room. He foraged through the cabin until he found a shovel in a utility closet and followed the others outside into a wooded area a short distance from the house. Each of the men took ten-minute intervals digging the grave. The ground was soft at first from the rain but began to become more and more difficult as they dug deeper into the earth striking roots mostly from the nearby pine trees. After an hour, the grave was completed. The grave was not as deep as the men would have liked, but with only one shovel and unforgiving soil, the men conceded to Mother Nature. The men placed Antonio's body in the shallow grave and covered him with the dirt they had just dug. They used pine needles and broken limbs to help conceal the freshly dug gravesite. Once their distasteful task was done, the men gathered around the grave, and Juan said a prayer for Antonio. Fortunately, the cabin they found was in a completely wooded area, far from anyone's sight. They found it on a previous trip to the area while planning their break-in. In fact, they had greeted the unsuspecting homeowners. They had driven down the long windy dirt road leading up to the cabin. When they found someone was home, they told them they were lost and requested directions. The homeowners were more than friendly and promptly provided the lost men with directions. They remembered that the long dirt road leading to the cabin would provide enough time for the men to scramble and hide should they hear anyone coming up the road. Now they were using the remote location for something they never could have imagined.

While the men buried Antonio, Juan took it upon himself to clean Antonio's blood off the boat. He found a hose next to the dock and found some old rags inside the cabin that he could use to help clean the boat. He took his time washing the blood off the boat. His movements were slow and deliberate. Juan used the time alone on the boat to allow him to collect his thoughts. Every time Juan felt tears begin to make pools in his eyes, he would stop what he was doing and berate himself. "I must be strong!" he would demand. He never lost anyone as close as he was to Antonio, but as the leader, he felt he had to be strong. This was not the time for him to be weak. He tried to encourage himself by saying, "Once this is over, I will cry for Antonio. Just let me be strong now."

Juan justified Antonio's death to himself by saying that Antonio would have wanted him to be tough for him and for Cuba's independence.

Once they completed the undesirable task of burying Antonio, the men showered, ate, and prepared themselves to continue their journey back to Miami. They cleaned up the cabin as best they could. They wrapped the mattress soaked in Antonio's blood as best they could with blankets and brought it on board the boat. They decided they would discard the blood-soaked mattress somewhere along the Intracoastal Waterway away from the cabin to try and lessen the obvious. The sun had risen when they finally started down the Intracoastal Waterway, moving once again at the same pace as other boaters. They did not want to rush. They planned stops along the way that were equally as secluded as the one where they had just spent the night. With the burial and other delays, they would arrive late at their next stop. It was not that they had to meet anyone, but they wanted to be off the Intracoastal Waterway before too late. They planned to travel with other boaters who were making their annual pilgrimage south. The plan was for the men to blend in with the other boaters as much as possible. If they traveled too late, they may draw unwanted attention. They continued down the Intracoastal Waterway, posing as snowbirds from the north doing their annual migration to South Florida for the winter. The boat was not too large to draw unnecessary attention but large enough to carry the weapons and the men comfortably. They had stripped the boat of its beds, kitchen appliances, and anything else that they felt they could do without. From the exterior of the boat, no one would notice the barren interior. They only wanted the essentials. Despite stripping the boat down, the boat, with the additional weight of the weapons, sat low in the water.

As they traveled, Juan began to soak up the beauty of his surroundings. It was early fall, and the leaves had begun to change into their fall colors. He noted the bright gold, orange, and red leaves against the backdrop of the stubborn green pine trees. He enjoyed the vista of the saltwater marsh with the light brown vegetation and the white egrets as they moved cautiously in the water in search of food. Pelicans and seagulls called out to the boaters as they flew overhead, requesting morsels of food to be thrown to them as they passed. Juan began to visualize people like Edward Teach, better known as Blackbeard, and his pirates sailing these very waters. He also reflected on Brigadier General Francis Marion, the Swamp Fox, who used the swamps of South Carolina to fight the British during the American Revolution. In these same waters, the *Monitor* and the *Merrimack*, two Civil War ships, did battle. While he was at the Murphys' house, he read an article about how Topsail Island was used as a testing center for jet propulsion during the Second World War. Juan enjoyed history. His hopes were to help write some of his own stories for his native Cuba.

Juan's thoughts of the history-rich area they were passing through soon faded and returned to Antonio. His cousin now lay in a shallow grave buried where he would never be able to see him again. What would his father think of him? He remembered the day his father brought Antonio home. Antonio's face was burned from the sun and his frail body dehydrated from the countless hours drifting in the open waters of the Florida Straits on his way to the United States. He spoke no English. It was he, Juan, who taught Antonio how to speak English. He remembered the dates the two of them went on together and their playing soccer or throwing the baseball in the backyard until it was too dark to see. Juan's father would scold them to come inside to do their homework or eat dinner. He wiped the tears from his eyes as inconspicuously as possible, hoping none of the men saw him crying. He was disgusted with himself. Antonio would never have done this to him, he thought. He wanted to tell the men to turn the boat around and go back so he could bury Antonio properly, in Miami or better yet an independent Cuba. He knew that it was impossible to go back now.

Tony Ermandez tapped Juan on the shoulder, startling Juan. "You had to do it." Tony was watching for the United States Coast Guard or possibly the local police that patrolled waterways adjacent to their municipalities as he navigated the boat down the Intracoastal Waterway. Tony would periodically scan the men in his company when he noticed the pensive Juan Mendoza. When he saw the tears in his eyes, he knew where his thoughts were. "In time the men will respect you for what you did. I know I respect you. It took a lot of courage. You're the leader of these men, and what you did was lead, as painful as it was."

Juan appreciated Tony's words. He quietly nodded his thank-you to Tony.

"Something has been troubling me," continued Tony. "Why did you shoot that man at the warehouse?" He was referring to Private Larry Shays. "He was helping us."

Juan quietly listened. He paused to collect his thoughts without divulging too much to Tony. "It was because he couldn't come with us." Juan gave Tony a moment for his comment to sink in before he continued. "The man killed his partner. If I didn't shoot him or he came with us, everyone would naturally assume he was in on the theft. His picture would be posted across the country as a thief and murderer. It would have made it dangerous for him and us if he'd come with us. It was better for me to shoot him, making him a victim of circumstance. This way we can continue on to Miami without any additional attention, and the MP I shot should go free."

"Aren't you afraid he will turn us in?" asked Tony. "Was he part of the plan?"

"I don't want to say too much. Yes, I'm afraid he may turn us in. He put us in one hell of a predicament by killing his partner. We had contingencies for everything except someone's murder. He did the one thing we did not need!"

Tony wanted to ask more questions, but he could see Juan was choosing his words carefully. He could see he was trying to avoid saying too much.

Juan stared out across the saltwater marsh, indicating his desire to end their conversation by his silence.

Tony recognized Juan's distancing mood and returned to navigating the boat back to Miami. The rest of the men occupied their time by playing cards, reading books and magazines, or making themselves comfortable as best they could to sleep or enjoy lying about soaking up the autumn day.

CHAPTER 24

They found a Dumpster next to a secluded dock and discarded the blood-soaked mattress. The men all felt some comfort in removing the last symbol of Antonio's demise. With the last symbol of Antonio's death behind them, the men felt they could focus on the mission at hand. They periodically stopped for gas and other essentials along the Intracoastal Waterway. Usually Juan would send two to three men into a nearby store for food and beverages while the others would stay with the boat helping to refuel and keeping curious onlookers at bay. Since the boat did not have a refrigerator since being stripped down in Miami, the men avoided buying anything perishable. The day dragged along as they slowly made their way south. Tension was still high since leaving Antonio behind, but the realization that they could not bring him along was rapidly setting in. As the sun began to slip into night, the men began to look for the river that would take them to their next night's stay.

Tony found a dock near Shell Point, Georgia, for the men to refuel. They wanted to fill up before they stopped for the night. Shell Point is at the mouth of the St. Mary's River. The river would take the men to the next scheduled house where the men would spend their final night before returning home to Miami. Juan found a pay phone at the gas station and called the disposable cell phone number he was given before leaving Miami. He was to call before the men arrived at each house to make sure the homeowners were away. As they had done before with the Murphys' house near Topsail Island, surveillance was done on the homeowners of the house on the St. Mary's River to avoid any unwanted surprises for the men. Juan knew very little about the house other than where it was. He and Tony had been there on a dry run to be sure they could find the house when they would return with the stolen weapons as they made their way back to Miami.

"Hello," responded the voice on the other end of the cell phone.

"It's me," responded Juan. "Is it a go?" It was the same plan that they laid out with the stranger during the break-in at Camp LeJeune. No names, only voices. All conversations would be concise.

"It's a go," answered the voice. Juan's phone went silent.

Juan returned to the boat.

Tony looked to Juan for the okay sign.

Juan gave a subtle nod. "It's a go."

While Juan made the phone call, the men refueled the boat. The sun was setting, and several other boaters were refueling for an early start the next day, which led to a slightly longer wait. Thus far, they had blended in with the other boaters who were making their annual pilgrimage to Florida for the winter months.

Gerardo and Hector went into a diner next to the dock and picked up meals for everyone. Juan made a point that he did not want any alcohol around until the mission was complete, so the men picked up a couple of six packs of soda to wash down the meals. Juan's fear was that the men would start drinking beer or liquor and then get careless. If they got careless, mistakes would happen, and in the end they would be caught.

Tony called to Miguel to untie the bow and to Jorge to untie the stern line of the boat. Tony put the boat into gear, and the men slowly pulled away from the dock. Tony steered the boat up the St. Mary's. He and Juan looked for the channel markers and landmarks to help guide them to the house where they would spend their last night away from their families and familiar surroundings. There was an air of excitement among the men that this long mission was drawing to a conclusion. There was also sadness having lost a close friend, and to Juan a cousin, in Antonio Mendoza.

As the men made their way west along the St. Mary's River, Juan noticed a red or sometimes light purple tint over the saltwater marsh as the sun gave way to the early-evening hours. Cranes stalked the marsh looking for their evening meal. When Juan looked over his shoulder to the eastern sky, he noticed the stars taking their place as the gradual darkening blue of the night took hold. He wished he could enjoy the scene instead of worrying about successfully completing their mission.

After their short ride on the St. Mary's River, the men found the secluded house near Laurel Bay. Like the Murphys' house, trees and a river surrounded this house. To access the house by land, one would have to drive a half mile down a remote dirt road, and once they left the main road, it was about another mile to the house. The nearest town was about two miles away, making the house ideal for their purpose.

Tony docked the boat, which was about two hundred yards up a gradual hill to the house. The men disembarked and made their way up to the house.

Juan gave instructions to the men on their respective shifts for guarding the boat and watching for any unwanted guests.

Juan took the first shift to have more time to reflect on his thoughts over what had transpired over the past two days. He still had not had time to grieve Antonio's death. All their other missions had been without incident. Now on their final mission procuring arms, two are killed, Antonio and a man he knew nothing about. He loved Antonio. They had grown up as brothers. He would never be able to replace him. He was determined that Antonio would die a martyr. Juan too felt compassion for the man he did not know. He hoped that the man would not be missed or that he did not leave behind a family. But Juan knew that his hopes were unrealistic. Surely the man had a family or someone who would miss him! Juan made himself comfortable in the captain's chair of the boat. He wiped the tears that filled his eyes. His tears were for both of the men. The night was cool, hinting winter was not far off. He put on a light jacket he had with him. He stared out at the distant lights. He noticed that hurricane Isabelle had left no ill effects on this remote place. The moon cast glimmers of light on the river's surface, bringing Juan a brief peace that he needed.

*   *   *

John Lawrence had gone into one of the holding cell rooms to grab a few minutes of rest. He was exhausted from the pace he set since the robbery. He realized he had been up almost thirty hours aside from a brief nap he was able to sneak in.

"Major?" one of the MPs called.

John was barely asleep when he heard the call. "In here." He sat up while he waited for the MP to enter the room. The small cot he was sleeping on never allowed him to get comfortable enough to fall completely asleep.

The MP entered. "They found the U-Haul."

"Where?" John was eager to pounce on any information, and right now to him, this was the Holy Grail. Until this break, his investigation had been a hurry up and wait.

"It was abandoned right here on base next to the river. It's at a recreational boating area."

This was good and bad news for John. He had hoped that the perps were in it, but the truck was a start. "Take me there, now! Have you contacted the Jacksonville forensics?"

"Not yet," replied the MP. "We were waiting for you to give the word."

"Call them now!" John led the way down the hallway toward the parking lot, pulling his shirt on and trying to walk and putting his shoes on at the same time. He stopped at a water fountain along the way. Cupping his hand under the stream of water, he accumulated enough cold water to throw on his face in an attempt to clear any remaining cobwebs from his brief sleep.

John and the MP climbed into a patrol car. The MP drove to where the U-Haul had been abandoned. John used the time to finish dressing himself. Fifteen minutes later, they were standing by the truck. The Jacksonville forensic team was just arriving when John and his driver pulled up.

"What do you have for me, Sergeant?" shouted John. As they approached where the truck was abandoned, John quickly scanned the scene to determine who was in charge. John could see from the distance a sergeant directing the subordinates.

The sergeant waved for John to join him. "Not much, but it looks as though your perps transferred the weapons from the truck here to a boat waiting over there."

A voice shouted, "Get the fuck back! You're destroying my crime scene."

John looked back at a man who appeared to be in his midthirties. He was wearing glasses. He was of average height. To John, he did not appear to be the lab rat one might expect to find on a forensic team. John thought to himself that the man was too young to possess the skills for an assignment of this magnitude. The man strolled to where John and the sergeant were standing. As the man approached, John noticed he was slightly overweight, and for a man his age, he was losing his fine white blond hair. He had a dark blue T-shirt with a bright yellow or to some gold lettering that read JACKSONVILLE FORENSICS.

"The name is Terence Ingram, but you can call me Terry." Terry stuck out his hand, waiting for John to shake his hand.

John shook the man's hand. "You may call me Major Lawrence."

"Very well then." Terry glanced at John's nameplate prominently displayed on his uniform: Major John A. Lawrence, "John." Terry walked off in defiance with his lab case in hand. Terry was ready to perform his duties.

John laughed to himself for a moment. He called out, "Terry."

Terry turned to look at John ready for some kind of confrontation.

John walked toward him. He reached into his pocket and pulled out Private Shays's knife and the two tranquilizer darts. "The knife was found at the ammunitions depot last night. An MP gave it to me. Can you check for fingerprints and test the blood against Lieutenant Dugens? See if you can find any fingerprints on the darts. The darts came from the surveillance center. You may want to have some of your people go over there and look for evidence as well."

"Thanks . . . I'll do that," replied Terry. Terry opened the envelope that John gave him to look at the new evidence just handed to him for testing. "So how many people have been handling the evidence?"

John felt a little annoyed at Terry. "Look . . . I tried to limit people touching the evidence, but we are not all as savvy as you. They handed me the evidence, and I tried to protect it as much as possible. I know where it came from, so can we try and be a little more flexible?" John knew he hadn't followed the protocol for evidence, but he had been more concerned about others learning too much too soon and jeopardizing his handling of the case. It was a risk he felt he had to take.

Terry started to attack John's retort and caught himself. "I think I can manage. Can I get you two to retreat back behind the yellow tape so I can do my part without you destroying my crime scene? The rain is already making my job near impossible without novices getting in the way."

John let Terry's last remark roll off his back. He attributed it to the hour and felt that when the time was right, he would set Terry straight. But right now he needed experienced allies. "As you wish." John motioned to the sergeant and the other MPs to move out of Terry's way.

John noticed the eddy where the boat was loaded. He also noticed footprints leading into the eddy. "Are you kidding me? During a hurricane when everything is shut down, a group drives a moving truck onto a military post, breaks into an ammunitions depot, steals approximately two tons of weapons, and loads it into that same truck. Then that same group unloads those same two tons of weapons onto a boat and leaves without anyone seeing them? Goddamn they've got some kind of balls!" John wasn't expecting an answer. He didn't realize he was talking out loud. John knew that hurricane Isabelle came ashore at Cape Fear. He also knew that Cape Fear was approximately sixty miles south of Camp LeJeune. This meant the worst of the hurricane was slightly south of where he was standing. The thought of a group being so gutsy to attempt such a thing was beyond his comprehension.

The sergeant stood by not sure if he was to respond or not. The sergeant started to reply when he realized that John was only taking out loud to himself. He became embarrassed about starting to speak when it was not expected.

John looked at the embarrassed sergeant and smiled.

"Sir," inquired the sergeant, "may I speak freely?"

"Go ahead."

"The absurdity of what you are describing is what makes this plan so beautiful. All these people needed was an opportunity . . . The hurricane gave them that opportunity. They knew everyone's attention would be on the storm. All they needed was the balls to execute."

"Sergeant, I think you may just be right. Have someone who knows something about boats and the local waters meet me at the office in an hour. I want to know what size boat we're talking about. Also, get on the phone with the people that open the bridges north and south of here. Hopefully they saw a boat that would dare these waters during what took place last night. One more thing, get some helicopters to patrol along the shoreline to see if they see any boats or access roads that our perps may have used."

"Yes, sir," replied the sergeant. The sergeant liked John's confirmation of his impressions and was eager to join John's team as a result.

John shouted out toward Terry, "Have we found any fingerprints yet?"

Terry shouted back, "Major, over here."

John lifted up the three-inch yellow-and-black plastic tape used by Terry's team to cordon off the crime scene and prevent further unwarranted intrusions. John walked over to where Terry was standing. He was cautious where he walked to avoid a second reprimand from Terry.

John was sickened at the thought of hiring civilian forensic teams to do the work once delegated internally. It was true that the military installations lacked the necessity of a forensics team routinely, but it would make it twice as difficult to keep things quiet within the corps when the work was being subcontracted out to civilians. Now here they were with a break-in on a military post, and the Jacksonville forensic team was scouring a military installation for clues. Jacksonville is the adjacent town to Camp LeJeune. If it was necessary, they could have the Jacksonville Police Department forward their evidence to the FBI in Washington, or if necessary they, could call the FBI lab in to do their own investigation. It had already been determined by those higher-ups that the Jacksonville Police Department Forensic Division would do the necessary forensic work, but if they needed to forward anything to Washington, it had already been approved by John's commanding officer.

"Anything to report, Terry?"

"No fingerprints yet, but it looks as though your lieutenant shot one of 'em. From the looks of the amount of blood I saw at the ammunitions depot and around here, I think he got him pretty good."

"How good?"

"Unless he got to a doctor pretty damn quick, my guess is he is probably dead or will soon be dead."

John felt a moment of triumph, one life for another. He called to the sergeant. "Sergeant, check all the hospitals within a one-hundred-mile radius and any other place around here that a person could get medical treatment for a gunshot wound. Also, find out if any doctors, including veterinarians, failed to report to work today."

John started to leave to return to his temporary office at the provost marshal's office. He called back to Terry, "Let me know what you find before you release any information to anyone else. I want you and your department to keep this close to the vest."

Terry looked at John. "No problem, Major." Terry had been around the military base long enough to know the political jockeying that took place. He also knew that the marine corps was a stickler about keeping things within the corps.

John detected a small amount of sarcasm in Terry's voice but let it go.

"Sure, Major." Terry felt that he was a scientist, and he needed to make allowances for those who were not. Terry knew that if he got in trouble for one more "fuck you" to any more officers, he would be kissing his forensic career *good-bye*. He had already been labeled a "troublemaker" by his previous employer and spent the next two years looking for a forensic job before he landed the position with the Jacksonville Police Department. It wasn't an illustrious position, but it was what he wanted to do and liked to do. He figured if he could impress his current boss, then maybe he could get a good reference and with a little luck find his dream forensic job. Terry also recognized that the investigation could go on for some time, as they often did, and good rapport with the investigating officer was a good place to begin. There was also the possibility that the FBI may get involved in the case. If that happened, he might just make the right connections with them during this investigation.

CHAPTER 25

Seth was lying in bed when the phone rang. He was half asleep. He fumbled through the darkness until he found the telephone. He awkwardly picked up the phone, and falling back onto the pillow, he grumbled, "Hello."

"Chief, you need to head out to the Murphys' place." It was Sarah, his deputy Ned's wife and the often-temporary Surf City police dispatcher.

Seth glared at the digital clock on the nightstand, trying to get his eyes to focus in on the numbers. He had slept well that night, making up some of the sleep lost the night before with all the pre- and posthurricane activities. I'm not sure I know where the Murphys' place is." For many of the Surf City locals such as Sarah, addresses were almost unheard-of. You went to a place based on who lived there or near where someone lived or near a local business. To Seth's dismay, even some of the local businesses were now defunct, but people still referred to the former business name. During his short tenure as Surf City police chief, Seth was learning many of the local nuances as well as the actual addresses. Eventually he would make the necessary changes to actually using addresses, but he inherited a good ol' boys' police station and was slowly implementing the changes he wanted. Too many changes too fast was not what the department needed. He needed the good ol' boys in the department to operate the police station as much as they needed him. "You need to cross the bridge and take the first left next to Johnson's Seafood House. Stay on the road for about two miles. You'll come to a fork in the road, bear left onto a dirt road for about another half mile. You can't miss it."

Seth mapped out the directions in his head as best he could. He knew where Johnson's Seafood House was, but that was pretty much it. "Sarah, isn't that in the Pender County sheriff's jurisdiction?"

"Yes it is, Chief, but the county can't get out there for a least a couple of hours. The sheriff is the one who told me to have you go out there until he can get someone out there."

"Is it an emergency?" Seth was more concerned with tending to the town's problems as a result of hurricane Isabelle. Taking on the county's problems was far removed from his thoughts and concerns.

"Well, the Murphys came down from Durham this morning to check on their property and found someone broke into their place. According to Mrs. Murphy, there's lots of blood, and they think something may have been buried in the woods behind the house."

Seth processed the information he was getting from Sarah for a moment before getting back to her. "What was that man's name at Camp LeJeune?" Seth was talking out loud to himself, not realizing Sarah was hearing him.

"Chief, are you there?" Sarah could barely make out Seth's incoherent mumblings. "Come again, Chief."

"Sarah, look on my desk for a message from somebody over at Camp LeJeune." Seth heard Sarah place the phone on the counter. He could hear her shuffling papers in the distance. A few moments later, Sarah went back to the phone. "I found a note from a Major John Lawrence over at Camp LeJeune requesting that you call him when you got back. Is that it?" asked Sarah.

"That's it. Call Major Lawrence over at LeJeune and tell him to meet me at the Murphys'. Tell him to bring a forensic team with him. Tell him the same things you just told me." Seth wasn't sure that the events at LeJeune and at the Murphys' house were related, but little happened in the area, especially at this time of the year. This was too coincidental for him. Surf City did not have a forensic team because the community was much too small to need one or for that matter could even afford one. This was too important to have a crime scene destroyed by his local boys, and he was a novice when it came to crime scene investigations. "Oh yeah, Sarah, make sure you give the major good directions. He's not from around here!"

"You got it, Chief!" Sarah said and hung up. Sarah prided herself on knowing all the town's gossip. Being a temporary police dispatcher and having her husband as a patrolman provided her with a wealth of town gossip. She was dying to know what was going on, and it took all her restraint not to ask. Sara knew Seth well enough that he was not going to tell her any more than what he had to. For her to have to call some major over at Camp LeJeune to meet him at a Pender County crime scene had to be big. Sarah placed the call to Major Lawrence. Maybe, just maybe, she could dig some information out of him.

Seth lumbered out of bed and started getting dressed. He was tired from the extra time he had spent at the police station. Seth flipped on some lights to help him find his way to the kitchen. Argo was on his heels waiting for a trip outside to do her morning chores. Seth put on some coffee and opened the door for Argo to go out. He looked through the cupboards for something fast to eat only to remember he hadn't been to the store in a while. He found some breakfast bars in the back of the cupboard. He opened one of the breakfast bars and took a big bite. "Shit," commented the annoyed Seth as he pulled out the trash can from under the kitchen sink and spat out the food. He looked at the package and noticed that the expiration date was six months earlier.

Seth heard Argo scratching at the door to come in. He let Argo in and offered the stale breakfast bar to her. She sniffed the remaining breakfast bar Seth offered her and then headed for her empty dog bowl. "Yeah, I don't blame you either," commented Seth. "I didn't like them when Maribeth bought them last year, and now they're even worse." Seth opened the pantry door where he had a sixty-pound bag of dog food. He took out a cup and placed it in Argo's dog bowl. He heard the sounds of the last few drops of coffee passing through the coffee filter. He took his spill-proof cup and filled it with coffee and a couple of spoonfuls of sugar before he headed into the bathroom to get ready to head over to the Murphys' house.

After Seth was dressed, he filled his coffee cup again and headed out to his Surf City Ford Bronco. Argo was hot on his heels. Seth opened up the door, and Argo leaped in. Seth got in after carefully placing his coffee cup in a cup holder conveniently designed by Ford. On his way out to the Murphys, he thought he would stop by the Fisherman's Café for a couple sausage and egg biscuits but remembered no one was allowed back on the island. As Seth approached the café, he saw it filled with locals and their respective vehicles parked in front. Seth decided to stop and get his sausage and egg biscuit after all. As he walked in, he found the locals sitting in the café reliving Isabelle and the horrors of past hurricanes. Seth shook his head wanting to say, "Who in hell allowed you back onto the island?" but realized it was a battle he was not going to win. They were the locals, and this was where they lived, so life was going to proceed with or without his consent. Mel and Eileen Jones owned the café. It was an early-morning fishermen's hangout along with other local tradesmen. Mel was the cook, and Eileen ran the register. Like clockwork they opened every morning by five and closed at three in the afternoon. The waitresses and busboys were either their own children or nieces and nephews. Isabelle to them was an inconvenience, but it was back to business as usual.

"Here ya go, Seth." Eileen handed Seth a paper bag with the biscuits. Grease was already beginning to stain the brown paper bag.

Seth started to reach for his wallet.

"Git on out o' here, honey. You don't owe me nothin'." Eileen gave Seth a wink.

"Thanks, Eileen!" It was a ritual that Seth and Eileen developed since Seth arrived in Surf City as the new chief of police. Seth would always try and pay, and Eileen would always refuse to accept his money. The café looked out for the fire, police, and rescue squad employees by offering discounts, but they never charged Seth or the fire chief.

Seth left the café and made his way to the Murphys' house. On his way Seth noticed a steady stream of traffic heading to Topsail Island. He heard on the radio as he rode along that at midnight last night, the governor announced that Topsail Island, where Surf City was located, and several other North Carolina islands affected by hurricane Isabelle were now open to the homeowners. Seth saw a couple of his patrolmen monitoring the bridge to only allow people that owned property back onto the island. They obviously got the update through police channels while Seth was sleeping. Before Seth had gone to bed, he imagined the caravans of people heading down to assess their properties only to get turned away. *What a mess!* he thought. Now the point was mute. It would be local carpenters, plumbers, and general handymen's dreams come true with more work than they would know what to do. Now he understood why Mel and Eileen had a full house. Their diner was a bonanza of carpenters, plumbers, and general handymen for the people coming down for repairs to their property.

As Seth pulled up to the Murphys' house, he noted how secluded the house was. It was down a long windy dirt road and surrounded by trees. The front of the house had a small porch with some rocking chairs that the Murphys were sitting on as he pulled up to the house. Seth also noticed a small river that flowed up to the back of the house where a dock was located. The side of the house overlooking the river also had a small screened-in porch with more rocking chairs looking out over the river. Seth parked the Bronco and walked toward the people he assumed to be the Murphys. Seth wiped the crumbs off his shirt from the sausage biscuits he ate on his way to the Murphys. He took a clipboard with a pad of paper off the backseat in case he needed to make any notes. He made sure both windows were open and gave Argo a stern "stay" as he got out of the patrol car. "I'm Chief Jarret with the Surf City Police Department," announced Seth as he approached the elderly couple with his hand out and the clipboard tucked under his other arm.

The Murphys were already walking toward Seth's car as it pulled into their driveway. They were dressed in jeans and T-shirts identifying a resort in Mexico, most likely their most recent trip. Seth could see the Murphys were eager to have some kind of law enforcement arrive. Mr. Murphy extended his hand. "Dave Murphy and my wife, Jill."

"It's a pleasure to meet the both of you. I'm sorry for the circumstance." Seth paused before he continued, "So I understand you had a break-in. I also understand you found some blood and something possibly buried in the woods behind your house." Seth was very businesslike. He realized he was not as tactful as usual. Right now it did not matter. This was not his case, and he had enough to do in Surf City as the chief of police.

"My wife and I were careful not to touch anything once we noticed we had had a break-in. Ya know we watch all those police shows on TV, so we made a point of not touching anything else. We figured maybe one of those crime scene scientists may want to look for evidence," commented Dave.

Seth smiled to himself as he listened intently to Dave. He liked the Murphys' attention to detail. Seth could tell they were well-educated. The possibility of the house being a crime scene and the Murphys' vigilance to preserving it was refreshing. He knew most people would have trounced through the house destroying evidence before bothering to call the police. Seth thought maybe those TV shows aren't so bad after all. "That was very good of you, Mr. Murphy."

Dave took Seth into the house with Jill Murphy following close behind in case her husband left anything out. The house was a one-story brick building. The house was simply decorated but well maintained. Paperback books were stacked everywhere, reinforcing Seth's notion that they were well educated and now well-read in many ways. He guessed the house was probably twenty years old. It had three bedrooms, one bathroom, a kitchen, a living room, and a dining area. Dave pointed to blood spots found in the kitchen and bathroom. There also appeared to be blood on a sofa in the living room. Dave directed Seth into a bedroom where he noticed the mattress was missing. Seth made several notes on the pad of paper that he made a point of bringing with him. Dave took Seth out into the yard and walked into some adjoining woods on one side of the house. Seth noticed an area freshly dug up and assumed, like the Murphys had, something had recently been buried there. Seth didn't want to say too much to the Murphys, but his mind began to ponder the possibilities. Seth recalled his conversation with a major at Camp LeJeune that an MP, most likely Hugh Dugen, may have shot one of the perps. The amount of blood at the Murphys and the possible grave site were good indications to Seth that the perps had used the Murphys' house as their hideout. Seth pulled some rubber gloves from his pocket and put them on. He opened a trash can as they made their way back to the house and found a plastic bag that was full of bloody towels. The perps were obviously hoping the garbage collectors would come before the homeowners arrived. From his days on the Charlotte police force, he remembered not to disturb anything, including carefully walking through a potential crime scene, in hopes of not destroying possible evidence for the forensic team.

"How did you find this dug-up spot in the woods?" inquired Seth. "I mean it isn't along any regular path I would have expected you to take."

Dave smiled to himself thinking about the television dramas he had seen. Now he was living his own television drama as he witnessed the chief of police asking him the appropriate probing questions. "My wife wanted me to cut some of those wildflowers for the dining room table," answered the calm Dave. Dave pointed to some wildflowers growing on the other side of the freshly dug soil.

"You know women, when they see something pretty, we're not going to get a moment's peace unless we go retrieve it for them."

Seth noted the beautiful purple and white flowers growing beyond the freshly disturbed soil they stood over. Maribeth would have made the same request of him had she seen the flowers. Seth nodded his understanding and continued, "Before I came over, I notified some people over at Camp LeJeune. They have an ongoing investigation, and I believe this may be related."

The Murphys were visibly disturbed that what appeared to be a simple break-in now appeared to be something larger. "What happened over at LeJeune?" inquired Dave.

"I'm sorry I can't disclose anything more than what I've told you." As Seth finished his response, he could see that Dave Murphy was upset, but at the same time, he was accepting Seth's answer. They made their way to the front porch of the small house. "We're going to need to stay out here on the porch until the forensic team from Jacksonville can come over and do a complete investigation."

"Are we in any kind of danger?" inquired Dave, who was trying desperately to read between the lines.

"No, I think you're quite safe," replied Seth. He tried using his most reassuring tone of voice. Seth felt confident that the perps were trying to put as much distance between them and the Murphys' place as fast as they could.

Jill Murphy made coffee before Seth arrived. He knew her coffeemaking possibly disturbed some evidence, but it was too late to do anything about it now. The three of them sat on the porch overlooking the river chatting until Major John Lawrence arrived with the Jacksonville Police Department forensic team. The approaching vehicles disturbed the casual conversation Seth was having with the Murphys.

CHAPTER 26

John Lawrence was the first one out of the car. He saw an imposing figure in a police uniform and assumed it was the chief from the Surf City Police Department, the man he had spoken to the previous day. John introduced himself as he walked toward Seth. "Major John Lawrence, this is Terence Ingram with the Jacksonville Police Department Forensic Division. You must be Chief Jarret!"

"Terry," interjected Terence Ingram. Terry was carrying a metal case containing much of the paraphernalia he would need to begin his forensic investigation. He extended his hand to Seth to greet him.

"Chief Seth Jarret, Surf City PD." Seth gave each of the men the standard firm handshake and stared directly into the eyes of the men he was greeting. He had heard it reflected confidence, and he liked coming across as confident no matter where he was.

"Tell me, Chief, what do you have for us?" asked John. Seth took John and Terry on the same tour Dave Murphy had given him. He periodically referred to his notes, making sure not to miss anything as he went along. Seth added the plastic bag in the garbage can and some other items he noticed from his tour of the Murphys' house.

"What have you touched?" demanded the inquisitive Terry.

"We tried to keep everything intact as much as possible. Mrs. Murphy already made the coffee before I arrived, but we stayed outside to prevent compromising anything else," stated Seth. He continued, "It appears that the Murphys are fans of forensic science because as soon as they realized there was a break-in, they made a point of not contaminating the crime scene any more than they already had."

"Excellent," responded Terry. "At least there are some people who know how to preserve a crime scene." He gave John a disgusted look and looked back at

Seth. "Good to see some of those crime shows are paying off and our local law enforcement boys are doing their part," continued Terry.

John ignored the accusatory comments.

Seth finished filling Terry in on what he felt was relevant. "I'm sure you have your own ideas on what you want to do, so I'll just get out of your way and let you boys take over," finished Seth.

Once Terry received Seth's information, he began barking out orders to his forensic team, which was comprised of two other men and a young woman. In a matter of minutes, the forensic team had roped off just about everything. They began the slow but deliberate task of gathering evidence. Terry split the team up so that some of the team combed the exterior of the house, and the rest took the interior. Terry snapped at John at one point when he felt he was getting underfoot. At that point John stepped back and joined Seth and the Murphys on the porch.

"Major, when do you think we'll get our house back?" inquired Dave.

"I don't think it will be anytime too soon. I'd have to talk with the forensic people to know for sure, and even then I think they would be guessing. If you would like, the marine corps would like to put you up in a hotel and take care of your meals. Here is my card along with my address, cell phone number, and I wrote a local phone number on the back where you can reach me over at Camp LeJeune. Please just keep your receipts for everything, just nothing too elaborate. Remember, it is the taxpayers' money. Send me the receipts and I will reimburse you."

The Murphys were not eager to leave their home to strangers, but considering they were policemen, they begrudgingly agreed to leave. Instead of accepting John's offer, they decided to return to their principal residence in Durham. John talked with Terry to see if it would be okay for the Murphys to gather up a few of the items they brought down with them. He agreed but called to one of the forensic team to escort the Murphys into the house to claim their belongings. Jill Murphy handed Terry a key to the house. She wrote her address and telephone number on a piece of paper and handed it to Terry. "Please call me when you are through, and I will come back to get my key," stated Jill. Jill started to walk away as she looked around her home. She noticed the forensic team spraying chemicals and black powder all over her home. She saw blood from the chemicals applied by Terry's forensic team. Jill looked back at Terry. "You're not going to destroy my home any more than what those men have already done, are you?"

Terry smiled to himself. "No, ma'am. I am going to ask if you wouldn't mind sticking around for a little longer."

"Sure," responded Dave. "Why?"

"I will need to fingerprint you to eliminate you as suspects. I also may need for you to answer a few more questions." Terry paused and looked back at Dave as an afterthought. "Maybe just an hour."

Dave nodded. He loaded their personal items the forensic investigator helped them gather into the trunk of their car. He walked over and joined Jill who was once again sitting in a rocking chair on the porch. Concern ran down her face. Dave sat down beside Jill in a rocking chair and took one of her hands. Using both of his hands, he caressed her hand. "Things are going to be all right."

Jill looked back at the man she had been married to for forty-two years and gave a look of thanks for his compassion. Eventually Dave sat back in his chair, and the two rocked slowly back and forth holding hands.

"Chief, do you think you could spare a couple of deputies to keep an eye on the house?" inquired John.

"I'm sorry, Major, with Isabelle we're already spread too thin. This isn't even our jurisdiction. Let me put a call into the Pender County sheriff's office, and I'll get them to send someone out to keep an eye on the place. Since this is a crime scene, they have an obligation to protect the integrity of the crime scene." Seth got on the radio to Sarah, his interim police dispatcher, and requested she contact the Pender County sheriff's office to get some deputies out to the Murphys' house to keep watch on the crime scene. After about a half hour, she called back to say that they were sending a couple of deputies and to stay until they arrived. It was almost two hours later when the Pender County sheriff's deputies arrived. John and Seth filled them in on the situation. Terry was quick to chime in on the conversation to be sure nothing was disturbed or tainted by the deputies.

Terry and his team spent the remainder of the day gathering blood samples, looking for fingerprints, and collecting anything else they felt could be used as evidence. They periodically inquired about items they found with the Murphys before they left. They fingerprinted the Murphys and Seth to know whom they could eliminate. One of Terry's forensic team spent a great deal of time interviewing the Murphys to determine who may have spent time at the cottage in order to further eliminate persons who may show up as a result of the fingerprints. They exhumed a body from the wooded area that Seth and the Murphys correctly assumed to be a grave site. The body was taken into Jacksonville to the medical examiner for a complete autopsy. Terry noticed that whoever had buried the body mutilated the fingertips to prevent identification from fingerprinting. They also removed any possible tags and labels from the man's clothing.

Seth felt he had seen enough; he was intrigued watching the forensic team at work, but he knew he had plenty to do in Surf City. Seth wanted to get back to town and find out if there were any other problems as a result of Isabelle. It was late in the afternoon, and the Murphys would be leaving soon. Darkness was soon approaching.

While Terry and his team diligently worked, John made his own observations. He noticed the dock behind the house. John made several inquiries of the Murphys before their return to Durham. "Dave, does this river access the Intracoastal?"

"Sure does. The access to the Intracoastal Waterway was one of the reasons we bought this property."

"Do you have a boat?"

"Yes."

"Where is it?"

"During this time of year, we keep it in dry dock in Surf City."

John called over to Terry, "Gotta minute?"

"Sure, what can I do for you?"

John took Terry to the side so the Murphys could not hear their conversation. John spoke. "Terry, I've been looking at that dock. I've spoken with the Murphys, and they tell me this river accesses the Intracoastal."

Terry looked at John remembering they surmised that when the perpetrators left Camp LeJeune, they left by boat. "John, this would be a great place to hide after leaving LeJeune. Nice secluded hideaway surrounded by woods with water access."

"That's what I've been thinking. Have your team—"

"I'm already ahead of you. We started with the house. I assigned one of my team to the outside. He just hasn't had time to get to it yet. You need to keep everyone away from the dock until we can get to it. Knowing that this is a probability of how they came and went, we'll give it extra attention." Terry left and returned to his work inside seeming to be annoyed that John would tell him how to do his job.

To John, the forensic work seemed to take an eternity. They were painfully slow; however, he was equally amazed at their attention to detail when they continued to find the minutest of possible clues. The final determination if an item was an actual piece of evidence would have to be determined at a later time. John called over to Terry, "When do you think you'll be through?"

"It will be several more hours. We're also planning on coming back tomorrow morning."

John decided he had spent enough time with the forensic team. He felt he could make better use of his time making additional calls and following up on other leads back at his makeshift office at the provost marshal's office at Camp LeJeune. He wanted to talk with Larry Shays again and see if he could rattle him. He was confident that Larry was hiding something.

John shouted into the house at Terry. He dared not go in for fear of upsetting the already-temperamental Terry. "I'm gonna leave now . . . When do you think you'll have something for me?"

Terry stopped what he was doing and met John on the front porch of the house. "Can't say, hopefully in the next couple of days. We have a lot of items to go over back in the lab, but if anything looks good, I'll give ya a call." Terry appreciated the fact that John didn't enter the house to announce his impending departure. He also recognized that he had been a little temperamental. "Look . . . I'll get on it right away. I'll make this a priority one for you. I know you're anxious to get moving on this."

"Thanks," replied John. He could see there was a change in Terry's demeanor, which was his way of apologizing. John said good-bye and went on his way.

CHAPTER 27

When Seth and Argo returned to Surf City, he stopped by the police station to find everything running smoothly. Ned had taken control of matters in Seth's absence. Ned frequently made Seth's life easier. The men knew Ned as a friend and respected him as a leader. He decided to go home a little early so he could straighten up the house and remove the plywood covering the doors and windows to his house. He knew if he didn't take care of it soon, it could get put off for several days.

It was dark when Seth finished removing the boards protecting the doors and windows to his house and put them away for the next hurricane. He saw the light on at Mary's house and decided to see how she was doing. Seth knocked on the door.

A moment later, an attractive young woman came to the door. The woman looked at Seth's Surf City police uniform. "May I help you?" she asked.

Seth could see Mary peering around the young woman. "It's all right," commented Mary to the young woman. "This is Seth. He is our—," Mary caught herself, recognizing that Hugh was dead, "my neighbor and the local police chief."

The young woman held the door for Seth to enter.

Mary continued the introductions, "Seth, this is Hugh's younger sister, Rachel."

Seth shook hands. "Nice to meet you. I didn't know Hugh had a sister."

"I work in Washington DC."

"I see you're in the navy." Rachel was still in her uniform. "When did you get in town?"

"Mary called me yesterday at the office, so I explained to my CO what had happened. I drove down late last night. I haven't had a chance to change clothes."

Seth had noticed the unfamiliar car in the driveway at Mary's house when he left for work that morning but did not give it a second thought. He was in a hurry to find out what was in store for him at the Murphys' house. "What do you do in the navy?" inquired Seth.

"I'm with Naval Intelligence." Rachel was somewhat vague as she responded to Seth's question. She made her way into the living room where Mary had made herself comfortable on the couch. Rachel sat next to Mary on the couch.

Seth joined the women in the living room and took a seat in a large cushioned chair facing Mary and Rachel. "Naval Intelligence," reflected an impressed Seth. Rachel was an attractive young woman with an excellent figure from Seth's point of view. Seth stared at Rachel as she spoke. He couldn't help himself. He found her looks intoxicating. He couldn't imagine what someone like this was doing in the navy, much less in Naval Intelligence. He thought she could have been a model and made a fortune as opposed to her salary as a naval officer.

Rachel had seen the look a thousand times working in the navy. Before Seth could say another word, Rachel headed off the question. "The navy helped put me through college, and now I'm putting my time in."

Seth felt a little embarrassed, and he began to blush. He did not think he was that obvious. He took a moment so he could regroup. "How long are you down for?" It was somewhat a foolish question. Seth felt he had to come up with something to ask to help alleviate his own uneasiness.

"Until I find out who killed my brother. I understand you have been in contact with someone from NCIS who is leading the investigation." Before he could speak, Rachel continued. "What is his name?"

Seth wondered who could have possibly given Rachel the information about Major John Lawrence. He had been aloof with his fellow officers. He thought, *It must have been Sarah, Ned's wife. She always had a big mouth.* "Major John Lawrence."

Rachel had been in the navy long enough to know anyone with the rank of major assigned to NCIS was in the marine corps. "I don't believe I recognize that name."

"He works out of Washington DC."

"Don't know him. Naval Intelligence and NCIS do not always cross paths in Washington. It is a big place you do realize. Do you know who his CO is?"

"No," replied Seth. "We never got into it that much."

Rachel followed up, "Well, what can you tell me about the investigation? Do you have any suspects, possible leads?"

Seth could hear the sarcasm in her voice. He knew it stemmed from her frustration with her brother's death and the helplessness she felt. Seth wanted to try and deflect her questions.

"I guess by your silence you have nothing," snipped Rachel.

Seth paused at her comment. "No, that's not what my silence is saying," replied the defensive Seth.

"Then you have something?" queried Rachel.

"My silence is my way of letting you know that everything at his juncture of the investigation is on a need-to-know basis only. You know that in an ongoing investigation, you can't disclose sensitive information," stated the annoyed Seth. Seth hoped that his comments would quell Rachel's incessant inquiries.

"But I do have a right to know. I'm his sister," replied Rachel in a crescendo of volume.

Mary tried to calm Rachel, but was promptly dismissed.

Seth hesitated. He was not sure what he could tell Rachel since John had asked him to keep everything on a need-to-know basis. He thought for a moment that since Rachel worked with Naval Intelligence and that since she was Hugh's sister, she did have a right to know. She could also find out on her own. Seth figured that she was not going to walk away from the investigation. He could see the determination in her face. Rachel was clearly a strong woman from Seth's point of view. She had been assertive since he walked into the house. He did not think Rachel could be easily snubbed by him or anyone else associated with the investigation. After a great deal of deliberation, Seth felt compelled to disclose to Rachel what he knew. During his deliberations, he came to the conclusion that maybe her connections in Naval Intelligence could help solve the mystery of who was responsible for Hugh's death. "Can we go somewhere where we can be alone?" asked Seth. Seth felt that he was stepping over the line disclosing what he knew to Rachel, but Mary was a separate matter. Both were emotionally involved, but Mary was a *civilian*, and Rachel was *militarily connected*.

Mary took the cue. "Look . . . I need to make some phone calls. I'll go into the bedroom so you can stay here and talk," announced the dejected Mary. Mary calmly got out of her seat and walked into the master bedroom. She wiped the tears welling up in her eyes as she headed out of the room. She thought to herself how cruel things could be since it was her husband. *Why is it only Rachel could know about the investigation?* Mary thought.

Rachel and Seth went into the kitchen adjacent to the living room. They sat next to each other at the small oval kitchen table in an effort to keep their conversation from earshot of Mary in the adjacent bedroom.

Seth started in, "We don't have much." Seth included himself in the "we" since he felt that since he was at the Murphys' house, he was now an active participant in the investigation. "What we do know is that there was a break-in over at LeJeune. Someone stole some weapons and loaded them into a U-Haul. Hugh was killed sometime during the break-in. It appears that Hugh and his partner were on a routine patrol when they happened upon the break-in. The perpetrators transferred the stolen weapons to a boat and escaped. Apparently during the break-in, Hugh shot and killed one of the perps. Today, we believe we may have found the perps' hideout. We found a man who had been shot and buried on the property. We believe his accomplices buried the man. The perps removed any items that would allow us to easily identify the man except for maybe his teeth." Seth was filling in much of the information he believed was fact from his observations at the Murphys' house. Major Lawrence could not substantiate all the information Seth was providing Rachel. Seth felt good about his hunches and wanted Rachel to believe he was an active part of the investigation. He felt an attraction to Rachel and was hoping to impress her with his knowledge of the investigation. "Forensics has been at the Murphys' house most of the day. They plan on going back tomorrow. That's everything except Hugh's partner who was with him on patrol when they stumbled upon the break-in. He said that the people were 'country,' whatever that means." During the afternoon with Major John Lawrence at the Murphys' house, John filled Seth in on these details of the investigation. Seth felt that John confided in him since Seth had been so prompt in notifying John about the Murphys' place.

Rachel pondered what Seth told her for a few moments. "Who's handling the forensics?"

"The Jacksonville PD."

Rachel shouted coming to her feet, "Jacksonville PD! Why not the FBI?" Rachel was fuming. She began pacing in the small kitchen. She could not understand why someone highly trained from the NCIS or the FBI was not handling the forensics; after all, weapons were stolen, and her brother was killed during the break-in. Furthermore, she had not even heard of Major John Lawrence from NCIS.

"The guy leading the forensic team's name is Terry Ingram. He seems quite knowledgeable. I've been with him most of the day, and I believe he'll do a great job," offered Seth.

Rachel held back from attacking Seth. She knew he meant well, but things were not adding up as far as she was concerned. She excused herself and left the room. She went into the bedroom where Mary had gone to make phone calls.

Seth sat at the kitchen table alone wondering now if Major Lawrence was going to string him up for divulging information about the investigation to Rachel. Mary walked into the kitchen to find the exasperated Seth.

"How about something to eat?" asked Mary. "I guess bad news travels fast in a small town. We've had people stopping by all day dropping off food." Tears again started to fill in Mary's eyes. "With all the destruction from Isabelle, people are taking the time to come by to look out after me. I didn't even know some of the people."

Seth got up from the table. Rachel had been hard on him, but it was Mary who was suffering the deepest wounds. Seth felt a little ashamed of himself for feeling self-pity from the scolding that Rachel put on him. He put his arms around Mary, her pregnant belly pushing against him. "These are good people around here. We all care about you, Mary." Seth spoke in a soothing voice.

Mary let Seth's warm embrace calm her. When his grip loosened, she stepped back wiping the tears from her face with her hands. "Now what can I get you to eat?" inquired Mary.

"Sit," demanded Seth. "I can get it."

Seth looked around on the counter and in the refrigerator. He was overwhelmed at the amount of food. He fixed a plate with some fried chicken and vegetables that he heated in the microwave. He poured himself a glass of ice tea and sat next to Mary, who was sipping a cup of coffee. "What else did you and Rachel do today?" asked Seth.

Mary smiled at Seth's weak attempt at idle conversation. "Funeral arrangements. Dealing with the bureaucracy at the marine corps and the like."

It wasn't long before Seth regretted the question.

Mary caught herself. "I'm sorry. You don't need to hear all that."

"No . . . go ahead. Bureaucracy, marine corps we've all been there before," replied the sarcastic Seth.

Mary laughed. His comment helped break some of the tension and the aggravation that she had been going on throughout the day. It wasn't long before the conversation changed to lighthearted conversation. It was something both of them needed after a long day.

Seth was finishing his meal when Rachel returned from the bedroom. They had heard her on the telephone carrying on a heated conversation. Rachel was fuming when she entered the kitchen and pulled a beer out of the refrigerator. Her eyes were red from freshly fallen tears. They could see her nose was red from constantly wiping it.

A loud silence hung in the air as they waited for Rachel to calm herself. She pushed herself back against the counter and took two long swigs of beer, almost finishing the bottle. After a few minutes, Rachel spoke. "I was on the phone with my CO in Washington updating him on what I knew about Hugh's death, and he became irate that I had gotten involved." Rachel thought to herself, *"Involved," I ask a few questions of a local cop about my own brother's death and I'm "involved."* "He told me to stay out of the investigation. Furthermore, he said that he had it on reliable information that Major John Lawrence was one hell of a NCIS investigator. The trouble is that it seems that he has no homicide training. He is more of a liaison between the military and the politicians on Capitol Hill. For Christ's sake, he's only got limited experience as a homicide investigator, and he's trying to solve a murder and arms theft. He's only a major after all the years he's been in service. For as long as he's been in the marine corps, he should be a fucking general by now. Hell of an investigator my ass." The room was cautiously silent as Rachel vented. "This whole thing reeks of a military cover-up but why? Is someone up for promotion that they don't want to tarnish their precious career at the last minute? Nothing I've heard makes a whole lot of sense."

"Cover-up . . . come on, Rachel, be serious. Aren't you getting a little paranoid? I'm sure your CO does not want you to become involved in the investigation since you're not objective," commented Seth.

Rachel ignored Seth's comments relating to a cover-up. Even she thought about her comment and realized it was a little over the top. "Damn being objective," grumbled Rachel. She paused realizing she was getting out of line with someone she had just met. "I know you're right, but I have a right to find out who killed my brother and why."

"I agree, but let the police or, should I say, NCIS do their job. Having family involved in an investigation other than purely for informational purposes only complicates an investigation," added Seth.

"Damn it, I know you're right, but things just don't feel right to me," responded Rachel. "This whole investigation seems strange to me how it's coming together. Ya know. You have a lead NCIS investigator that is more of a military politician than an investigator. It just doesn't seem to add up."

Though Mary was also upset, she wanted to change the subject and did so by changing the direction of the conversation. She tried to draw Seth into the conversation by asking about the hurricane and the resultant damage to the local area. Mary had been listening to the local news, but she figured Seth could provide information that was left out of the news. She also inquired about how the various divisions of law enforcement were coming together to assist in the cleanup and all. After a while, Rachel calmed down, and everyone talked idly. Seth saw the direction Mary was going and tried to create a less stressful evening by interjecting some humor that helped soothe Rachel. Before midnight, Seth excused himself and went home.

CHAPTER 28

When Seth arrived home, he let Argo out onto the beach for a run and to do her chores. Argo had been with Seth all day, and a run on the beach was what she was craving. When Seth returned from the beach, he saw there was a message on the answering machine and played it. As soon as he heard the voice on the answering machine, he recognized it as Major John Lawrence. John's voice came across as urgent. He left his office number and a cell phone number. Seth scribbled the information on a pad of paper that he always kept next to the phone.

Seth looked at his watch trying to decide which number he felt was more likely to catch John. He settled on the cell phone number. Seth sat down and dialed the number. After the first ring, she heard John's voice again. "John, Seth Jarret."

"Seth, where the hell have you been? I've been trying to reach you all night. I received a call from Washington. They said they had a lead on who broke into the ammunitions depot. They said they believed it to be a militia in western North Carolina. They call themselves the . . ."

Seth could hear John shuffling some papers looking for the name.

"Ah, the hell with it," commented the annoyed John. "Look . . . they're sending a team of FBI and ATF agents there as we speak. I'm ready to go. I was calling to see if you wanted to tag along with me. The downside is we have to drive all night to get there before the raid takes place. They are planning a raid at dawn."

Seth could not believe his ears. He realized how much he missed the excitement of a dawn raid or just a good chase in order to put some lowlife scum behind bars. Working as the chief of the Surf City Police Department was never going to lead to anything like this. "Count me in! What do you need for me to do?" asked Seth. He could barely contain himself.

"Nothin'," replied John. "I'll be there in a half hour. Just be ready to go when I get there. I'm in my car headed your way. I figured you'd want to go, and if you didn't, I was going to make you go anyhow. I need someone to help me drive. This area is all new to me. By the way, tell me how to get to your place."

After giving John directions to his place, Seth raced into the bedroom gathering what he thought he would need for the next few days. He called Ned to update him. He asked him to manage the police station for the next few days and look after Argo.

Ned was always thrilled to be in charge. It rarely happened because there was little need for Seth to go out of town unless it was on vacation or some kind of police training.

CHAPTER 29

John Lawrence arrived a little before one in the morning. John had a marine corps-issue sedan, dark green with yellow writing on the sides clearly indicating that is was a marine corps sedan. John wore a yellow T-shirt with the marine corps logo on the crest in bright red and a pair of jeans. He had a red marine corps Windbreaker and was wearing marine corps-issued boots suitable for war or a hike in the mountains.

Seth looked at John and thought, *There is no mistaking this guy as marine corps government issue.*

Seth had his personal belongings for a few nights on the road stuffed in a gym bag. He grabbed his gun and attached the clip-on holster to his belt. Seth wore a white T-shirt with the Surf City Police Department logo in navy blue on the chest and a pair of jeans. He too was wearing his marine corps-issued boots from his days in Desert Storm. He had a blue Windbreaker with the Surf City Police Department logo on the right crest as well. "I'm ready," Seth shouted as he hurried down the steps of his beach house to the sedan.

"I can see," replied John. "Nice house. Have you lived here long?"

"Long enough," answered Seth. He wanted to avoid the whole story about how this was Maribeth's and his house but she had died almost ten months prior. "Where are we going?" inquired Seth.

"It's a small place just west of Cherokee, North Carolina, up near the Tennessee state line."

The two men heard some commotion followed by footsteps from Mary's house next door. Then a woman's voice called down to them. It was Rachel standing on the deck of Mary's house looking down at the two men getting ready to leave. "This is about my brother's death, isn't it?"

John and Seth were caught off guard by Rachel's question. Seth looked at John and then back at Rachel. "I'm afraid that it is."

—

"Then I'm going with you!" demanded Rachel. Rachel was already on leave as a result of her brother's death, so a side trip to wherever these men were going in search of her brother's killer certainly was not about to hold her back.

"The hell you are!" replied Seth. "This is a police and NCIS matter. The reason we are going is because of our insight into this investigation." Seth did not think what he was telling Rachel was necessarily the whole truth, but he felt it sounded good and maybe the deterrent they needed to exclude her. Seth certainly did not want a family member involved in a police investigation.

Rachel returned, "He and I are both naval investigators. If he's going, I'm going." The fact that John was actually in the marine corps didn't matter since the marine corps is a branch of the navy.

"Who the hell is this, Seth?" inquired John.

"This is Rachel Dugen. She is Lieutenant Hugh Dugen's sister. She happens to be with Naval Intelligence in Washington DC," replied Seth.

"Major John Lawrence," John introduced himself. Rachel had come down the steps of the beach house while they were exchanging conversation so she could face the two men. John extended his hand to greet the young naval officer.

The rush to get on the road and brush off Rachel exasperated Seth. He looked over at John. "It's your call."

"Hell, I don't care. Let's just get doing," answered John. "We've got a long way to go, and I'm not sure if we are going to get there in time as it is. She can share in the driving."

"I'll only be a minute," replied Rachel. She race back up the steps of Mary's beach house. She threw a change of clothes and some bathroom items into a knapsack. She said good-bye to Mary and raced out the door. She caught herself at the door and went back to her room for her Beretta. She checked the clip to make sure it was loaded as she ran out of the house.

John and Seth were sitting in the car waiting for Rachel when she jumped into the backseat of the sedan. "You know this is a bad idea to have a relative of one of the victim's coming along," commented Seth.

"Yeah, I know. Hell, by the time we get there, this whole thing will most likely be wrapped up anyhow. I can use the time to maybe get some background information from her."

Seth sat in the sedan shaking his head as he listened to John. "It's your call."

Rachel jumped into the backseat of the sedan. "Okay, guys—let's roll!"

As they started out, Rachel and John exchanged a few more customary military designations. He had heard the exchanges in the past, but since his discharge from military service, he had made a point of ignoring the exchange.

"Ensign Rachel Dugen," commented Rachel from the backseat. Seth had only introduced her as Rachel Dugen, and without her uniform, she wanted John aware of her rank, though a low grade in the officer corps. Rachel gave John a soft, subtle smile as she made herself comfortable that would have brought John to his knees had he been standing.

"Nice to formerly meet you," commented John.

"Now that the introductions are over, were you spying on us?" inquired Seth. Seth was annoyed. He was looking forward to doing some *real* police work, and having a victim's sister tagging along was not in his plans.

"Ease up, Chief, I don't think she means any harm," announced John.

Seth heard the comment and wanted to respond vehemently, but he felt if the major was okay with her involvement, then it was not his place to interfere. It was still John's investigation after all.

"No," replied Rachel, responding to Seth's comment. "When I heard a car pull up at this hour and noticed that it was military issue, I had to find out if it was about my brother."

John had started the car and put it in drive as soon as Rachel got in. They headed for Cherokce, which is in the far western part of North Carolina. John raced through the small town of Surf City trying to reach any kind of highway as fast as he could.

Seth asked, "What about your sister-in-law and the funeral arrangements? Is she going to take care of it alone?"

"Relax . . . my mother will be here first thing in the morning. They can keep each other company and make all the arrangement. Besides . . . I've never been good at that kind of thing." Rachel had always been a bit of a tomboy despite her attractive appearance.

"How the hell do we get to Cherokee?" asked John as he headed out of town.

Seth heard the question and looked around the car for a map.

"What the hell are you looking for?" inquired John.

"A map. All I know is that Cherokee is in the far western corner of North Carolina, and if we are going to get there for a dawn raid, you had better floor it! I'm not originally from North Carolina, so I am going to have to look at a map."

"Lovely," John commented in a sarcastic manner.

Seth heard the comment and realized the comment, though sarcastic, was meant in jest. He found a map in the glove compartment. The map was a few years old, but it was all Seth needed to get them headed in the right direction.

Rachel soon fell asleep. She had driven down during the previous night from northern Virginia and was exhausted.

Seth noted how quiet the backseat was. He looked back to see Rachel peacefully sleeping. He felt she could use the rest from everything that had happened.

As they rode along, the two men noticed the inland damage caused by hurricane Isabelle from the car's headlights. There were small lakes on either side of the road on what was once farmland. A number of tree limbs had snapped from the wind, or the trees had toppled over as a result of the saturated ground loosening the soil around the roots of the trees. Several homes had lost their roofs most likely from tornados spawned by the hurricane. As the men got farther and farther inland, they could see most of the damage was water and wind related. The water damage was most likely from flash floods.

CHAPTER 30

It was six-thirty in the morning when FBI Agent Mike Kelly glanced down at his watch. He had been up since six o'clock in the morning the previous day at his home in Bethesda, Maryland. He received a call that awoke him giving him instructions that he would be leading a raid on a militia compound near Cherokee, North Carolina, the following day. He had been making telephone calls all day long. He traveled by helicopter to Cherokee, North Carolina, since there were no convenient airports. He coordinated the early-morning raid on the militia while en route to the small western town. The North Carolina and Tennessee branches of the FBI had been sent to assist him in the impending raid. He also had support from the ATF for the raid. In all, he had almost one hundred FBI and ATF agents going along with him on the raid. Mike was impressed with himself; he had never had this many people under his command at any one time. He had been in the FBI for almost twenty years, and thus far this was his biggest command. He had had other more important assignments, but they never required this kind of contingent.

He had received information that there were approximately one hundred members of a militia in a compound in western North Carolina. There was rumor that the militia had a number of automatic and semiautomatic weapons and grenades. Based on an informant's information, a judge issued a search warrant at the bequest of the FBI because the militia was viewed as an "imminent threat" to the United States. The FBI and ATF agents were dressed in military fatigues or jeans and navy blue T-shirts along with navy blue jackets identifying them as either FBI or ATF in yellow. The consensus among the agents was to hit the militia before dawn, hopefully catching them off guard and saving the lives of all concerned.

The Cherokee locals had not seen the likes of this many federal agents since the capture of Eric Rudolph behind a grocery store in Murphy, North Carolina, some years earlier. Eric Rudolph was the man convicted of the bombings of an Atlanta nightclub, an abortion clinic, and the 1996 Olympic bombing at Centennial Park. The only thing missing this time was the bounty of media hanging on anything uttered by the lowest—to the highest-ranked federal agents or local cops. The media chased after anyone that ever knew of Eric Rudolph. That included his elementary schoolmates as they tried to get a perspective of what kind of person he was or what drove him to commit the bombings. Murphy is just a short scenic drive from downtown Cherokee.

The air and colorful surrounding foliage of an early autumn hung heavy along with the morning dew that glistened on the foliage and in the grassy meadows. The dampness of the dew made the federal agents' clothes feel damp and cold. As each person spoke, they could see their breath. The task force, comprised of the FBI and ATF agents, had surrounded the militia's compound and was awaiting Agent Kelly to give the word to move in. It was six thirty go time. As the agents closed in, they caught several sentries sleeping or drinking beer despite the early-morning hour. Others in the militia were deep in conversation of military hardware they had or hoped to one day own, one man boasting over the next. The remainder of the militia was caught in their bunks, and some were found using the makeshift bathrooms dispersed among the bunkhouses. The plan had worked better than Agent Kelly hoped. No shots were fired, and the militia members seemed surprised by the sudden appearance of the federal agents. As Agent Kelly started his count of the number of militia prisoners, he counted only forty members, far less than the informant's estimates. The agents confiscated about two hundred automatic and semiautomatic weapons, a small number of grenades, some fifty pistols in varying calibers, and almost thirty thousand rounds of varying ammunition. Agent Kelly was fascinated by how sophisticated the militia was. They found a number of new high-speed computers and peripheral support equipment connecting to a network of computers throughout the United States and Canada. The militia had disconnected the Internet connections prior to retiring for the evening. The entire system comprised of a series of passwords throughout to prevent unauthorized access if the militia's compound was ever compromised.

CHAPTER 31

Seth was driving when they reached Cherokee shortly after seven in the morning. They were worn-out from the long drive from the coast to the mountains. They originally got directions from a clerk with the FBI prior to leaving the coast. However, Seth stopped at a convenience store to get some further directions from a local resident. The locals knew they were headed to the militia's compound from their inquiries. No one professed to know anything about a militia's compound. It was an understood fact known to the locals but never open for public discussion; it was safer for everyone that way. When the plethora of federal agents arrived, the locals assumed they were there to raid the militia's compound—especially since Eric Rudolph was already in federal custody, what else was there for them to do? Though the entire town had guessed there would be a raid by the FBI and ATF, the town's people did not care to alert the militia. The locals viewed the militia as a nuisance, and their elimination from the community would be a welcomed event.

Seth was disappointed to hear from the convenience store clerk that the raid had already taken place. He was surprised by the commonality of information among the locals of what was to be a surprise raid. Seth was frustrated not to be a part of the raid but was glad to still be a part of the investigation. They drove out of Cherokee following the convenience store clerk's directions until they came to a roadblock. The roadblock was next to a dirt road leading up into some hills via a series of switchbacks in the dirt road. Also, next to the roadblock was a welcome sign for Camp Laurel. John reached across Seth to flash his badge and spoke to a man who was wearing a jacket that identified him as an FBI agent. The FBI agent looked at John's credentials with a wary eye. He stepped back from the car as he called someone on his two-way radio while another FBI agent made sure John did not proceed before gaining authorization. The first FBI agent concluded his conversation and moved back to the car where John, Seth, and Rachel waited. The FBI agent bent over looking into the car to give

---

125

John instructions as to where to proceed and whom he needed to contact once inside the compound. He then motioned for Seth to proceed. They proceeded driving up the dirt road following the numerous switchbacks for about a mile and a quarter. The road emptied into an area surrounded by crudely built cabins and a target range. A number of men and a few women were standing around in fatigues and jackets that identified themselves as either ATF or FBI. Seth parked the car. He noticed several ATF and FBI agents standing guard over approximately fifty men and women dressed in jeans, T-shirts, and fatigues sitting on the ground.

As the three of them got out of the car, John called over to one of the men wearing a navy blue jacket with the yellow FBI print on the back, "Who's in charge?" The FBI agent standing closest pointed to another man about twenty-five yards away. John approached the man and identified himself, "Major Lawrence with NCIS."

"Agent Mike Kelly, what can I do for you, Major?" Agent Kelly was dressed sharply despite the inexpensive jacket identifying him as an FBI agent. He had on dress pants instead on jeans or fatigues like many of the other field agents that were prepared for a wilderness adventure.

"Excuse me?" replied an incredulous John. "We were informed by one of your agents that there was to be an early-morning raid of a militia. We were told by one of your offices to join in the raid."

Agent Kelly looked at John a little surprised by the new information. "I'm not sure why. This was to be an entirely federal agency raid without any military involvement." Agent Kelly cast a wary eye toward Seth, dressed in his Surf City police jacket, and Rachel who was also dressed casually. Rachel was not wearing anything to identify her as being with Naval Intelligence. Agent Kelly continued, "We were sent here to raid these guys as gunrunners and a possible threat to national security."

John chimed in, "Your office told us to assist you in an early-morning raid. These guys may be the ones responsible for the break-in at Camp LeJeune that killed an MP." John was becoming agitated by Agent Kelly's dismissive response.

"I'm sorry, but I received no such word regarding your involvement or about any related break-in at Camp LeJeune," continued Agent Kelly. "Who specifically contacted you?"

"I'm not sure," replied an exasperated John. "I received a call at my temporary office at Camp LeJeune from someone identifying themselves as an FBI agent in Washington DC."

Agent Kelly ignored John's vague reply. He decided to follow up on who may have called John at a later time. He had been up more hours than he cared to think about. For now the FBI and ATF agents, both under his direct command, had captured a potentially dangerous militia without incident, and he wanted to move forward with the investigation. Agent Kelly decided that since John and his entourage were affiliated with law enforcement in some capacity, from his brief conversation with the FBI agent at the roadblock, a few extra law enforcement bodies couldn't hurt. "That must have been some drive coming up from Camp LeJeune," said Agent Mike Kelly. "Look, let me deal with a few things, and I will call Washington and try and get to the bottom of all this. Can I see some ID from you before I let you start wandering around my crime scene?" asked Agent Kelly. Agent Kelly wanted to cover his bases one more time before he gave too much latitude to some unknown persons.

John, Seth, and Rachel produced their badges once again for Agent Kelly. Agent Kelly looked at the respective badges and into the faces of the tired people standing before him comparing the pictures on the badges to the faces. Once he was satisfied, he gave a cautious warning, "I know you want to get involved, but before I can get to the bottom of all this, I'm going to have to ask that you just observe. I need for my men to do their work without any outside interference. Are we in agreement?"

Reluctantly Seth, John, and Rachel verbally agreed.

"Good." Agent Kelly handed the badges back and started to walk away.

Rachel could wait no longer. "Can't you tell us something?"

Agent Kelly paused and gave Rachel an exasperated look. He held up his hand to indicate he would deal with her and her questions at his disposal.

Rachel started to pursue Agent Kelly before John and Seth stepped into her path to detain her. John started in, "Rachel . . . this is his crime scene. We better give him some room before he escorts us out of here."

Rachel was angry. She wanted something to help solve her brother's untimely death, but she knew John was right. Either she played along or it would be a quick escort off the premises followed by a long ride back to Surf City. "You're right. I'm sorry. I just . . . just am . . . !

"I know. You're angry," answered John. "But we need to play it his way." John was referring to Agent Kelly.

CHAPTER 32

John, Seth, and Rachel tried to relax after their long ride to Cherokee; they were frustrated for being late for the raid and for being greeted with such surprise. They talked among themselves about Agent Kelly's confusion with their presence. John apologized for the confusion. Seth and Rachel deflected his apologies by chalking it up to government bureaucracy. After about an hour, Agent Kelly returned and approached John. "I called Washington, and no one there knows anything about a call to you much less about assisting us in today's raid. They are well aware of the break-in at Camp LeJeune, but they don't think the two are related." Agent Kelly waited for some kind of reply from John.

"I don't understand," answered a dejected John. "I received a message from the FBI late last night to rush up here to take part in this raid. I was told by the bureau to take part in the questioning because there was a strong belief that the militia was responsible for the break-in at Camp LeJeune. How else could I have known about the raid? Did you ask around who may have called me?" John was perturbed with the lack of professionalism within the FBI. He had made the long drive to the mountains of North Carolina only to find out it was a waste of his time.

Agent Kelly saw the disappointment on John's face. "Yes, I had them ask around. Look, you're welcome to stick around and help out if you think it will help in your investigation. You can sit in on the interrogations. Who knows, maybe you'll get lucky after all and find out these guys were responsible." As Agent Kelly was talking, he thought about John's comment about how they may have found out about the raid. It could only have been some foul-up in Washington. "Hell . . . if they didn't do it, they may have some knowledge about who did. Things like that can happen. It takes just one person to give us a lead sometimes, and the whole thing can fall into place."

"Thanks," responded Seth, who jumped in for John. Seth could see John was confused from what had transpired and was diligently trying to piece everything together in his head. John tuned Agent Kelly out as he opened a notebook to review his notes on who from the FBI may have called him about the raid on the militia.

Rachel started in again, "So what do you have so far?"

Agent Kelly looked warily at Rachel. He proceeded to give a long story of how they secured a parameter position before moving in. He took his time explaining that the entire raid had gone without incident, a proud moment for him considering the magnitude of the raid and the amount of weapons found. No shots were fired. He included how they had caught the militia completely off guard. John, Seth, and Rachel wanted to know what Agent Kelly and his men found related to possible military weapons that could indicate there was some kind of link to Camp LeJeune. John put his notebook down while he listened intently to Agent Kelly to determine if any of the evidence connected the militia to the break-in at Camp LeJeune. After the long-winded recap, he realized there was nothing he could link to the break-in. *More time wasted!* he thought.

"Do we know where they got the new weapons from?" inquired John.

"No, but we have reason to believe the men purchased the weapons from a Russian arms dealer out of St. Petersburg, Russia. The arms were routed through Costa Rica before arriving at a private airport in Wilmington, North Carolina. These guys then probably transported them here by truck."

John spoke. "Who is in charge of the militia?"

Mike pointed to one of the men in handcuffs. "His name is Al Stewart."

"Would you mind if I questioned him?" John was eager to accomplish something out of the day. He was hoping Agent Kelly was right in that he may get lucky by walking away with some kind of a lead from the militia.

Agent looked indignant at first. Who was this NCIS officer to make such a request? Reluctantly, Agent Kelly offered, "I suppose not, but I want one of my men in on the interrogation."

"No problem," replied John. John was surprised that Agent Kelly would be willing to allow him to conduct his own interrogation, but thus far nothing about the investigation was making any sense. If the only way he can conduct an interrogation relating to what happened at Camp LeJeune included an FBI agent sitting in, then why the hell not thought John?

Mike called one of his men over, who helped John usher Al Stewart into one of the crude cabins. John heard Agent Kelly comment to the agent, "Stay with him while he interrogates Mr. Stewart." John could see the agent nod his acknowledgment. The two men exchanged some additional words that John could not hear before Agent Kelly signaled to John for him to join them in the cabin.

Agent Kelly looked down from the cabin at John and Seth. "We already read them their rights." Seth continued into the cabin and took a seat with Rachel close behind.

"Thanks for the update," replied John. John stopped at the door before entering. He called over to two FBI agents who were taking a smoke break together and asked for a cigarette and a light. One of the FBI agents walked over to John, reached into a breast pocket, and produced a packet of Camels. He shuffled the pack allowing John to grab a cigarette from the pack and then lit the cigarette for John.

"Thanks."

"Don't mention it." The FBI agent left John standing at the entrance to the cabin.

John stood just outside the cabin smoking the cigarette alone.

Seth wondered what happened to John. He walked back to the entrance. He saw John just outside the cabin smoking a cigarette. He opened the door to the cabin and looked over at John. "We're ready when you are." Seth waited for some kind of acknowledgment from John but received none. "I didn't know you were a smoker," added the irritated Seth.

John took a deep drag on the cigarette and gave Seth a stern look. "I'm not but I used to be. I just wanted one to buy a little time to collect my thoughts."

"Oh . . . sorry." Seth felt a little uncomfortable for disturbing John.

John noticed Seth's reaction to his comment. "Forget it. Let's crack this son of a bitch wide open." John gave Seth a wink and a confident and cunning smile. Seth nodded in agreement. Seth stepped aside to allow John into the cabin.

———

CHAPTER 33

The cabin was sparsely furnished. It was a cabin in every sense of the word. The floor was made of crude strips of wood. The ceiling reflected exposed beams, and the same crude strips of wood that made the floor was the staple that comprised the support for the roof. The cabin consisted of two rooms. The main room was the kitchen and bedroom. There were several bunk beds throughout the bedroom, and a large pine picnic table in the center of the room completed much of the furnishings. There were a few crudely but sturdily built wood chairs spread throughout the cabin. The kitchen included a refrigerator, stove, and sink. John assumed that the cupboards consisted of food and dishes. The only other room was a bathroom separated by a plywood door with a metal handle. The bathroom had two sinks, side by side; three toilets partitioned off with a door for privacy; and an open shower with six nozzles. John casually went over to one of the cupboards and found a tin of coffee. He did not ask Al Stewart, who was now sitting in one of the crudely built straight-back chairs with his hands handcuffed behind him, if he minded that John helped himself to making the coffee. Al was sitting in the kitchen area with the FBI agent that helped usher him into the cabin, standing along a wall keeping close watch. John looked at Al without expression. "What is your name?"

The FBI agent had identified Al Stewart earlier to John. The FBI agent looked at Al and then John and replied, "His name is Al Stewart." Al was wearing a pair of jeans that were torn at the knees and was worn where his wallet rested. He had a T-shirt with the name of a local bar. He also wore a pair of scuffed-up black army boots. He had a disheveled look as he peered at John and the FBI agent.

Al ignored the question since the FBI agent had beaten him to the answer. After John got the coffee going, he found another chair and sat down across from Al. Rachel, Seth, and the FBI agent sat down at the picnic table in a position so they could watch the interrogation. Once the coffee was ready, John poured himself a cup and returned to his seat. John sat and stared at Al for the longest while without saying anything and slowly sipped his coffee. Everyone grew quite uncomfortable, but Seth could tell John was very much in control and that Al was more uncomfortable than anyone. After about thirty minutes, Agent Mike Kelly entered the room and motioned for the other agent to leave the cabin while Mike took his place. Still no one had uttered a word. Agent Kelly's entrance seemed to help matters as he nodded to John seemingly to communicate something. John returned the nod expressionlessly. Mike took a seat next to Rachel and Seth at the picnic table.

During the long silence, Seth watched John. To Seth it seemed as though John was pondering the right questions to ask without coming across as though he did not know what questions to ask or in what sequence to ask them.

Al broke the long silence, "You're not getting shit out of me, so you can take this silent crap and stick it." When Al broke the silence, he startled Rachel, and she jumped slightly, giving herself away as new to the interrogation process. She looked at John in fear she may have somehow broken some sacred interrogation oath. John did not acknowledge what had happened. He just sat there continuing to stare at Al and enjoying his cup of coffee.

Al saw Rachel jump out of the corner of his eye and chuckled. "A newbie? I guess your girl is finally getting out in the real world."

John ignored Al's comment. "Mr. Stewart, my friend over there brought some FBI agents that are very accomplished computer hackers. They are practicing their trade on your computers as we speak. When they are through, any chance of making a deal will be long gone."

Al looked back in a matter-of-fact glance. "Big fuckin' deal . . . ain't gonna get shit from me or those computers!" John smiled and sat back as best he could in the homemade wooden chair, clasping his hands behind his head. After a while he got up and poured himself yet another cup of coffee. Al called over, "How 'bout a cup?" John grabbed another cup, poured the coffee, and put it on the floor next to where Al was seated. Al looked at John and offered the handcuffs from around his back for to John to unlock them. John ignored the entire exchange and sat down. "Well, how 'bout unlocking these fuckin' handcuffs?" inquired an annoyed Al.

John sat for a moment and then spoke. "You give me something, and I'll give you something."

"Fuck you!" snapped Al as his left foot shot out from under his chair, knocking over the cup of coffee John had placed on the floor next to him.

John once again ignored Al's remark and returned to the silence. The room was so quiet that everyone could hear the coffee seep through the crude flooring and onto the ground beneath the cabin. John sat back and slowly drank his coffee, giving the illusion that he was enjoying the cup of coffee more than usual. John glanced at his watch; the day had slipped away from him. The room started to chill now that the day was drawing to a close as the day gave way to the mountain evening. The air was once again filling with a cool mountain dampness that had greeted the task force that earlier in the day raided the compound in the early-morning hours. The only light in the room was from a lamp strategically placed behind John and the open door. It looked like someone had lit a fire outside to warm the task force and the militia still sitting on the ground.

CHAPTER 34

Rachel and Seth left the room to stretch their legs and go to the bathroom. They elected to not use the bathroom in the interrogation cabin but one in another cabin. They were not eager to return since the silence had grown excruciating at times. They watched FBI agents and forensic teams comb the remaining cabins searching for guns and anything else connecting the militia to *subversive* activity. Everything they did was slow and deliberate. A group of forensic agents combed through trash cans and other items collected by the FBI agents. Another group of FBI agents was processing the militia members one by one. They were taking digital pictures of each militia detainee and any tattoos that could later be used for identification. The FBI was fingerprinting each person and entering it into a database linked to a mainframe in Washington DC to determine if there were any outstanding warrants, etc., on the militia members. Rachel and Seth looked in on the FBI computer hackers as they accessed files and tried accessing other militias throughout the country. They said nothing as they worked. Occasionally they would to take notes and print out pages and pages of data they accessed. Two other agents sat with the computer hackers reading over the documents as they printed them out. They used yellow highlighters and felt-tipped red pens as they highlighted or circled things they felt were significant. They exchanged only information that either of them felt was immediately relevant. Someone ordered food and brought enough for everyone, except the militia who continued to sit on the ground watching as their personal belongings were combed through by the federal agents. Periodically a couple of the other agents would bring a man or woman back and take another away to interrogate them in one of the other cabins made into an interrogation room. Their methods seemed to work more expediently than John's, yet John had seemed to be in full control. Rachel found the other interrogations more productive and elected to remain outside the silent cabin. Agent Kelly had not

---

134

made any comments toward John other than to periodically make subtle gestures to pick up the pace, none of which seemed to induce John to move any faster.

Seth returned to the cabin to find John still conducting the silent interrogation. As Seth entered the cabin, John looked up along with Agent Kelly. Al could see who entered the room. John looked at Al with contempt; he got up and came over to Seth. John took Seth by the arm and led him out of the room. As he did, he motioned to Seth not to say anything. Seth was alarmed; now he felt as though he had broken some interrogation code too. Once out of range from Al to hear anything, John spoke. "How's it going?"

Seth was surprised by the question. "What do you mean, 'how's it going'? You're the one who has been in with him for an eternity now without saying anything. What is it with the silent interrogation? Is this some new kind of interrogation technique you guys in Washington came up with?"

"Yeah, I know. It's not fun, but I think when I go back, he'll be willing to give us something. I wanted to try a different approach to interrogating him, not that I've had a whole lot of experience with interrogations. I figured he was expecting the traditional yelling and screaming type of interrogation. That or the good-cop bad-cop method, so I wanted to try something that I thought he wouldn't know how to react to. Ya know, keep him off balance. It's my own theory. You see, someone like Mr. Stewart in there who is used to a captive audience that hangs on his every word needs to talk. He also knows that we need him to talk, so he'll give us information through his own errors or by tripping over his own words. He is already predisposed to a line of questioning probably from similar circumstances. By me keeping silent, he will eventually talk because he just needs to be heard, and he needs to talk on his own volition. You see, he is incredibly impressed with himself and by us showing up at 'his' compound he needs to rub all this in our face. Once he starts talking, he will tell us something of value."

"Interesting theory. How can you be sure he'll say something worthwhile when you return? I mean, it's not like you're moving along with much of anything."

"Well, we've been at it for over an hour now, and I know I have to pee, so I'm sure he does too." As John came to a close, he turned and headed back into the cabin.

Seth wasn't sure what the hell John's comment about having to pee meant, but he followed John back into the cabin where Al quietly sat staring at the wall and Agent Kelly sat sipping a cup of coffee.

"Well, now that you're back, how 'bout removing these handcuffs so I can go take a piss?" shouted Al to John.

John stood in front of Al and looked over at Agent Kelly. "Do I have to take him out for a piss?" Not waiting for an answer from Agent Kelly, John looked back at Al. "You give me something, and I give you something."

"Fuck you!" shouted Al.

"As you wish," responded John. John slowly empted the cold coffee from his cup onto the floor in front of Al, allowing it to make as much splattering sound as he could. Much of the splattering coffee found its way to the bottom of Al's jeans. Once his cup was completely empty, he shook it a couple of times in Al's face. John went over to the counter and poured himself another cup of coffee.

"All right," Al called out. "What's your fucking question?"

John paused a moment in triumph before acknowledging Al's call. "I'm interested in some arms that were stolen from Camp LeJeune a couple of days ago," inquired John.

"Don't know anything about it," replied Al.

"Okay then." John sat back down and sipped his coffee in front of Al.

Al was disgusted; he had to urinate, and he could tell John was not about to give in unless he gave John something tangible. He was not sure who else was in the room or could hear what he was about to say, but the information he was about to give did not affect his militia. "You guys are so fuckin' stupid. You can't figure out who stole your guns, so you figure we had to take 'em. Ya know we're not the only ones who are in the market for arms. It could be drug dealers, your basic thief, gunrunners, or someone else."

"Now why should we believe you? Hell . . . we got a tip that you and your comrades up here stole the arms." John didn't want to disclose too much about what was stolen or how cleanly the men had gotten away.

"Bullshit! Who's the fuckin' asshole that would make that crap up? My guess is your own people gave you that cock-and-bull story to give you some bullshit reason to raid our place. You've been itchin' to get in here for a long time. Did you even think that maybe your own people are selling you out? You guys gotta fuckin' wake up!"

"What do ya mean?" replied John. He knew he sounded naive, but now that Al was talking, he felt he had to dig for as much information as Al was willing to give. John still believed that once Al got to talking, he would go on and on about how great his organization was, but he also didn't want to take a chance that Al would clam up, and they would be starting the waiting period all over again.

"We got word those LeJeune arms were gonna get ripped off at least a month ago. We thought about takin' those guys out after they did the job, but figured we'd get whacked if we got in the middle. There was some strong muscle behind that rip."

John listened intently. He was not sure if Al was just blowing smoke or if he was on the level. "So if you didn't do the job, who did? I can't imagine there being enough muscle to run you boys off." John hoped that he offered Al enough of a challenge to bait him into continuing the dialogue.

Al paused looking down at the floor. With a long grin on his face, he slowly raised his head to look John in the face and, in a gruff voice, said, "Fuckin' Cubans, you morons!" He paused for a moment and looked John coldly in the eyes. "Hell, even your own people were in on it."

John was baffled by Al's response. Agent Kelly hurriedly scribbled some notes on a pad of paper he had next to him. John thought to himself, *Is he making this stuff up, or was he on the level? "Own people," what could he possibly mean by it?* John digested Al's comments for the moment. He didn't want to appear too eager in case Al was stringing him along. He tried to put up a facade that he already knew the information Al was providing but was just getting confirmation. "What do you mean 'my people' and the 'Cubans'?" asked John.

Al was enjoying himself. He could tell by Agent Kelly's scribbled notes and John's hesitations that he was giving them everything they could want and more. He also knew the information was almost unbelievable. "Ya know, Cubans, like in Miami! That's what I mean!" Al was smug; he was enjoying the puzzled look on John's face. He could tell John was not sure if he was leading him on or not. He intentionally held out on "your own people" to draw John in.

John could not believe what he was hearing. None of what Al was saying made any sense. "What do you mean 'my people'? Where are you gettin' this stuff from?" John asked incredulously as he tried to regroup. He knew Al was reading his expressions, but he did not care; he just wanted as much information as he could get out of this son of a bitch.

Al ignored John's questions. "Hey, I don't give a fuck if you believe me or not. Just let me take a piss. You agreed that if I gave you something, you'd give me something." Al twisted in his seat, extending his handcuffed wrists so John could remove the handcuffs.

John stood over Al for a moment. He could see in the corner of his eye that Agent Kelly wanted to talk with him, and this was as good a time as any to make it happen. John leaned forward and unlocked one side of the handcuffs. Al started to get up to walk away, but John pulled back firmly on the handcuffs and replaced the handcuffs in front of Al as opposed to where they were behind him. Agent Kelly sat up to help guard Al in case Al made any sudden moves during the unhandcuffing and rehandcuffing of the prisoner. John opened the bathroom door and stepped inside for a long, deliberate look around the empty bathroom. After the brief look, he stepped back out of the bathroom and motioned for Al to enter. He held the door open for Al to enter. John looked back at Seth and Agent Kelly waiting for some signal on how to handle the situation, but he received none. He stared back at Al with a determined look. The two were face-to-face just inches apart, both forceful individuals staring each other down. It seemed almost silly that two grown men were establishing their turf next to a bathroom.

Al gave John a smug look as he entered the bathroom.

John smiled back. "I think you can manage."

CHAPTER 35

Seth, Agent Kelly, and John immediately congregated around the picnic table inside the cabin to quietly discuss the possibilities of Cuban involvement and what other information Al could provide. No one had ever considered the possibility of Cuban involvement. There was no indication that this was even a possibility. They were baffled by what Al said about "your own people." They decided when Al returned that the focus of the interrogation would be on specifically who the Cubans were and who "your own people" were. Agent Kelly insisted on taking over the interrogation, and John finally acquiesced because of Agent Kelly's detailed knowledge of Al's criminal background. Maybe this was just a ruse conjured up by Al, but the only way they were ever going to figure out if it was truth or fiction was to demand things from Al that they could substantiate. It was not beyond Al to conjure up some lies for his own amusement. Agent Kelly received a profile of Al in Washington indicating, among some of his many less desirable traits, that he was a pathological liar. The FBI profilers had classified him a sociopath. Al was born to two attorneys who specialized in personal injury litigation in Upstate New York. About the time he was ten, he started associating with some youths in his school that were chronic petty criminals from what could be best described as from the wrong side of the tracks. By the time Al was thirteen, he had a history of shoplifting arrests. When Al turned fifteen, he graduated to grand theft auto and did a year in a juvenile detention. His parents fought vigorously with each arrest, but with the grand theft auto, the local court system had had enough. When he was released from juvenile detention, it took less than a year before he was arrested for breaking and entering and the rape of a college coed at the nearby college. He was sent to prison for three years. After the last arrest, Al's parents washed their hands of him. When he was released from prison, he disappeared before he had completed his parole. He stayed under law enforcement radar until he was identified as a member of the militia. This data helped prompt a judge to issue a warrant along with an informant's inside information about the weapons.

CHAPTER 36

The door swung shut behind Al once he was in the bathroom. He stepped up to a toilet and urinated. He had waited far too long. A slight tingle ran down his back from the long-overdue relief. Now he was literally pissed and ready for bear. Al walked over to the sink and turned the faucet on as fast as it would go. Water sprayed everywhere, but Al could care less. He peered over his shoulder to make sure no one had come in while he was in the stall to check on him. He calmly reached under the sink and found a revolver that had been hidden away for a moment like this. With the faucet still running, Al cocked the revolver and proceeded to the door. He could hear the men discussing what he had told John during the interrogation. Al opened the door to see where everyone was. As he peered through the crack, he took a deep breath and then made his move.

Agent Kelly glanced up from his conversation with the others to see Al coming out of the bathroom with a revolver in his left hand and pointed at John, who was the first in Al's line of vision. Agent Kelly dropped the cup of coffee he was drinking as he reached for his standard-issue Colt revolver resting in its holster. By the time Agent Kelly had his hand on his revolver, it was too late; Al had taken aim at John and fired.

The force of the shot sent John tumbling forward. He just missed Agent Kelly as he fell against a wall on the opposite side of the room from where Al was standing. John felt a searing pain in his upper body as he adjusted himself on the floor, seeking refuge behind some bunk beds. "Jesus Christ, I'm hit!" shouted John. John looked down at his right shoulder and then with his left arm pulled his shoulder forward to look at his back. The bullet had hit him in his shoulder and exited just above his chest. John looked back toward Al from behind the bunk beds as he reached for his gun with his right hand.

Agent Kelly's shot had gone wide hitting the wall to Al's right. Al dove behind another set of bunk beds before Agent Kelly could fire a second shot.

Seth dove for the floor behind the picnic table as he reached for his gun, also a Colt revolver. He caught glimpses of the continuing gun battle as he found a safe position from which to return fire.

The next shot fired by Al passed through a small opening in the two-by-fours, which made the bunk beds and hit John in the middle of his forehead. As the bullet entered John's head, blood spurt in all directions as John slumped toward the floor. Agent Kelly fired a second shot, this time catching Al in his upper left arm. Al twisted sideways as he fell against the bunk beds. Agent Kelly took aim yet again, but before he could fire, Al had regained his balance. Al now had the gun in his right hand and fired a direct shot in the middle of Agent Kelly's chest. Agent Kelly had taken his bulletproof vest off once the ATF and FBI had everything under control early that morning. Seth could hear the air collapse from his lungs. Agent Kelly fell toppling over some nearby bunk beds and finally came to rest on top of the beds. Al turned to take aim at Seth, but it was too late. Seth had already risen from behind the picnic table and taken aim. Seth shot once directly into Al's chest. Seth heard the familiar sound of air rushing out. He fired again, this time hitting Al's right arm, the one holding the gun. The adrenalin was pulsing feverishly in Seth. The gun Seth was holding seemed to fire by itself; a third shot hit Al once again in the chest, ripping a second massive hole in him. Seth fired one final shot again, striking Al in the chest. This time there was no air left. Al fell back against the bathroom door nearly causing the crudely built door to crack down the middle, and he fell forward, coming to rest on the floor. Blood consumed the floor, walls, and ceiling. Seth felt sick and dropped to the floor. He was shaking from the adrenalin. Seth used a nearby chair to help lift and prop himself up. The room abruptly filled with FBI and ATF agents, their guns drawn. What seemed like a lifetime to Seth had taken place in only seconds.

Rachel pushed past several FBI and ATF agents and ran toward the only familiar face in the room standing, Seth's. "Are you all right?"

Seth took a moment and assessed his situation. "I think so." He was still shaking. Rachel helped lead Seth outside where they were both greeted by what Seth and Rachel assumed to be the second in command.

The man introduced himself as Agent Jack Cooper. "Sir, could you please tell me what happened?"

Seth surmised by the way Jack asked his questions he was not a suspect and the fact he was wearing his Surf City Police Department jacket. Seth explained what had happened in as much detail as he could remember. He was still shaking from what had happened. It all seemed surreal. The melee of the situation left him still a little confused by the chain of events. The sequence of events that transpired was not as detailed as he would have liked, but he felt that most of his account was accurate. Seth left out what he had heard about the Cubans and your own people since he was not sure how much of it was true. He couldn't remember if John had even made notes during his interrogation of Al because he was so shaken. Seth felt that if John did make notes, the FBI would certainly review them and draw their own conclusions. Seth also assumed that if it was true, he was not sure who could be trusted. What weighed heavily on Seth's mind was Al's comment on "your own people selling you out"; who specifically was Al referring to? Was it the CIA, the FBI, the military, or all of them? And why the Cubans?

CHAPTER 37

At eight in the evening, everyone finally began packing. An ambulance was leaving with Agent Kelly, John, and Al. Seth looked around and could see everyone was physically and emotionally drained from the course of the day. A somber mood lingered over the FBI and ATF as they prepared to leave. Earlier they were excited about capturing the vast number of militia without incident, which now seemed a fleeting memory. Seth felt the fatigue from the long drive and the reality of his near-death experience after being caught in a hail of bullets. The militia was to be detained in the Cherokee Police Department jail until the FBI and ATF could figure out what to do with them. There were still several members of the militia that had yet to be processed. Sheriff's deputies and the state police had been brought in to guard the militia's compound until the forensic team would return in the daylight hours to continue their work.

Seth looked over at Rachel. "What do ya say we get a couple of rooms for the night along with a bite to eat?"

Rachel smiled as best she could. "Sounds good to me. How 'bout I drive?"

Seth looked into Rachel's tired face. "It's all yours." He reached into his pocket and pulled out the keys to the marine corps sedan. He tossed Rachel the keys.

It wasn't a long drive before Rachel pulled up to a motel in Cherokee. As Rachel put the car into park, she realized that they had not spoken a word since they left the militia's compound. She had been thinking about how crazy the past few days had been. She looked at Seth. "I'll get us a couple of rooms for the night."

"Okay, how 'bout one overlooking the lake?" Rachel laughed at his response since there was no lake. The small town was inundated with casinos, tourist traps, motels, and diners. A small river flowed through the community surrounded by mountains.

"How 'bout a view of the pool and mountains?" Rachel called back as she made her way to the motel office. The town had some beautiful views of the Smoky Mountains that Seth noticed when they arrived earlier in the day, and the motel had a small pool that was closed for the fall and winter.

After a few minutes, Rachel returned with two keys. "You're in room 6, and I'm in room 7."

Rachel headed for her room. She was tired. The past few days were taking a heavy toll on her. "How about we skip that bite to eat? Instead I think I'm going to take a hot bath. I'll see you in the morning."

"Okay with me. How about I meet you in the diner about seven tomorrow morning?" There was a diner adjacent to the motel Rachel had chosen.

"Let's make it eight."

"Okay, eight it is."

CHAPTER 38

It was a little before four-thirty in the morning when Juan Mendoza and his men woke. They quickly dressed and headed out to the boat. Gerardo Zapata was already on board readying the boat for the long day on the Intracoastal Waterway. The men had had a restless night of slumber thinking about Antonio Mendoza's body in a shallow grave in North Carolina, the mission to free Cuba, and getting back home to family and familiar surroundings. It was going to be their last day cruising down the Intracoastal Waterway with the other northern boaters making their annual pilgrimage to South Florida for the winter. As each man climbed aboard, they found a place that they could make themselves comfortable for the predawn start. A few of the men made themselves comfortable with some blankets as they tried to sleep a little before sunrise. Tony Ermandez, the self-appointed captain, made his way to the helm. Once all the men boarded the boat, Juan made one last pass through the house that they used for the night's stay to make sure they did not leave anything that may connect them to the house. The men had been informed before they left Miami to remember everything they touched and to wipe down every house they stayed in for fingerprints. Once Juan felt comfortable that everything was as they had found it, he headed down to the dock. He untied the bowline and leapt aboard. Gerardo had already untied the stern line. Gerardo and Juan pushed the boat away from the dock while Tony steered the boat into the St. Mary's River toward the Intracoastal Waterway.

Juan looked through the still-dark morning noticing the red and green channel markers that helped guide the boat through the river. Juan could tell where the shoreline began from the distant lights illuminating the homes alongside the river. He also noticed many of the docks with their own unique lighting to help guide the homeowner on a dark night.

It was not long before the boat made its way to the Intracoastal Waterway. They noticed that several other boaters were also getting an early start, presumably to make South Florida the final stop before the day's end. The sun was beginning to rise as the boat entered the waters near Savannah. Juan noticed the air had a crisp coolness to it in late September. Once the men reached south Florida, the fall air would evaporate into a memory. It would be warm and sunny. Foliage would turn from autumn leaves to palm trees and orange groves.

Tony, Juan, and a few of the others began chatting with the men that had been sleeping inside the cabin. The men were beginning to feel a little happier since they would be in their own beds at the end of the day. Their part of the mission would soon come to an end. The men knew that another group in Miami would soon take the arms they had stolen to liberate Cuba. This mission had cost so much more than any other mission. It hurt each of them to look at what they had on board knowing the pain it caused. They were glad to soon distance themselves from what caused their pain. They did not even know who comprised the team in Miami; they just wanted to separate themselves from the symbol of their pain and return home to familiar surroundings. Juan knew a limited amount about the future plans of the weapons but not enough that if he were caught during the break-in, it would jeopardize the entire mission.

Juan could tell that each man was thinking of Antonio Mendoza, their friend and fallen comrade. Resentment toward Juan lingered though it was beginning to subside now at the denouement of their long, arduous mission. Juan wondered how his family and organization members would react to the news about what happened to Antonio. He wondered if he would be recognized as a brave leader making sacrifices for the good of all or if he would be seem as a cold, insensitive bastard hated for what he had done. They had not made any telephone calls to anyone in Miami. There was a fear that if anyone's telephone was tapped, news would spread, and the ultimate mission would be a bust. Everything was done to prevent any link between what had happened at Camp LeJeune and their friends in Miami. No one was to be trusted unless it was absolutely necessary.

* * *

Periodically, Tony made stops along the way to refuel and get some food and drinks. He knew the men were anxious to return home, but Tony felt the periodic stops helped relieve some of the tension. Whenever they stopped, two people stayed with the boat to deter anyone from accidentally finding out what they had on board the boat. Most of the people greeted them with open arms, glad that they were making the pilgrimage to South Florida and glad that they were spending their money along the way. Cash was always used to prevent tracing any credit card charges and minimize the chances of being caught.

It was almost lunchtime when the boat reached the Jacksonville, Florida, waters. The volume of boat traffic had picked up considerably. Tony could tell that they would make it to South Florida a lot later than he hoped. When they crossed the St. Johns River, they were almost struck by some novice boaters on wave runners. Children and young adults sped around on Jet Skis. Tony, being the professional fisherman, assumed the marine patrol was already working overtime to help control the swollen boat traffic, and yet it was only late September. He could only imagine what the boat traffic was going to be like in a couple of months during the peak tourist season. Tony began to plan for what the boat traffic in the Miami area was going to be like when they returned. He and the others had been gone a little over two weeks. Much of their time away was planning and waiting for everything to fall into place. In two weeks' time, it seemed like the entire northern boating armada made their pilgrimage to the warm waters of Florida. South Florida, Tony envisioned, during the day would be worse than the Jacksonville area. Arriving late would be a small favor with the boat traffic.

It was almost one o'clock in the morning when Tony and the others entered Biscayne Bay. Tony could see the downtown Miami skyline off to his right, and to his left was Miami Beach, made famous by Jackie Gleason and the Honeymooners. Like the waters around Jacksonville, Biscayne Bay was inundated with boat traffic, only worse. Tony could only guess that the new arrivals, the northern snowbirds, were kicking up their heels late night to let everyone know they had arrived. Eagerness began to permeate throughout the boat. The men would soon be home with their families or their girlfriends. The long trip filled with tragedy and success was finally coming to a close. The return trip had been mostly quiet aside from the outside distractions. There was a great deal of reflection on the price they had to pay for their long-term goal. Antonio Mendoza, a family member and friend, was dead. The men had to bury Antonio in a shallow grave in the middle of nowhere, no tombstone, only a few prayers.

CHAPTER 39

Miami-Dade police officer Marshall Jamison and five other officers were patrolling the waters in a twenty-four-foot scarab. The Miami-Dade police officers were in and around Biscayne Bay looking for potential drug smugglers and drunken boaters when Marshall caught sight of Juan and his men. Marshall commented to one of the other officers navigating the boat, "Does that boat look a little low in the water to you?" One of the notable signs of possible drug smugglers was a boat riding low in the water due to it being laden with marijuana or cocaine.

The other officer took his binoculars and directed them to where Marshall was pointing. "Now that you mention it, it does."

"Let's go take a look, shall we?" commented Marshall.

The other officer increased the boat's speed and headed in the direction of Juan and his men. Marshall thought about turning on the patrol boat's siren and flashing lights but thought better of it, using the element of surprise in the congested waters. As the boat neared Juan and his men, they heard a loud explosion coming from the area they just left. Marshall and the other officers turned in the direction of the explosion in time to catch a fireball explode into the night's sky.

"Turn around!" shouted Marshall over the series of explosions that followed.

The officer turned the boat in the direction of the fire now painting the water in front of the scarab while pieces of flaming wreckage from two boats fell onto the dark night waters of Biscayne Bay. Marshall looked back in the direction where he last saw Juan and his men in hopes of getting the boat number off the bow. The plethora of boats obstructed his view, allowing the boat in question to subtly blend into the night and disappear from Marshall's sight. "Damn it," commented Marshall under his breath. Marshall hated drugs and those that peddled them. He had grown up in Miami and remembered the days when cocaine became a toy for any and everyone with a few extra bucks in their pockets. Drug cartels fought for territory, and bodies began to pile up in Biscayne Bay, in the streets of Miami, and washing up on the Miami beaches. When he was a senior in high school, Marshall lost his older brother to a heroin overdose during the Christmas holidays. He also saw several of his friends get mixed up in drugs in one way or another. Before Marshall graduated from high school, he contacted the Miami-Dade Police Department about becoming a police officer. Upon his graduation from high school, Marshall joined the Miami-Dade Police Department. He graduated second in his class and requested to be assigned to the drug task force.

Marshall and the other police officers gradually approached the sight of the fire. Shouts called out from various directions from the survivors now frantically treading water in the darkened waters of Biscayne Bay. A few other boaters cautiously joined in the search for survivors. Marshall could see boat debris throughout the water. Marshall called to one of the police officers, "John, get Marine Emergency Rescue out here now. Make sure we get some ambulances to evac these people out of here. Have dispatch call Jackson Memorial Hospital and let them know what happened and that we have survivors headed their way." Marshall could hear the officer on the radio with the dispatcher. Moments later, Marshall could hear sirens howling into the night from other police boats and the Coast Guard boats screaming toward them. On the horizon he could see sirens flashing from the direction of Downtown Miami moving as close to shore where Marshall and the others were now rescuing the displaced boaters.

The first person rescued was a woman. She was wearing what appeared to be a chic dress at one time, now torn, and her appearance was disheveled as the result of her being a victim of the boating collision. Her shoes were missing, no doubt due to the impact of the two boats colliding or discarded once she found herself swimming in the bay. The next person rescued was a man dressed smartly for a casual cruise along the bay, but now also appeared disheveled with his clothes wet and torn. The last person rescued was a man dressed in a suit with tears in his clothes. He was visibly intoxicated and seemed bewildered.

The first man rescued continued to call out into the night for his wife. His eyes were red and filled with tears as it became apparent that his continued efforts were going to be unanswered. There would be no response to his unrelenting calls. An officer on board tried to put a blanket over the disconsolate man to comfort him. He rejected the blanket as he continued to call. His view was obscured by his tears and his eyes swollen and red from wiping them. The blackened water only added desperation to his efforts.

Marshall heard people joining in the rescue and calling out to some of the other survivors. Officials had recovered bodies but no survivors. Marshall talked with the woman they rescued, in trying to ascertain the number of people involved and what had happened. After some discussion, she explained the tragic circumstance. She and her boyfriend had gone to a dinner party at a house along Biscayne Bay with two other couples. One was the man calling out for his wife, and the other couple was the owner of the boat, the disoriented man rescued. The party was heading back to her boyfriend's condominium overlooking Biscayne Bay. On their way back, the owner of the boat was kissing his girlfriend when they hit the other boat. The woman indicated that she saw the other boat a split second before the two boats collided. Marshall asked if she felt the owner of the boat she was riding on was going too fast, and her response was yes.

It was just after dawn before Marshall and the others left the site of the accident. As Marshall rode along in the scarab, his mind wandered back to the boat they were headed toward when the accident occurred. *Were there drugs on that boat?* he thought. "Damn it!" He could only wonder because any thought of finding drugs was just a wild wish.

CHAPTER 40

Tony guided the boat toward its final destination as far as the team was concerned. The final destination was just a little trip up the Miami River. Tony never noticed the police scarab that had been following them. Juan and his men heard the explosion. They saw the ball of fire leap into the sky. Tony's instinct as the captain of the boat was to turn and assist in the rescue. He had participated in many rescues in the Caribbean and in the gulf as a fisherman but knew he had to stay the course this evening. It went against everything he knew as a ship's captain, but many things that had happened in the past two weeks went against his character.

Tony docked the boat at the home of Julio Chavez. It was almost one thirty in the morning. Tony had been to the house many times before but never on as important an occasion as this. Julio heard the diesel engines of the boat docking next to his house and went out to greet Juan and the men in his company. Two men followed closely behind Julio as he headed to the dock. Juan recognized the men as Julio's bodyguards. The dock and the area next to the dock had sufficient light for security purposes, so everyone could identify one another. Julio called to one of the bodyguards to turn out the lights. Reluctantly the bodyguard turned off the lights for security purposes. There was enough light cast off from the house and nearby docks to allow the men to see. Julio greeted each man as they stepped from the boat to the dock with a hug and kiss on each cheek. He escorted Juan and the men into the house. Julio wrapped his left arm around the shoulders of Juan as they followed the men into Julio's house. Julio was as giddy as a child on Christmas morning.

Julio was ready to celebrate the success of Juan and his men's mission. "Let us toast to your success!" shouted Julio. He walked behind the mahogany bar that added to the masculine decor of the entertainment room. Heads of varying animals decorated the walls along with a collection of old guns and several paintings of the countryside in Cuba. Julio drew out four bottles of Dom

Pérignon and began uncorking them. He placed a Waterford Crystal bowl filled with fresh strawberries on the bar. Juan and his men approached the bar, but fatigue was written across their faces. Julio could see the men wanted to go home. It was almost two thirty in the morning. He poured a glass of champagne for each of them. "Drink this now and tonight after you have rested, you'll return, and we shall celebrate your success in grand style," added Julio. The men picked up their glasses and held them high; then in unison they drained their glasses. They ignored the strawberries that would only enhance the flavor of the Dom Pérignon. Julio made arrangements through one of the bodyguards and some of the household help that lived with Julio to take the men home. Within minutes, Julio's home was vacant of the new guests.

CHAPTER 41

Rachel woke up about six in the morning despite getting to bed at such a late hour. Since she had been in the navy, she had not been able to sleep late like she once had in her college days. She plugged her computer into a telephone outlet she found in the sparse motel room. She planned to check on her e-mail messages that she might have missed during the past couple of days. She also wanted to see what she could find in the Naval Intelligence files on Al Stewart and the North Carolina militia. Rachel also thought of Al's comments about the possibility of Cuban involvement, so she also wanted to try and follow up on that angle. She entered her password into the computer to access her account. Most of the e-mail messages were from coworkers and a few friends but nothing urgent. She tried to access the Naval Intelligence files to investigate Al Stewart and the North Carolina militia. As she entered her password into the Naval Intelligence files, she received this message: "Access denied." She repeated the process over and over. After her repeated attempts, Rachel decided to shut down her computer and reboot to see if maybe there was some kind of glitch when she logged on. After logging in again, she tried to access the Naval Intelligence files but was once again denied access. This was not the first time her access to the Naval Intelligence files had been denied. In previous times, it had been due to some overzealous clerk who erroneously had her deleted, or often it was a computer glitch. *So much for military efficiency!* she thought. Rachel decided to try again later. It was now almost 7:00 a.m., so she decided to call Mary, her sister-in-law, to find out about the funeral arrangements for her brother Hugh.

"Hello." Mary was asleep when the phone rang. The phone had startled her from her sleep. Since Hugh's death, Mary had gotten little sleep, but when she could finally fall asleep, she slept hard.

"Mary, it's me, Rachel." Rachel could tell she had awoken Mary. Her voice was gruff from being awoken from sleep.

"Hey, Rachel, what is it?"

"I'm calling to find out about the funeral."

"It's tomorrow at eight a.m. You're going to be here, aren't you?"

"Yeah, of course I'll be there. Is there anything I can do for you?" asked Rachel. "Did my mother make it there?" inquired Rachel.

"Yes . . . your mother made it. And *no*, there is nothing I need for you to do. Your mother arrived yesterday to help with the funeral arrangements. She's been great. What's happening on your end? Did you find the bastards that killed Hugh?"

"I don't think so," replied Rachel. "We caught up with the militia here in Cherokee. We had a lead that they may be behind Hugh's death." The break-in was not what concerned Rachel, and she knew it was not what Mary would be interested in. They both wanted to know who killed Hugh, and so she ignored the break-in part of the conversation. "I don't think the militia had anything to do with Hugh's death."

"Shit!" responded Mary. "I was hoping to have some closure on this. How's Seth?" asked Mary. "Sarah, Officer Ned's wife, asked me that if I heard from the two of you to have him call in. Seth hasn't called his office, and they need a little direction, I'm guessin'."

Rachel could hear the subtle humor in Mary's voice. She was glad to hear Mary starting to get her life back on track after Hugh's death. "Yesterday was a long day," answered Rachel. "We didn't get to our motel until after one this mornin'. I'm supposed to meet Seth for breakfast at eight. I'll have him call the station. Look, I've gotta finish getting ready so I can meet him. I'll see you tonight."

"Bye."

Rachel hung up and rushed to finish getting ready so she could meet Seth at eight.

CHAPTER 42

Seth woke up a little before seven in the morning since his biological clock would not allow him to sleep late. He remembered he had forgotten to call the Surf City police station to check in with his staff. *Shit*, he thought. *I need to find out where we are with posthurricane Isabelle and just day-to-day activity.* He rolled over to the phone next to his bed and called.

He greeted Sarah, who was still answering the phone, before he asked for Ned. Seth assumed that she was still needed because the staff was still running short with the additional duties his deputies were taking on as a result of Isabelle and now his absence. Seth waited for Ned to get on the line. After a minute, he heard, "How's it going, Chief?" Seth gave Ned a brief synopsis of what had transpired in Cherokee. He left out most of the details and just hit the highlights. Seth was fearful of too much information leaking to the general public. If there was going to be any kind of leak about what occurred in Cherokee, he would rather it come from the FBI or ATF, and not some small-town cop. Seth knew that Ned would undoubtedly tell Sarah, his wife and town gossip, and the entire story would be all over town within hours. Seth did not want the fallout from the brass at Camp LeJeune coming down on him either. Seth did mention arriving late with the militia already in custody. He mentioned watching the interrogation by John and other FBI agents. He told Ned that they found a number of firearms and grenades, but gave no specifics. He also mentioned the FBI hackers and the elaborate computer Internet system devised by the militia. Seth made a point of intentionally leaving out the shoot-out leading to the deaths of Al Stewart, Agent Mike Kelly, and Major John Lawrence. It would only add fuel to a fire that no one needed to light. Ned filled Seth in on the funeral arrangements for Hugh. Seth assumed Sarah had given Ned the information since she was helping Mary out along with her own temporary assignments at the police station. Ned updated Seth on the island developments posthurricane Isabelle.

—

After a while, he told Ned he would be back for the funeral by nightfall and hung up. Seth had never been one to chat on the telephone, especially when he knew he would see the person later that day. He raced into the shower so he could meet Rachel by 8:00 a.m.

CHAPTER 43

Seth was the first to arrive at the sparse diner. Rachel came in and found Seth sipping a cup of coffee and reading the local newspaper. There was nothing in the newspaper regarding the raid on the militia's compound. Seth surmised that the newspaper had already gone to press before the raid, the editor had gone home to bed early, or the FBI made sure nothing was in the newspaper.

"Have you ordered?" asked Rachel. Rachel seated herself across from Seth in the small booth. She picked up the menu clipped next to a supply of napkins and condiments. Rachel scanned the menu. Breakfast consisted of eggs, scrambled or over easy; bacon, sausage, or country ham; grits; and biscuits.

"No, I waited for you." Seth folded the newspaper and put it on the table.

"Did you call your station house?" asked Rachel.

Seth looked incredulously at Rachel.

Rachel said, "I called Mary this morning. She said Sarah had asked if she had heard from us. Shame on you, as the chief of police you need to keep an eye on your town."

Seth noted a little sarcasm in her voice. He also noticed a little smile creep out of the weary woman sitting in front of him. Seth smiled back. "I'll have you know I called the station this morning."

Rachel looked kindly at Seth. "You're such a good boy."

Seth became a little embarrassed. "Shut up and order."

Rachel recapped her conversation with Mary. They decided to leave after breakfast for Surf City. They knew it would take them most of the day to make the drive back to Surf City.

After they ate, Seth paid the check. Rachel had insisted until Seth promised to charge it back to the Surf City Police Department. They both returned to their rooms and completed packing the few articles of clothing and toiletries they brought with them.

—

Seth was loading his bag into the car when Rachel came out. "Throw your bag in the back, and I'll settle our room bill," called Seth.

"I can't let you do that. Let me at least pay my share." Rachel reached into her purse and pulled out enough for the room and her telephone call to Mary. "I mean, I did invite myself along."

Seth nodded his agreement. "All right all ready." Seth took the money and headed out to pay the clerk. Seth returned with the receipt and handed Rachel her change.

"You know we're going to need to return this car to the Camp LeJeune motor pool when we get back," commented Rachel. "The military hates when civilians run off with their stuff, especially these handsome sedans."

"Yeah, it's not the color I would have chosen," replied Seth. They both laughed and started out for Surf City.

Rachel and Seth shared the long drive back to Surf City. There were periods of long lulls followed by general conversation that often ended in a disinterested silence by one or the other. The long day followed by the long drive home with no accomplishment had taken its toll on the two of them. They felt defeated. "Do you know if John was married?" asked Rachel.

"I don't know. He never said anything to me," replied Seth. "I don't even remember if he had on a wedding ring. But then again that is not something one guy tends to notice about another guy."

Rachel smiled at the guy-to-guy comment made by Seth. She thought to herself how surprised she was that she never noticed if John wore a wedding ring or not.

They thought about the time they spent with Major John Lawrence and realized they knew nothing about the man. Seth knew John served in Desert Storm. He knew that John was sent down from Washington DC to do some investigative work regarding the security at Camp LeJeune, but that was all he really knew. All their interaction had been about the break-in and who killed Hugh.

"It's pretty sad that we spent as much time as we did with John, but we really knew nothing about him," offered Rachel.

"We weren't friends," replied Seth. "We were basically cops that came together one way or another to solve a case." Seth heard his comment that "they were not friends but cops" and wished he could take it back. It was callous. He had spent some time with John, and he respected the man. He would have liked to have been friends with John, but he also didn't want to feel the sadness he felt when his wife died. The thought that they were not friends seemed to somehow make his death a little easier to swallow.

Rachel and Seth rode along for some time mulling over the past forty-eight to seventy-two hours. Neither person spoke. They were tired and deflated. They just sat quietly thinking.

Rachel disturbed the silence. "Do you believe there could be any truth to what Al Stewart said about Cuban involvement?" Rachel asked cautiously.

"I've been thinking long and hard about that one," answered Seth. "But why Cubans way up in North Carolina? There are several military installations between here and Miami," continued Seth.

"Didn't John say there had been numerous break-ins at military installations throughout the southeast?" replied Rachel.

"Come to think of it, I believe you're right. I've been mulling over the whys." John sat driving the military sedan staring out at the road and letting the previous days of conversations with John run through his mind over and over. He was looking for any clues John may have slipped out that he somehow overlooked.

Rachel let the conversation die. She could tell that Seth was deep in thought and decided to let him use the time, hoping that he may be able to come up with something that they could use to find out who killed her brother.

CHAPTER 44

It was well after dinnertime when Seth pulled the military sedan into the driveway of his home at the beach. They had taken their time returning. They had reflected on the past couple of days until they were physically and emotionally exhausted. It was dark, cold, and late. The air was heavy with salt from the ocean mist hanging in the late evening. A fog had begun to roll into the quiet community that was still reeling from the wounds of hurricane Isabelle.

"Thanks for letting me come along. Well, maybe I should say thanks for putting up with me since I invited myself," commented Rachel as she exited the sedan. She leaned across the seat to give Seth a kiss on the cheek.

Seth was startled by the sudden show of emotion. "Good night, I guess I'll see you tomorrow." Seth was taken aback by Rachel's slight sign of affection. She had been all business until now.

Rachel got out of the car and raced up the steps into Mary's house. Rachel's mother started crying as soon as she saw Rachel come through the door. Seth lumbered out of the sedan. He climbed the steps to his house and opened the front door. He was greeted warmly by Argo. He picked up the small creature and held her to his face while she licked his face. As Seth held Argo in one arm, he noticed a note on the counter from Ned. The note included information letting Seth know the last time he had taken Argo out for her chores and that the funeral for Hugh was the next day. He also asked Seth to call him to let him know that he was back so he wouldn't have to come over later that night to take Argo out for another walk.

Seth put Argo down and called Ned. He thanked him for taking care of Argo. Ned updated Seth on the day's activities. Seth could hear Sarah in the background reminding Ned of things he left out. After what seemed like a long conversation about nothing, the two men concluded their conversation. Seth took a beer out of the refrigerator and went into the bedroom to unpack his small bag. He spent the rest of the night wrestling around with Argo and depleting the refrigerator of its beer supply and some stale munchies.

CHAPTER 45

It was shortly after seven in the evening when Juan and his men returned to Julio's house to celebrate their success in North Carolina. They were there for a celebration of success, but in their hearts, they were lamenting Antonio's tragic death left behind in a shallow grave in North Carolina. Juan's men returned not so much as to celebrate their success, but to immortalize Antonio as a fallen hero. Julio Chavez was the vice president of the Cubans for a Free Cuba organization. The president was Carlos Hernandez. Julio had liked Juan Mendoza from the beginning. He saw Juan as a new generation of movers and shakers eager to return to a free and democratic Cuba. Much of the new generation felt strongly about their Cuban roots but felt they had started a new life in the United States and did not seem as passionate to return to an impoverished Cuba. They also were not enthusiastic about rebuilding the beleaguered country after so many decades of rule under Fidel Castro. Additionally, the organization did not have the financial resources to pay large salaries to the new graduates coming out of college, and so much of the new generation sought jobs that would pay them compensation to support a more extravagant lifestyle. Miguel, Juan's father, had the financial resources to help support Juan in his liberation efforts.

Juan and his men had left Miami two weeks ago. They had traveled to North Carolina. They had broken into a military installation and stolen arms they felt could be used in urban and guerilla warfare. The kind of warfare they realized would be fought in Cuba in these more modern times. Their friend Antonio Mendoza was now viewed as a martyr for the liberation of Cuba. Juan and his crew, having guided the boatload of stolen arms through the Intracoastal Waterway the past few days, were being hailed as heroes by Julio for their efforts.

Carlos Hernandez felt his organization was strong. When he took control, it was comprised of about five hundred members in the mid-1960s. Now the organization was comprised of over seventy thousand dues-paying members throughout the United States and several foreign countries. The growth was due in large part to the younger generation taking advantage of the Internet and other modern methods of communication. Gone were the days of mass mailings, which were slow and cost prohibitive. Though the organization had grown impressively since the 1960s, there was internal discontent rising among a small, but growing, fragment of the organization. The small fragment was Julio Chavez and his young sympathizers. Julio fostered the discontent within the organization. It was his belief, along with his followers, that they wanted more immediate and assertive action. Julio and his following had grown tired of the diplomatic measures instituted by Washington that had gone on for decades without any substantive results. They felt more extreme measures were necessary.

Julio's ascent within the leadership of the Cubans for a Free Cuba was not by accident. He made his way to the vice presidency by making claims that the Miami Cubans had grown weak by not pushing Washington DC to remove Castro. He argued long and hard that the administration of the Cubans for a Free Cuba had not tried hard enough to pressure their representatives in Washington to take action against Fidel Castro. His voice steadily attracted a number of followers, young and old. As Julio's voice was heard, the membership grew rapidly, and with the membership came money and lots of it. It was those followers that helped make him the vice president. Carlos and his more conservative followers felt that by making Julio vice president, it would help avoid splintering the organization and weakening what had taken decades to build. Julio originally made his money in banking. He established a strong bank that many believe was the result of laundering money for the drug cartels during the seventies. The comptroller for the Federal Reserve Bank had requested an investigation that was mysteriously squashed by several members of Congress.

CHAPTER 46

As Juan's men and other loyalists to Julio arrived to celebrate the triumphant return, Julio came up to Juan. Julio embraced Juan, and as he leaned toward Juan's ear, he said in a quiet whisper, "Come with me." Julio led Juan to an office in the back of the house that had a view of the Miami River. Juan had been in the office numerous times before. The room was ornately decorated for a man. It had mahogany trim and shelving. The countertops were dark green granite. The furniture was brown leather, and Persian carpets covered a dark tiled floor. There was an abundance of old black-and-white framed pictures that adorned the walls of Cuban countrysides, of Julio's family, and signed pictures of Ernest Hemmingway. Juan assumed the signed pictures of Ernest Hemmingway were originals from Ernest Hemmingway's years living in Cuba. There were several old books on the mahogany shelves written by Cuban authors, some that Juan did not recognize. He recognized the names of the books written by Ernest Hemmingway. On one side of the room was a small bar that had several crystal decanters of cognac. There was also a wooden humidor that Juan new housed Cohibas.

Once inside the room, Julio closed the door so the two men could be alone. Julio embraced Juan and kissed him on each cheek. "How did it go?" asked Julio. As Julio asked his question, he made his way to the bar and poured two brandy snifters with cognac for the two of them. Julio continued, "I know about Antonio. That was tragic, I know. I would like to hear from you how it happened." Julio returned to where Juan was standing and handed him the snifter of cognac.

Juan took the glass from Julio. The two men tapped their glasses. Juan gave the cognac a deep sniff and then took a large gulp. He knew he was doing it to muster his courage as well as hold back his emotions.

"Easy," commented Julio. Julio then directed Juan to sit on the leather sofa. Juan sat at one end and Julio the other.

Juan paused once he was seated to regain his composure. He took another gulp of the cognac, almost finishing it, and then began telling Julio what happened at Camp LeJeune. Tears filled his eyes as he told Julio the details of what had happened. Juan wanted a moment like this right after it happened. He knew back then as the leader of men he had to be strong. He knew the men hated him for the decisions he was forced to make under the extreme circumstance, but he also felt a certain amount of respect from those same men. He had wanted a friend and confidant like Julio to unburden his heavy heart of what had happened and how he felt about it. That time had finally come. It was decided that before Juan and the others left, there would be no contact under any circumstance. It was feared that because of Julio's more extreme views, federal organizations and even their own organization may be watching them. Julio made a point of keeping the mission on a need-to-know basis. Only a handful of people knew about the mission, and most of them were with Juan in North Carolina.

Juan started, "Everything went as planned, but while we were loading the weapons into the truck, an MP showed up. Antonio pulled his gun out and fired a round in the general direction of the MP. The MP returned fire and shot him in the stomach. He died during the night at our first stop. How he hung on as long as he did was sheer will on his part. I've seen people die in less than an hour with the same kind of wound. We buried him behind the house after we removed anything that may disclose who he was, including mutilating his fingerprints."

Julio listened intently as Juan spoke. He never interrupted. Julio knew most of the details, but he wanted to hear it from his friend Juan. Julio hoped that as Juan spoke, his own obvious grief did not show on his face. Julio appreciated Juan's attention to detail in regard to the mission. Most of all, he respected Juan's strength. He knew Antonio's father had sent him to live with Juan's family in Miami. He knew Antonio's father, Tito, had remained in Cuba to help liberate Cuba from Cuba's own shores.

Julio listened to Juan as tears filled in his eyes. He knew Antonio and Juan were cousins. He knew they had been inseparable since Antonio came to live with Juan and his family in the United States. "I want you to know that I sent a message to Tito informing him what happened to his son. I let him know how much he had contributed to the cause and how much he will be missed. Is there anything else I need to know?" inquired Julio.

"Yes . . . I think your inside man stabbed an MP in the back. I think he may have killed him. I'm not positive he was your inside man, but he seemed to act like it when we confronted him."

"Fuck!" Julio stood and wiped the tears from his eyes. He paced the floor. What was once sadness now turned to anger. "No one was to be hurt—no one." Julio looked back at Juan.

Juan could sense Julio's anger. "It couldn't be helped. Antonio's gun was an accident, and everything seemed to spiral downward from there. I shot your man in the shoulder to make it look as though he got caught up in the middle but was lucky enough to survive. I was hoping that it may take some of the heat off him while we try to figure out what to do with him."

Julio paused as he listened intently to Juan's comment. "That was good thinking about shooting our inside man," responded Julio. "By the way, that man's name was Private Shays." Julio looked around the room trying to figure out what he was going to say next. Juan could tell that Julio was finally getting the full story, and it was obvious it was not the one he was hoping to hear. "Has anyone heard from Mr. Shays? Do we know if he is sticking to the plan?" Julio was talking out loud trying to figure out if months of planning were going to fall apart due to a loose cannon, Private Shays.

Juan could see Julio was distraught that things had not gone as smoothly as they all had hoped. He was wrestling with losing his cousin, but the reality was that they were playing a high-stacks game, and their luck had run dry. Private Shays had upped the ante for all of them.

The plan was for Private Larry Shays to stay at Camp LeJeune until his military discharge, which was due within the next few months. For his services, Private Shays was to receive $10,000 upon his discharge from the marine corps to be paid in Miami. Julio instead paid him $5,000 up front, and he was to receive the balance of $5,000 when he arrived in Miami. He was the only person to receive any compensation and the only non-Cuban American participating in the operation. A man Julio only referred to as the Insider recruited Larry for the assignment. The Insider felt that they needed someone inside the military police at Camp LeJeune. Larry was selected because the Insider felt he could easily be bought since he lacked any ethical responsibility. Larry was brought in to help keep the MPs at bay and to prevent any potential fatalities. It was thought that having a non-Cuban American may help to avoid any common links to the organization. The fact that Larry and the other MP showed up at the ammunitions depot while Juan and his men were still there was contrary to what Larry was paid to do.

Juan waited to see if Julio was going to answer his own question. He could see Julio's disgust at the thought of Private Shays showing up at the ammunitions depot. Juan started to answer, but Julio cut him off. "Of course, you have no idea what Shays is doing. You just got back. Hell . . . you didn't know who it was until I just told you. Thank God your instincts told you he was in on the break-in in a split second." Juan was relieved that Julio answered his own question. The two men sat in silence before Julio continued, "Do you want a refill?"

Juan was surprised by the disjunctive question. "S'cuse me?" responded Juan.

"Your drink, would you like me to refill it?" asked a recomposed Julio.

—

Juan was still a little bewildered at how the conversation was going as he replied, "No, I'm okay . . . thanks." Juan was amazed to see Julio go from anger and rage to calm and composed in almost the blink of an eye. He could see why people followed him. He was a leader of men.

"Okay then, let's join the others, shall we?" asked Julio. Julio stood and graciously motioned for Juan to lead the way back to the festivities. "I think we can take this conversation up later." Juan stood and Julio placed his arm around Juan's shoulders as they left the office to join the others. As they joined the others in the living room, Julio released his grip on Juan. "Tonight, after the celebration, we'll unload the weapons and warehouse them with the others. We can't have that boat sitting out there next to my dock deep in the water . . . Someone may think we have a boatload of drugs." The two men casually laughed as they separated to greet the guests. Julio looked at Juan with a congratulatory smile once more and said, "It is time to celebrate your triumph."

CHAPTER 47

While Juan filled Julio in on the details of the trip to Camp LeJeune, the house had filled with some one hundred guests. All the guests were there cheering the return of Juan and his men. Few knew the true circumstance of the celebration, but a party at Julio's house was not to be missed by those who knew him. The housekeeping staff ushered trays of food and drinks for the guests. A bartender was on hand to mix drinks for the celebratory guests.

Most of the guests had left when Juan looked at his watch; it was just after three in the morning. Juan was still exhausted from the trip to Camp LeJeune and back. He was thinking about going home when Julio led him into the kitchen. Juan looked around the room, and the only remaining guests sitting in the kitchen were those that Julio considered to be his most staunch supporters. Julio opened the refrigerator and took some pork and ham, cheese, and bread on the counter. There was a sandwich press sitting on the counter for making a Cuban sandwich. He also asked those remaining if they would like something to drink. Julio had Marguerite, his live-in housekeeper and cook, assist in the kitchen making the Cuban sandwiches for the guests. Julio turned toward the remaining guests and loudly announced, "Tonight we celebrated the success of Juan and his men. We also salute a fallen hero and friend, Antonio Mendoza."

Cheers rang out from everyone in the room. A few of the remaining guests began to tear up with a mix of elation and loss.

It was shortly before four in the morning when Juan noticed Julio holding a flashlight. "Expecting a power outage?" inquired Juan in a jovial manner. Just then Juan noticed the power go out in the entire neighborhood. Juan turned to Julio. "Is there anyone in Miami that isn't tied to you somehow?"

Julio gave a thunderous laugh along with several in the room, "My son . . . didn't you know . . . Miami is Cuban? And those that I do not know aren't worth knowing." Julio gave a wink and a nod to Juan.

Juan reverently closed his eyes as he bowed his head; he knew he was in the presence of a great leader of men.

All the men in the kitchen made their way in a very businesslike fashion to the dock divided into efficient teams of two. Juan heard a truck pull into the driveway, and then he saw it making its way toward the dock in Julio's backyard. The men began transferring the weapons from the boat to the delivery truck amid a line of lanterns. The truck had a logo on the side indicating "Miami's Freshest Coffee." Juan recognized the delivery truck as owned by one of the members of the Cubans for a Free Cuba. Juan could not believe how quickly they unloaded the boat and loaded the truck. In the North Carolina rain, as a result of hurricane Isabelle, it seemed to take forever to load and unload the weapons. The river water from the New River had rocked the boat despite being docked in the eddy. Now it was a beautiful fall evening in Miami, and the water barely rippled on the Miami River.

Juan enjoyed the fall, despite the infrequent hurricanes, in Miami. He also enjoyed the winter and early spring. For him it was the best time of year. There was almost no humidity and very little rain. The nights were comfortable to go out in long pants and a short-sleeve shirt. The only negative thing to him was the vast influx of tourists everywhere. The truck left as soon as the men transferred the weapons from the boat to the truck. A few of Julio's men left right after the truck was loaded. There was no discussion, but just a very businesslike transaction. A couple of Julio's men were to drive the truck to the warehouse. They would unload the truck alone. Only Julio and a few men knew where the weapons were stored. Juan knew wherever the weapons were to be stored, the place must have been good size. They had accumulated a vast number of weapons from various military installations throughout the southeastern part of the United States. The accumulation had gone on for a little over a year accumulating certain weapons from this military base and another kind of weapon from this military base. They made sure never to always take one thing or too much of another. Until the trip to Camp LeJeune, no one had been harmed. It left a bad taste in Juan's mouth.

It was slightly before five in the morning when the remaining men returned to the house to have more drinks at the bar before heading home. Julio asked Juan to wait until everyone left. The last person left as the sun was rising across Biscayne Bay. Julio put his arm around him to reassure Juan that it was not his fault that Antonio died. He also reassured Juan that if he needed anything that he, Julio, would be there for him. Julio had one of his men waiting in the driveway to take Juan home when he was ready. Julio walked Juan out to the waiting car; "I want to thank you for a job well done."

Juan appreciated the kind words he received throughout the evening. It was a joyous evening back in Miami. The celebration was long overdue and a welcomed relief to the guilt he had been carrying around since Antonio's death. Juan started to choke up with tears when Julio stopped him. "It couldn't be helped. We were lucky on our previous missions. This was bound to happen. It was a high-risk venture. Fortunately, it was our last mission. Unfortunately, it cost Antonio his life." Julio embraced Juan and gave him another kiss on the cheek. "Don't let his death be wasted! He died because he believed in what we were doing. He knew the risks."

Juan felt some of the burden of Antonio's death lift off his shoulders as he got into the car to go home. He waved good-bye to Julio, and Julio motioned to the driver to leave with a hard pat on the roof of the car with his hand. Juan sat in silence and pondered the last two weeks in his mind. He knew Julio was right. The driver tried to strike up a conversation with Juan, but he ignored the attempts. He felt alone in the world. His wife, Alexis, had died several years earlier from cancer. Their two children had gone to college and married. Both had their own families now and lived in the Tampa-St. Petersburg area. Antonio had been with him through the good times and the bad times. It was Julio's plans for the Cuban people that had rekindled his enthusiasm for life, and Antonio had been his crutch to continue living.

CHAPTER 48

Seth woke when he heard the alarm go off; it was six in the morning. He glanced at the window and could see it was still dark outside. Coolness hung in the morning air with the fresh scent of salt air. Argo was on the bed curled up next to him soaking up Seth's warmth from his body heat.

Seth went into the kitchen and started the coffee. He opened the door and stepped out on the deck of the house with Argo overlooking the ocean. Argo raced out onto the beach to do her morning chores. Seth kept a watchful eye on Argo to determine if he would need to follow after her to do any cleaning up! From the deck of his house, he saw the lights were already on next door at Hugh and Mary's house. He caught himself in his thoughts; it would just have to be Mary's house now. Seth went down the steps of the beach house and made his way to the mailbox to retrieve the newspaper. Argo was on his heels, having returned from her morning chores. The local newspaper was the *Wilmington Morning Star*. Seth always enjoyed poring over the newspaper with a cup coffee in hand. He made his way back onto the deck of the beach house noticing several locals drifting up and down the beach. Seth stood in the cool morning air watching the few locals scour the beach for shells, a ritual that somehow had eluded him. The past several days had not allowed Seth the time to relax and read the newspaper. He briefly tried his morning ritual in Cherokee, but it was not the same as his local newspaper and the ocean atmosphere that was home. With the hurricane and then rushing up to Cherokee with Major John Lawrence and Rachel, his time for relaxation was put on hold. He figured that now that he was back, things could return to normal. Seth made his way into the house with Argo close at hand. Seth poured himself a cup of coffee and opened up the newspaper. As he sat down to glance at the headlines, he remembered the funeral was at eight.

"Shit!" grumbled Seth. He was hoping to have a relaxing moment when he realized he was going to need to hurry to make it to the funeral on time. Seth dejectedly put the newspaper down and took his coffee with him to the bedroom. As he entered the bedroom, he remembered it was not all that long ago that he buried Maribeth. He remembered when he would come back from letting Argo out and gathering the morning newspaper only to return to their master bathroom to find Maribeth getting ready. He fondly remembered enjoying watching Maribeth dry herself off. She was beautiful even with all her minor imperfections that he used to tease her about. God, how he missed her!

As Seth shaved with each deliberate stroke, he thought about what he was going to do after the funeral. He figured everyone would go back to Mary's house after the funeral. He hated the thought of going. People would be standing around feeling uncomfortable making small talk. He felt he should make an appearance and then politely excuse himself. He needed to go by the office since he hadn't been there in a few days if nothing more than to go through the mail and return some overdue telephone calls. Seth also knew he needed to check with Ned to see how things had been going the past few days. Seth finished shaving and wiped off the residual shaving cream from his face. He turned on the hot water in the shower and stepped in to the shower, hoping to calm the frantic pace he had been on, and think a little bit more about what he needed to address. After several minutes of random thoughts, he decided to start slow and see where the day leads him.

After Seth showered and dressed, he decided to grab a quick bite before he left for the funeral. He knew it was going to be yet again another long day. Seth was shoveling in a bowl of Cheerios when he heard Mary, Rachel, and Hugh's mother leave for the funeral. Seth glanced at his watch; it was almost seven thirty. He knew he needed to get moving because he did not want to get stopped at the swinging bridge that was sometimes opened for passing boats going up and down the Intracoastal Waterway. He opened the door for Argo to do her chores before he left for the funeral. Argo charged down the steps of the beach house to do her chores with Seth close behind with a small shovel and bag. It was only minutes before they were back on the deck enjoying the vista. Seth looked down at the lonely eyes of his companion. "Hell . . . why don't you come with me." Seth locked up the house and headed out to the Ford Bronco with Argo on his heels. He opened the door, and the excited dog leaped into the passenger's seat.

Mary and Hugh's mother had found a funeral plot about a twenty minutes' drive from Surf City. It was near Hampstead, a small town not far off the island. They decided to have the entire funeral at the graveside. Neither Hugh nor Mary had joined a local church since arriving in the area. They also did not have a lot of friends in the area. Most of their friends were comprised of a few locals, including Maribeth and Seth and the people with whom Hugh worked.

Seth drove his Surf City police Bronco to the graveyard. As he pulled in, he saw people already gathering by the grave site. A tent had been erected next to the grave site with the name of the funeral home imprinted along the edges. Flowers were placed next to the casket draped in the American flag. He parked the Bronco under a tree for shade and opened the window enough for Argo to relax comfortably while he attended the solemn ceremony. Seth walked over to join the others. There were about fifteen people at the funeral. Seth recognized a few of the locals, including his assistant Ned and Sarah. They did not know Hugh but were attending out of respect for Seth. Most of the others were in their military uniforms that Seth assumed were people Hugh worked with at Camp LeJeune. Seth paid his respects to Mary, Rachel, and Hugh's mother before the funeral began.

CHAPTER 49

During the funeral, Seth noticed a Jacksonville Police Department van pull up. Seth could barely make out "Jacksonville Police Department, Forensic Division" on the side of the van. Terry hopped out and made his way over to the grave site and stood behind Seth.

Terry discretely leaned over to Seth's ear and whispered, "I need to talk with you," during the eulogy.

Seth waved his hand to politely acknowledge Terry's comment as if to say, "As soon as this is over."

As the minister made his closing comments, Terry took Seth by the arm and led him to the side. Apparently what Terry had to say was important, and he could wait no longer.

The marine corps color guard entered the tent as Terry and Seth exited the far side of the tent.

"What is it?" remarked an annoyed Seth.

"Look, I've been working on the break-in over at Camp LeJeune where Lieutenant Hugh Dugen died. I've also been working on the break-in at the Murphy's house. I've been trying to track down John, but I'm not getting anywhere, and your office said you were here. I figured if I find you, maybe I'd find John too," barked Terry in response to Seth's apparent annoyance.

Seth was surprised by the obviously irritated and unknowing Terence Ingram. "Terry, John's dead. Didn't the people over at LeJeune tell you?"

"No, I can't get anybody over at LeJeune to call me or even talk with me on the phone. Even Colonel Charles Radford seems to have disappeared."

"Who the hell is he?" inquired Seth.

"He is, or was, the provost marshal—you know, the chief of the military police at Camp LeJeune."

Having served in the military, Seth was quite familiar with who the provost marshal was. "I know who the provost marshal is. But what do you mean he's disappeared?" "Well, after the break-in at LeJeune, John called us in to do the forensic work. You know, with military cutbacks and all. Well, at that time, Radford was the provost marshal. I tried to talk with John, but when I couldn't get him, I asked for Radford. Apparently, he has been reassigned back to Washington DC after a short three-month stint at LeJeune." All in the same breath, Terry asked, "What do you mean John's dead?" Terry was bewildered by the data he was receiving.

"We went up near Cherokee, North Carolina, and were to join in a raid of a militia along with ATF and the FBI. The FBI received a tip that there were some automatic weapons and grenades. We were led to believe that the weapons were the same ones stolen from LeJeune. When we arrived, the FBI and ATF had already completed the raid of the militia's compound. Somehow one of the members of the militia got hold of a pistol and shot John during what was to be a routine interrogation. Turns out the militia bought the weapons from a third party and shipped them through Costa Rica to Wilmington." Seth could see Terry was upset.

For the brief time they spent together, Terry had grown fond of John. John was an easy guy to like, he thought.

"Terry, what did you find out?" inquired Seth. His police background was starting to take control of the situation.

"Hey, no one seems to know much about anything at LeJeune. All I get is the runaround. They act as if they have no idea what we've been looking into." The mound of military protocol that was constantly being placed in front of him aggravated Terry.

"Did you talk with the chief of staff? If anyone knows anything, it's him!" Seth's experience in the military made him well aware of the hierarchy of the military and how the game was played.

"I tried . . . all I got from his office was to send our bill to them and that our services were no longer necessary as it relates to the break-in. I was also told to forward all my records to his office as soon as possible." Terry continued, "John, excuse me, Major Lawrence gave me a knife that was found at the break-in to test. We determined the knife was the murder weapon. One of the MPs found it in Private Shays's pocket when he was checking the unconscious Private Shays's wounds at the scene." Terry was looking through his notes as he recounted what he knew from his forensic work. "The knife had traces of Lieutenant Hugh Dugen's blood on it. The knife also matched the wounds in Lieutenant Hugh Dugen's body. A second blood type was also found at Camp LeJeune, at the ammunitions depot. We matched the blood we found at the Murphys' house next to their dock to this second blood sample, which was also found in a U-Haul believed to have transported the weapons. It was the same blood from the body they dug up at the Murphys' house."

"Who is Private Shays?" asked Seth. This was a new player that he had not heard of, yet the man's name kept coming up in his discussion with Terry.

"He was Lieutenant Dugen's patrol partner," responded an incredulous Terry. "I thought you would have known."

"No, that is a new one for me. John didn't give me all his information. Remember, it was a need-to-know basis for all military information." Seth was trying to place all the players as Terry spoke. He was also trying to figure out why Terry was so willing to give so much information to a Surf City police chief.

"I also spent a lot of time trying to determine the identity of the body you found. You know, the one with the matching blood to the U-Haul, the ammo depot, and the Murphys' house. I haven't had any luck with who he is as of yet, but I did find something interesting."

"What's that?" Terry was drawing Seth into the investigation without knowing it.

"The fingerprints were mutilated, as we all know, and he had no other identifying marks. What I did find was that he did have fillings."

Seth looked at Terry in an odd way. "No kidding, any crowns too?" replied Seth in a sarcastic manner.

"The fillings were made from Russian gold. The man was Hispanic. My guess with the Russian gold, he's got to be Cuban."

Seth smiled.

Terry could see something finally struck a nerve with Seth.

"That makes sense," commented Seth.

Terry was curious by Seth's casual remark. "It does? What makes sense? The gold?"

"When we were in Cherokee, one of the members of the militia said we were being played. He said it was Cubans that were responsible for the break-in, not the militia."

Terry enjoyed what he felt was confirmation for his forensic work. "By the way," added Terry, "the MP guy, Private Shays, has also disappeared. When I was askin' about everyone else, I asked about the other MP who was shot. They told me he was AWOL. I wanted to inform them that it was Shays's knife that killed Lieutenant Dugen. I figured that way they could arrest him, and maybe part of this menagerie of a case could have been solved. I don't think John ever trusted that guy."

"Well . . . so much for asking if they arrested Private Shays. I guess his disappearance will just add another layer to our mystery." Seth was intrigued by all this new information and what appeared to be a botched investigation on the part of military. "Jesus . . . this whole thing stinks from beginning to the end."

Terry silently agreed to himself that Seth was right about the investigation but didn't want to say it out loud for fear of getting himself into a situation that he couldn't get out of. "Look, I'm getting pressure to end this thing from upstairs especially since LeJeune wants the bill for our work." He paused looking down at the ground. Terry looked back at Seth. "You know this is no longer and never really was, your case."

Seth was curious having heard all the developments from Terry. "Yeah, I know."

"What are your plans?" inquired Terry.

It occurred to Seth why Terry was unburdening himself of all this information. He could see Terry wanted the investigation to go somewhere; however, on its present course, it was about to get buried in military bureaucracy. "I don't know. Do me a favor. Stall LeJeune as long as you can. Make copies and photos of anything you can and give them to me." Seth was surprised that Camp LeJeune was so quick to dismiss so much and wondered why people were disappearing with no explanation.

"I'll do my best. Let me know if you need anything else. It will have to be on the QT." Terry reached into his pocket and pulled out a business card along with a pen. He scribbled two numbers on the back of the card. "Here is my business card. I put my cell phone and home phone numbers on the back. Call me if you need anything!" Terry started for his car when he looked back. "I'll let you know if I find out who this guy is with the fillings." As Terry walked to his van, he clenched his fist raising it toward his chest, indicating that between he and Seth, the fight was going to continue.

As Terry headed for his van, a bugle began to play taps. Terry, Seth, and all those at the gravesite stood frozen. As the bugler concluded playing taps, the color guard fired a twenty-one-gun salute.

There was a brief pause after the moving ceremony; then Seth called out to Terry, "Thanks." Seth liked Terry's enthusiasm in determining the identity of "the guy with the fillings." The two men parted. Seth got in the Bronco and saw Argo look up. "It's okay . . . we're goin' home." Argo wagged her tail, and Seth headed back for the postfuneral gathering at the Dugens'.

CHAPTER 50

Seth rode home in silence, no radio and the police radio turned down barely audible. His mind was processing the many unanswered questions that Terry raised at Seth's funeral. Seth pulled the Bronco into his driveway. He headed into the house as Argo raced off to do her chores. Seth sat at the kitchen table scribbling a few notes on a piece of notebook paper. He felt he needed a few more minutes away from the others before heading to the postfuneral gathering. Seth wanted to think more about Terry's comments about Camp LeJeune's disregard for Terry's forensic work and the apathy related to the break-in. "Damn this doesn't add up," Seth was talking aloud. Seth heard Argo bark at the door leading to the deck, requesting to come in. Seth decided he was getting too close to the investigation, and he needed to back off. He locked up the house and joined the others at Mary's house.

Rachel cornered Seth as he walked into Mary's house to pay his respects. "Who was that man at the funeral?" demanded Rachel. "And don't lie to me. I know he is with the Jacksonville Police Department. I couldn't help but notice 'Forensic Division' on the side of his van. And why would he drive all the way out to Hugh's funeral when he didn't even know him aside from his forensic work? He had something important to tell you that he couldn't tell you over the phone."

Seth could see the curious and determined look on Rachel's face. He motioned for Rachel to follow him as he led her out onto the deck of Mary's house overlooking the ocean. Seth sat on a swinging chair so they could enjoy the view of the ocean. Reluctantly Rachel took a seat next to Seth. Seth filled her in on his conversation with Terry. He could tell by her reaction that she felt as he did. There were too may coincidences and too many unanswered questions. There were the sudden disappearances of Private Shays, Hugh's partner, and Colonel Charles Radford, the provost marshal. Camp LeJeune's appearance of trying to bury the investigation in bureaucratic red tape made matters worse.

—

178

Rachel looked at Seth. "I've been trying to access the Naval Intelligence files since being in Cherokee without any success. They're denying my access." Seth could see the frustration in Rachel's face. Rachel continued, "I called my office to find out why and got the runaround." Rachel took a deep breath. "I'm going to Miami." She paused for a moment, waiting for Seth to react. When he didn't, she asked, "What are your plans?"

"I've been getting that question a lot lately. I think Terry was banking on wetting my appetite to carry the ball in this investigation ever since I told him that John was dead." Seth sat for a moment, staring distantly out over the ocean. "I guess I'm going with you to Miami."

"Good. We'll take John's car. The marine corps will never miss it." Seth remembered that since their return from Cherokee, he never got around to calling someone over at Camp LeJeune to come and pick up their sedan. The car had been sitting in Seth's driveway since their return from Cherokee—not that it had been all that long.

Seth loved Rachel's determination. He also loved the idea of taking the marine corps' car for an investigation they were attempting to bury. Seth stood up and looked down at Rachel still seated in the swinging chair. "I've gotta run over to the house. I made some notes that I would like to go over with you. I still have John's notes too. Maybe he made some references to Private Shays and the knife." Seth started to leave when he turned back toward Rachel. "Maybe we should wait and do this tomorrow. This is your brother's funeral."

A glint shone from Rachel's eyes. "I made some notes too that I would like to go over with you as well. And no, I don't want to do it tomorrow. The longer we wait, the colder this thing gets, and besides, Hugh would want us to tackle it right now. You knew Hugh well enough . . . tell me I'm wrong!"

Seth stood there stunned by Rachel's determined response, yet at the same time he somehow knew she would be ready to charge ahead. Her intuitions were right thus far. He was happy to hear that she was ready to pursue the investigation right then and there. Seth nodded his agreement to Rachel and went over to his house. He found his notes right where he left them on the kitchen table. Seth noticed Argo giving him a look for another trip outside that he promptly obliged. Seth called Ned to let him know he would be heading out of town soon and asked him to look after Argo and to fill in at the police station in his absence.

In a matter of minutes, Seth was back at Mary's house eagerly looking for Rachel. He found Rachel in Mary's bedroom on the phone. She looked at him and motioned for him to come in, close the door, and wait. Seth sat down on the edge of the bed and waited for Rachel to finish her phone conversation.

Rachel hung the phone up in a deliberate manner. She paused long enough to gather her thoughts. Things were beginning to move quickly, and she didn't want to come across to Seth as some naive little girl who had no real direction. "Look, that was a friend of mine's sister. The friend, Sky, lives in Atlanta. He is a computer whiz. If there's a computer system out there, he can crack it open like a ripe melon. I had asked Beth, his sister, to have him look into what Cuban organizations in Miami may be bold enough to steal arms from a military installation. I also told her we were coming to Atlanta on our way to Miami and wanted to meet with her brother in person to talk with him. I couldn't speak directly with him. My friend and his buddies are"—Rachel paused to find the right words to describe her friend—"fugitives of the FBI. They are being sought for their hacking prowess. I suggest we pack and leave within the hour for Atlanta. We can go over our notes on the drive down."

"But you have a house full of people from the funeral." This was somewhat of an overstatement, most of the people had left, but Seth hoped to spend the night and start fresh in the morning. It had been less than a week since their all-night drive to Cherokee, and now Rachel was talking about another long drive to Atlanta. Seth also thought she may want to spend some time with her grieving mother and sister-in-law.

"Look, I love my family, but I want to find the bastards that killed my brother. Standing around here consoling my family and socializing with my brother's friends aren't going to find them. The trail is getting cold as we speak. The sooner we pursue the bastards, the better luck we're gonna have finding them. Besides, my mother is a strong and nurturing woman. She'll take care of Mary better than I ever could. They want this thing to just end, and I need to find out the truth. No matter where it takes me, I will end this!"

Seth knew she was right. It was always best to stay on a fugitive's trail while it was hot. For the little time Seth had spent with Rachel, he knew she was not about to let this thing end until she got to the bottom of it. He loved her fervor for the pursuit of whoever was responsible for her brother's death. "Okay. I'll meet you at the car in thirty minutes."

"Twenty!" scolded Rachel. Seth went into the living room to say good-bye and to offer his condolences once again to Mary and Hugh's mother. He headed back to his house. He packed what he thought he might need. Seth called Ned back to let him know he was leaving immediately and as such he need him to assume his responsibilities right away along with looking out for Argo. Twenty minutes later, Seth met Rachel at the car.

Rachel was dressed in a pair of blue jeans, a bright red blouse, and a light jacket. She was leaning against the car with an impatient air about her. When she heard Seth coming up behind her, she looked up in disgust. "And men dare to comment how long it takes women."

Seth countered, "You said twenty minutes."

Rachel was agitated by his reply but did not want to let Seth see it. She ignored his comment and got into the passenger's seat of the marine corps sedan.

Seth shook his head as he got behind the wheel of the car trying to figure out Rachel's agitated state.

CHAPTER 51

Sky adopted the name while he was a freshman at Georgia Tech. All his friends had adopted strange names. The names were adopted so they could operate over the Internet without their true identities known. Eventually it became a game to try and fit a person's Internet name with the actual person as the number of participants grew. Skypilot was the full name Rachel's friend adopted. Most of his friends just called him Sky for short. He was Rachel's computer whiz.

Sky and his friends were computer hackers and had become increasingly competitive with one another. Each hacker tried to hack into a bigger and ever more challenging computer system than the next. Neither corporate America nor any government agency was safe from Sky and his band of computer hackers. The hackers formed an informal club where they would share some of their respective secrets but still reserving their best secrets for themselves. The club's members quickly distinguished themselves from the amateurs and were hated for their arrogance by their peers in the school of computer sciences. The dean of the department despised them the most because of their suspected nefarious activities and his own inability to teach them anything new. Sky and several of his friends had been able to access the FBI, National Security Agency, and CIA computer files. The school's reputation for producing computer wizards had become well documented throughout corporate America and the federal government.

Grants were offered to the school's computer science department to help create computer firewalls against people like Sky and his friends. Sky and a few of his inner circle believed the grants were more of an excuse to keep them preoccupied so they would not have time to hack into corporate America's computer mainframes that they had become notorious for accessing. As a result, Sky and his buddies had snubbed the grants and went out on their own freelancing for various corporations wanting inside information about their competitor's records or to protect their own interests. The money had been quite lucrative for Sky and his buddies. The money was always in cash, so Sky and his buddies never reported it to the IRS or anyone else for that matter. It was fine for the corporations that had hired Sky and his companions because it helped avoid a paper trail. They did not want anyone to find out about their own illegal tactics for gaining inside information about a competitor.

Aside from the money corporate America was willing to pay them for their nefarious activities, Sky's and his friends' greatest pleasures were describing in painfully slow detail to one another how they hacked into a system or watching their computer science professors thrash about in their own ineptness. Sky lasted as long as he could at Georgia Tech before the lure of the easy cash dominated his interest, and he dropped out. Sky's values, when it came to computer ethical responsibility, died when corporate America approached him with handfuls of Ben Franklins and fifty-year-old scotch. What others called illegal he justified as corporate greed and entitlement and amusement.

Sky grew up in the greater Atlanta area. His father, Aaron McGavin, was a partner with one of the largest law firms in Atlanta. Aaron worked in corporate law. Sky's mother was a homemaker and a country club regular. Sky's parents were enthusiastic when he was admitted to Georgia Tech because of its reputation for academics. They were later disappointed when they found out that he dropped out of college and learned what he was doing for a living. Aaron had aggressively gone after computer hackers such as Sky and his friends for illegally accessing computer databases for insider information. It wasn't long before Sky started missing Christmas, family birthdays, and other celebrations with his parents for fear of being arrested. Aaron, on numerous occasions when Sky would call, asked Sky to turn himself in to the authorities and offered the services of his law firm to help him with all his legal matters. Sky always refused any suggestion of turning himself in.

CHAPTER 52

It was well after midnight when Seth and Rachel arrived on the outskirts of Atlanta. Rachel called Sky's sister, Beth. While Rachel was calling Beth, Seth found John's briefcase and suitcase from their earlier trip to Cherokee still in the truck of the car. Seth had already sorted through John's briefcase for his notes on the investigation and left what appeared to be personal effects alone. Seth had had no interest in going through John's personal effects; he felt that should be left to his relatives. After a gut check, Seth decided he should comb through both of John's bags to make sure there wasn't anything he overlooked related to the investigation. He was upset with himself when he spoke with Terry to find out about Private Shays and the knife. Seth felt he made a rookie mistake by not checking John's notes more thoroughly. Seth combed through John's suitcase and his briefcase once again. He reviewed John's notes this time in more detail for anything directly related to the investigation. Seth paid particular attention to the areas where it mentioned Private Shays and/or the knife. The notes concluded with the words "Cubans and Miami" followed by question marks. Seth found a pen in the glove compartment of the car. He made some notes on a pad of paper he found in John's briefcase as he read through John's notes. He noted that John had found Private Larry Shays's account of the break-in as "unbelievable." John indicated that he felt Private Shays was a "person of interest" in Lieutenant Dugen's death. He went on to note that he felt somehow Private Shays was linked to the break-ins but had nothing concrete with which to charge Private Shays at that time. John also indicated there had been a number of break-ins at military installations throughout the southeastern part of the United States, which was why he was initially sent to Camp LeJeune. His notes suggested a reluctance to go to Cherokee because he believed that an informant indicating that a North Carolina militia had committed the break-in was too convenient. The informant's account seemed sketchy to John based upon his conversations with his direct supervisor. However, he decided to go to Cherokee to placate his superiors. He also felt that it might give him time to rehash much of the information he had on the long drive to and from Cherokee with a neutral party, the chief of the Surf City Police Department. John's notes indicated that Seth appeared to "have good instincts for a small-town cop." John also questioned why he was put in charge of this type of investigation with his limited experience.

As Seth read through John's notes, he was amazed by John's instincts and his ability to read people. The forensic evidence gathered by Terry with the Jacksonville Police Department confirmed much of John's assumptions. Their trip to Cherokee further confirmed John's hunches about the militia. Seth felt John had excellent investigative skills to carry out the investigation. Seth did notice that though John appeared confident, there were times he seemed to need validation from Seth, a cop.

CHAPTER 53

Rachel found a public telephone off the interstate next to a service station. Sky insisted that all calls be made from landlines, never from a cell phone. It was his reasoning that the airwaves were too easy to compromise. Sky would not give his telephone number to anyone for fear of government agencies and other persons looking to do him harm or pursuing him for his nefarious hacking activities. Beth could not even call him directly. Rachel was not sure how Beth contacted Sky; she assumed by beeper, disposable phone, or random rendezvous, all casual events without any specific information provided. All Rachel knew was that no one she knew could contact Sky directly. When someone came looking for Sky, it had to be through Beth. She would take their name and number, indicating she hadn't seen Sky in years, but if she did, she would give him their number. Rachel knew it was a lark in case Beth's telephone was tapped, but she would somehow contact Sky with their information.

"Hey, Rachel, I ran into Sky at the mall. I told him you were coming to Atlanta. He is looking forward to seeing you. I think secretly he had a thing for you."

Rachel laughed at the thought of her and Sky. He was never her type of guy, but she was flattered by Beth's compliment. Rachel was one of the few people outside of Sky's cohorts that got along with him. Sky was attracted to Rachel, but the feeling was never mutual, and Sky knew it. Rachel loved Sky's sense of humor and intelligence while he seemed to find her charming yet upfront. He was well-read and could talk intelligently on almost any topic. It was these characteristics that led to a strong friendship.

Beth continued, "I also told him to look into the items you requested."

Rachel noticed Beth always kept conversations short and to the point. She never repeated previous conversations but would refer to them in passing. She made sure never to use words that would link their conversations. Most of all,

Rachel noticed that Beth never alluded to the fact that she would necessarily see Sky or meet with him. All her meetings with Sky were chance encounters.

"Great! When can I meet with him? Do you know if he found anything out?"

"Let me update you later. There are those listening to our conversations." This was Beth's polite way of letting Rachel know her phone was being tapped possibly by government agencies. Also, if she confirmed that Sky found something, their chance encounter could be considered as planned by investigating agencies. "There is a McDonald's in Downtown Atlanta at First and Peachtree. Meet me there at eight tomorrow morning."

After Beth's abrupt response to her question, Rachel realized how foolish she had been with Beth to ask such direct questions. There was also the implication that Beth had had follow-up meetings with Sky, which meant their meetings with each other were less than casual. "See you then," replied Rachel. Rachel hung up the phone reenergized. She knew that if she could get up with Sky, he would find something she could use.

Rachel returned to the car where Seth was reading over John's notes and making some of his own. He had also refueled the car while Rachel called Beth. "So what's the plan?" asked Seth. Seth recognized Rachel's newfound enthusiasm. He, on the other hand, had a more "wait and see" attitude. Seth was hoping to temper Rachel's enthusiasm so she wouldn't be let down too hard if they couldn't get up with Sky or if Sky ended up with nothing that they could use.

"We meet tomorrow morning at a McDonald's in Downtown Atlanta," answered Rachel.

"So I guess what we need to do is find a motel." Seth pulled out of the service station where they found the pay telephone. He got back on the interstate heading toward downtown Atlanta. One of the information signs on the interstate indicated about five motels at the next exit. Seth followed the signs off the interstate and pulled into the nearest motel. They went in and got two adjacent rooms on the first floor. They were both exhausted from getting up early for the funeral and then their long drive to Atlanta. They decided to meet and leave for downtown at seven in the morning. They were not sure how long it would take to find the McDonald's in downtown Atlanta, so they decided to eat once they got there. Their fear was that if they were late, Beth could already be gone by the time they got there.

CHAPTER 54

Rachel was finishing getting ready the next morning when Seth knocked on the door a few minutes before seven. "Are you about ready?" pleaded Seth. Seth was feeling a little impatient. He hated traffic and hated the thought of negotiating downtown Atlanta during rush hour when they didn't know exactly where they were going. "Two minutes." Rachel shouted through the door as she finished throwing the last few things into her bag. Once Rachel was finished getting ready, she left the room to find Seth sitting in the marine corps sedan going over a detailed map of Downtown Atlanta that he picked up the night before at the service station.

Rachel was hardly in the car when Seth chimed in on what he felt was the best way to get to the McDonald's where they were to meet Beth. Rachel gave Seth a slow smile. "You forgot I went to school at Georgia Tech, right here in Atlanta. I spent four years in this area! I know how to get around."

Seth was a little embarrassed that he forgot how Rachel had met Sky. "I forgot," he responded.

Rachel gave Seth a teasing punch on the shoulder and a smile. "You're a man. Reading a map is second nature, and asking for directions, especially from a woman, is taboo."

Seth liked Rachel's quick wit and politely responded, "And with that, my dear, you can kiss my ass."

They both laughed as Seth pulled around to the front of the motel to check out.

The motel was just off Interstate 85 and the beltline. After a short drive, following Rachel's directions, they were in Downtown Atlanta. It did not take long for Seth to remember why he avoided cities. Seth had not seen traffic like this in years—and he didn't miss it. Even on Charlotte's worst traffic day, it did not rival the traffic Seth encountered driving into Downtown Atlanta. When he needed to make a turn, there were signs posted that he could not turn. He and

Rachel made what seemed like an endless number of turns before they found a parking lot near the designated McDonald's in Downtown Atlanta.

"Wow," commented Rachel. "It's been awhile since I was here, and has this gotten complicated."

Seth couldn't resist the chance to rib Rachel after she teased him about looking over the map. "I thought this was all second nature to you."

"All right, you got me," replied Rachel.

They walked several blocks back to the McDonald's where they hoped they would meet Beth, Sky's sister. It was two minutes to eight when they arrived. They were both out of breath walking as fast as they could so they would not be late. Rachel suggested that Seth go in and order food and coffee for the both of them. Rachel wanted to wait outside for Beth. She did not want to take a chance on missing her. Rachel also felt that if Seth were nearby, Beth might be hesitant to meet with her. She knew if they somehow missed each other, it would be at least another day before they could set up another meeting. It began to rain when Seth returned with the food and coffee, sooner than what Rachel had hoped for. It was the first day of October, and a cold front had moved into the area, making for a miserable day. She was hungry but wanted the extra time to try and meet with Beth before Seth's return. Rachel inched as close to the building as possible to take advantage of the small overhanging awning, compliments of McDonald's, to keep out of the rain.

"Looks like we're in for a nasty day," commented Seth.

Rachel politely agreed, but it was clear that her mind was on their meeting Beth. It had been almost four years since they had last seen each other, and even then it was only a brief encounter. Rachel feared that since it had been so long, would Beth even recognize her? Would she recognize Beth? Rachel took the breakfast biscuit and coffee that she had asked Seth to get her. She gulped down the breakfast biscuit and sipped the hot coffee while trying to keep warm and dry. Rachel kept looking at her watch and scanning the proximate area; it was almost eight thirty. Had they missed Beth? Was Beth wary of meeting with them because of Seth, or had something else spooked her? Rachel's clothes were starting to get soaked from the rain when a woman bumped into her.

Several items from the bags the woman was carrying fell to the ground when she ran into Rachel. To Rachel, it looked like the woman just left a supermarket. There were cans of soup and vegetables, assorted frozen goods, and fresh vegetables. Rachel bent down to help the woman pick up the groceries she dropped when the woman spoke in a soft whisper. "Leave here and make sure no one follows you."

Rachel was startled at first when she heard the woman speak. She recognized Beth's voice from their telephone conversations. Beth was wearing a three-quarter-length coat that was successfully repelling the rain. She had on an Atlanta Braves baseball cap, a pair of jeans, and some work boots. Rachel continued to casually assist Beth picking up her belongings.

Beth continued quietly providing instructions to Rachel, "Get on Marta and head north to Lennox Square. There is a small coffee shop there called Computer Perks. Sky will meet you there." Rachel hardly recognized Beth as they stood and faced each other for the brief moment. Beth, still making the appearance of a casual encounter, thanked Rachel for her assistance. Rachel placed the items she had picked up in one of the bags. "My apologies," commented Beth.

"It's quite all right," replied Rachel.

Beth politely gave Rachel a nod and briskly walked away, blending into the rush hour crowd.

Rachel wanted to try and say more but could see by Beth's actions that the discussion was over. Rachel watched Beth as she melded into the vast throng of people as they raced to their jobs or appointments. Rachel thought to herself how casual and how smooth everything transpired. *Damn, is she good!* thought Rachel. Rachel took a moment to digest her ever-so-brief encounter with Beth and looked at Seth with a sense of urgency. "We need to go. Now!"

"What the hell do you mean we have to go?" incredulously asked Seth. "We haven't met your friend yet!"

Rachel grabbed Seth and pulled him close so she could get directly in his face. "Trust me! We have to go and keep your voice down." Her voice was just barely audible, and her face was as stern as Seth had ever seen. Rachel started walking in the opposite direction in which Beth departed.

CHAPTER 55

They headed north until they came to an entrance to Marta, the Atlanta subway system. They started down the steps and began meandering through the busy subway before taking another exit that put them west of where they originally entered. They headed north once again along another street before Rachel found a small coffee shop. She shoved Seth into the entryway of a coffee shop, almost knocking him over. Her action was one of two people seeking refuge from the rain. Rachel helped Seth regain his balance and then threw her arms around him. She gave him a big hug and kissed him passionately on the mouth. Seth was taken aback by this spontaneous display of affection from Rachel. He did not fight her; in fact, he was enjoying the moment. She had never expressed any kind of interest toward him, and after her "in his face" attitude just a few moments earlier, he was caught off guard. While still tightly embraced, Rachel whispered into Seth's ear as she continued her long, slow romantic embrace, "The woman who bumped into me was Beth. She told us to head to a coffee shop called Computer Perks north of Lennox Square. She told us to make sure we were not followed and to be sure to take Marta to get there."

Seth pulled back from Rachel. He looked at her with surprise before Rachel threw herself against him once again. As Rachel pulled herself close, she whispered into his ear, "You're a lousy poker player."

Seth pondered in his mind, *Why are these people so cautious? Who are Beth and Rachel working with that these people needed to take such elaborate precautions to mask a seemingly harmless meeting? Is all this necessary to meet some computer hackers? They are not some kind of international spies. They are computer nerds for Christ's sake!* It seemed to border on the ridiculous to Seth. How much of a threat could a bunch of computer nerds be?

Seth caught his mind wandering and refocused his attention back to Rachel. He took a stronger, more romantic hold of Rachel as he slowly gazed around the room and into the street. He knew Rachel was doing the same in the opposite direction. Everything seemed copasetic to Seth. He was not sure what or who he was looking for, but he tried to be as casual as possible. Seth was not sure how long they were holding each other before they both relaxed their grip on each other.

Several of the customers and staff in the small coffee shop seemed to look at them as if reminiscing of being a young couple very much in love. A few of the couples inside the coffee shop gave each other a similar glance of affection before returning their attention to where Rachel and Seth were still standing in the doorway. Rachel became a little embarrassed once she noticed the throng of people looking back at them with interest because of the demonstrative display of affection they showed each other. They continued to hold each other as they departed from the coffee shop and back into the rain. As Rachel and Seth left, a lingering sense of warmth hung in the air of the small coffee shop as the remaining couples smiled at each other and held hands.

Rachel and Seth vigilantly glanced around as they made their way down the busy street trying to avoid the men and woman dressed in business attire walking against them. Once they felt they were not being followed, they found another entrance to Marta. They took the first metro heading north toward Lennox Square. They made one transfer before they arrived at Lennox Square. As they exited Marta, they saw several signs directing them to Computer Perks. The bounty of businessmen and women had dissipated dramatically since their early-morning start in Downtown Atlanta. They were no longer holding each other as they once were at the small coffee shop. As they approached Computer Perks, their affection for each other was just a brief memory; they were there to find Sky and get information. Both were eager to find out what Sky had for them, especially after all the cloak-and-dagger process it took to get them this far.

Seth could see the name in white on a black awning for Computer Perks a half a block away. It was on a corner. On either side of the coffee shop, the sides were open to allow people to freely enter. It created an open-air coffee shop. It seemed out of place on a cool, rainy October day. As Seth and Rachel got closer, the coffee shop appeared new with lots of wood trim and countertops. The floor was black-and-white tile. There were approximately ten small wooden round tables with matching chairs. Near the counter were stools and a narrow bar top. There were several pastries under a glass countertop. Seth noticed six or seven people sitting independent of one another drinking their coffee and staring into their respective computer screens. Occasionally one of the patrons would move the mouse on their laptop. On the side of the street that Seth and Rachel approached was a small bookstore with small-framed windows and a black door that was the sole visible entrance to the bookstore. The name was Van's Vintage Books. Next to the bookstore and across from where Rachel and Seth were standing was an English pub called Her Majesty's Pub. It had a Tudor facade. Over the windows and door just below the name of the pub were painted a Union Jack opposite the Stars and Stripes. Between the two flags were painted a gold lion standing on its hind legs and a bald eagle.

"Hold it," blurted out Seth as he grabbed at Rachel's arm, pulling her back.

"What?" cried Rachel. She was angry that Seth grabbed her arm so hard. "That hurt!" She looked angrily into Seth's face, but he was not looking back. He was staring just down the street.

Seth ignored Rachel's painful cry. He took her in his arms, and they acted like lovers once again. This time Seth slowly turned Rachel in the direction of Computer Perks while embraced. Two men in dark suits with trench coats were forcing a young handcuffed man into the back of a dark four-door sedan. Seth knew the sedan was a federal car by the license plates. The man was fighting the two men as much as possible to no avail. Seth whispered into Rachel's ear, "Is that Sky?"

Rachel looked hard at the figure the men were forcing into the sedan. She was almost frozen in Seth's arms. It had been a long time since she had last seen Sky. When she and Sky were in college together, he had dirty blond hair that he always wore in a ponytail. He always wore tinted eyeglasses along with T-shirts and worn-out jeans.

Suddenly the handcuffed man bit the hand of one of the federal agents who immediately let go of Sky. The second man tried to get a better grip of Sky but instead received a stern kick to the groin. As he bent over, Sky gave him a big shove with his shoulder, driving the man to the ground. Sky glanced up to see Rachel and gave her a big smile and then took off running in the opposite direction of where Seth and Rachel stood embraced. Two other federal agents who were assisting in the arrest chased after Sky down the puddle-ridden sidewalk. Once the first two agents regained their composure, they jumped into their sedan and joined the pursuit, squealing tires as they raced down the street. That was when Rachel knew it was Sky. She tried to run after him, but Seth held firm.

"You can't go. You know Sky wouldn't want to involve you." Seth spoke in a soft soothing voice. Rachel paused when she noticed the sedan pull in front of Sky as he ran down the sidewalk. A loud thud rang out from the impact of Sky running into the side of the dark four-door sedan. The two men that were chasing Sky picked him up off the ground and forcefully loaded him into the backseat of the sedan. Sky glanced once again across the roof of the sedan and briefly stared at Rachel. The sedan quickly sped away once again, squealing tires on the wet asphalt. The other two federal agents walked back to their sedan and sped away.

Rachel gasped when she caught Sky's glance. "He knew I was here!" She felt a sting of guilt for bringing Sky out in the open where the federal authorities could catch him.

"It was him, wasn't it?" Seth was caught up in the moment. He remembered that when he was a policeman in Charlotte, there was many a times that it was him forcing a prisoner into the backseat of a patrol car.

Rachel replied, "Yes." She felt deflated. They were so close, and now they were walking away with nothing.

CHAPTER 56

Rachel and Seth turned to make their way back to the Marta station exasperated by what they just witnessed. Empty-handed! Their trip to Atlanta was a bust. While dejectedly heading back to the Marta station, they noticed that a dingy man kept impeding their progress.

Seth gallantly stepped forward to confront the man. "Can I help you?"

The dingily clad man ignored Seth and focused his attention on Rachel. "Are you Rachel Dugen?" asked the man in a soft-spoken Southern drawl.

Rachel looked the man over cautiously. She was not sure how she should respond. Would a yes answer put her in harm's way? What would happen if she said no? The man was of average height, wearing a tattered pair of jeans, a Batman T-shirt, and an old navy blue trench coat that Rachel assumed to be a second from a local Army Navy store. The man had long dark oily hair pulled back into a ponytail and glasses that needed to be cleaned. Rachel felt herself having an out-of-body experience when she heard herself blurt out, "Yes . . . I'm Rachel."

Rachel noticed Seth bracing himself for potential confrontation with the man as he waited for him to respond. Rachel could see Seth's previous marine corps training take over the situation as his body tensed up waiting for the man to lunge.

The man stared at Rachel for a brief moment and then reached inside his trench coat. As the man reached inside his trench coat, Seth reached for his gun. The man produced a large manila envelope. He extended his hand offering the manila envelope to Rachel. Rachel cautiously stepped forward to accept the envelope and promptly stepped back to create more room between her and the stranger. The man calmly turned and walked away.

Without looking inside the envelope, Rachel ran after him and grabbed his arm. She snapped, "I don't understand!"

The man shook loose from Rachel's grip; as he did, he took Rachel by her arm in a tight grip. He ushered her into the entrance way of a nearby four-story apartment building. Seth followed closely behind. Before he could grab the man, he saw that the man had drawn a gun and pointed it at Seth. Seth responded in kind by pointing his gun at the man holding Rachel.

As the two men faced each other with their guns drawn, the man spoke. "I'm one of Sky's friends. We hack together. Sky hacked into some government files and found some things he thought you should have. That's what's in the envelope. Sky told me he set up ghosts all over the globe to keep from being traced during the hack. He told me the feds were knocking down the ghosts like he had never seen before. Hell . . . when he was telling me about it, I thought he was yankin' my chain. Then last night after Beth beeped him, he went out to a pay phone to call her. While he was talking with Beth, he noticed some people watching him. He figured they had to be the feds. Since he knew he was being followed, he e-mailed me after he talked with Beth. We set up our own little misdirection with a few of our friends so we could lose the feds. I met him late last night when he gave me this envelope to give to you. He knew the feds would be back onto him soon. We cooked up this nice little plan to get you the envelope without anyone noticing. He also wanted to be sure to lead them away from you to give me this chance to get you the information. I like Sky and all, but I ain't goin' to prison for you or him."

"How did he know the people watching him were feds?" asked Rachel.

The man gave a half laugh. "That Sky is a sneaky bastard. While he was on the phone with Beth, he wrote down the license plate numbers of the cars the men were sitting in. After he got off the phone, he went online and tracked the plates down to the FBI office in Atlanta. He figured you were gonna ask that question. That Sky is one smart son of a bitch. And lady he knows you 'cause he said that he got all your questions answered before you could even ask 'em."

"So what's in the envelope?" asked Rachel. Rachel had a pretty good idea what was in the envelope. It had to be the information she requested Beth get from Sky. She wanted to know how much this stranger knew and if he could help.

"Beats the hell out of me," the man replied. "All I know is that it must be big. Sky set up this scheme to get this information to you without the feds tying you in. The feds are hungry to get to the bottom of what's goin' on, and they want someone's ass. Early this mornin', a bunch of feds turned up at Sky's place around four. Sky and his friends heard the fed cars pull up. They trashed the computers to keep the feds from getting any good inside info on our hacks and then bugged out before the feds could get their hands on 'em. They probably searched what Sky and the boys left behind, which wasn't much. They left just enough information behind, so the feds thought they had something to work with. That Sky thinks of everything! When Sky gets back, he's gonna have to replace the computer shit the feds confiscated. If he doesn't, he's gonna have some pissed-off friends to answer to."

The man looked over at Seth. "Your arm getting tired of holdin' that piece?"

Seth nodded. "Now that you mention it, yeh . . . my arm is getting a little tired."

The man cautiously put his gun into his lower back, wedged inside his belt, and started to walk away when Rachel called to him, "What's your name?"

The man waved his hand in the air as he shouted back, "Lady, you're too much fuckin' trouble. I don't want you to know who I am." The man walked off into the rain. He turned down an alleyway across the street and was gone as casually as he appeared.

Seth put his gun back into his holster. "Do you want me to go after him?" asked Seth.

"No . . . I think he's done enough," replied an exhausted Rachel. "I think we should let him well enough alone." Rachel stuffed the envelope the man gave her into her coat to keep it dry. "I don't think there is anything else here in Atlanta for us to do right now. Let's head on back to the car and start making our way to Miami."

Seth knew Rachel was right. The feds had Sky, and a local cop from Surf City wouldn't carry any weight with them. Rachel, the naval ensign, who was on leave for a funeral, would most likely find herself in the stockade for getting entwined in a federal investigation. The fact that the investigation involved stolen arms and someone who hacked into federal computers on her behalf seeking information would not go over well with her commanding officer.

Seth and Rachel returned to the Marta station to make their way back to the downtown parking garage and their marine corps car. Rachel pulled the envelope out from under her coat while they were riding along in the subway. She looked around the subway car to see if anyone was watching her or possibly the information she just acquired. She was not sure what she had, but Sky was going to jail for it, so whatever it was, it must be important. Rachel cautiously opened the envelope and withdrew the contents. There was an article from a Web site called Cubans for a Free Cuba. The article mainly discussed the purpose of the organization, who the main officers were, and other general information, including the organization's activities and its organizational structure. There were what appeared to be three internal memorandums from government agencies based upon the letterhead that Sky provided. He apparently acquired the memorandums by hacking into federal agencies. One was from the Office of Naval Intelligence. Rachel chuckled to herself to think some hacker who had eluded federal authorities until now could access the Naval Intelligence files, and yet she, who at one time had a high-level security clearance to much of the files, was now denied.

The memorandum from the Office of Naval Intelligence consisted of little more than the general information about the Cubans for a Free Cuba that she read from the organization's Web site, compliments of Sky. The other two memorandums were from the Federal Bureau of Investigation and the Central Intelligence Agency. Rachel read the memorandum from the CIA first. The memorandum focused on the organization, Cubans for a Free Cuba, and its current proactive efforts to overthrow the Cuban government by the use of political pressure. The memorandum was written by a field agent that quietly snuck in and out of Cuba. He spent his Stateside time blending into the Miami Cuban population. The memorandum also discussed Julio Chavez, the vice president, and his efforts to undermine the current president of the organization, Carlos Hernandez. According to the memorandum, the CIA was sympathetic to Julio Chavez because he had grown impatient with Carlos Hernandez's slow and deliberate progress to oust the current regime. The CIA was enthusiastic about entertaining more aggressive angles on dethroning Fidel Castro. Rachel could tell the memorandum was a little dated since Fidel's brother Raul had since taken control of Cuba. It made sense to Rachel that the CIA would be entertaining new angles on dethroning Raul Castro. She knew they never got over the debacle of the Bay of Pigs incident when Cuban exiles landed at Playa Giron in the Bahia de Cochinos, on Cuba's south coast, hoping to instigate a coup. The whole plan went awry when U.S. bombers failed to neutralize the Cuban air force. Rachel read on when she noticed that the page she was reading turned to a series of garbled numbers and letters. Apparently, the CIA had noticed someone hacked into the system and scrambled the information. The FBI memorandum too covered most of what the CIA memorandum covered but mentioned an Operation Razorback. The FBI memorandum also turned into a series of garbled numbers and letters that Rachel assumed was the same reason as the CIA memorandum she was reading.

CHAPTER 57

As Rachel read the documents she received from Sky's friend, Seth scanned the subway car. Like Rachel, Seth was not sure what he was looking for. Seth knew how cops and federal agents dressed, but if they were real undercover cops, all bets were off. He settled on looking for people who kept looking their way. As Seth stood watch, he began to wonder why the FBI, the military, Sky, Rachel, and he could not work together to solve Hugh's death. Why were they trying to avoid the FBI and maybe the CIA? Hugh was a marine. It only made sense that they should all be working together.

By the time Rachel finished the FBI article, they had already made their one transfer and were now back at the downtown Marta station from which they had started. Rachel and Seth exited the station and walked in the direction where they parked the car. While they headed for the parking garage, the sun was pushing past the clouds, slowly warming the day.

Rachel looked sternly at Seth. "We need to get to Miami—fast!"

"I had a feeling you were going to say that," Seth responded very matter of fact. "We were heading there all along if I remember." Seth felt put out with Rachel when she emphatically demanded they get to Miami *fast*. "Hopefully the information you got from Sky was worth this little side trip."

Rachel sensed that Seth was annoyed about something. "Is there something you're not telling me?" inquired Rachel.

Seth wanted to tell Rachel that they should have gone directly to Miami bypassing Atlanta but thought better of it. How valuable was the information Sky accumulated anyhow? Why couldn't he have just e-mailed her the information? He began to tell Rachel about his concerns about why the federal agencies and they couldn't work together but thought better of that too. He also was curious about what she read in the articles that Sky put together for her. The entire ride back from Lennox Square, Rachel seemed engrossed in the information she received from Sky, yet she had shared nothing with him. Seth also felt that he and Rachel were accomplishing something important, but what? He wasn't quite sure what it was other than solving Hugh's death, but he felt somehow there was something important that they would need to figure out before they could solve Hugh's death. He would need to read the documents that Rachel had been poring over, so maybe he could steer the investigation in the right direction.

"No," responded Seth, interrupted from his thoughts. "It's just that with Sky now out of the picture, we have no other reason to stay here in Atlanta. We certainly can't bail him out. If we do, we say good-bye to this investigation." Seth paused as he heard himself talking out loud. "When we were at Hugh's funeral," continued Seth, "Terry told me that he thought the dead guy found at the Murphy's house near Surf City was Cuban. In Cherokee, Al Stewart eluded to the fact it was Cubans from Miami. Miami keeps popping up. Miami with its large Cuban population makes sense. I just think we should have gone directly there without this side trip to Atlanta. Remember, Rachel, we came to Atlanta to see your computer pal."

"I agree that we have no reason to stay here in Atlanta. I said we needed to go to Miami. I also agree we can't do anything for Sky. His dad is going to have to get him out of this one." Rachel began to tear up. It was the first time she had shown any real emotion. She was tired from the past several days. Maybe it was the fatigue finally catching up to her along with her brother's death and now an old friend arrested by the feds while assisting her.

Seth realized he had been callous with his comments, but he had felt all along they should have gone directly to Miami. Seth felt that they could have just as easily had Sky call them or e-mail them the information. He felt that with all the covert meetings, it was wasted time in Atlanta. His police and military instincts were now taking over, just get the job done! He knew that it was more important to stay on a trail while it was hot.

Seth slowed the brisk pace they had set while returning to the car and took Rachel in his arms to comfort her. She seemed to melt into his embrace. "I'm sorry. The policeman and maybe the ex-soldier in me took over, and when that happens, I am sometimes too direct. I know you said we needed to go to Miami after you had a chance to go over the information Sky gave you. I just thought he could have e-mailed you or called you to give you the information."

Rachel calmed herself. She pulled away from Seth. "No, I'm sorry. I'm a military officer, and becoming all whiny is no way for an officer to act."

Seth took her back in his arms. "Sometimes it's okay to be a little human and sometimes even a girl."

Rachel glanced up at Seth as if to say thank you, but she continued. They walked almost a block when Rachel pulled herself from Seth's comforting arms in order to confront him. "You're right about the information we got from Sky . . .

We could have gotten it over the phone or by e-mail. But what we also got are documents that show the FBI and the CIA knows something. One other thing, one of those agencies is hiding something, and that's what we're going to need to figure out." Rachel used the one-block walk to regroup, and now she was fired up. She turned and hurried her pace to the garage.

It was now Seth who had his back to the wall. He caught Rachel just as they entered the lower level of the parking garage. He was impressed with her instincts and how she was putting the information together. "Hold on! You've got a point, but you have the advantage of reading over Sky's documents. I haven't seen them yet!"

Rachel felt she made her point, but Seth was right in that he had not read over Sky's documents. Maybe once he read them, he would be as fired up as she. Hopefully he, too, would come to the same conclusions as she once he read Sky's information.

Seth continued on, "Let's go to Miami together, and while you drive, I can read over what you have. Maybe we can put out heads together and come up with a plan when we get to Miami."

Rachel was pleased with Seth's idea of formulating a plan for how they would proceed once they got to Miami. It was a long drive that they should be able to brainstorm and come up with a game plan. They could also use the time to rehash the information they had. "Fair enough," replied the triumphant Rachel.

When they got to the car, it was almost four o'clock in the afternoon. They both jumped in the marine corps sedan and pulled out of the garage. Seth had the Atlanta map in front of him before Rachel could pay to leave the garage. Rachel asked the attendant for directions to Interstate 75 south as she paid to leave the parking lot. The attendant gave Rachel the directions that Seth promptly confirmed. After about fifteen minutes of various turns and the early rush hour traffic, Seth and Rachel were on Interstate 75 bound for Florida and Miami. Traffic was heavy until they drove beyond the greater Atlanta suburbs. They decided to drive as far as possible before pulling off the road for the night. Seth reviewed a Florida map that he found in the glove compartment, and they decided to spend the night in Ocala, Florida.

CHAPTER 58

During the early part of the drive to Ocala, Rachel drove while Seth read Sky's documents. He made notes on things he felt they needed to follow up on when they got to Miami. Eventually, Seth and Rachel opened their conversation to more personal matters. Seth talked about the time he spent in the marine corps and his role in Operation Desert Storm in Iraq. He discussed the months he spent away from Maribeth and the toll it took on their marriage. He also talked about his time with the Charlotte Police Department. He told Rachel about the time he was in a shoot-out in Charlotte. Seth and his partner had responded to a failed bank robbery. The would-be robbers were caught when a savvy teller activated the silent alarm. Seth and his partner were around the corner and caught the robbers coming out of the bank. When they identified themselves as the police, one of the robbers opened fire. Seth wounded one of the robbers, and the other immediately surrendered. Seth explained that after telling Maribeth about the shoot-out, she demanded that he leave the Charlotte Police Department as soon as possible. She feared for his life when he was in Operation Desert Storm, and she would not go on any longer worrying about him every day he left for work. His departure from the Charlotte Police Department eventually led to his position as chief of the Surf City Police Department per a friend's recommendation. Seth told Rachel that initially he felt he was underqualified for the position, but after the interview, he felt it was a position that he could handle. It was not long after he was interviewed that they made him an offer for the position. He also told Rachel how Maribeth was killed by a drunk driver on their way home from a Super Bowl party.

Rachel talked about her duties with Naval Intelligence in Washington DC. She did not get into too much detail because much of what she did was classified but provided Seth with enough information to impress him. Rachel also talked about growing up in the Cleveland, Ohio, area with her brother Hugh. They were the only children their parents had. Periodically, she would tear up reminiscing about Hugh and periodically had to stop talking to regain her composure.

Eventually Seth and Rachel talked about Major John Lawrence and what they knew about him, which was very little. What they did know about Major John Lawrence was that they liked him. They felt he was passionate about what he did. It caused them to look at their own careers and wonder if they were as passionate about what they did as Major John Lawrence. They sensed that he was not necessarily the best person suited to investigate the break-in at Camp LeJeune and the resultant murder of Rachel's brother Hugh, but they loved his attention to detail and his determination to solve the crimes.

When they reached Ocala, they found themselves worn-out from the early-morning start. They pulled into a Hampton Inn just off Interstate 75 and once again got adjoining rooms.

"Hey, what do ya say we go out and get something to eat before it's too late and things start shutting down around here?" asked Seth. Not knowing the area that well, Seth felt that his immediate surroundings lived and died with what Interstate 75 was doing at a particular hour.

"Sounds like a plan. How 'bout Mexican? I'm in the mood for a margarita," replied Rachel. Her spirit was upbeat despite the fatigue.

"Good idea! I could use a good margarita." Seth called the front desk to ask about some of the nearby restaurants, more specifically Mexican restaurants. As it turned out, there was a Mexican restaurant within walking distance of the motel. Once they freshened up, they went to the restaurant. Within a few minutes, they arrived at a restaurant called Ole and took a booth toward the back of the restaurant. They took a booth that was more private in case they wanted to discuss the investigation.

"Are you ready for a couple of margaritas?" inquired Rachel. She was almost giddy.

"Order away!" When the waitress arrived, Rachel ordered margaritas for both she and Seth. The waitress recommended ordering a pitcher since the restaurant was having a special on them that evening. They ordered a pitcher of margarita and began drinking. After they ate, they decided to stay and order another pitcher of margarita. They laughed and commiserated about things that had happened to them since they had met and about their lives in general. They toasted Major John Lawrence and Sky. They also toasted Terry for his forensic work. They toasted Sky's friend with the gun. Eventually, they noticed they were the only customers remaining in the restaurant. They noticed an exasperated waitress and several of the other staff beginning to eye them in hopes that they would soon be leaving. Seth looked at his watch; it was past midnight.

Rachel awkwardly, leaning across the table, motioned for Seth to lean toward her. "I think they're ready for us to leave," remarked Rachel as she burst into laughter.

Seth leaned back and panned the room. "I believe you're right." No sooner did Seth wave to the waitress before he noticed the bill in front of him. Seth looked over the bill and realized he and Rachel had had four pitchers of margaritas. Rachel insisted on splitting the check. After several banters, Seth agreed to split the check. After they paid and exited, they heard the manager close and lock the door behind them. They looked at each other and laughed out loud.

They made their way back to the motel following the path they took to get to the restaurant. They found themselves staggering and each helping to hold the other up. As they reached Seth's room, he unlocked the door, and they both fell through the doorway onto the floor and on top of each other. Rachel gazed into Seth's eyes. He looked back into her eyes and pressed his lips to hers. She responded with exuberant passion. They climbed to their feet as they continued kissing each other passionately. Seth lifted Rachel, and she wrapped her legs around Seth's waist and her arms around his neck. Seth clumsily pushed the door closed with his foot, and Rachel snugly wrapped around him. Seth stumbled to the nearest of the two double beds in his room, and they both fell onto the bed. They slowly began undressing each other as they continued to kiss passionately. Seth began caressing Rachel's body, and she his. It wasn't long before the passionate kisses turned to making love to each other. Seth felt a touch he had missed since Maribeth passed away. When they were done, they fell onto their backs exhausted. They both were lying next to each other gasping for a breath, and neither saying anything.

Rachel quietly got up and went into the bathroom. She stumbled as she made her way. The margaritas were still in control of her intoxicated body.

Seth remained lying in bed. His mind began to race. He thought about everything that had happened between them the past several days. He was still very much inebriated, and it wasn't long before his attention turned to Maribeth. Was it too soon for him to get mixed up with another woman? His mind raged, *What have I done?* Rachel returned from the bathroom and curled into Seth's arms. Seth dared not move for fear that Rachel would know what he was thinking or did she want to talk about a relationship. He would not know what to say if they started talking. He needed time to think with a clear head before he could carry on such a deep conversation with her. Before long, they both drifted off to sleep.

CHAPTER 59

Seth awoke and looked at his watch. It was just past seven in the morning. It was the latest he had actually slept in days, maybe months. He could see the morning sunlight peering around the edges of the drapes. Seth could hear Rachel in her shower in the adjacent motel room bathroom. The doors separating the two rooms were still open from when they checked into their rooms the previous day. Seth's mind drifted back to what had happened when they returned from the restaurant. He was quickly consumed with guilt. He was reliving the same guilt that ate at him until he forced himself to fall asleep. He got up and pushed in the door that separated the two rooms, leaving it only slightly ajar. He went into his bathroom to start to get ready for the rest of the trip to Miami. They would drive to Miami and pursue the people that killed Hugh and stole the arms from Camp LeJeune. Seth was in front of the mirror with lather covering his tired face, ready for his morning shave with a towel wrapped around his waist, when Rachel entered the room.

Seth was startled when he saw Rachel behind him in the mirror as he prepared to take the first swipe with the razor across his face. His hand was quivering. Was it his anticipation of what she was going to say, or was it too much tequila from the night before? He couldn't help noticing how beautiful she looked standing there in a white T-shirt, a pair of fitted blue jeans, and cowboy boots. Her hair was still wet from her shower, and she had no makeup on.

"Good, you're not quite dressed," remarked Rachel.

"Excuse me," responded the surprised Seth. Seth turned to face Rachel as he placed the razor on the counter.

"I wanted to talk with you while you were in a somewhat"—Rachel gave a long pause and a smug grin—"awkward situation." She gave Seth a gentle jab to the stomach with her fist as she took a seat on the edge of one of the beds in the room nearest to where Seth was standing. "I know you feel guilty. I feel guilty too. You and I have had several stress-filled days. I think the booze tore down some of our defenses, and we had sex, pure and simple sex!" Seth started to talk when Rachel promptly cut him off. "Don't say anything. I rehearsed this over and over in my mind this morning. I'm not asking for anything. We just both needed something last night, and it happened. I know you loved Maribeth and probably still do. I'm not interested in being the replacement or the transitional girl, so don't feel obligated."

Seth stood there speechless at first. After a brief moment, he finally uttered, "Okay." He felt stupid. Was that the best he could come up with?

Rachel could see that Seth was struggling with what to say. She had rehearsed everything in her mind, and now she had caught him off guard. Rachel felt pleased with how she handled herself and Seth. She decided to make an excuse to leave him while he collected his thoughts. "I'm going over to the diner. You want me to get you anything?"

Seth was still trying to gather himself together. "Sure . . . how 'bout a cup of coffee and maybe a bagel with cream cheese." "You got it." Rachel turned and left the room. As she walked to the diner, she began to chuckle to herself at what had just taken place. She never felt so in control with any man. She clearly caught him off guard, and she liked it! Rachel couldn't help herself she jumped into the air; as she did, she punched her fist into the air. She felt so alive!

CHAPTER 60

Seth finished getting ready. He was packing the car when Rachel returned from the diner. While he was getting ready, he digested his conversation with Rachel. He was grateful for her candor, but he felt he had to say something, but what? He knew he still loved Maribeth and always would. Seth tried to figure out something to say to Rachel, but he realized he wasn't sure of his own feelings for her. He wondered if his interest in Rachel was because of their working relationship or if his feelings were real. Seth had heard how people of the opposite sex become intimately entangled as a result of their working relationship. He also wondered if it was too soon for him to become involved in another relationship. For the time being, Seth did not want to be trite with Rachel, so he decided to say nothing. He felt that somehow between now and before they returned to Surf City, a situation would present itself for him to figure out his feelings and express himself appropriately. Seth also felt that to rush to say something, anything, may come across as retaliatory or just wrong, and he would feel foolish for having done so. He needed time to think.

Rachel returned from the diner and handed Seth his coffee and bagel. "Let me get my things, and we can get on our way." Rachel returned to her room and gathered the remaining items still left unpacked.

Seth got in the car and ate the bagel with cream cheese and drank the coffee while he waited. He found the map of Florida and began reviewing the directions to Miami. For the most part, Seth felt that if they got lost, it was because aliens moved Miami. It was almost a direct route to Miami from where they were. He also took a look at the Miami map on the reverse side of the Florida map. Getting around Miami was going to be a challenge.

Rachel returned from her room. She took the keys from Seth to unlock the trunk of the marine corps car and threw her bag into the trunk. She jumped into the passenger's seat returning the keys so Seth could start the car.

Seth looked at Rachel. He could tell she was enjoying herself. He gave her a smirk and put the car in gear. He pulled the car up to the lobby area for them to check out. They each paid their bills.

They found a nearby service station and filled up with gas before entering Florida's Turnpike. Seth noticed behind the cash register that the Florida Lottery was up to $10 million dollars and couldn't help but buy a five-dollar lottery ticket. He looked at Rachel holding up the ticket so she could see it. "I'll split it with you when I win."

"I'm gonna hold you to it," replied a still-gleaming Rachel.

Rachel's mind returned to the task at hand, finding out who killed her brother. "When we get to Miami, I think we should go see Carlos Hernandez. He's the president of the Cubans for a Free Cuba. I have an address that I found in the information we got from Sky. They're located just off Calle Ocho in Little Havana."

"I agree," commented Seth. "That's where I was thinking we should start."

They stopped near Orlando for a bathroom break and to stretch their legs. Rachel asked if she could drive for a little while. Seth welcomed the opportunity so he could get a second glance at the information Sky accumulated for Rachel and once again review John's notes. He found that the more he read the same information, the more he would pick up additional little items that he missed on a first or even second pass—not necessarily in the words themselves but the implied meanings. Seth read the information quietly and deliberately for almost an hour before he looked at Rachel. "According to Sky's information, the take at Camp LeJeune was the largest of any of the armories."

"And that bothers you?" asked the incredulous Rachel. "I mean, aside from the fact there are fanatics running around with high-powered, military-grade weaponry?"

"Yeh. All the installations offered the same opportunity to steal pretty much the same types of weapons. They all had almost the same quantities of weaponry." Rachel watched as Seth pondered his next statement. His face presented a bewildered expression. "They always had access to larger quantities but went for smaller amounts although they did go for the big enchilada this time," commented Seth.

"But they were interrupted by Hugh and his partner," replied Rachel, trying to help Seth decipher his thought process. "What are you thinking, Seth?"

"I know but that's not it. If you're stealing to sell the weapons, every time you go out, you try and get all you can. But not these guys, they only take same amounts until this last time. They're just too . . . disciplined."

"Disciplined" was not the word Rachel was expecting to hear about the people that killed her brother. "Yeh . . . so! Maybe they were just getting bolder since they got away with the previous times."

"It says to me that the LeJeune robbery was probably their last. I think they were at the end of whatever they were trying to accomplish," stated Seth. He felt proud of his hypothesis. He now needed to find a way to prove that he was right.

The remainder of their drive consisted of idle conversation while Seth scanned a detailed map of Miami that they picked up at the service station prior to entering Florida's Turnpike. Seth enjoyed some of the quiet time they had in the car while Rachel drove. It gave him time to mull over in his mind the previous night's events and his feelings for her.

CHAPTER 61

Rachel and Seth stopped a couple more times along the way before they arrived in Miami shortly after two thirty in the afternoon. As they rode around Little Havana looking for the office of the Cubans for a Free Cuba, Seth could not believe everything he saw was in Spanish. "Amazing to me, everywhere you look it's in Spanish. This is America."

Rachel could not help but laugh. Seth appeared so naive for someone that had served in the marine corps, a policeman in the largest city in the Carolinas and traveled to the Persian Gulf. *Maybe he had been in Surf City too long?* Rachel thought. "This is the heart of the Cuban American people," replied Rachel. "How do think they're going to display their signs?"

"Yeh, I know but this is still America!"

"Just park the car. We're here," replied Rachel. Rachel was growing tired of Seth's naive look at America. She felt he needed to be more in touch with an ever-changing America.

Seth parked the car in front of the building. They got out of the car, and Seth gave one more look at the local population and decor of the buildings. He felt that if he were in Havana, that was what it would surely look like.

Rachel and Seth entered the two-story building for Cubans for a Free Cuba. They stepped inside the old wooden door leading into a foyer. There was an old desk covered with papers just inside the doorway where a person apparently had been working. There were two flags that decorated the sparse foyer—the Stars and Stripes and a Cuban flag. The terrazzo flooring dated the building. The walls were painted a mint green. A polite, well-dressed woman approached them from one of the hallways leading into the foyer. Recognizing the two as Anglos, the woman spoke English with a slight Spanish accent. "May I help you?"

Rachel quickly spoke up. "We're here to see Mr. Hernandez."

The woman quietly responded, "Is he expecting you?"

Seth spoke up this time. "We're here on police business."

The woman politely nodded her understanding and said, "Please wait here." She directed Rachel and Seth to an adjacent room. The room was decorated with some rattan furniture and pictures that they assumed were of Cuba. Seth could hear the woman climb a flight of terrazzo steps he noticed earlier from the foyer.

Seth looked at Rachel. "Well, she was so nice."

Rachel laughed at Seth once again. "Yes. And she speaks English too."

Seth caught Rachel's sarcasm and ignored the remark.

A couple of minutes later, the woman returned with a man wearing a nice shirt and slacks; he definitely had the air of someone who was living in the tropics. "My name is Carlos Hernandez. May I be of help?" Carlos spoke with a heavy Spanish accent, but Seth could tell the man was well educated.

Seth and Rachel were pleased he was accessible. "Is there somewhere we can go so we can speak in private?" inquired Seth.

"Certainly, we can go to my office," responded Carlos. "Please follow me." He started down the hallway leading up to the terrazzo steps. "I'm sorry, but our elevator is not working. We'll have to take the stairs."

They walked down a narrow corridor and went up the stairs the woman had previously climbed on their way to Carlos's office. While Seth and Rachel walked along, they noticed several more black-and-white pictures on the walls of what they assumed to be Cuba. There were pictures of sugar fields, coffee fields, men tending to their nets next to boats, various pictures of urban areas, etc. The building itself appeared to have been built in the 1950s. There was a sign next to an elevator indicating in Spanish something that both Seth and Rachel assumed meant that it was not working. The rooms had terrazzo floors, jalousie windows, and ceiling fans and open windows in place of air-conditioning. They both felt it was very warm even for this time of year. The walls in Carlos's office were laden with pictures of various award ceremonies Carlos had attended. Most of the pictures reflected him receiving some kind of award. There were also numerous pictures yet again of what Seth and Rachel assumed to be Cuba. Behind Carlos's desk were the American and Cuban flags. Carlos motioned for Seth and Rachel to be seated in front of his desk as he took his seat behind his desk.

Carlos opened a wooden box on his desk and offered Rachel and Seth a cigar. "They're hand-rolled right in here in Miami on Calle Ocho," commented Carlos. Seth took a cigar, but Rachel declined. Carlos pulled out some clippers for the cigars. He offered the clippers to Seth. Seth used the clippers and then returned it to Carlos. Once both men were ready, Carlos produced a large wooden match and lit it. He leaned forward and lit Seth's cigar and then his own.

Carlos made himself comfortable behind his desk as he took a few long drags on the cigar. "My secretary said you are here on police business. May I see your badges?" inquired Carlos. He leaned forward, puffing on his cigar in anticipation of receiving police badges for his inspection.

Seth loved Carlos's panache. He was obviously quite comfortable in *his* surroundings and was unmoved by any police interest in his affairs. Seth smiled politely as he produced his chief of police badge for Surf City, North Carolina. Rachel was annoyed with Carlos's attitude but begrudgingly produced her identification indicating she was an officer with Naval Intelligence. Seth could tell that Carlos was going to play games with the two of them. With all of Carlos's pomp and circumstance, he was playing the role of a powerful Cuban representative with all the political muscle, and they were the lowly policemen. Seth had seen the attitude before, but today he was going to play along. Seth felt confident Rachel had never experienced this kind of person in her duties with Naval Intelligence. He was going to enjoy watching her become aggravated with Carlos. If Rachel hadn't been such a smart-ass with him when they arrived in Little Havana, maybe he would have been less enthusiastic to watch her get played.

"Curious badges for here in Miami," commented Carlos. "What seems to be the problem?"

Seth continued to enjoy Carlos's demeanor. He knew that most often when people displayed this kind of personality, they were hiding something and eventually would do something stupid. He wasn't sure if it was going to happen today, but Seth was willing to play along and wait for Carlos to make a mistake.

Rachel and Seth started to talk at the same time. Rachel stopped herself, and Seth continued on. "We are here investigating a robbery of some arms at a military base in North Carolina in which a young MP was killed. We were wondering if you had any information that may be helpful to our investigation."

Carlos looked inquisitive. "I'm not sure how a robbery in North Carolina and someone's death would be linked to me or my organization."

Seth paused briefly to collect his thoughts before replying. "Mr. Hernandez, we are not implying that you or your organization was involved. During the robbery, one of the thieves was killed. We have not identified who he is as of yet, but we do know he is of Cuban descent, possibly Cuban American," commented Seth.

Carlos sat back is his chair and took a couple of slow methodical drags on his cigar. "You have a dead Cuban shot during a break-in in North Carolina and suddenly you find yourself in the Cubans for a Free Cuba office in Miami. Why is that? Do you have a picture of this person?" inquired Carlos. "I'm sorry, but I do not know every Cuban in America. You watch the movie *Scarface*, and suddenly all Cubans are all drug dealers?"

Seth started to reply when Carlos cut him off.

—

"Am I to know every Cuban in America?"

Seth could tell that Carlos was playing the wounded victim and was trying to put them on the defensive. Seth smiled in an effort to help break the tension rising in the air. "No, sir, it is not that way at all. We also have reason to believe that someone, not necessarily affiliated with your organization, may be involved in stockpiling arms for some other purpose. We are asking for your assistance to apprehend a killer or killers. We would also hope to prevent arms falling in the wrong hands. We would hate to see anyone else hurt. We felt that your organization would be eager to assist and prevent the Cuban American people from falling into an unfavorable light with the rest of the American people." Seth was proud of the way he turned the conversation back on Carlos. He took a puff of his cigar and waited for Carlos to react.

Carlos sat forward. "I'm sorry for the break-in and the loss of a MP. But I do not have any information for you. I also have a duty to help to protect my fellow Cubans here in Miami"—Carlos looked into Seth's eyes—"no matter what the rest of the American people may think."

Rachel spoke up. "The person who was killed was my brother."

Carlos paused and said to a sullen Rachel, "I'm very sorry for your loss, but I do not have any knowledge of this travesty."

Seth knew the conversation was over. He knew that he would get no further information from this bantering. It was Carlos's town, and they had no authority. What was worse, Carlos knew it. Seth stood up disgusted but did everything in his power not to let Carlos see it on his face. He thought round 1 goes to Carlos. "Well, thank you for your time," commented Seth as he extended his hand.

Carlos stood and shook Seth's hand. "You're very welcome. Come back if I can be of any further assistance."

"We'll do that," replied Seth cautiously.

Rachel was annoyed as she stood. She started to ask another question when Seth cut her off. "I'm sure Mr. Hernandez has answered all our questions," commented Seth. Seth politely remarked, "Thank you again for your time." Carlos acknowledged Seth this time with a slight nod of his head.

Rachel shook Carlos's hand but said nothing. Once they were outside, she turned on Seth. "He knows something!"

"Maybe he does, but he wasn't going to tell us anything right now. We have nothing to link him to any of this other than a dead Cuban, and that is certainly not enough to make him talk. We need to find something to rattle him so he'll talk or make a mistake." Seth was a little aggravated with Rachel for not maintaining her cool in front of Carlos. Seth knew his job well from police instincts and training, and maintaining one's cool was paramount.

Rachel knew Seth was right. For all his naive reactions toward Little Havana, he had good police and people skills. "You're right," conceded Rachel.

CHAPTER 62

"Is there anyone else in Sky's information that you think we should see?" asked Seth. He was racking his brain trying to remember the information he had so deliberately read over on their trip to Florida. Seth felt that Carlos was not a dead end but that they should explore other avenues. Hopefully, Sky's information had something more they could try and sink their teeth into.

Rachel sifted through the papers Sky put together for her along with her notes she had compiled. She skimmed the pages as quickly as she could. "There is this guy named Julio Chavez. According to Sky's information, he is involved with some kind of splinter group within the Cubans for a Free Cuba organization as well as being the organization's vice president."

Seth absorbed what he heard from Rachel before he spoke. "Yeah, I remember that name. I guess Carlos is keeping his enemies as close as he can." Seth paused to gain direction on where he thought they should go next. "Does Sky's information indicate what kind of relationship the two have with each other, other than the obvious?"

"Not that I see," replied Rachel, hoping for a little more information from Seth.

"I have a choice for you. One of us needs to stay here and shadow Mr. Hernandez. I think he knows more than what he is willing to say. The other should go have a talk with Mr. Chavez."

Rachel pounced. "I'll go see Mr. Chavez!"

Seth smiled. "Be nice to Mr. Chavez. Do you know where to look for him?"

Seth was rather sarcastic in his retort. He did not want Rachel to make the same kind of scene with Julio Chavez that she made with Carlos Hernandez.

"I have an idea," replied the enthusiastic Rachel. She reached into her handbag and retrieved her cell phone. She called the Cubans for a Free Cuba main telephone number she had scrawled on a piece of paper. A woman answered the phone. Rachel assumed it was the same smartly dressed woman they had just seen. "Is Mr. Chavez there?"

"No, Mr. Chavez has left for the day. May I take a message?"

"No, thank you." Rachel hung up and returned to the car.

"Well, what did you find out?"

"He has left for the day."

"Well, I guess that takes care of that," responded Seth.

"Maybe not!" Rachel pulled out the information she received from Sky. She skimmed over the information once again. "Shit . . . there's nothing here." She was disheartened to be stymied once again. "Wait . . . I have another idea. Follow me," commanded Rachel.

She headed for a coffee shop that had some computers. "Are any of these hooked up to the Internet?" inquired Rachel to a young Hispanic-looking man behind the counter.

"Yeah, all of 'em," replied the young man.

"How much to use them?" asked Rachel.

The young man pointed to a sign that was written in Spanish and English saying "Free Internet Use to Customers."

Rachel turned to Seth. "Get us something to eat while I do a little Internet searching." Rachel headed for a computer against one of the walls. Seth headed for the counter to order some food and drinks. After he ordered, he found a chair opposite from where Rachel was sitting. He handed Rachel her drink and took a sip out of his.

"Any luck?" asked Seth.

"I almost have it. Got it!" Rachel was thrilled to find Julio Chavez's address on the Internet. She also noted the address of the restaurant they were sitting in and did a MapQuest for directions.

Just as Rachel got the directions, the shopkeeper announced their food was ready. Seth returned to the counter and brought the food.

Rachel gulped down half of her sandwich when she announced, "I'm going to his house. Should I take a cab?" She gave Seth a wounded-animal look hoping he would relinquish the car keys. Rachel thought about leaving Seth stranded in Little Havana without a car. "You may need the car if Carlos leaves."

Seth looked at the pout on Rachel's face and then handed her the key. "You take the car. I'll manage. I'm hoping with all his contacts, he'll be on foot. I'll just meet you back at the motel. No later than seven!" Seth stared sternly into Rachel's eyes as he spoke. They decided earlier to get a couple of rooms at the Marriott Bayside in Fort Lauderdale. Rachel had been pricing motels and hotels from brochures she had picked up riding along Florida's Turnpike. She decided on the Marriott Bayside because she was not familiar with either

Miami or Fort Lauderdale, and the pictures in the brochure made the hotel look enticing. "Yes, Dad."

Seth looked as Rachel in disapproval. "Just try and not piss anybody off!"

Rachel headed out to the car, leaving Seth to finish his sandwich. She pulled out a map of Miami to get her bearings along with the MapQuest directions. She figured out the roads she needed to take. She waved good-bye to Seth, still sitting in the restaurant and trying to keep an eye on the front door to the Cubans for a Free Cuba. Rachel put the car in gear and headed for Julio Chavez's home.

—

CHAPTER 63

Julio Chavez was meeting with Juan Mendoza and several other people that were part of the splinter group of the Cubans for a Free Cuba. Julio had spent years methodically organizing those people that he felt he could count and rely on to orchestrate something of the magnitude that was coming to fruition. They had spent nearly eighteen months stockpiling stolen arms from various military installations throughout the southeastern part of the United States and were now making their final arrangements to move the arms covertly into Cuba.

Larry Shays attended the meeting. He was the only Anglo there. Larry was not well liked by many of the Cubans, not because he was an Anglo but many thought he was a loudmouth. Many feared that because of his loud mouth, he would inadvertently reveal their plans or draw unnecessary attention to their organization. The Cubans, especially those who had emigrated from Cuba, knew that Fidel Castro had spies throughout South Florida. Those same spies were now Raul's, Fidel's brother. Often at Cubans for a Free Cuba meeting when plans were made to undermine Cuba on an international level, a special meeting would be held to reduce the participants to a select few to prevent pro-Castro sympathizers from foiling their plans. Larry was allowed to remain with Julio's group solely because of his limited contribution at Camp LeJeune, prior to Hugh's death. Larry helped lay out much of the groundwork for the break-in as communicated to the group through Julio's mystery Insider. This Insider was known only to Julio and obviously had access to the central surveillance system at Camp LeJeune. The access was pivotal to the break-in. Larry had walked out of his hospital room at Camp LeJeune and caught a plane out of Jacksonville, North Carolina, for Miami. Everyone was surprised to see him, especially Julio. In addition to having contributed to an MP's death, he was now AWOL, which drew even more unneeded attention to their group. His flight plans from Jacksonville, North Carolina, to Miami made him easy to trace by the military police. The only thing helping to avoid his capture right now was the fact he could blend into the vast population of Miami along with the greater Fort Lauderdale and Palm Beach areas. Everyone figured Larry would stay his remaining two months in the marine corps until he was discharged, but Larry wanted to be a part of the "mission" and get the recognition he felt he deserved. Several of Julio's men were now eager to expel him from the group, but did not know how. He knew too much, and if he were expelled, they feared he would go straight to the police or, worse, the media in retaliation.

Julio's plans were to go forward the next evening with the shipment of the weapons. Larry's surprise visit was not going to be a deterrent. His unexpected showing was going to be an inconvenience and would have to be dealt with immediately. He would need to assign someone to keep Larry out of sight and, if necessary, use force to do so.

The shipment would go out late Saturday night or in the early hours Sunday morning. Julio had divided the group into two smaller groups. One group was to coordinate the acquisition of trucks to move the arms from the warehouse location, which only a select few in the group knew, to the location that was to transport the arms to Cuba. Julio personally made the arrangements for transporting the arms from Miami to Cuba with the assistance of his Insider. No one knew from where the arms were to leave Miami or how. From Key West, Florida, it was only ninety miles to Cuba; from Miami, it would be farther. It would be easy to move the shipment by boat or plane. Julio only told the men that the trucks should be prepared to travel within a one-hundred-mile radius. Saturday night after the trucks were loaded was when he planned to tell the men how the arms were to be delivered to Cuba. The men felt that they would most likely be airlifted into Cuba, but a boat or boats were still within the realm of possibility. Several of the men that were part of the warehouse group had flying experience and were eager to put their flying experience to use if called upon. Many of the men received their training flying combat missions over Vietnam, and some of the younger guys got their training during the Gulf Wars.

A second group was to travel by boat to the Bahamas. They had left earlier in the day. Those traveling by boat were to meet up with a small group of Cuban nationals about one hundred and fifty miles east of Havana in a cove. The second group, comprised mostly of younger men with recent military training, would join up with the Cuban nationals and help provide training and logistics. There was a considerable amount of opposition to the team travelling through the Bahamas to carrying any weapons because their "pleasure boats" would have been easy pickings to Cuba's navy. The ruse was to have them slip into the melee casually.

The group in Cuba was to be lead by Tito Mendoza, Juan's relative. The plans slowly culminated over the past year and a half. Since a limited number of flights were going from Miami to Cuba, messengers slowly passed information back and forth. Nothing was ever to be written. The messengers would memorize paragraphs of nonsensical information and relay the information to someone on the other end. Each side would then decipher the nonsensical information. In fact, none of the messengers had ever even seen Tito. Tito himself used couriers who met the people from Miami in predetermined open-air shops and cafés to prevent from being tracked down by the interior ministry, the Cuban equivalent of the FBI. He did not like the idea of using couriers but was concerned that if he were captured, the plans would certainly fail.

CHAPTER 64

Rachel found her way to Julio's house. Along the way she negotiated countless traffic jams, stoplights, and a few wrong turns. It didn't take long for Rachel to recognize the problems foreign tourists would encounter trying to get around Miami. As she pulled up in front of Julio Chavez's home, she was amazed to see that his beautiful home was set on a waterway that she assumed led to Biscayne Bay. Rachel had driven along the perimeter of Biscayne Bay on her way to Julio Chavez's home. She enjoyed watching the numerous boats on the bay, the people scantily dressed as they roller-bladed along a path skirting the water's edge along the public access, and the beautiful vistas. She saw several cruise ships readying themselves for a voyage. Rachel started to pull into the driveway but saw that it was already occupied with two Mercedes Benz, a Cadillac, and a Range Rover. The street was inundated with cars of similar caliber as those in Julio's driveway. Rachel parked the conspicuous military vehicle in the street between a BMW 540i and a Hummer. She walked to the front door along the ornate brick walkway trimmed with bright colorful flowers. She rang the doorbell that produced radiant chimes. A few moments later an elderly woman dressed in maid's clothes answered the door. In Spanish she asked Rachel something that Rachel assumed meant, "What did she [Rachel] want?"

"Mr. Chavez?"

"Si, Senior Chavez." The woman closed the door leaving Rachel waiting outside. She didn't mind since the humidity was almost nonexistent for this time of year, and it gave her a few minutes to digest her surroundings. Rachel had already made a mental note of the cars in the driveway, but she also thought about the accessibility for boats. She remembered from John's notes and the military police reports that it appeared the thieves had gotten away by boat. Why not drive the boat up to Julio's back door? She started to walk around to the side of the house to see if there was a boat dock and possibly the *boat* when she heard the front door start to open.

The front door opened, and Rachel saw a well-dressed man in his early to midthirties, guessed Rachel, at the door. Before the man could say a word, Rachel inquired, "Are you Mr. Julio Chavez?"

"No, he's in a meeting. May I be of help?"

"No, I must speak with Mr. Chavez." Rachel appreciated the man's polite rapport, but she was determined to speak directly with Mr. Chavez. She felt she was entitled.

"He's in a meeting right now!" The man was quickly becoming annoyed by Rachel's persistence.

"Do you know how long he'll be?" countered Rachel.

The man was utterly annoyed with this pushy woman. "No! He is in a very important meeting, and it could last for hours."

Rachel decided she would not take no for an answer. "Well, I'll wait right here if I have to."

The man gave Rachel a stern look. Without saying anything, he closed the door. The man returned to the meeting that Julio was directing. He motioned to Julio, who then excused himself and walked over to the man. The man whispered, "Julio, there is a woman at the door who says she has to speak with you. I told her you were in a meeting, but she refuses to leave until she speaks with you."

Julio was aggravated by the interruption. "Okay." Julio calmly addressed everyone in the room, "Excuse me, gentlemen, it appears we have a guest who will not leave until she meets with me. I will be right back. Please . . . make yourselves at home." As Julio exited the room, the men began milling about and talking among themselves.

Julio motioned to his housekeeper to come to him. "Please get my guests something to eat and drink. I will be right back."

Julio went toward the front door where Rachel was waiting for him. He called to the man who had summoned him to meet with Rachel, "Call the police." Julio continued to the front door where Rachel waited. Julio opened the door. He looked almost eye to eye with Rachel. "I am Julio Chavez. What seems to be the problem?"

Rachel looked at yet another well-dressed slightly older man with a calm demeanor. She could tell he was well educated. "My name is Ensign Rachel Dugen, I have been sent here by the Office of Naval Intelligence to investigate the theft of arms from a military base and the death of a military police officer during that robbery." Rachel felt that if she came from a position of authority, even though she lacked actual authority, Julio may give her the respect she needed to get answers.

Julio smiled. "Ensign, if you are conducting an investigation representing the Office of Naval Intelligence, why are you standing in my doorway in a blouse and a pair of jeans? I would assume that if you were operating at the behest of our government, you would be dressed appropriately, in uniform." Julio was a master of finding ways to keep a person off balance when in a confrontation.

Rachel was shocked by his response. It was not the retort she expected. She had to think quickly. "I can appreciate your expectations of my attire. However, I have spent the past several days investigating this case. I have been from Washington DC, to Atlanta, and now here in Miami investigating the perpetrators. I can assure you, my appearance is not the most important thing to me right now." Rachel did not feel it was important to include the detour to Cherokee. In fact, if Julio were involved, the lark to Cherokee would give him an advantage. "Now . . . what can you tell me about the theft?" Rachel felt vindicated by the way she turned the questions and answers back to Julio.

"Why do you feel that I may have any information relating to a theft of some arms?" responded Julio. "I am a well-respected businessman here in Miami, and for you to imply I had anything to do with nefarious activities, I find insulting!"

"Well, a man was found dead whom we believe was directly involved in the robbery." Rachel ignored Julio's comment regarding his social status, charging forward with her inquiry. "The man was a Cuban immigrant. Furthermore, we know he was associated with the Cubans for a Free Cuba more specifically, your tight little group within a group." Rachel was reaching for anything she could, trying to get some response from Julio. She didn't want to say "splinter group" for fear that he would take exception. She was already pushing the limits.

As Rachel was concluding her probing questions, she heard a car pull up behind her. She turned to see two Miami-Dade police deputies get out of their squad car. They calmly approached Rachel and Julio. One of the deputies inquired, "What seems to be the problem, Mr. Chavez?"

Rachel was surprised the policeman was so familiar with Julio. She promptly turned to speak to the deputy, "I'm with the Office of Naval Intelligence investigating the theft of arms at a military installation and the death of a military policeman during that theft." Rachel flashed her badge to make things look more official. Rachel felt that by taking the initiative, it may help to deflect their inquiry of her.

The deputy nodded to acknowledge that he heard Rachel and glanced at her badge. The deputy proceeded to look at Julio, expecting some kind of response.

"I explained to her that I knew nothing of any theft at any military installation. This woman has continued to harass me. I have been polite, but she has been rude to my guests and me. I have politely requested that she leave, but she refuses." Julio waited for the deputy's reaction. He hoped that his response would bring an end to Rachel's questions. He did not have time to deal with her. They were doing their final planning, and her unexpected arrival had interrupted those proceedings. Rachel noticed that the man she had initially spoken with had now returned. He attested to everything Julio said. The deputies got on either side of Rachel and ushered her over to her car. Julio started to dismiss Rachel to the deputies when Rachel shouted out, "What can you tell me about Operation Razorback?" "Operation Razorback" was a name she picked up from the governmental information she received from Sky. Sky's information became garbled right after the name. Rachel figured that since she was getting escorted away, she might try one last effort to get some kind of reaction from Julio.

Julio gave Rachel a disturbed look as he entered his house, closing the door behind him. He started to return to the meeting, but Larry Shays stepped in his way. "Get out of my way, Larry!"

"Sounds like that bitch knows too much," commented Larry.

Julio looked crossly at Larry. "Stay out of it! She doesn't know anything. She is trying to get a reaction from us. Leave it alone and she will go away."

CHAPTER 65

Rachel was outside defending herself from the two deputies. She had shown them all her military identification, but they continued to question her.

The deputy who seemed to be in charge was Deputy Pedro Fernandez. "Ensign, if you are investigating what you say you are, why didn't you notify the local police? That's protocol. We would have assisted you."

Rachel was thinking as fast as she could. She and Seth were clearly operating on their own volition. "We are under strict orders to keep our investigation on a need-to-know-only basis. A break-in at a military installation where weapons are stolen could cause a nationwide panic. We also need to rule out that it may have been an inside job. Ya know, a conspiracy. We are not sure how far this mess reaches." Rachel was trying to impress the deputies and worm herself out of a precarious situation. She figured part of her story was true, so why not stretch it a little to see how far it would take her.

Deputy Fernandez started to grin but held back. "Conspiracy? Come on!"

"Seriously, a conspiracy?" Rachel held firm.

Deputy Fernandez had heard enough. "Ensign, I don't care what orders you have. You are to stay away from Mr. Chavez. He is a well-respected member of the community."

"And that gives him the right to hinder a federal investigation?" Rachel refused to back off.

"Look, Ensign, I don't want to get ugly. If you want to question Mr. Chavez, you're going to have to do it through proper channels. That means city hall and kissing all the right asses along the way." Deputy Fernandez stepped back, indicating the conversation was over and to allow Rachel to get in her car.

"All right, I will leave Mr. Chavez alone for now," responded a disgruntled Rachel.

"Thank you, Ensign Dugen," replied Deputy Fernandez. The two deputies headed to their patrol car.

Rachel felt some sense of relief that they were allowing her to go. She was elated that they didn't check her story with Naval Intelligence in Washington DC or with her commanding officer. She also felt she had gotten some positive feedback from her Operation Razorback comment from Julio. It wasn't much, but it was a start. Rachel started to get into her car and then paused and looked at the deputies. Using her best distressed-girl voice, she asked, "Can you tell me how to get to the Marriott Bayside in Fort Lauderdale?"

Deputy Fernandez walked back over to where Rachel was standing and gave her directions. He also instructed her to follow him because he had to get on Interstate 95 since they were both headed in the same general direction.

As Rachel drove away, she noticed Carlos Hernandez take the parking space she just vacated in front of Julio's house. Rachel paused to look for Seth following Carlos, but did not see him anywhere. She pulled out a map to provide an excuse for the waiting deputies. Deputy Fernandez backed the patrol car up next to Rachel. Rachel waited as long as she could. She motioned to Deputy Fernandez that she was ready to go. Rachel made a mental note to talk with Seth about seeing Carlos arrive at Julio's house.

CHAPTER 66

In the interim, Seth started to become familiar with the local Cuban coffee and cigars. He found a local establishment on Calle Ocho that rolled the cigars by hand in the shop. Seth remembered Carlos Hernandez talking about it when he and Rachel met with him earlier in the day. He snacked on Cuban pastries with guava and made friends with a few of the locals while trying to blend in as a tourist, not that it took a lot of effort.

After almost two hours of waiting and watching, Seth saw Carlos exit the Cubans for a Free Cuba headquarters. Seth followed Carlos for a few blocks before he entered a parking lot and got into his BMW 740 series car. Seth turned to hail a cab. About a block away he saw three cabs. The cabdrivers, all Cuban American, were deep in conversation and never noticed Seth motioning to them. He ran over and tried to stir them into action so as not to lose sight of Carlos. The cabdrivers could not be concerned with rushing into anything. Banging on the roof of the foremost cab finally caught one of the drivers' attention; however, by this time Carlos was long gone.

With Carlos's disappearance, Seth felt the day was over. He decided he would meet up with Rachel to find out what, if any, luck she had with Julio Chavez. Seth came to the conclusion that they needed to reevaluate their limited information and come up with a new strategy on how they should proceed with their investigation. Seth had the cabdriver take him to the Marriott Bayside in Fort Lauderdale, the hotel he and Rachel elected to stay based on some brochures they gathered while driving to Miami. He knew he had to make some overdue telephone calls, especially to Ned, his trusted deputy in Surf City, once he got to the hotel.

—

CHAPTER 67

Carlos Hernandez arrived at Julio's house as Rachel was pulling away. He did not expect to see her. He noticed her taking a long determined look at him as he pulled into park on the already-congested street with the driveway already full. Carlos parked his car leaving the rear of the car slightly protruding into the street. As he approached the front door to Julio's house, three men ran out, almost knocking him over. Carlos recognized two of the men from the Cubans for a Free Cuba meetings. The other man that Carlos did not recognize was an Anglo. He dismissed the encounter because he was more concerned with the meeting he had had earlier in the day with Seth and Rachel. Was Julio up to something that could endanger the goodwill of the organization he created? Carlos rang the doorbell. The door opened, and the elderly maid who greeted Rachel earlier stood in the doorway.

"Maria, is Julio home?" Carlos knew Maria from his previous visits with Julio over the years since they had been working together. Their conversations were always in Spanish as was the custom for many of the traditional Cubans in Miami. Spanish was the only language spoken at the Cubans for a Free Cuba meeting unless a non-Spanish speaking person was invited to attend the meeting.

"Yes, please come in," responded Maria. "Please wait here." Maria left Carlos in the foyer and interrupted Julio's meeting. Maria informed Julio that Carlos was there. Julio once again politely excused himself. This time he adjourned the meeting and found Julio standing in the foyer. He knew that whenever he and Carlos met, it was a minimum of an hour.

Julio greeted Carlos in the same informal manner they had grown accustomed to. "What can I do for you, Carlos?" inquired Julio.

Carlos noticed several members of the Cubans for a Free Cuba file out of the living room and head for their cars. He remembered them because he knew they had had an allegiance to Julio's splinter group. It was this reason for

Julio's appointment to vice president of the Cubans for a Free Cuba. It was not uncommon for Julio to have people over at his house, but with the unexpected visit of Rachel and Seth at his office and now this meeting, Carlos was confident Julio was up to something. But what?

Carlos said, "Today two people came to see me regarding a theft of some weapons at a military base in North Carolina. One was from the Office of Naval Intelligence, and the other was a policeman from some town in North Carolina. They also said that a Hispanic man was killed during the break-in. Do you know anything about this?" As Carlos spoke, he grew even tenser with each passing word.

Julio recognized Carlos's agitation. "Relax, Carlos." Julio put his arm around Carlos's shoulder and led him to the patio area behind the house overlooking the river and the boat docked next to the house. A gentle waterfall adjacent to the patio area was made for a tranquil setting along with the abundance of fresh flowers that recently bloomed. He called to Maria to bring a couple of Hatuays, a popular Cuban beer, to them. Julio took a seat next to Carlos. They exchanged idle conversation until Maria returned with the Hatuays and a slice of lime to complement the beer.

Carlos sensed that Julio was stalling. "Tell me, Julio, what is this all about?" demanded Carlos, once Maria left the men alone.

Julio took a deep breath and then leaned forward looking at Carlos with a disdained expression. "A few of my men and I—"

Carlos interrupted, "A few of YOUR men?" He was annoyed that Julio would dare refer to any members of the Cubans for a Free Cuban as "my men."

"Yes, a few of my men and I have acquired a small arsenal that we are sending to Cuba to help overthrow the Cuban government. Your efforts, old man, are too slow!"

Carlos began to interrupt again when Julio put his hand in Carlos's face to signal him to stop interrupting. As Julio talked, he appeared to gain confidence and take control of the conversation. Julio was debasing Carlos of his power. Carlos felt helpless to do anything but listen. He could feel the fear rising within him. Julio was becoming more powerful in both Miami and in his organization, Cubans for a Free Cuba.

"We have plans to send the weapons soon. Tito is already waiting for delivery."

Carlos knew who Tito was and his relationship with Julio. Their relationship was another thorn in Carlos's side. The Cuban nationals recognized Tito as a powerful freedom fighter. Carlos always knew that if Cuba was ever overthrown, Tito would most likely be the cause, and Julio would stand to gain considerable power because of their relationship.

"Antonio was the man killed during the acquisition of the weapons in North Carolina." Carlos noticed that Julio avoided terms like "break-in," "theft," etc., when referring to what he and his men were doing. Julio seemed to be justifying his criminal activities with terms like "liberated," "for a greater purpose of," and "the liberation of Cuba."

Carlos could not believe what he was hearing. "Tito is in on this? His son is dead?" Carlos stood to leave. He knew things obviously had gone beyond his control. "Julio, if this thing falls apart, I want your word that you, and you alone, will take full responsibility."

Julio stood and looked Carlos directly in the eye and said, "Done!" Carlos began to leave when he turned to Julio one last time. "Who else is in on this?"

"No one!"

Carlos knew Julio was hiding something. "No one?"

"No one!"

Carlos left Julio on the patio slowly drinking his Hatuay and basking in the glow of his forthcoming accomplishments. He could tell that Julio was enjoying the control he had over him.

CHAPTER 68

Rachel continued to follow the sheriff's deputies as they made their way toward Interstate 95. Once on Interstate 95, they found themselves in the midst of rush hour traffic. Rachel tried to stay close to the patrol car driven by Deputy Fernandez, but cars periodically forced their way in front of her. When the Dolphin Expressway, another major artery, merged with Interstate 95, her car slowed to a crawl and then stopped.

Wham! Rachel was startled by the sound and shards of shattered glass spraying throughout the interior of the military sedan. Rachel turned to find a young boy reaching across the backseat of her car and grabbing her purse. She lunged at the boy to grab him; as she did, the car lurched forward careening into the back of a white Lincoln Town Car stopped in front of her. When the car lurched forward, the boy momentarily was knocked off balance and dropped her purse. The boy stabbed at the purse once again, taking hold of the strap. Rachel lunged while trying to keep her foot on the brake and snatched hold of the other end of the purse strap. The boy, scared, let go of the strap and ran down an embankment adjacent to the interchange.

Deputy Fernandez had been watching Rachel periodically in his rearview mirror. He shouted at his partner, "Jesus Christ, she's in a smash and grab!"

"Who? Where?" shouted Hernandez's partner, uncertain as to where Deputy Fernandez was referring.

"Ensign Dugen," Deputy Fernandez yelled as he pulled the car out of traffic. They leapt out of the car. Fernandez saw a young boy running down the adjacent embankment. Rachel had put her car in park and was giving chase after the young boy.

"Hold it!" shouted Deputy Hernandez.

Rachel heard the shout and stopped.

Deputy Fernandez's partner continued the pursuit.

Deputy Fernandez approached Rachel. "Where do you think you're going?"

—

"After that boy!" responded an exasperated Rachel.

"Ensign Dugen, the Miami Police Department doesn't even go down there unless they have to, and even then, they take an army with 'em," commented Deputy Fernandez.

"Your partner is down there," rebutted Rachel.

"And I'm keeping an eye on him," answered Deputy Fernandez. "He won't be going very far."

Rachel and Deputy Fernandez began looking over the fender bender damage while the deputy chased after the young boy.

"Anything missing?" asked Deputy Fernandez as he moved on to the broken car window.

"No," answered Rachel. "I think when I rear-ended the car in front, the boy lost his grip on my purse. When he tried the second time and saw that I wasn't going to back down, he took off."

Deputy Fernandez's partner chased after the boy, who leapt over a second guardrail and disappeared into a neighborhood. The partner continued the chase but lost sight shortly after the boy leapt over the second guardrail. He questioned some of the kids in the neighborhood who promptly denied any knowledge of anything, including questions that the deputy never even posed. The partner returned where he found Rachel and Deputy Fernandez examining the damage as a result of the accident.

"Sorry but I lost him. Anything of value stolen?" inquired the partner.

"No. It appears that when Rachel hit the car, the boy dropped her purse and took off running," responded Deputy Fernandez.

The owner of the Lincoln Town Car was an elderly woman. She was still behind the wheel of the car trembling from the low-impact accident. She cautiously got out of her car and walked over to where both Deputy Fernandez and Rachel were standing. The elderly woman assessed the damage to her car and then irately approached Rachel. She was shaking her finger and yelling at Rachel in German and periodically English with a German accident.

Rachel looked at Deputy Fernandez as if to ask, "What is this woman saying?" The woman's continuous yelling incensed Rachel. She started to retaliate when she noticed concentration camp numbers tattooed on the woman's forearm. She felt that she needed to let the woman speak her peace, and then she would let Deputy Fernandez and his partner deal with the agitated woman.

Deputy Fernandez turned to his partner. "How about getting this nice lady's license and registration information, and I will get the same information from this woman," referring to Rachel. Deputy Fernandez did not want to let the elderly woman know that he knew who Rachel was. He feared she would accuse him of conspiring with her regarding the accident.

Rachel excused herself and returned to her car. There she fumbled through her purse and glove compartment looking for her driver's license and the car's registration for Deputy Fernandez. After several frantic minutes of searching, Rachel found the information and handed it to Deputy Fernandez.

Deputy Fernandez took the requisite information and subsequently handed everything over to his partner. "How 'bout writing up the report?" Deputy Fernandez turned his attention back to Rachel. "It appears that you had a full day, young lady."

"Not one I care to repeat, thank you," responded an exasperated Rachel.

"You know, we're going to have to give you a citation."

Rachel was flabbergast. "What the hell do you mean? That son of a bitch throws a brick through my window trying to rip me off, and because the car lunged forward, you're going to give me a ticket?"

"The problem is you hit that elderly woman. If it was up to me, I'd let you go, but somebody has to pay for that lady's car."

After a moment, Rachel settled down. She was clearly rattled by what occurred. She looked at the deputy and apologized for losing her temper with him. Deputy Fernandez gave a half laugh. "I hear it all the time. You know these smash and grabs can be dangerous. People get hurt and sometimes killed."

Rachel looked back at the deputy. "After the day I've had, he's lucky I didn't shoot him."

Rachel pulled out her Berretta and showed it to the deputy.

"Nice gun. You better put it away before someone thinks a cop is getting assaulted and calls in a SWAT team," jabbed Deputy Fernandez.

They both laughed. Rachel put the gun back in her holster, and the two continued to idly chat until Deputy Hernandez's partner completed writing up the report.

Deputy Fernandez handed Rachel her part of the report after she signed the citation. She walked around and got into the car. Deputy Hernandez leaned in the window on the passenger's side and whispered to Rachel, "I'll see if we can't lose the citation."

Rachel smiled and thanked him. She got directions once more from Deputy Fernandez.

"Do you want us to follow you to the hotel?" asked the deputy. "We'd hate for you to have any more problems.""No, I think I can stay out of trouble until then." Rachel put the car into drive and continued on Interstate 95. The traffic had had a chance to subside somewhat while Deputy Fernandez's partner wrote up the accident report. The traffic was now moving smoother. There were people darting in and out of traffic at what Rachel thought was at breakneck speeds, but everyone seemed to take the driving in its stride.

CHAPTER 69

Larry had heard Julio's conversation with Rachel and the two deputies from inside the front door. When he heard Julio coming in, he retreated around the corner into the living room so that Julio wouldn't know he had been listening in on his conversation with Rachel and the police deputies. Larry motioned to the two men he arrived with earlier at Julio's house.

Larry spoke to the two men in his company. "Look, Julio is having a problem with that woman who is just leaving. He wants us to put a little scare into her. You know, to get her to back off." Larry was feeling invincible since his escape from Camp LeJeune and the unsubstantiated lies he told Major John Lawrence. He wanted to make an impression on his two Cuban companions. The men raced out almost knocking over a well-dressed man coming up the sidewalk. They waited outside of Julio's house in a Mercedes owned by one of the Cuban men in Larry's company. It seemed that Rachel was going to take forever to get going. They watched as she reviewed a map and had a follow-up conversation with the police deputy. Eventually they followed Rachel as she made her way through the neighborhood and onto Interstate 95.

"Jesus Christ," shouted Larry. He watched as a teenager smashed Rachel's window with a brick. "This woman is going to take an eternity to get where she is going at this pace." He instructed the driver to continue up Interstate 95. Once they were out of sight of Rachel and the patrol car, they pulled off onto the shoulder. They waited once again for Rachel to make her way up Interstate 95. It was close to an hour before they saw her pass them with the broken window heading north on Interstate 95. They pulled onto the interstate as soon after she passed. They followed her to the Marriott in Fort Lauderdale. They found a parking space near the hotel entrance and followed Rachel into the hotel lobby.

CHAPTER 70

Rachel found the hotel a little before eight in the evening. She was exhausted from the long day she put in. She couldn't help but think that since embarking on the pursuit of her brother's killer, it was the hardest she had worked in years. She parked the car in adjacent garage to the motel. After walking through a maze of corridors, Rachel found the front desk and asked about her room. Seth had already checked both of them into the hotel in separate rooms. They had hoped for adjoining rooms like before, but there was a boat show in Fort Lauderdale. Rachel had no idea how lucky she and Seth had been in getting the rooms at all in Fort Lauderdale. There were two last-minute cancellations, and Seth's timing could not have been more fortuitous. The lady at the front desk handed Rachel her key. Rachel thanked the lady and asked for directions to the elevators that were tucked around the corner in an alcove. As Rachel made her way, her mind began to wander to the day's events. She was eager to tell Seth about seeing Carlos Hernandez at Julio Chavez's house. She was also anxious to find out what Seth learned while trailing Carlos Hernandez. She was also curious why she had not seen him at Julio's house, but then she remembered he would have had to take a taxi to get there. Rachel pressed the button for the elevator that seemed to take an eternity to arrive. She stepped into the elevator along with three polite men in suits who raced on at the last second. The elevator slowly made its way to the fifth floor. Rachel and the three men stepped off the elevator when it arrived at her floor. Rachel made her way to her room and opened the door. As she stepped into the room, the three men shoved her into the room and onto one of the double beds nearest the front door. Two of the men held Rachel down on the bed and covered her mouth with duck tape. The third man who looked to be in the military with his short haircut punched Rachel across the right side of her face. He then punched her in the stomach and face over and over again. Rachel was limp with pain yet still conscious.

The military-looking man leaned over Rachel and whispered into her ear, "Get the fuck out of South Florida. You don't know what you're in the middle of, bitch." The man then produced a knife and in a very calculating moment nicked her under her left eye about a half-inch long.

Rachel felt the sting as the blade tore through her delicate skin. She held back the tears that tried to force their way out. She would not let this bastard see her cry. She could feel the warm dampness of her blood stream down the side of her face. Rachel looked defiantly into the man's face. She wanted to remember every detail of his face.

Larry leaned over and whispered once again into Rachel's ear, "If you don't leave, I'm gonna cut you into little pieces and dump your whore ass into Biscayne Bay. The sharks and crabs will enjoy feasting on you." Larry found a telephone book in the nightstand. He struck Rachel on one side of her head and then the other with the telephone book. With the force that Larry was using, the telephone book began to come apart. Fortunately, Rachel fell unconscious after the first blow.

Larry walked around the room before he saw a small trash can. He picked up and tossed it to one of the men. "Here . . . fill it up 'bout halfway," commanded Larry. The man took the trash can into the bathroom, returning within minutes with the trash can half filled with water when he gave it to Larry. Larry stood over Rachel, who was lying bloodied on the bed. Larry callously poured the water over Rachel's head, reviving her.

Rachel felt the rude awakening of the cold water being dumped on her head. She managed to raise her head enough to turn it to see three men staring down at her. *Damn*, she thought. *This hellish nightmare still isn't over.* Just then Rachel saw a phone book coming down across her head.

Larry struck Rachel several more times with the phone book until she became limp and unconscious once again. The final blow caused Rachel's unconscious body to roll onto the floor. He tossed the shredded phone book onto one of the beds. Larry looked at the two men staring in awe. "I think she got the message. Let's get the fuck outta here."

CHAPTER 71

Seth had been in his room for several hours. He tried calling Rachel in her room and on her cell phone repeatedly without success. He looked at his watch and wondered why he had not heard from her. It was after ten in the evening. He wondered what could have happened to her. He thought surely she would have called if she were going to be tailing someone this late. Had she gotten lucky at Julio Chavez's house, and he was helping her solve the case? Instead, a cool chill came over him, and he began feeling uneasy. He called down to the front desk to inquire if Rachel had called and left any messages. The woman at the front desk put him on hold and then courteously replied that she did not have any messages for him. Seth began to hang up when another woman came on the phone. The woman spoke with a slight Spanish accent. "Ms. Dugen came in almost two hours ago. She asked for directions to the elevators and headed up to her room."

"Hang on." Seth put the phone on the nightstand. He opened his door to step across the hall to her door and pounded, but no one answered. He ran back to his room where he found the extra key he received when he checked them in to the hotel. Seth opened the door noticing that the room was in disarray. He saw a telephone book on the bed almost in shreds and covered in fresh blood. Seth stepped cautiously into the room, fearing that the intruder that caused this disturbance could surprise him at any moment. He found Rachel lying on the floor on the other side of the bed. She was unconscious. Her face was swollen, with several cuts and bruising that begun to show. Seth force Rachel's eyelids open so he could look into her eyes, which were both bloodshot. Seth raced back to his room and yelled into the phone, "Get me a doctor—now!" He hung up the phone and raced back to Rachel's room. He made sure the door was left ajar and then went to the bathroom to grab some towels that he soaked in the sink. He wet the towels with cold water and knelt on the floor next to Rachel's side, leaving the water running. He wiped her face repeatedly. The towels were covered in blood as fast as Seth could wipe her battered face. A man representing himself as the hotel doctor came in with two other men who identified themselves as hotel security. Seth noticed official-looking blazers indicating "Marriott Hotel Security" on two of the men. The doctor wore a button-down shirt and slacks. Seth noticed a large case more commonly carried by paramedics.

The men began to question Seth who promptly held up his hand to stop their questions. Seth turned his attention to the doctor, who was kneeling next to Rachel treating her wounds. "Is she going to be all right?"

The doctor replied, "I can't tell yet. I'll let you know." The doctor began taking her vitals. He placed a call to 911, requesting an ambulance for someone who had been "severely beaten," and the Fort Lauderdale police.

Seth could tell by the doctor's expression that he was gravely concerned about her condition. Once he felt that Rachel was being properly attended to, he began to accept the questions from hotel security men. At first, they felt maybe Seth and Rachel had had a domestic dispute. Seth could tell from their questions that he was their principal suspect. He didn't blame them; had he arrived on the scene, he felt he would have followed the same line of questioning. Seth showed them his police badge and found Rachel's Naval Intelligence badge in her purse that was lying on the floor. Most of the contents of her purse had been dumped onto the floor as if someone was looking for something. He explained that they were on an investigation but kept everything very general to avoid probing questions that were not for discussion with security guards at a local hotel. Seth asked if the hotel had surveillance cameras. The two men from hotel security stated they did. Seth inquired if he could view the surveillance tape, hoping to catch a glimpse of who might have assaulted Rachel.

"Hey, Doc . . . would ya mind if I left for a few minutes?" Seth called to the hotel doctor.

"No, but don't go too far. I'm gonna need to get some more information from you. The hospital is gonna have a few more questions for you as well," replied the doctor, never looking up as he attended to Rachel's wounds.

Seth and the two hotel security guards left the room and headed for the hotel surveillance room while the hotel doctor continued attending to Rachel. Before they left, Seth jotted down the doctor's cell number and gave him his cell number. Seth made it known to the doctor that if he needed anything, he was to be notified immediately. When Seth and the security guards arrived at the surveillance room, Seth was happy to see the number of cameras covering the entire hotel and surrounding grounds. They found the video that covered the hall where Seth's and Rachel's rooms were located. In a matter of moments, Seth and the two guards were watching three men forcing Rachel into her room.

Seth looked angrily at the security guards. "Why didn't someone see this take place?" he demanded. The two guards looked at the man assigned to the surveillance camera room. The man sat quietly in his chair. It was obvious to everyone in the room that the man was trying to create some conceivable explanation. Seth could see the man was consumed with guilt. It was obvious to Seth that the man had not been watching the surveillance screens.

One of the guards demanded, "Well, answer the man!" He was looking sternly at the man who was attending to the video they were watching and responsible for the surveillance.

There was a long silence. The man felt the tension level rising in the room. "I got called away!"

The other security guard responded, "By whom?" The lead security guard felt certain the man was lying.

There was again a long uncomfortable silence. "My girlfriend called me!"

The hotel manager arrived as the two security guards queried the man assigned to watch the surveillance cameras. "Well then, you can collect your personal belongings. You're fired!" the hotel manager curtly resounded.

One of the other guards printed out several copies of the men's faces and an array of other photos for Seth to take with him. They printed extra copies for the Fort Lauderdale police who were just now arriving and for their own files. The hotel manager commented that he would follow up with the Fort Lauderdale police on the information they discovered and have them view the surveillance footage. He alluded to their insurance carrier's requirements that once a crime was reported, an insurance report and notification to the local authorities were required. Seth ignored the hotel manager's comments regarding the insurance carrier, figuring he was posturing for protection against a lawsuit. He was more concerned with talking to Rachel before the Fort Lauderdale police got too involved. Seth wanted to determine if the men who had beaten her were somehow linked to their investigation.

CHAPTER 72

Before they left the surveillance room, Seth wanted to call Terry Ingram, the Jacksonville police forensic investigator. He found his business card in his wallet and called him at home, figuring due to the hour he was most likely to be there.

A groggy Terry answered his phone on the second ring, "Yeh." He was tired, but it was not unusual for him to get calls in the middle of the night.

"Terry . . . it's me, Seth, Seth Jarrett with the Surf City Police Department."

Terry yawned trying to remember who Seth was in his groggy state. After a brief pause, he perked up, "Oh yeh, Seth, what's going on?"

"Rachel Dugen, the Naval Intelligence Officer, was beaten up last night, and I have some hotel surveillance photos of the guys we think did it. I'd like for you to try and run them through your system and see what turns up." Seth was hoping that the Jacksonville Police Department had the computer resources to connect with federal and state law enforcement agencies across the country.

"Is she all right?" asked Terry.

Seth appreciated Terry's concern, but he wanted to keep the conversation short and get back to Rachel before the Fort Lauderdale police arrived. "Yeh, she's all right. Can you do this for me?"

Terry sensed Seth's impatience. "Sure, but like I said, before we've got to do this on the QT. Can you e-mail the pictures to me?"

Seth looked at the security guards in the room with him. "Can I e-mail him the pictures?"

One of the security guard smiled broadly back. "You bet! What's the address?" He sat down at one of the computers in the room and prepared the information for e-mail.

Seth got the information from Terry who had the security guard e-mail the pictures to Terry's home e-mail address. "Where can I reach you?" asked Terry.

Seth gave Terry his cell phone number and the hotel's number as well. He demanded the hotel to track him down if Terry should call back. The hotel staff was extremely compliant after everything that had happened. Seth left the guards in the surveillance camera room and returned to Rachel's room.

CHAPTER 73

Much to Seth's disappointment, the room was filled with police officers, detectives, and some forensic investigators. The doctor was still attending to Rachel along with some paramedics that arrived while Seth was with the security guards. The paramedics had placed Rachel on a stretcher. Seth could see Rachel was now somewhat conscious. "You okay?"

A policeman stepped in front of Seth as he approached Rachel. Seth started to become defensive when the hotel doctor intervened. "He is with the victim," commented the doctor to the policeman.

Seth let the incident pass and moved next to Rachel. "I've had one hell of a day." Rachel was groggy from the beating she had taken and the sedative the doctor gave her. She could only speak out of one side of her mouth due to the swelling.

Seth looked over at the doctor and the paramedics. "Could you give us a couple of minutes?"

The doctor was reluctant. After a brief pause, he answered, "Sure, but only a couple of minutes!" The doctor gave Seth a wary look as he and the paramedics moved away from the stretcher.

Seth leaned over the stretcher so he could get closer to Rachel. "Do you know who did this?" Seth purposely did not show the surveillance pictures to Rachel so he could get a gut reaction from her.

Rachel painfully nodded yes. Tears streamed down the side of her face as she recalled each violent blow the three men inflicted on her delicate skin before she lost consciousness. She winced as she remembered being awakened with cold water being dumped on her face only to be struck down again so violently.

"Did you see their faces?"

She shuddered and then painfully nodded yes once again.

Seth found some tissue and wiped the tears from Rachel's face. He could see it was taking everything Rachel had to focus on his questions. "Do you want to do this later?" asked Seth.

Rachel shook her head no as adamantly as she could muster under the circumstance.

Seth gave Rachel a reassuring smile and produced the pictures.

Rachel shivered as she looked at the faces of the men. She was reliving the beating, blow by blow, as she looked through her tears at the pictures. She winced in agony and returned her attention to the pictures in front of her.

Seth knew it would be rough, but he felt Rachel wanted to see everything through. From the first time they met, Seth could see that she was not a person that would wait around. He knew time was precious, and he needed her focus now.

Rachel nodded that it was the men that had beaten her. Rachel called Seth down closer to her lips so she could whisper into his ear, "I saw Carlos at Julio's house before I came here."

"You're kidding!" Seth was enthusiastic. He felt that maybe they had applied enough pressure on Carlos to force him to make a mistake. Seth was still not sure of Carlos's level of involvement. The fact that their questioning of Carlos sent him straight to Julio, the leader of the Cubans for a Free Cuba splinter organization, was a good sign. Seth felt confident that if someone affiliated with Carlos's organization did the break-in at Camp LeJeune, Carlos would seek him or her out. Seth figured that by Carlos's immediate response, he either knew who did it or had a good idea who did. Seth felt sure that one or both had to be involved, but which one? Now the question for Seth was, how to force one of them out? Seth felt things might start to take shape now that they got some reaction out of Carlos.

Rachel slowly shook her head that she was not kidding. Rachel's confirmation was unnecessary since he knew that she was in too much pain to fool around. With each move of her head, Rachel grimaced.

Seth was holding and caressing Rachel's hand when the doctor returned with the paramedics. She had fallen asleep. The doctor called Seth over so they could talk without waking Rachel. Seth carefully let Rachel's hand go and walked over to where the hotel doctor was waiting.

"She needs her rest now," commented the doctor. "They're going to take her to the hospital emergency room for some x-rays and treatment. I can only do so much for her here. She'll probably be in the hospital for at least the night. My biggest fear is she may have internal bleeding and a concussion from the head trauma that she received."

Seth was receiving confirmation from what the doctor was telling him. From the bruises and swelling that Seth could see, he had come to his own conclusions that Rachel's situation was serious. Seth had seen a lot of similar trauma from his days in the marine corps and with the Charlotte Police Department. He started to follow the paramedics to the lobby when a policeman stopped him.

"We have some questions for you," stated the policeman.

Seth noticed the two security guards from earlier standing next to the policeman, who was holding copies of the surveillance photos.

"Sure," replied Seth.

The policeman was polite but direct. "She confirmed the photos, didn't she?" asked the policemen.

"Yes," answered Seth. Seth was a little surprised that they had not addressed their questioning directly with Rachel.

"We saw you talking with her and showing her the photos. We understand that you're a policeman in North Carolina. We felt that because of your relationship with the victim, you may make the inquiries a little less intimidating," stated the policeman. "Look, we're gonna try and get these pictures on the local news stations and in the local papers. Someone has to know who these guys are."

Seth was thrilled to hear the aggressive approach the Fort Lauderdale Police Department was taking. He figured their approach would catch whoever had beaten Rachel and flush out Carlos or Julio. But which one would be flushed out?

"Can you ask me your questions on the way over to the hospital?" asked Seth.

The policeman sympathized with Seth's concern for Rachel. "I don't see why not."

They made their way to a patrol car in front of the hotel. Seth got in the backseat. The policeman that had been doing the inquiry got in the passenger seat while another policeman drove. It was a short trip to the Fort Lauderdale Hospital.

Seth walked into the emergency room and asked a nurse behind the counter where Rachel Dugen was. She checked her chart and asked what relationship he had to Rachel. The lead Fort Lauderdale policeman intervened on Seth's behalf; after which the nurse looked into Rachel's situation. A doctor called shortly after they took Rachel into the emergency room. "Who is with Ms. Dugen?"

Seth shouted back, "I am!"

The doctor asked Seth what had happened. He looked at Seth the same as the hotel security people, assuming it had been a domestic spat gone awry. The doctor also asked Seth if Rachel had taken any medications. Seth informed him that the hotel doctor had given Rachel some medication and that was the only medication that he knew of. The doctor returned to the emergency room to resume treatment.

It was almost two in the morning before Seth could see Rachel again. She was in a hospital room by herself sleeping. A nurse in the room informed Seth that Rachel was heavily sedated and that it would most likely be morning before she would awake. Seth sat down in a chair beside Rachel's bed. He wanted to hold her, but he knew he shouldn't. She was hooked up to IVs. There were bandages around her head and hands. Seth assumed that her hands were bandaged because she had used them to shield herself from the blows. A nurse eventually came in and asked Seth to leave. He knew it was for Rachel's own well-being and politely agreed. As Seth exited her room, a chill came over him. He wondered if the men that had beaten Rachel had tried to kill her or scare her. He wondered that if they had tried to kill her, would they come back now that she was in the hospital and finished what they had started? Seth noticed Rachel's room was directly across from the nurses' station; and, as such, he decided there were too many people around for someone to cause her any further harm.

Seth elected to return to the hotel and get some sleep. He was exhausted. He would return first thing in the morning. He also felt that with a clear head, he could better plan his next move. It was obvious to him that he would continue alone. Rachel was too badly battered to continue with the investigation.

CHAPTER 74

Bam! Bam! Bam!

Seth awoke when he heard someone pounding at his door. Seth drew his gun as he softly made his way to the door. He peered through the peephole in the door and saw two men dressed in suits. Their suits looked to be of a higher quality normally worn by police detective, so he immediately eliminated the possibility of police detectives. The men were both about six feet in height and weighed about two hundred pounds. Seth could not help but think clones were now after him. He did not recognize either of them. He wondered if they knew that he was connected to Rachel and were coming after him now to try and close up any loose ends. He tried to figure out alternatives to confronting the men when he heard them bang on his door again.

Bam! Bam! Bam!

Seth threw on a pair of jeans and then raced over to the sliding glass door on the opposite side of the room leading out to a balcony overlooking the Intracoastal Waterway. He stepped out onto the balcony remembering he was the second to the last room on the hallway, but he was on the fourth floor. Seth climbed over the railing to an adjacent balcony and looked around the corner, hoping for a back way into the building. "Dammit," exclaimed Seth. As he looked, he saw there was no other way out of the building. He returned the way he came. He would just have to confront the men directly. Seth peered through the peephole once again. He was gripping his Glock in his right hand. His heart was pounding. He noticed that the men had turned to walk away but had stopped a few feet from his door to discuss something. Seth pressed his ear to the door to try and hear what they were saying, but it was muffled. Seth felt the time was right. Seth threw open the door, stepping into the hallway. "Hold it right there!" shouted Seth. Seth was aiming his gun at the two men.

"Jesus Christ," called out one of the startled men. They were both caught off guard. They both started to reach for their guns.

"I wouldn't do that if I were you," commented Seth.

Both of the men stopped reaching for their guns and slowly raised their hands. They were frozen in position.

"Who the fuck are you?" shouted Seth.

Both men slowly turned to face their adversary.

Seth looked at the two anxious men. One of the men looked like he belonged in Miami. He was a tall lean individual. His skin was tanned and weathered from several years in the Miami sun. His suit was lightweight, suitable for the warmer weather one would expect in Miami. The other man had a fair complexion, but Seth could tell given the right set of circumstance, he too would have a nice tan. His suit was made of a heavier fabric, indicating that he was most likely not from Miami. As Seth gazed upon the two men, the man with the fair complexion began to look somewhat familiar. Seth just couldn't place him.

The man that looked familiar to Seth responded indicating that he was Jack Cooper and the other man identified himself as Tom Osgood. They both indicated that they were with the FBI. Jack Cooper slowly lowered his right hand in front of him as if to say, "Stop." They were surprised to see some local yocal cop get the drop on them. "If you'll allow us, we have badges," commented Jack in a deliberate manner.

Seth nodded in the affirmative. "Be very slow."

The two men cautiously reached into their coat pockets and produced their badges for Seth.

Seth leaned slightly forward to get a better view of the badges and carelessly commented, "You dress like FBI agents," as he lowered his gun and then tucking it between the middle of his back and his jeans.

Jack continued, "I don't know if you remember me, we were never actually introduced, but I saw you in Cherokee. I'm with the North Carolina FBI office out of Charlotte, and Tom here is with the local Miami office. Could we step into your room?"

As Jack introduced himself, Seth remembered him from Cherokee. Seth found Jack to have a calm demeanor and be well educated. He was not an imposing individual but was easily likeable. "Sure," answered Seth. He motioned for the two men to enter and then followed them into the room. Tom adjusted the only chair in the room in order to face the other two and sat down. Jack sat on the bed that was still made up. Seth had been sleeping when they knocked on his door. He pulled the bedsheets back on the bed to try and make himself more comfortable. It was a cozy trio.

CHAPTER 75

Jack started the discussion. "We've been trying to keep up with you since Cherokee. Between you and Ms. Dugen, you've gotten pretty damn far with this thing."

Seth quickly became irate. "This thing?" Seth was almost shouting as he came out of his chair. "And what the hell do you mean you've been tracking us and we got pretty damn far?" Seth was tired from the relentless pace Rachel and he had set, so it didn't take much to set him off. "Seth, if you would bear with me for a few minutes, I'd like to explain."

Seth eased back down in his chair, trying to calm himself down. He was seething. He was anxious for Jack to explain his comments.

"We've been pursuing a group of people breaking into military installations throughout the southeastern part of the United States. Ms. Dugen's brother was just an innocent victim. As far as we can tell, he was the only person killed during any of the break-ins. With your efforts, those of Skypilot"—Jack paused and shook his head with a smile as he thought of Skypilot—"and Terry from the Jacksonville PD, we came to the same conclusion as you that it is tied to some Cubans here in Miami. We're confident that someone or a group of individuals within the Cubans for a Free Cuba are involved. We don't think it is the organization as a whole." Jack walked over to the sink and filled a glass of water. He took a long drink and started in again. "We were also amazed, once we got onto the militia's computers in Cherokee, how much information they had on the Cubans' network. What we need is for you to give us the information you have so far, and we'll see this thing through."

Seth was curt with his reply, "Fuck you!" Seth continued, "We've been shot at, and Rachel's been beaten half to death and rests in a hospital bed here in Fort Lauderdale. Major John Lawrence and Lieutenant Hugh Dugen, Rachel's brother, are both dead, and now you just want me to hand everything over to you and step back. I don't think so!" Seth continued, "Why don't you give us what you have, and we'll see it through. We seem to have made better progress than you with only two of us. Otherwise, I don't think you'd be standing here asking for what we've put together."

Jack saw he was getting nowhere without some give-and-take, "All right, we'll do this together." Tom started to say something to Jack when Jack cut him off. "Tom, I'll accept full responsibility." Jack motioned for Tom to take over the discussion.

Tom pulled the same photos Seth had acquired from the security guards the night before. He pointed at the two Hispanic men in the picture. "These two men are associated with the Cubans for a Free Cuba. More specifically, we think they are closely aligned with what we believe to be a splinter group formed by the organization's vice president, Julio Chavez. The other man was Lieutenant Hugh Dugen's partner, Private Larry Shays, now AWOL. We believe Private Shays"—Tom tapped his finger on Shay's picture—"was the one that killed Lieutenant Dugen."

"Shit, so that's where the bastard disappeared to," commented Seth. Seth remembered his conversation with Terry at the funeral. Terry told him that Hugh's partner, Private Shays, had disappeared along with the provost marshal, adding to the number of coincidences surrounding Hugh's death and the break-in.

Tom continued, "The Hispanic man found dead at Dave and Jill Murphy's place is Antonio Chavez. He is Juan Mendoza's second cousin who came here via the Florida Straits from Cuba. Juan Mendoza is a well-respected man within the Cubans for a Free Cuba and has a lot of clout here in Miami. We know Juan is closely aligned with the splinter group and Julio Chavez. Juan and Antonio grew up together in Miami. We believe, through our informants, that Julio and his sympathizers are planning on flying the weapons that they've stolen throughout the southeast to Cuba tonight. Our plan is to raid the whole operation and arrest everyone involved."

Seth listened intently to Tom. He remembered his and Rachel's drive from Ocala to Miami and the discussion they had that he thought that the robberies were leading up to something big. He remembered telling Rachel he thought the theft at Camp LeJeune was probably the last, and he was right, a shipment of arms to Cuba!

"Well, what do you care if arms get to Cuba, and they overthrow either Castro? It's not like we've exactly been getting along with the Castro family for all these years," Seth commented sarcastically.

Jack jumped back in, "True, but relations with Cuba have been less stressful than they have been in years. The biggest reason is Carlos Hernandez."

"The president of the Cubans for a Free Cuba organization," commented Seth.

Tom, the Miami FBI agent, chimed in, "Right! I understand you've already met Mr. Hernandez. He has a lot of muscle, and he has been calling in favors all over Washington to put the kibosh on Julio and his gang."

"Seems strange that the leader of the Cubans for a Free Cuba would want to squelch an attempt at overthrowing Raul Castro," replied Seth.

"I don't disagree," answered Tom, "but Carlos believes Fidel Castro's days are running out. The man is eighty, and Carlos believes it won't be that much longer. He doesn't want any more Cubans killed, and his supporters in Washington don't want another black eye. Their fear is that it will come back and kick us in the teeth globally."

Seth listened to Tom talk about Fidel Castro. "Tom, Fidel's brother, Raul, has taken over the reins in Cuba."

"Seth, we know Raul has taken over the reins, but we still believe Fidel is calling a lot of the shots right now. We believe that once Fidel dies, Raul will be in a position to open things up more with the United States, which is another reason we don't want to see Julio's plans take off. Hell, Russia can't keep funding Cuba like it once did. We think that once Fidel is out of the picture, Raul will want to start fostering negotiations with the United States to help build infrastructure there."

CHAPTER 76

Seth started in again, "So why are you here, and how is it you caught up with us?" He felt that Tom and Jack had enough information that they didn't really need his help or information.

Jack jumped in, "We tracked you down through your credit cards. Also, the security guards for the hotel are required by their insurance company to file reports on any crimes reported on the hotel premises."

"Shit," commented Seth. "That happened only last night." Seth guessed the hotel manager filed his report immediately after he left the security room on some kind of online reporting with the insurance company. "So from the record of Rachel being beaten last night and through our credit cards, you're here. So where do we go from here, gentlemen?" inquired Seth.

Tom continued, "What we need is to get any additional information from you on what you learned from Skypilot and his pals. We do know one of Skypilot's pals gave you some information that Skypilot had accumulated on Rachel's behalf. As Jack mentioned, we've accumulated quite a bit of information on our own from following your sources. We were shocked by what Jack acquired from the militia's computers. The militia had information on the Cubans for a Free Cuba, several other organizations, including the CIA and FBI. Some of the information we hope isn't true. Rachel's friend, Skypilot, wow, is he unbelievable! I understand you call him Sky. We rescued him from the CIA. We've moved him to Washington DC and have him working for us now. He won't be able to hack into some of the stuff he has been hacking into without a warrant, but he is good! Damn good!" Tom looked over at Jack, and the two men gave a slight chuckle.

"What do you mean, hope some of the information isn't true?" inquired Seth.

"From the militia's information and from what we got from Skypilot, we believe this Cuban group is getting assistance from within our own government.

We're not sure if it is our people in the FBI, CIA, NSA, or whom. So what we were planning on doing is staking out an airfield that we believe the Cubans are planning on using to export the stolen arms out of the United States. When the Cubans load the plane bound for Cuba, we step in and hopefully nab everyone we can. From there we hope we can get a few of the people to roll over on others and lead us to the major players. If it is within our own government, someone will burn and burn bad," stated Tom.

Jack started in, "Tom has gathered several non-Cuban-affiliated FBI agents to help in the raid tonight. It's not that we can't trust anyone Cuban. It is just that I am not sure of whom to trust anymore, and we don't have time to play around with it anymore. Everyone has been instructed to keep their mouths shut. Additionally, everyone was recruited outside of the bureau office in Miami to prevent anyone not involved from becoming a suspect. Since we don't know how far this thing goes, we have been tight-lipped with everyone. We believe all our Miami FBI agents are good people, but we can't afford one mistake with only one chance at catching this splinter group with their hand in the cookie jar."

"Okay . . . but I want to be a part of things when it comes down on these guys!" Seth took a deep breath and took the plunge. He filled Tom and Jack in on what he and Rachel found out. They pretty much had the same information. Much of what they accumulated was from following Seth and Rachel's leads anyhow as Tom and Jack stated. He included the two of them confronting Carlos and then Rachel seeing Carlos later in the day at Julio's house.

The three men spent the rest of the day making plans for the evening raid. Tom made several calls during the day to the FBI agents that would be taking part in the raid. At ten o'clock the three men departed for the Opa-Locka Airport. Seth was gratified to be fully involved in the planning of the raid and now the execution. The FBI agents taking part in the raid followed in separate cars and staggered their departures from the staging area so no one would see a swarm of official-looking dark sedans ascend on the Opa-Locka Airport and surrounding area.

CHAPTER 77

Larry Shays and the two Cuban men that were responsible for beating Rachel arrived at Julio's house just before eleven thirty in the evening. The three men had stopped by a strip club off Lincoln Road after assaulting Rachel for a few drinks. They had bragged about their efforts targeting the Naval Intelligence officer.

Julio could smell liquor on the men's breath. "How many drinks have you had?" asked Julio, looking at the men in disdain.

Larry grinned. "What's the big deal? We stopped and had a few drinks before the big night."

Julio put his hand on the back of Larry's neck and pulled him close. "We can't have any fuck-ups because we had a few guys that had one drink too many." Julio noticed the other two men beginning to look uncomfortable. Julio noticed some blood splatter on Larry's shirt. Pointing at the blood, Julio asked, "Where did this come from?"

Larry began to laugh. "We went to see that nosy bitch that came over here and told her to mind her own business."

Before he knew it, Larry saw Julio's hand flying toward his face. The backhanded hit caught Larry off guard more than it hurt him. But it did cause Larry to lose his balance and fall backward onto the floor. Julio turned and looked at the other two men with Larry.

"That was the confirmation I needed." Julio was furious. The two men in Larry's company helped Larry off the floor. Julio called to Pedro Moreno, one of his closest allies outside of Juan. "Pedro!" shouted Julio. In a moment Pedro arrived with two other men. "These are the two you were telling me about?" asked Pedro in a businesslike manner.

"Yes." Julio looked at the two men who were Larry's cohorts. They looked back with trepidation. "While you were in the bar, your faces were making the headlines for the eleven o'clock news."

"But how?" began one of Larry's men before Julio shut him off.

"They have cameras in the hallway. Because of your stupidity, the police may have already linked you to us. Pedro has made arrangements for you two to fly to Costa Rica tonight on one of his private jets."

Pedro motioned for the men to follow him to a car waiting out in front of Julio's house.

Julio called after them, "Don't plan on coming back until you hear from me!"

Larry looked cautiously at Julio wondering what his fate would be. He cautiously spoke. "We went to scare her off."

Julio angrily responded, "She was no problem. She had nothing to go on. With the help of the local police, she was not going to be coming around here again. Now, thanks to your stupidity, she and the cops have every reason to come here. Let's just hope we can get this thing done before the cops come around again." Julio looked at Larry. "I told you before we ever started this mission no one was to be hurt! What part of that did you not understand?"

Larry stood defiantly with a handkerchief in his hand wiping the blood from his lower lip from when Julio backhanded him.

Julio was trying to maintain his control, staring coldly at Larry. "Who the fuck gave you the authority to go after that woman?" inquired Julio.

Larry had had enough. He spat out, "I don't need any authority!"

Julio became exasperated with Larry. He knew he could not just let him leave; he may retaliate, or he may do further damage. He wanted to send him to Costa Rica but knew he needed to keep an eye on him. He shouted to Juan Mendoza in the other room, "Juan! Come here."

As soon as Julio spoke, it seemed that Juan was standing next to him. Julio looked at Juan. "Keep him with you the rest of the night. Don't let him out of your sight for a second!"

Larry cut back at Julio, "You can't tell me what I can and cannot do!"

As soon as the words left Larry's mouth, Julio grabbed Larry by his shirt just under his chin and got in his face. "Shut your fucking mouth! Do you hear me?"

Larry started to respond when he heard the other men gathering behind him. He let his anger briefly diminish. "Yeh . . . I hear ya." Larry pushed his way past the throng of men that had gathered and made his way into the living room, eventually making his way to the bar.

Juan looked at Julio and nodded. "No problem." Juan looked at Julio for further instructions.

"Do whatever you have to do. Just don't let him out of your sight!" commanded Julio.

Juan moved next to where Larry was seated at the bar and poured himself a Cuban coffee from the silver decanter sitting on the bar.

Larry found a bottle of Cuervo Gold Tequila behind the bar. He poured it into a shot glass, spilling some onto the bar. His hands were shaking. After the first shot, he poured himself another before turning his attention back to Julio, who was following the horde of men entering the room.

Julio had paused in the hallway after Larry and many of the guests dispersed to calm himself. He made it a point never to address the men while in anger though Larry had just driven him to the brink. Julio went into the room where the men had gathered, awaiting further instructions. He went over additional items. The housekeeper brought in bottled water, soft drinks, and Cuban food to munch on and drink before they left for the long night ahead.

CHAPTER 78

It was a little after midnight when the men left for the warehouse where Julio had stockpiled the arms. Julio had to give directions to the drivers since only a couple had known the warehouse location. Julio wanted the men to carpool to keep anyone from straying and to keep an eye on one another. This would help prevent any tip-offs in case someone had infiltrated the team. The warehouse was located in Kendall.

Larry sat next to Juan in the backseat of a Chevy Tahoe on the ride over to the warehouse. Larry had to laugh as they pulled in front of the warehouse when he realized it was in Kendall, just a few blocks from where he grew up.

The warehouse was for a plumbing supply company that had several retail stores located throughout Miami-Dade County with a few locations in Broward County as well. The Cuban owner originally bought the warehouse larger than he felt he would need for some time but felt he could sublet the extra space in the interim. Julio needed it to stockpile arms for his own war with the Cuban government, and the owner graciously wanted to help out. He felt certain that Julio would be Cuba's next leader, and he was honored to have the opportunity to assist.

Since the Opa-Locka Airport is a small airport open only to noncommercial traffic, there are only a few hangars to accommodate about thirty private airplanes and one relatively small warehouse. The remaining fifty or so private planes are parked on the tarmac. When threatening weather approaches, the owners typically fly the planes inland or to other private airfields to the north. The area was developed in the sixties and seventies. The local shops surrounding the airport are comprised mostly of Hispanic restaurants, convenient stores, and pawnshops. It is situated in a largely Hispanic population of South Florida that is yet another reason Julio wanted to use the Opa-Locka Airport; it was in "friendly" territory.

When the men arrived at the remote warehouse, Julio directed them to begin loading the trucks. Julio made sure he got delivery trucks to help blend into the community. Members of the Cubans for a Free Cuba provided all the trucks. The delivery trucks were comprised of food delivery, office supply, and plumbing goods. Julio met with the owner to make sure all the telephones were temporarily disconnected in the building. He had also informed all the men that they were not to bring any cell phones. Once again, it was Julio's way to avoid any tip-offs.

It was one thirty in the morning when the trucks were loaded. Once the trucks were loaded, the men sat and waited for Julio to receive a call on his cell phone to instruct him when the plane was scheduled to arrive at the Opa-Locka Airport. The men knew Julio was receiving instructions from someone else, but no one knew who that person was. They only knew that they had to wait for a call before they were to leave for the airport. They did not want any trucks loaded with arms sitting around the small Opa-Locka Airport until it was absolutely necessary. Their fear was that someone might become suspicious with delivery trucks parked at the airport in the middle of the night and call the police. The men sat around and made idle conversation as they waited for the call. The gentleman that owned the warehouse provided Cuban coffee, water, and soft drinks along with some pastries. He was honored to be involved in such a historic moment he wanted to be there when the trucks started rolling. Some of the men smoked cigars and exchanged stories while enjoying the food and drinks.

It was after two in the morning when the call finally came through to Julio. Only then did Julio announce that they were heading for the Opa-Locka Airport. The plan was that everyone would follow the same path about one-half-mile apart. Julio would lead the caravan, and Juan would be in the last truck to arrive. Julio gave each driver a small radio with a range of no more than five miles. If anyone encountered any problems, they were to radio to the others to change their course immediately to help avoid foiling the entire mission. Aside from emergency purposes, the men were not to be using the radios. The radios Julio gave each driver were preset to the same frequency. Julio also notified some of the local police that were affiliated with his splinter group that there would be four trucks coming through the area and to make sure that they were not hindered. The local police were not notified as to what the trucks would be carrying, but they knew Julio well enough that the trucks would not be carrying drugs, so they agreed. It was shortly before three when the last truck reached the airport. Julio, along with the men and trucks, waited next to a warehouse near the runway awaiting the plane's arrival.

The Opa-Locka Airport is typically open during the day to smaller air traffic. The airport at this time of night was closed, but the runway lights were still on. The airport kept the runway lights on for emergency purposes only, and two men were assigned to the control tower for just that purpose. Julio made sure those two men were members of the Cubans for a Free Cuba and, more importantly, his men.

CHAPTER 79

Seth, Jack, and Tom sat in Tom's unmarked FBI car waiting for Julio and his splinter group sympathizers to arrive. They had arrived shortly after the airport closed to the usual noncommercial air traffic to ensure that they did not miss anything. They also wanted to secure a spot that would have a vantage point to see everything coming and going, but not draw attention to themselves.

Seth questioned Tom several times as to whether his informant was reliable. They were growing restless when they noticed a commercial delivery truck coming into view. Before they knew it, three other varying delivery trucks were arriving at the small airport. Although initially surprised by this form of transportation, Seth realized it was a practical plan. As each truck entered the airport, Tom's grin grew bigger. He became as excited as a kid in a candy shop. Jack was equally thrilled. He had followed the case from the mountains of North Carolina to South Florida, and now his efforts were coming to fruition. The informant was right.

Seth was filled with excitement. What had started as a small break-in at a vacationer's home had blossomed into a federal investigation and the possible smuggling of arms into a thorn in America's side for decades, Cuba.

It was after three in the morning when they first caught sight of a mammoth C-130 Hercules cargo plane beginning its decent into the Opa-Locka Airport. At first, they could only see the approach lights of the beast in the distant sky. It seemed almost surreal watching the huge plane ease onto the tiny runway of the Opa-Locka Airport. Seth couldn't imagine this huge beast landing on such a small airfield, but the plane seemed to be determined to do so without too much difficulty. Seth remembered a similar sight during his stint in the marine corps during Desert Storm. He noted the plane's nondescript appearance. It was white with black numbers on the tail of the plane. Seth's first thoughts were that it appeared to be CIA. Only they could create something so generic and get away with it. Most likely the numbers on the plane's tail would lead to some nonexistent offshore corporation in the Cayman Islands.

Once the plane touched down, it made its way toward the sole warehouse where the delivery trucks were waiting. The cacophony of the plane's engines disturbed the tiny airport. The plane came to a stop, and the pilot slowed the engines. One of the men who had protected his ears with a headset ran over and chalked the tires. The rear gate opened to allow the delivery men to load the plane. The trucks took turns backing up to the plane's massive gate. Seth was amazed at the efficiency with which the men moved. As soon as one truck was emptied, the next one was moved into position and promptly unloaded.

The last truck was almost unloaded when Tom gave the order for his men to move in. Ten dark FBI sedans loaded with FBI agents came from several directions, squealing tires as they stopped, taking their position around the delivery men, their trucks, and the enormous C-130. Tom raced the sedan into position; as he did, he noticed Julio Chavez in the throng of delivery men. Tom made a point of pointing Julio out to Jack and Seth as he drove. The FBI agents had their guns drawn and directed at Julio's men in a matter of minutes. Seth was astonished to see how the FBI agents could swarm in so quickly. The FBI's actions reminded him of his tour during Desert Storm. Julio's men stopped loading the plane, scrambled for position, and prepared to return fire if the FBI agents initiated shooting. The FBI agents and Julio's men soon found themselves in a standoff, each waiting for the other to take some action.

CHAPTER 80

Tires squealing, another car raced into the standoff between the FBI and Julio's men. Carlos and a stranger jumped out of the car. The unknown man was known only to Carlos and Julio. Carlos and his companion had been watching the events unfold in a nearby parking lot. For Carlos, it was his worst fears coming true: the potential slaughter of several members of his beloved organization by federal authorities. Carlos bravely walked between the two combatants appealing to Julio's men to put down their arms and give themselves up. Julio encouraged his men to hold their ground despite Carlos's plea.

The stranger calmly looked around and shouted in the direction of the FBI agents, "Who's in charge?"

Two FBI agents simultaneously shouted back, "I am!"

The stranger laughed and walked in the direction where he heard the two FBI agents call out. He was slow and deliberate as he made his way toward them. He jokingly said, "This must be a government operation." Standing directly in front of the FBI agents in charge, he reached into his coat pocket. As the man did so, he could feel gun barrels direct their attention toward him. The man raised his other hand as if surrendering. He pulled out a badge holding it in front of him so the FBI agents could read it as he identified himself as "Ed Logan of the CIA." Ed was just over six feet four and fit. It was obvious to all that he worked out regularly.

Chapter 81

Jack and Tom both looked stunned. Seth had drawn as close as he could to hear the man now identifying himself as CIA Agent Ed Logan.

Seth could not contain himself. "What the fuck?"

"Who the hell is this man?" asked Ed.

"Never mind," countered Jack. "What's this all about? Is the CIA running a covert op without notifying the FBI?"

"This is a CIA operation," confirmed Ed.

"If so, why the hell haven't you guys approached us on this?" challenged Jack.

"We couldn't!"

Before Ed could continue, "That's because this is being done outside the normal boundaries," commented the agitated Tom. "This is without the knowledge of anyone on Capitol Hill for that matter, isn't it? You're off the grid!"

"Hey, I don't make policy. I'm a field agent carrying out orders," responded Ed in an effort to defend himself.

Tom moved closer to Ed. "What exactly are your orders?"

"To make sure these men are not interfered with and that these arms find their way to the Cuban resistance on that plane. With a little luck, Castro and his brother, Raul, will be overthrown, and the world will be a better place." Ed pointed toward the almost-loaded cargo plane.

CHAPTER 82

While Tom, Jack, and Ed spoke, Julio had stepped out from behind a truck that he had used as a shield against the FBI agents and looked at Carlos. "What are you doing here?" inquired Julio.

"I'm making sure the Cubans for a Free Cuba don't lose a number of our members needlessly because of your stupidity," sounded a perturbed Carlos.

"My stupidity? You ass, you probably lead these men here." He was motioning toward the FBI agents.

Carlos pointed to Ed. "That man came to my house to bring me here tonight. He explained on the way here what you were doing behind my back. He asked for my support, and from the looks of things, we got here just in time."

CHAPTER 83

Ed called to Carlos and Julio to discontinue their heated debate. He motioned for them to come to where he was standing. They begrudgingly agreed and made their way to where Ed and the others were standing. Julio and Carlos looked each other over in contempt as they joined the others.

Ed looked at Jack and Tom. "Can we talk . . . privately?"

Jack and Tom looked incredulously at Ed as if to say, "So talk."

"In private!" Ed was annoyed with Tom's and Jack's cavalier attitude toward him.

Tom, Jack, Ed, Julio, and Carlos walked away from Seth and everyone else. Seth followed the men. Ed looked at Seth to prevent his pursuit. Jack interceded, looking at Ed, "It's okay . . . he is with me. He is probably the only one here with any objectivity."

Ed gave a disapproving nod, but Seth ignored the exchange and joined the men.

Once the men distanced themselves from the rest, Ed realized the absurdity of his request for a "private" conversation. He had hoped to exclude Seth from his conversation along with Julio and Carlos, but all were standing in front of him waiting for his "private" conversation to begin. The only ones excluded were the FBI team agents and Julio's men, all tucked safely behind barriers in case shooting broke out. None of the ones excluded could have heard his conversation without him shouting. Ed gathered himself and continued, "Time is running out, gentlemen. We've gotta get that bird in the air. The Cubans in South Florida have grown tired of the hapless boycotts and laissez-faire political pressure. A few people in Washington have grown tired of the process as well and came up with this covert op. The CIA, with Washington's consent, has been aiding the Cubans in acquiring arms from military installations in the southeastern part of the United States to be airlifted to the local Cuban resistance plotting an overthrow. This has taken years of planning. We have guys in Cuba right now that have been assisting with this coup who have stuck their necks out, not to mention the Cubans waiting in Cuba with their asses in the air with nothing to show right now except a prayer." Julio nodded his agreement.

Tom laughed. "Help from Washington? You know you're in violation of Congress," commented Tom. "Hell, if you had Congress's support, why in the world are you having to 'acquire' it through nefarious means? And if you have political muscle, who are they? I sure as hell would like to know so I can stick it in my files to cover my ass on this far-flung op."

Ed had grown tired of Tom's flippant attitude toward the covert operation. "Hey, I'm a field agent . . . I take orders just like you. Besides, I don't give a fuck if Washington does or doesn't support what we're doing. You and I both know that there is a bunch of tight asses on Capitol Hill too fucking scared to take a chance on an operation like this. Those bastards screwed the military in Nam. We've been working on this operation for well over a year now. It's called Operation Razorback. I've been in on it from the get-go—planning, organizing, and helping wherever I needed to make it happen! These guys needed a little backing. They're going forward to liberate Cuba and throw that bastard Fidel and his brother into the fucking Atlantic."

CHAPTER 84

Jack was tired and wasn't sure if Ed was on the level or not. He had the identification of a CIA operative. The fact he was operating in the United States without FBI knowledge didn't make him feel comfortable, but this wouldn't be the first time something like this happened. He also knew they weren't going to get any kind of quick confirmation in the early-morning hours. "I don't care if that bird flies or not," responded Jack referring the parked C-130.

Tom looked at Jack with disapproval. "For something of this magnitude, we should run it by someone with the FBI in Washington as a minimum," commented Tom.

Jack responded, "I can appreciate where you're coming from Tom, but as I see it, this is a CIA op, so its success and failure rides with them. If we talk to your boss, we can expect to spend the next several hours waiting on someone to make the final decision. By then, their window to get these arms to Cuba will certainly have closed. I think I would like to stay out of this as much as possible and let the CIA roll the dice."

Tom paused to think about Jack's position. "Ed, it's a go for me too," answered Tom.

Jack looked at Ed. "Before we let that bird fly, just tell me who killed that MP at Camp LeJeune. If you turn him over to me, your bird flies without further delay. Also, when this whole thing goes south, you and the CIA are gonna take full responsibility." Jack looked scornfully at Ed. Jack thought about the dead FBI agent, Mike Kelly and Major John Lawrence, but they were killed by Al Stewart, who was in the militia and not by the Cubans for a Free Cuba.

"Agreed," replied Ed. Ed looked at Julio. "Julio . . . give him the one who shot the MP."

Seth jumped in, "I want to know who beat up Rachel."

"Gladly," commented Julio. "It was all Larry Shays. What a pain in the ass! Please, just take that bastard away."

Ed looked at Julio. "Enjoyed his company, did you?"

The men laughed in unison and returned to join the others. As they approached the loading area next to the plane where the men had gathered, a single shot rang out. Tom grimaced in agony as he gripped his chest. His knees buckled. Tom dropped first to his knees and then fell face-first onto the tarmac. Jack and the others dropped to the ground instinctively. Jack took his right hand and placed it on Tom's neck to feel for a pulse. There was none; Tom was dead.

Jack was stunned. He mumbled aloud, "I can't believe he didn't wear a vest for the raid."

CHAPTER 85

Hearing a shot ring out, Seth dropped to the ground and crawled to a position behind a car opposite from the direction that the shot appeared to come from. Several FBI agents returned fire in the direction of the nearby airplane hangar, shattering windows and piercing the thin metal siding. Julio's men had taken cover, not sure what to do or who was shooting.

Off in the distance, Seth could see a lone gunman's silhouette from inside the airplane hangar. The man was now firing random shots in the direction of Seth and the FBI agents. Seth recognized the sound of an M-16 from his days in military training and the Gulf War. He could see a faint image of the gunman moving from one open window to another. Seth crawled along the ground until he made his way alongside the warehouse out of sight of the gunman. He could feel his heart pounding in his throat and sweat formed down his back. Seth didn't like what he was feeling; it was fear and too much fear is what gets one killed. He found an unlocked door on the reverse side of the hangar. As Seth entered the hangar, he could hear the lone gunman exchanging gunfire. The sounds resonating from his M-16 reverberated through the structure. The gunman's feet shuffled on the imperfect hangar floor. The return fire from the FBI agents was sporadic. He could see the wayward bullets striking the metal structure, leaving small holes in the thin metal. Seth knew he didn't want to get hit by a stray bullet or have the gunman put him away. It appeared that the hangar had become more of a storage facility for worn-out old parts and other debris than a place to store someone's plane. The poorly lit hangar indicated that the debris was either someone's organized madness or just haphazard storage.

Seth was gradually making his way toward the gunman when he tripped. Before he knew it, he heard an empty can hit the floor to his left as he fell to the ground. The gunman turned and fired in Seth's direction. Seth could hear the errant shot hit something behind him. When the gunman's firing paused, Seth moved to a kneeling position. An eerie silence rang out over the darkened hangar. Seth panned the warehouse while straining to listen for the gunman. Seth could feel his heart beating as he tried lining up his sight on the gunman. Finally, Seth caught the brief glimpse he needed and fired. A loud crash echoed as the figure off in the distance fell backward onto some debris. The figure was still standing, but stumbling. Seth could hear the odd sound of the man gurgling and gasping for air; he knew he hit the gunman in the throat. Seth was glad that when he tripped and fell, he fell to his left, making his gun available to his right hand to return fire. Seth fired again, this time striking the man in the chest. He knew he hit him because he could see vague images of the man holding his chest and moving erratically from a light shining into the hangar. The gunman fell backward, stumbled, and fell to the ground. Seth heard several cans and other debris crash onto the concrete floor of the hangar. The room was dark except for the obscure lights coming in from outside. He waited trying to listen for movement from where the lone gunman once stood.

The shots continued coming from outside. *Damn*, thought Seth, *I can't hear a thing.* Seth shouted from his couched position, "Hold your fire!" The outside barrage of bullets waned and then stopped. The airplane hangar fell eerily silent once again. Seth approached the gunman slowly. He feared that one last ounce of strength like a wounded animal would be reserved for his foe—him. He found the gunman lying on his side. Seth cautiously removed the gun from the man's still hand. Seth kneeled beside the man and felt for a pulse, but found none.

Seth shouted to the men outside, "It's okay—he's had it."

Seth heard someone shout back, "Who's had it?"

Seth realized that few were familiar with his voice, and so he identified himself. "It's me, Seth, your friendly Surf City police chief."

Everyone, FBI agents and the Cubans, made their way toward Seth and the dead man. One of the FBI agents found a switch to open the bay doors, offering more light into the dark airplane hangar. Julio pushed the others aside so he could see who had dared to cause so much difficulty. "That's your man."

Jack countered, "What man?"

"The man who killed your MP and beat up your friend."

"I'm afraid Julio is right," commented Ed. "We recruited Private Shays at Camp LeJeune. We figured he was the kind of guy we could use. Regrettably, he thought he was more valuable than he really was. He became more of a nuisance."

Seth became indignant to the careless way Julio and Ed referred to Hugh and Rachel. "Look—they have names. That MP was Lieutenant Hugh Dugen of the United States Marine Corps. He was a neighbor, a friend, a husband, soon to be a father, and Rachel's brother. His sister, Rachel, is the 'friend who was beaten up.' She is an officer in the United States Navy. And let's not forget Major John Lawrence, also of the United States Marine Corps. He was killed by the militia, but had it not been for the break-in, he would never had been in Cherokee in the first place to be shot."

Julio felt the loathing in Seth's voice.

Ed too could hear the anger in Seth's voice stirred by their insensitive comments.

"I apologize for my behavior," responded Ed. "Sometimes we agents can get too caught up in the operation to realize that we are talking about real people."

Julio chimed in, "I'm sorry for your friend, Lieutenant Dugen, and my apologies to Rachel. Mr. Shays acted on his own accord. The two men that assisted him are hers to prosecute if she chooses. I will personally turn them over to her and the authorities. No one was to get hurt. No one! We were determined to get the arms to Cuba, but everyone was advised that if confronted, they are to turn themselves in before bringing harm to anyone. I regret what has happened, but I too have lost someone, Antonio Mendoza. He was like family." He pointed toward Juan Mendoza. "Antonio was his cousin."

CHAPTER 86

Ed looked at Jack. "If we're going to finish this thing, we need to get going before it is too late and the sun comes up."

Reluctantly, Jack gave an approving nodded.

Julio, hearing and seeing the exchange between Ed and Jack, turned and shouted to his men to finish loading the plane. He threw his right arm into the air and started rotating his arm in a circular motion to start rolling.

Jack told one of his agents to call an ambulance for Tom and Larry. He briefed the FBI agent standing next to him to provide as little information as possible to the paramedics when they arrive with an ambulance. "The FBI will follow up in due time." Jack caught himself, "Correction—the CIA will follow up in due time." Jack looked at Ed, who nodded in agreement. Jack relieved the other FBI agents who were eager to go home. The entire evening seemed cast in a maze of governmental leapfrog with the Cuban intrastruggling of the Cubans for a Free Cuba thrown in on top to add another layer of bickering and confusion. Jack instructed the FBI agents not to disclose anything that happened at the airfield to anyone.

Ed approached Jack after the FBI agents were dismissed. "I would like for you to come with me. We've set up a satellite telecast to view the fruits of our efforts." Ed looked in the direction of Seth, Julio, and Carlos and motioned for them to come along as well and witness the impending success.

Ed got into a car with Julio and Carlos. Seth, Tom, and Jack followed in a separate FBI car. Jack followed Ed's into a warehouse district not far from the airport. They parked next to a nondescript white warehouse in Hialeah. The outside of the building did not bear any signs indicating the name of a business. If not for the several cars parked adjacent to the warehouse, it would have appeared to be an abandoned warehouse. There were several nearby warehouses that were in fact vacant and unlikely to have inquisitive neighbors. Seth couldn't help but think the cheap rent helped close the deal for the CIA. Several empty beer bottles and cans were strewn about the parking lot. The landscaping shrubs were over grown and consisted mostly of weeds with pieces of trash interspersed. As the men started into the warehouse, Ed motioned for everyone to keep silent until they were inside. He was trying to keep as low a profile as possible to much of the indigent population that considered the parking lot their home. Two muscular men with their hair shaved close, adding to their ominous presence, each holding grease guns and .45s, guarded the entrance to the warehouse. The high-tech equipment adorning the nondescript warehouse enamored the men. Several men dressed in white shirts and dark ties manned the equipment. There was little conversation among them. It was covert business, pure and simple. Against one end of the warehouse attached to the wall was what appeared to be a large-screen television. The screen was showing nothing but garbled images when they entered the room. One man was startled when he saw Ed and the other men enter the room, "Hey, Ed, what's goin' on?" There was a brief pause as the man made his way to Ed's side. "Who are these people?"

Ed replied, "They are all closely tied to the operation. It's okay . . . I'll vouch for them."

Ed's response seemed to give the agitated man some solace. The man shot back, "We're almost there. We've followed the plane on radar the entire way."

Ed explained the anticipated chain of events needed to complete the CIA mission. To prevent the possibility of being discovered, the plane would maintain radio silence the entire way to Cuba and return. The plane was to head out over the Bahamas. Once the CIA jammed the Cuban radar, the plane would turn and fly into Cuban airspace to make the drop at a designated place. The plane would be in Cuban airspace for only a matter of minutes. The CIA would contact the Homestead Air Force Base to send out some Tomcat fighters in the general direction of Cuba. Once the cargo was dropped, the plane would need to return to Bahamian airspace. This was extremely dangerous since once the radar frequency was jammed, the Cubans would scramble their MIG fighters and search the skies over Cuba. To find a cargo plane would be an easy task; hopefully, having the Tomcat fighters in the area would add some confusion for the Cuban MIGs.

CHAPTER 87

Tito Mendoza gathered about twenty men and women in a sugarcane barn in the Villa Clara Province. The barn was about one hundred and fifty miles east of Havana. From the barn, they were about another fifteen miles to Sol Beach located in a cove where the plane carrying the arms to overthrow the Castro government were to be dropped. The cove was in a remote part of Cuba. Most of the locals were sympathetic to Tito and his contingency. The sympathetic environment was one of the factors that prompted Tito to choose Sol Beach as the drop site. The men and women came from diverse backgrounds. There were farmers, doctors, scientists, and others enthusiastic to overthrow the Castro government. Those that could not come and help Tito sent money, food, and drinks. The fact that those that could not come sent money, food, and drinks touched Tito and those in his company. He knew that much of what was sent was made or came from governmental rations. To many in Cuba, the rationed food was barely enough to survive, which made the contributions that much more significant.

Tito gazed around the room. He felt a bit of irony. Many of the people were from Santa Clara, the provincial capital of Villa Clara. Santa Clara was the city captured by Che Guevara in a decisive victory over Batista. Che's victory was instrumental in Fidel Castro's rise to power. Now Tito was using the same arena to overthrow Fidel's government now run by his brother Raul Castro. While the men and women anxiously waited to depart for the cove, they sat, drank Cuban coffee, and ate guava pastries. There was little conversation. Several were saying prayers and others resting for what was already a long night and about to become even longer.

Tito asked only those he felt were physically capable and he could trust 100 percent to come. Tito was the only one who knew the specifics of the evening's mission. The mission was far too important to his efforts to overthrow Castro to have anyone leak any information to the minister of the interior. He also needed trucks that were provided by local farmers and small delivery companies. People also arrived with tools, flashlights, ropes, and anything else they felt they could use. Several brought guns; though obsolete by today's standards, they were the only guns anyone could put their hands on. Those on hand were eager to see the night end. There was so much to gain, yet so much to lose if caught. Certainly death would await anyone caught in Tito's company.

Tito stayed in communication with Julio in Miami via a ham radio that had been airlifted years earlier. Tito and Julio, with the help of the CIA, had devised a code for sending messages back and forth. Initially, changing the code to prevent the interior ministry from breaking the code had been difficult. Now with regular flights from Miami, the CIA, with the help of couriers, brought new codes to Tito regularly so they could change the codes. Couriers memorized new codes, and while visiting family, they would pass the new code along to someone who in turn would relay the code to Tito. Even the messengers had no idea what the code was. The couriers only relayed additional numbers and letters that were added to or subtracted from the previous code. The code was elaborate, but Tito was considered a major threat to the security of Cuba by the minister of the interior. If the code was broken, it would lead to Tito's capture. It was through the ham radio that Tito first learned of his son's, Antonio's, death. Tito passed along his son's death to the men and women that had arrived earlier in the week. They wanted to dedicate the evening quest to him by wearing black armbands in his honor.

Some Cubans seeking to dare the Florida Straits knew a little of Tito's communication assets. They would sometimes request Tito to contact family members in Miami to send boats out and look for them in the Florida Straits. The CIA frowned on Tito using the radio for this type of communication, but they knew they could not stop him. The CIA justified it by viewing it as saving lives and keeping a pro-American asset in Cuba.

Tito was very optimistic about the mission to recover the arms. There was just a sliver of the moon on this clear, cool night. At three in the morning, Tito had the first group of people leave for the cove. He felt that if everyone left at the same time, they would surely draw attention to themselves. Especially at that time of the night, a large group of people headed toward the cove would draw too much attention and arouse unwanted suspicion despite the pro-Tito sentiment among the local population. Those arriving early were to find a somewhat-secluded spot and stay in their truck. The next group would do the same though not using the same parking lot, yet visible to the other trucks. Tito figured that three different delivery trucks and the twenty men and women would be sufficient to carry out the mission. Too many trucks and too many people would draw unwanted attention. The end result would doom the mission. Tito's other fear was that they would not have enough time to retrieve the arms from the cove and load them into the trucks before dawn. It was a chance that they would have to risk.

CHAPTER 88

Seth, Tom, and Jack were watching from inside the warehouse in Hialeah when they were startled as the images flickered on the large television screen as it came to life. The satellite feed reflected humans as fluorescent green and red images. The plane was primarily viewed as red due to the heat from its engines of the C-130. As the plane neared its destination, more images appeared. Everyone in the room assumed them to be Tito and his Cuban makeshift army awaiting the plane's drop. The radar noted the plane banking before its descent into the cove for the cargo drop. The men could now hear Tito communicating with the C-130 in the final seconds before the drop over the speakers spread throughout the small warehouse. The plan was for the plane to make the drop inside a cove close enough to shore for Tito's freedom fighters to quickly take hold of the cargo and load it into waiting delivery trucks. The boats Julio sent earlier in the day were to lend support to the freedom fighters. Some of those on the boats requested to stay and become active participants in the imminent fight. From the view everyone was watching in the room, it appeared that the drop was going better than anyone expected. It was accurate enough that the freedom fighters could wade into the warm shallow waters and reclaim the dropped cargo.

CHAPTER 89

Tito stood waist deep in the shallow warm Cuban water of Sol Beach. He could hear the engines from the MIGs hiss as they approached the lumbering C-130. Each of the MIGs fired rockets into the helpless beast. There were two loud explosions as the rockets struck the enormous C-130. Tito heard the sonic boom as the MIGs departed the immediate airspace.

Before Tito could react, he saw soldiers running at his team of freedom fighters from several directions on the beach. He haplessly fired his antique revolver toward a group of soldiers. There were too many. Soon he felt bullets ripping at his chest. He fired until his relic was empty. He tried to reload but found he no longer had any bullets. He had so few to start the evening. His eyes filled with tears. His shirt was soaked in his own blood as he watched his fellow freedom fighters gunned down in front of him one after another in a hail of methodical gunfire. He tried to cry out, but he couldn't; there was no air in his lungs, only fluid. Tito saw a brief flash of light in the sky followed by a loud explosion as the cargo plane disappeared into oblivion. The plane's remnants of steel drifted to the ocean's surface.

While the cargo plane and Tito's men were being slaughtered, a small armada of gun boats attacked the flotilla of boats filled with fellow Cuban sympathizers from Miami. The small boats from Miami made easy targets for the powerful gunboats. As the gunboats fired at the Miami boaters, the pleasure craft turned into shards of fiberglass.

Tito watched the fate of his sympathizers. He gasped one last time as his lifeless body collapsed face-first into the water of Sol Beach. What had taken over a year of precise planning and calculation came to a disastrous end in only a few brief moments.

A silent hush fell over the once-quiet remote cove as the gunfire and cannons had no other targets. Occasionally a *rat-a-tat* was heard from an AK-47 or Makarov when one of Colonel Ochoa's men found a wounded or dying dissident. There would be no prisoners on this night. There would be no press to document this evening's tragedy. Tito's legacy would have to be carried on by men and women in the streets, over a quiet meal, or in a cantina. Eventually someone would take Tito's place among the dissidents, but not in the near future. There were no lights from the windows of the local residents. They wanted to remain anonymous.

Colonel Ochoa's men gathered the bodies of the dissidents in and around the cove and placed them in a pile on the beach in the cove. Floodlights were brought in to ensure that no bodies drifted off with the ocean current to be later found and provided fuel for a new group of freedom fighters. Colonel Ochoa smiled when he recognized Tito's body among the dead. He would certainly be handsomely rewarded for killing the infamous Tito Mendoza. Several of Colonel Ochoa's men shouted their happiness and fired their weapons into the air to celebrate their conquest of such a notorious outlaw. The local town's people peered through their tattered curtains or through the smallest crack in their doors during the melee to view the sickening celebration. They did not want to join the festivity, but they knew what the festivity was about.

One of Tito's delivery trucks, driven by one of Colonel Ochoa's men, backed up to the shoddy pile of dead bodies. Colonel Ochoa's men tossed the bodies carelessly into the back of the delivery truck where they would eventually be mass buried in an unmarked grave—discarded like waste at a dump. Colonel Ochoa watched from the confines of his car as the truck pulled away. A tepid rain began slowly and then gained momentum. Colonel Ochoa smiled even brighter. The rain would wash away the bloodstained beach. It wouldn't be long before the evening's events would be nothing more than a distant memory and a tale to be told by the locals.

CHAPTER 90

As Colonel Ochoa watched his men rid the beach and cove of the dissident dead bodies, he reflected on the day's events. The assistant deputy minister of the interior, Juan Jimenez, had briefed him of Tito's well-orchestrated plans to get weapons to Cuba in order to overthrow the aged Fidel Castro. The assistant deputy minister had ordered Colonel Ochoa to move his troops into position in anticipation of the plane's cargo drop. Once the plane made the weapons drop and Tito's freedom fights began retrieving the cargo, Colonel Ochoa's men would move into attack. Tito's men would be an easy target for Colonel Ochoa's well-trained soldiers.

The assistant deputy minister also ordered Colonel Ochoa to have MIG jet fighters at the ready in order to destroy the slow-moving cargo plane. The MIGs were to stay back to prevent the U.S. radar operators from spotting their position. The last coup de grâce was to have several gunboats at the ready to take out the boats coming in from Miami. This was the day Colonel Ochoa had been awaiting for years.

CHAPTER 91

As the realization dawned, the faces of the observers in the Hialeah warehouse began to show varying shades of shock, horror, and sadness as unexpected new images started firing at the freedom fighters. The MIGs were scrambled, and the gunboats were sent into action. By all indications, the freedom fighters were clearly caught off guard. What had originally been a major operation for the Cubans in Miami and the CIA was now turning into nothing more than a massacre carried out by the minister of the interior. Shouts came over the plane's radio as the MIGs darted by. As abruptly as the airplane's radio sounded when the pilot and crew spotted the MIGs, it went silent. The stillness of the Hialeah warehouse was deafening.

The freedom fighters with their obsolete weapons were no match for the well-equipped, heavily armed Cuban troops. The weapons that the freedom fighters would use in their quest for freedom sat floating in the water in front of them, still neatly packed in their crates. The Miami Cuban freedom fighters were on their boats shouting over their respective radios for help that would not and could not come. The satellite feed that showed a flash of red light, which was once the cargo plane, now disappeared from the infrared screen. The boats carrying Cubans from Miami flashed indicating their tragic end. The room watched in silence as the Cuban military gunned down the last of the Cuban nationals and Miami citizens. The operation was a disaster.

Carlos's and Julio's eyes filled with tears as they watched Tito and his freedom fighters slaughtered before their very eyes on the huge monitor in the obscure warehouse. Julio walked over to Ed. "I've seen all that I care to." And he excused himself.

Carlos looked at Ed with the same forlorn look and sighed, "I think I've also seen more than I care to see." The two men tearfully said good-bye to Jack and Seth. Carlos and Julio left together in silence. The two men who had so vehemently opposed each other for so many years were now leaving as grieving allies. Their sharp tongues for each other were held in check. They were both clearly devastated by the evening's disastrous outcome with neither one pointing an accusatory finger at the other. On this tragic night they would not let their differences tear them apart any further.

Jack motioned to Seth. "We too must be going." The two men looked at a despondent Ed. Ed, still standing in front of the monitor, said his farewells. Seth and Jack too left quietly.

CHAPTER 92

Seth requested that Jack drop him at the hospital so he could update Rachel on the evening's tragic events. He wanted to let her know who was responsible for her brother's death. The sun was rising to welcome the new day. Seth noticed the sunlight glowing between the buildings set along the Intracoastal Waterway. Jack looked at Seth. "Get some sleep." Seth smiled in agreement. Jack went on, "When are you leaving?"

"It depends on Rachel. As soon as I know something about how she's doing, then we can make plans. I'm hoping we can get out of here this evening."

Jack continued, "Before you leave, I'm going to need statements from you and Rachel. You know how it is. I gotta have something for the file. I'll meet you and maybe Rachel at your hotel around four this afternoon. You can make your statements, and then I'll put you on a plane back to North Carolina at the FBI's expense." Jack waved and left. Seth headed inside the hospital anxious to tell Rachel about all that happened.

CHAPTER 93

Seth walked into the hospital and headed for Rachel's room. When he had last seen Rachel, she was lying in pain covered in bandages with black swollen eyes. A woman whom Seth had never seen before was lying in the bed once occupied by Rachel. The woman was as startled to see Seth as he was to see her. "Excuse me," announced Seth. "I must be in the wrong room." Seth promptly left the room and located the nurses' station on the floor. "Excuse me, Nurse," called Seth to the older woman sitting behind the desk.

"May I help you?" answered the annoyed nurse.

"Yes, I'm looking for Rachel Dugen. She used to be in the room over there," Seth pointed to the room he had just excused himself.

The nurse looked incredulously at Seth. "We don't have a Ms. Rachel Dugen here."

Seth was annoyed with the lack of patient knowledge by the nurse. "Well, she was here last night. I brought her here in an ambulance."

"Let me look for you." The nurse looked at the prior evening's register and found Rachel's name. She got on the telephone and called the front desk. After a series of exchanges with someone on the other end of the line, she looked up at the distraught Seth. "Ms. Dugen checked herself out before my shift change. That would be about an hour ago."

"Well, do you know where she went?"

"I'm sorry I don't."

Seth was more annoyed now that he had no idea where Rachel went. He found a telephone booth and called the hotel. A hotel operator answered and connected him to Rachel's room.

"Hello," Rachel answered the telephone on the second ring. She had an awful headache from the prior day's beatings. She was still heavily medicated.

Seth was glad to hear Rachel's voice even though it was rough. He was happy to know that she was getting around on her own. "Rachel, I'm at the hospital looking for you. They said you checked yourself out a little while ago."

"Yea, I couldn't stand another minute in that hospital. The food is horrible. And damn if those nurses don't have the coldest hands on earth." They both laughed. Rachel, despite her condition, got quickly to the point. "Well, what did ya find out?"

"Give me time to get there, and I'll tell you all about it. Is anyone there with you?" Seth was still worried about Rachel. Though he was somewhat calmer now that he knew the man who had beaten her was no longer with the living, Seth was still concerned about her safety after being so severely beaten.

"No, I'm all right. Just get your ass back here and tell me what the hell's goin' on!"

Seth said good-bye and exited the hospital. He hailed a cab and arrived at the hotel twenty minutes later. He headed up to Rachel's hotel room. He knocked and heard Rachel race to open the door.

"So what happened?" asked Rachel. Seth looked around the hotel room as he and Rachel made their way into the room so they could sit. The room had been clearly straightened up by a vigil housekeeping staff. The bloodstained towels were removed and the room returned to an almost-pristine condition. A large bouquet of flowers and some Godiva chocolates sat on the small desk in the room, compliments of the hotel.

Rachel sat on the bed propping herself up with some pillows. Seth sat in a chair next to the bed. Seth looked at Rachel for the first time in almost thirty-six hours. He wanted to cry as he looked into her battered face. Her beautiful face was still swollen almost beyond recognition from the beating she had taken. Her lip was stitched in a couple of places. He remembered how stunning she was when he first met her. Now she looked like the loser from a sixteen-round bout from a prizefight.

Seth told Rachel about the evening's events. She showed relief when he told her about shooting Larry Shays, the one that had killed her brother. She was saddened to hear about the tragic ending to Tito and his Cuban freedom fighters that were mercilessly gunned down in some remote cove in Cuba. Her anger flared when she heard how the CIA had manipulated everyone to orchestrate the covert operation. The CIA had placed key people in the military to help facilitate the thefts by the Cubans. They arranged a cargo plane to make the drop in Cuban airspace.

Rachel sat quietly listening and absorbing everything that Seth was telling her. Once Seth paused, she commented, "This was never my brother's fight, but he was the first to die, and no one will ever know why." Tears filled her majestic blue eyes.

Seth felt her pain and moved toward her. He sat on the edge of the bed and held her as gently as he could in his arms to comfort her. She promptly fell into his arms, accepting his sympathy. It wasn't long before they both fell asleep with Seth holding Rachel in his arms.

CHAPTER 94

Jack called around three in the afternoon to get a status report from Seth to determine when he and Rachel had planned on leaving. He had already called the hospital and learned that she had already checked herself out earlier in the day.

At four in the afternoon, two men identifying themselves as FBI agents knocked at Seth's door. Rachel heard the knock from across the hall. She raced into Seth's room following the two FBI agents. One of the men spoke. "Jack sent us for you."

Rachel and Seth were both packed and ready to go. The nap that they had taken was long overdue. The past several days had left the two of them exhausted, and with the anticipation of seeing this thing almost through was more than they could stand. One of Jack's FBI agents helped Rachel gather her belongings and carried them down to the dark four-door sedan that would take them to the local FBI office for a final debriefing.

They met Jack at an FBI office in downtown Miami. They could tell Jack had not yet had any sleep. He was still in the same clothes Seth had last seen him in, and he now had a slight beard showing. "I need to get statements from each of you."

Since Seth was a policeman, this seemed routine. Rachel, however, became more inquisitive. "What do you need our statements for? Hell, just ask the fucking CIA!"

Jack could see Rachel was livid about the circumstance behind her brother's death. He too was angry because of the amount of time he and about a hundred other FBI agents wasted chasing Ed and his Cuban operatives around. Jack responded, "This is routine, we just need to dot the i's and cross the t's." After some prodding, Rachel consented to do a statement for the FBI and then signed off. Seth had already signed his statement.

"You know, Jack . . . I've been thinking a lot about what happened last night," commented Seth.

"And what have you been thinking about?" asked Jack.

"The way the Cuban army was all over the freedom fighters."

"And your point is?"

"It looked like the Cuban army was waiting for the whole damn thing to unfold before them. I mean, they were all over the people in the cove, the MIGs right there to take out that C-130, and the boats from Miami were sitting ducks," commented Seth.

"It bothered me too, but where would the leak come from? We talked with Julio Chavez and Ed Logan about possible leaks. They were the only people that had enough information to cause such a disaster. Julio had the most to gain by the mission's success, and Ed isn't going to sabotage his own op. Hell, even Carlos, who had the most to lose with Julio's success, isn't going to get his own people killed."

"I guess you're right," responded a dejected Seth. "It is just that the cop in me keeps rehashing this whole thing over and over. How about you take us to the airport and get us a couple of first-class tickets so we can go home?"

Jack gave a smile. "I'm one step ahead of you this time." Jack held up two airline tickets. "Coach is the best the FBI can afford. One to Wilmington, North Carolina, and one to our nation's Capitol."

"Coach it is!"

CHAPTER 95

After what seemed like an eternity, Jack, Rachel, and Seth arrived at the Miami International Airport. Jack had an airport courtesy cart take them to Rachel's gate. They sat until it was time for her to board her flight to Reagan International Airport.

When they called Rachel's flight, she stood on her still wobbly legs. Seth supported her as she readied herself to board. He held her in his arms and gave her a few gentle kisses on her cheek. "Give me a call once you get settled," commented Seth.

Rachel stepped back so she could look into Seth's face and then kissed him on his right cheek. "You bet I will." Rachel then headed down the concourse for her plane.

Jack and Seth talked while they waited for Rachel's plane to pull away from the gate. Rachel had spoken earlier in the day to her mother and Mary. Rachel's mother and Mary had driven up to Rachel's place in Washington DC. They felt they needed to get away from Surf City because it fostered such a horrific memory of Hugh's death. They hoped going to Rachel's place would prompt a new beginning for them.

Jack escorted Seth to the Charlotte, North Carolina, gate as soon as Rachel's plane pulled away. Seth's flight back to Wilmington was routed through Charlotte. The men spoke about general sleuth ideas as they waited. Seth called his office to say he was flying into Wilmington, North Carolina, the closest airport to Surf City. He spoke with his loyal officer and second in command, Ned. Ned agreed to pick him up since it would be late in the evening when his flight was to arrive, and most local operations would have shut down by then.

Indeed it was late when Seth's small fifteen-seat commuter plane arrived in Wilmington, North Carolina. Ned was waiting for Seth at the gate. There was only a small skeleton staff on hand to greet the late-night flight. Seth only had one small bag that he retrieved from the tail section of the plane. The two men made their way quickly through the sparse airport to Ned's patrol car waiting next to the airport's front entrance. He felt somewhat privileged parking his patrol car in front of the terminal. Ned brought Argo to greet his master. Argo was beside herself when she saw Seth. She leapt into his arms and managed to get her face close enough to Seth's to bathe his face in moist kisses. Once they got in the car, Argo jumped into Seth's lap, seeking and receiving some overdue attention.

As Ned drove north to Surf City, he filled Seth in on what had been happening, which was not too much. The damage to the private residences and commercial property was being repaired, thanks to the financial resources of FEMA and the reluctant insurance companies, as a result of hurricane Isabelle. Ned dropped Seth and Argo off at their house and went home.

Seth entered his beach house with Argo on his heels. He dropped his bags on the living room floor and got Argo some treats out of the cabinet to bribe his neglected companion. He reached into the refrigerator and opened a bottle of cold beer. Seth looked and saw there were no messages on his answering machine. He wondered if Ned had played the messages and deleted them or if he was just not important enough for anyone to call.

Seth picked up his bag and went into the bedroom and unpacked. He threw on a pair of cotton bed pants and an old T-shirt from one of the local surf shops. Seth returned to the living room and sat on the couch. Argo leaped up on the couch and climbed into his lap. "I guess I haven't been giving you enough attention." Seth started rubbing Argo; in a matter of minutes Argo was on her back absorbing all the attention Seth would give her. The two moved onto the carpeted floor and began roughhousing. Before the evening was through, Seth had a couple more beers and sorted through his pile of mail.

Chapter 96

The Boeing 707 made its final approach into Orly at shortly before seven in the morning. The plane originated in Mexico City. It was the only direct flight from Mexico City to Paris. Vladimir Petrov had purchased his one-way ticket in cash the day before it was to leave; prior to that he had driven from Miami to Houston, Texas. He had taken several flights in between before he caught an Aeroméxico flight into Mexico City.

Once the plane arrived at the gate, Vladimir headed to baggage claim. He did not really care if he even got his baggage and thought about just leaving it. With the money he made, he could afford to buy a whole new wardrobe. He was reeling with excitement after the CIA cargo plane exploded over Sol Beach and Tito Mendoza and his freedom fighters were massacred on a little known beach, in the cove and in their boats.

He eventually picked up his bag and took a cab to the Deux Fontaines, a small restaurant on the Champs-Elysees. He took a seat at a table in front of the quaint restaurant. He ordered a cappuccino and pastry; it was now almost ten in the morning.

"Good morning, Vladimir. Or is it Colonel Radford, or is it Special Agent Robert Carrington, or CIA Operative Ed Logan?" It was Juan Jimenez, the assistant deputy minister of the interior for the Cuban government. The assistant deputy minister was smartly dressed in a custom-made suit he had tailored since arriving in Paris the day before.

"Good morning," responded Vladimir. He stood and motioned for Juan to take a seat opposite him at the small table. He motioned for the waiter, who promptly arrived, and took the assistant deputy minister's order. "Please call me by my given name, Vladimir Petrov."

"Very well, Vladimir," replied Juan. The two men smiled and nodded at each other with mutual respect. Juan continued, "I want to congratulate you. Thanks to you, the CIA nor anyone else in Washington would dare fund another project to remove Fidel or Juan from power for a very long time. We are starting to watch the congressional hearings, thanks to C-SPAN, daily. There will surely be a number of people who will lose their jobs, thanks to our little ruse."

Vladimir was ready to dispense with the pleasantries. He wanted to get down to business. "Do you have my money?" asked Vladimir. He was eager to collect his hard-earned money and move on to better times. His funds were somewhat depleted from moving from city to city using only cash to mask his disappearance.

"Yes, here is the confirmation of your $5 million deposited to the Swiss account you gave us. Tell me, Agent Logan"—Juan caught himself—"excuse me, Vladimir, how is it you were able to infiltrate the CIA and be so integral in the mission?" inquired Juan.

Vladimir cautiously looked over the deposit confirmation. He politely smiled and took time to pause. Once he felt comfortable with the confirmation's validity, he folded it and put it carefully inside the breast pocket of his jacket. Vladimir took a sip of his cappuccino and then turned his attention back to Juan. "My parents immigrated to the United States in 1952. The United States and Soviet Union were at great odds at that time, I'm sure you remember. You probably better remember it as the Cold War. My parents immigrated to the United States through Canada. The KGB prepared excellent documents that gave them the opportunity to blend into the job market in Washington DC. As KGB agents, they spoke English better than most Americans. My father took a job as an appliance repairman. My mother stayed home and ran the errands. She eventually was my tutor, both with my schoolwork and, when I was old enough, in how to be a Soviet spy. The plan was for them to be sleepers, stay anonymous until the KGB needed them. I was born in 1962. They did not tell me my real name until I was eighteen. By then my father had started a business selling computers and servicing them for businesses and the government. When I applied to join the CIA, my father contacted a friend in the CIA for whom he had done some computer work. The friend helped push my application through. I was accepted and have been a good operative for the CIA until now. Well, as good as I could be with a Soviet allegiance. Whenever they needed a volunteer, I was there. My mother died just as I was graduating from college and before I joined the CIA. Up to a year ago, my father had five computer stores throughout the Washington DC area. He died this past year. So I sold the stores for $5 million. With the money you're giving me, I plan to live here in France for the rest of my life, quite comfortably." Vladimir smiled to himself once again; he had been so calculating, and here he was receiving his final payoff. "You know, the KGB had excellent spies but bad negotiators."

"What are your plans now, Vladimir?"

"To enjoy the good life!"

Juan stood and extended his hand to shake Vladimir's. "Thank you again, comrade. I must leave. I have a plane to catch back to Cuba."

Vladimir stood and shook Juan's hand. "No, thank you." Vladimir continued sitting in the café drinking his cappuccino and eating his pastry while watching Juan hail a cab to the airport.

CHAPTER 97

Jack had taken Seth and Rachel's reports along with his own report to the FBI office in Washington DC. It wasn't long before reports made their way to the U.S. Senate Oversight Committee. For the next several months Jack, Seth, and Rachel independently testified before a congressional panel. Several members of the CIA, and FBI were called upon to testify. Numerous people were terminated, with no pensions. After a number of first-year FBI agents had the opportunity to delve into the remotest of archives and did a tireless search were they able to come up with the name Vladimir Petrov. The extensive research included manual state and county records stored in ledgers and five-by-seven-inch cards. The name Ed Logan was eventually tied to the name Vladimir Petrov. Thanks to glasnost, initiated by Mikhail Gorbachev in prior years, the CIA and FBI had access to archaic KGB data linking Vladimir Petrov's parents to the KGB agents. There were several documents indicating that Vladimir's parents immigrated to the United States during the Cold War years. The documents reflected their extensive training before they left the Soviet Union and the seed money used by Vladimir's father to start his computer company that availed him access to government files.

During the period the FBI was immersed in the deluge of domestic and former Soviet Union documents, the CIA began its plan of defense. Ed Logan's immediate boss was terminated with the promise of preserving his pension if he agreed to follow a scripted defense. He was to agree to the standard denial of any and all actions. He was further instructed to claim whenever and wherever possible that he could not answer questions because of potentially jeopardizing ongoing covert operations.

A congressional panel was created from the FBI data to investigate the CIA's domestic actions with regard to Ed Logan's participation in what became known as the Cuban Miami fiasco. They were bound and determined to have someone's head by the conclusion of the inquiry.

The press core covered the story of the Op Gone Bad. The CIA and FBI were paraded before the public as buffoons, and the congressional panel was going to make heads roll. The press corps camped out on the lawns of high-ranking CIA and FBI agents' homes to stick cameras and microphones in their faces. Everybody asked the same probing questions, but everything could "neither be confirmed nor denied," or it was "in the best interest of national security to not say anything at this time."

Carlos and Julio, through some legal maneuvering of their own, avoided the congressional panel's inquiries and were hailed in Miami by the Cuban community as heroes despite the failed attempt. The membership in the Cubans for a Free Cuban rose dramatically. Some believed that not all the membership increases were good. There was a reason to believe that some of the increase was due to pro-Castro infiltrators.

CHAPTER 98

It was late February when Sky called Rachel. "We need to meet." Sky had been working for the FBI in Washington DC for the past several months. His job was to hack into computers under warrants procured by the FBI from federal judges across the county.

"How 'bout tonight for dinner?" replied the intrigued Rachel. She had not heard from Sky since he was nabbed by the FBI in Atlanta. Rachel had called Sky's sister, Beth, in late November to find out what had happened to Sky. Rachel's own life had been in turmoil after Naval Intelligence questioned her about her activities in Miami. The FBI called her in on repeated occasions to query her about what took place in Miami. The CIA also tried to question her, but the FBI intervened. Rachel never understood how she avoided the CIA questioning, but she had had enough of the same questions posed to her by so many federal organizations with different slants.

The two met for dinner on M Street in Washington DC. They greeted each other in the lobby of a small seafood bistro and chatted about incidental things until they were seated. Sky asked for a small table in the back of the half-empty restaurant. Rachel could tell from Sky's actions that he wanted a secluded setting before he was going to get to the heart of why he called her. She knew it had to be related to the Cuban Miami fiasco, but what? The CIA, FBI, and a bunch of other federal agencies had beaten the issue to death. Rachel knew Sky didn't have questions for her, but she felt confident that he had information she wanted to hear.

The restaurant was a Mediterranean-style seafood restaurant. Since the restaurant was new, it had not developed a large clientele, and so it was only half full. The decor was upscale with red, green, and white colors. Votives were placed on each table to provide light for the dimly lit restaurant. It was the environment that Sky wanted, quiet with a sparse crowd. The two of them could talk without anyone overhearing their conversation. They were directed to a booth toward the back of the restaurant.

Once they were seated and the hostess dismissed herself, Sky handed Rachel a large manila envelope that he had tucked under his jacket. "Here's some information that I thought you might be interested in. I shouldn't be doing this ya know."

Rachel couldn't believe the risk Sky was taking. He had broken so many laws that the only way the authorities could control him were for the FBI to hire him. "When did you get religion?" sheepishly inquired Rachel.

"Shit, I was just kiddin'." Sky tried to disguise his newly felt fears of incarceration for violating FBI rules of conduct. In the past, he was fearless. Getting caught hacking into corporate mainframes, school records or any government agency wasn't even an afterthought.

Rachel looked at Sky inquisitively. She felt that maybe he had turned his life around since working for the FBI.

Sky couldn't control his excitement. It had been months since he had last spoken to Rachel. Now that the FBI had set him up in Washington DC, he no longer needed his cloak-and-dagger lifestyle. His parents were proud of him working regular hours and with such a respected organization. "These guys I work with are so green. Compared to what the old gang and I did. It sometimes feels like I'm in Computer 101. These warrants crimp my style. Hell, they give me these assignments that are supposed to take a week, and I knock 'em out in a half day. So while I had the extra time, I did a little work for ya. Ya know, for old time's sake." Sky almost blushed as he looked at Rachel. His crush on her from college still lingered.

Rachel started to open the envelope until Sky asked her to put it away.

A young waitress appeared and took their drink orders and left, leaving them with menus to look over while she got their drinks.

As soon as the waitress left, Rachel asked, "What's in the envelope?"

In a whispered voice, leaning over the table, Sky spoke to Rachel. "The man you are looking for is Vladimir Petrov. He worked for the CIA as Special Agent Ed Logan. He put the whole fiasco together pilfering military bases in the southeast. Then he orchestrated that massacre in Cuba. He was also Lt. Colonel Charles Radford, who was briefly the provost marshal at Camp LeJeune. Vladimir used fraudulent military documents that he got through his position in the CIA to temporarily assign himself to each location prior to a theft to help coordinate the thefts from the inside. His parents were KGB. They came to the United States during the fifties. Vladimir was actually born here in the United States. When he was old enough, his parents started training him to be a KGB agent to follow in their footsteps. His father built a computer company that managed to get U.S. government contracts. Through the contracts, he cultivated contacts inside the CIA and used those contacts to help get his son, Vladimir, a job in the CIA. The CIA and FBI know all this. That's how I got you the information. There's a bio on his life, including his parents, in the envelope."

Rachel looked incredulously at Sky. "Sky, much of this has become public information. It has been all over the media for months. I have been testifying about this. Where the hell have you been?"

Sky was hurt. He never paid much attention to media. His life focused around hacking into computers. He knew some of what had happened was in the media, but he didn't know much about the specifics.

Rachel realized how callous she had been to Sky. She knew the media was something he pretty much ignored. If it didn't happen with a computer, he just ignored it. "I'm sorry, Sky. This whole testifying and everything has worn me out. Let's get something to eat and try to enjoy each other's company."

The waitress reappeared with their drinks. "Would you like to order?" asked the bubbly waitress.

Sky politely responded, "Could you give us a few more minutes?" The waitress nodded and left to attend to four men who just arrived dressed in suits.

Sky loved it when she recognized his little idiosyncrasies. "Well, I did a little more than the rest of them," commented Sky.

Rachel was looking at the menu. She slowly lowered the menu and stared into Sky's eyes. "You know where he is . . . don't you?" asked Rachel. She was almost giddy with excitement; if anyone could use a computer to find someone, Sky was that person.

CHAPTER 99

A big smile appeared on Sky's face. "Yeh. He's outside Toulouse, France. He bought an old farmhouse. Did you know he speaks four languages other than English, fluently? He speaks his former motherland's language of Russian as well as French, Spanish, and German."

"No," answered Rachel. She wasn't interested in Ed Logan's language skills but showed as much enthusiasm as she could muster in hopes of rekindling Sky's damaged ego. She wanted to know where the bastard who was responsible for her brother's death was. "How the hell did you track him down?" inquired Rachel.

"Your boy is a tricky bastard. I tracked him to Houston. Apparently, he drove there and took a plane to Mexico City. That was the easy part. He bought a ticket to Seattle and then another to Tokyo all using names that were easy to track. He was baiting us. He actually rented a car under another name and drove to Vancouver where he flew back to Mexico City and then to Paris, Orly more specifically."

"But how did you track him?" asked an incredulous Rachel. "I mean, with all the name changes, different flights, and everything else."

Sky could see Rachel's curiosity. Only a few minutes before, she was bashing him for burying himself in to his computer hacks while ignoring the rest of the world. And now she was eager to hear the details of his conquest. Sky was thrilled that Rachel was so intent. He paused a moment to enjoy the sensation. "Well, once I got Ed's—I mean Vladimir's bio, I had something to go on. Credit cards were a start. I figured a government employee would only have so much cash availability until I found out he sold his father's company. Yeah, I know spies are supposed to have caches of cash throughout the world, but I took a gamble and figured Vladimir wasn't that bright. My gamble paid off."

"He sold his father's company?" interrupted Rachel.

"Yeah, I'll get to that. I traced the funds from the sale of the company to an account in Switzerland that still left him cash poor except for the three thousand he took in cash."

"How do you know he kept three thousand in cash?" asked Rachel.

"That was easy. I found out who his attorney was because the transfer of the commercial property is public record. His attorney, who handled the closing, had all of the closing documents on his computer. I hacked in and found out how much the sale was for. The closing documents indicated how much was for attorney fees, commission, and so on. I traced the wire transfer from the bank here in the United States to Switzerland. It was short three thousand dollars."

"You are amazing!" Rachel asked, "But credit cards?"

"Yeah, he's a government employee, which meant he didn't have a lot of cash lying around. Even though he was working for the Russian government, they don't pay a whole lot, so I didn't think he would have that lying around either. My guess is most of that money is also offshore since if the CIA checks on its own people, you don't have a big, fat bank account. I figured he hadn't received his payoff for what happened in Cuba, so he would have to charge everything until he got his payoff. To buy last-minute tickets on an airplane gets expensive. I knew how much cash he had. The rest of the cash I knew was offshore, and he had to get offshore to get to it. He sure wasn't going to transfer it back! I wrote a program once I hacked into the airlines' mainframes to look for the names he used in his past life with the CIA. I figured he probably hadn't dumped those credit cards because . . . hell the government was still payin' for 'em." Sky sat back and let out a big laugh.

The waitress appeared once again to take their orders. Sky ordered a seafood medley over linguine, and Rachel ordered mahi mahi over angel-hair pasta. They ordered a bottle of Pinot Grigio to go with the meal. The waitress was excited to have customers springing for a bottle of wine running up their tab. She promptly returned and uncorked the bottle. After Rachel examined the cork, she poured a small amount into her glass to taste. Once Rachel gave her the okay, she poured Rachel and then Sky a glass full of wine.

Sky started talking again after the waitress left. "His bio indicated that he was a cheap bastard. I guess that sometimes comes with being a government employee. So I employed a process of elimination. What I did was look for single passengers and how they paid for their tickets. Then I tracked the people who bought last-minute tickets and watched their credit card activities while they were in town. I also cross-checked the passengers to see if they resided in that particular city or state. I got a few of the old gang to help out. I told 'em it was for you. After that I had to get them to slow down. I don't know what you said or did to my friend who gave you that envelope while you were in Atlanta, but he was definitely on your side. We looked for the ones where they were staying in a hotel, eating out, and renting cars. The process of elimination eventually tracked him to Paris."

"Hell, that could be anyone," responded Rachel.

"Yeah, it could have been, but it wasn't. Your boy is white and has fucked over everyone he knows to cash in. So where could he go? He can't stay in the United States. He needs a place he can blend in because if he stands out he'll draw attention to himself. He knows the CIA is looking for him, so he has to stay below the radar screen but still enjoy his money. That rules out the Far East. Russia doesn't have enough posh stuff to attract him. So voila, that leaves Europe or maybe South America. I ruled out South America because even though he speaks Spanish, I thought Europe was a better fit. He is looking for the finer things in life such as good food, drink, and places to see and things to do. Besides, what red-blooded Russian doesn't want to go to Europe?"

Rachel sat listening amazed at Sky's process of elimination. She thought he had spent his whole life wrapped up in computers, and here he was, educating her on how he tracked down Vladimir Petrov, a trained KGB and CIA agent who spent his entire life working for the other side right under the CIA's nose.

Sky couldn't wait to continue. It seemed as though he hadn't taken a breath since he started his harangue. "I also figured that someone from Cuba would meet Vladimir with his payoff, so I monitored flights with high-ranking Cuban officials flying out of Cuba shortly after everything went down. Only one guy from Cuba fit the profile that also went to Paris." Sky was feeling in command, cutting Rachel off each time she tried to intercede.

Rachel thought a little more. "How can you be so sure it is him?"

"You're gonna love this part. I helped out this French computer nerd a few months back, so he owed me a favor."

Rachel dismissed Sky's comments about a "computer nerd." Sky could have been a poster child for the Computer Nerds of America.

Sky continued his story. "I asked my French computer nerd for the video of the port of entry at Orly for the time when Vladimir's flight arrived. He was reluctant at first, so I threatened to send a virus to the French government's computers with him as the primary source of the virus. It scared him to death, so he helped out. He figured I had the know-how. Once I got the video, I cross-checked his picture with the CIA records using facial recognition. It's him, Rachel. It's really him! Open up the file, I put his picture on top."

Rachel opened up the envelope and slid an eight-by-ten-inch black-and-white picture out of the envelope. Rachel stared at the CIA picture of the Russian man that had caused her family so much heartache. "You're a fucking genius!" Rachel started laughing when it occurred to her what Sky had done. "You cross-checked his picture with the CIA records?"

Sky started to laugh too when he thought about what he had just said to Rachel. "I hope they don't mind me hacking in!" Sky got somber and leaned close to Rachel. "You can't tell anyone I told you this. I could go to prison. Rachel, I couldn't handle going to prison!"

Rachel could see the terror in Sky's face. She had never seen it before. He had broken so many laws before that it seemed strange to hear the fear in his voice about the possibility of going to prison. She wondered if working with the FBI made him realize there were serious consequences of his actions, or maybe he had finally started growing up once he got away from his computer buddies in Atlanta. "I will take it to my grave." Rachel leaned toward Sky and gave him a kiss on his cheek. "Thanks!"

Soon things between them settled down, and the waitress returned with their meals.

Sky continued to fill Rachel in on information to which the media was not privy. "The CIA and FBI know Vladimir is in France, but they don't know exactly where. They have been trying to get the French government to extradite him here but no such luck. I don't think the French will ever give him up. They're still pissy about the whole Iraq issue . . . there's more."

"What else could there be?" inquired Rachel.

"I traced where the Cubans paid him five million dollars for the information. As you already heard, he also cashed in his father's business for an additional five million dollars. I know the money went into a Swiss account, but I can't access the account without the code numbers. If you find him, get me the account numbers, code numbers and anything else you can find about that account, and I'll get the money back."

Sky finally breathed a sigh and allowed Rachel to digest everything he told her. "He used the money to buy the farmhouse. I bought a condo down on the Potomac River not too long ago. That's when I started thinking about what Vladimir might do with his money. All of a sudden his credit cards slowed to a halt. I thought maybe he was now spending his newfound cash. Then I started tracking real estate purchases and eventually found his little farmhouse in Toulouse."

Rachel was shocked and angry. Rachel thought for a moment. "I've gotta go!"

"But we haven't even finished eating," responded the dejected Sky.

"I know. Can I owe ya one?"

"Sure," answered Sky. He sat there eating his meal alone.

Rachel headed for the door and then stopped. She hurried back to the table where Sky sat alone pouring some of the Pinot Grigio into his glass. Rachel leaned over and gave Sky an affectionate kiss on his cheek, startling him.

Sky looked at Rachel standing over him. He was once again giddy. "You owe me one hell of a meal."

"Gladly," answered Rachel, who was proud of herself for restoring Sky's faith in her.

CHAPTER 100

Even though it was late, Rachel returned to her office at Naval Intelligence. It was quiet. Most of the office staff was on assignment out of the office or had gone home for the day. Rachel looked into acquaintances she had come to know in France from her current and previous assignments. She grabbed a few things from her office and went home.

The next morning Rachel went into to her office as usual. She went to her commanding officer and requested a short leave of absence to clear up some family matters relating to her brother's death.

She called Sky. "We need to meet after work."

"Okay. Where?"

"Meet me at Reagan International. I have a seven thirty-nine flight to Paris on Air France."

At the end of the day, Rachel took a cab to Reagan International Airport. She had bought a one-way ticket to Paris and waited for Sky.

Rachel waited as long as she could for Sky to meet her. Eventually she had to head for the gate.

As she approached the gate, Sky grabbed her by the arm. "I've been looking for you," commented Sky. "Do you know how many people there are in this airport? It's like looking for a needle in a haystack."

"Sorry, I guess I should have been a little more specific," responded Rachel. "Here." Rachel handed Sky a large manila envelope. "There are instructions in this. I'll call you later." Rachel proceeded to the gate.

"Hey, Rach . . . be careful."

Rachel turned and gave Sky a wink and left.

CHAPTER 101

Rachel's plane arrived in Paris time at six thirty in the morning. As Rachel headed for the Air France baggage claim, she noticed Seth walking toward her.

"What the hell are you doing here?" asked Rachel.

"Sky called me. He thought you might need my help. He told me I better hurry, and he was right. My plane got here ten minutes ago. Ya know, Sky had a first-class ticket waiting for me when I got to the airport. Somehow I think he bought the ticket through the government with his computer prowess."

"Seth," demanded a stern Rachel, "stay out of this!"

"Rachel, Sky's worried about you, and so am I. I came here not because I thought you'd need my help but to keep you from doing something stupid. I was about to reach through the phone and kill Sky when he told me you were on your way here. But then he told me you called him at the last minute to let him know you were headed to Paris, so I was willing to let him off the hook."

Rachel was irate and disgusted. She walked away from Seth, heading in the direction of baggage claim.

Seth paused in anger as Rachel walked away. Then chased after her and grabbed her arm to cause her to stop.

Rachel turned at Seth, ready to chastise him and caught herself realizing that all he wanted was to help keep her out of trouble.

"I love you," stated Seth in a matter-of-fact manner. "I don't want you to do something stupid because then I'll have to move to France to visit you on weekends."

"No, you don't you love me. You love your wife's memory!" Rachel realized how insensitive she was. Rachel dropped her head to try and regroup. "I'm sorry. That was way out of line."

Rachel's comments stung. Seth took her comments hard. He knew he would always love Maribeth, but he also knew that he loved Rachel. Seth didn't know what to say. He just looked at Rachel, hoping she would help him pick up the pieces.

Rachel could not believe what she had heard. She had seen Seth countless times during the Senate oversight hearings, but it was only in passing. They were asked not to talk with each other until after the hearings. The prosecutors were concerned that if they were together, they would discuss their testimony, potentially giving the defense grounds to overturn the panel's decision. Rachel hugged Seth and then gave him a long, slow kiss. It was the first real kiss they shared. There were the casual pecks on the cheek here and there and the drunken night in Ocala, but this was real. When Rachel stopped, she looked him in the eyes. "Well then, can we start over?"

"Sure," replied the relieved Seth. "Tell me, what are your plans, and I hope you're not going to tell me you're planning to kill Vladimir Petrov?"

Rachel looked unyielding at Seth. "I want to bring that son of a bitch to justice!"

"I want to see that happen too, but we're gonna have to let our respective governments fight that one out," replied Seth.

"The hell I am," snapped an agitated Rachel. "I'm going after him right now! I know where he is."

"Whoa," answered Seth. "You can't just go and pick up Vladimir Petrov and haul him off to the U.S. to stand trial. It just can't happen."

"Look . . . I'm not going to wait umpteen years for the U.S. to bring him to justice like that guy who killed his girlfriend in Philadelphia. That girl's family waited forever for the French government to finally send that asshole back to serve out his sentence after his conviction in absentia."

"I remember. Einhorn, Ira Einhorn. The police found her body stuffed in a trunk in his apartment. It took like twenty years before the French government finally sent him back."

"That's him. And I'm not waiting twenty years!" Rachel started again for baggage claim. Once again Seth grabbed hold of Rachel to keep her from walking away. "Tell me that you at least have a plan," remarked the frustrated Seth.

Rachel paused as she gave Seth a devilish grin. "Do I have a plan? Of course, I have a plan, but I don't want to talk about it here."

"Well then, let's get going," commented the curious Seth.

They both headed for the baggage claim. Rachel locked her arms around one of Seth, pulling herself in close. "So ya love me?" teasingly asked Rachel. She had not felt this giddy since high school.

Seth could tell the feeling was mutual by Rachel's actions though she never said she loved him.

They headed on to baggage claim to claim their luggage. Then they headed on to the Eurocar car rental company. When they arrived at the Eurocar counter,

Rachel gathered her thoughts together. She dropped her luggage and threw her arms around Seth's neck. She put her face as close to Seth as she could but still looking at his entire face. "Are you sure you really love me?"

"Yes," replied Seth with a reassuring stare.

Rachel leaped up throwing her legs around Seth's waist, still with her arms locked around Seth's neck. Although Seth was caught off guard by her sudden display of affection, he fiercely held her close to his body. She kissed his lips and his face. "I love you too!" Tears filled her eyes. With everything that had happened in their lives that was so terrible, this was a shining light.

CHAPTER 102

Seth insisted on driving the four-door Renault sedan. Rachel took the roll of navigator. She knew where to go, but neither had driven around Paris before. As they drove along, Rachel explained to Seth her plan on capturing Vladimir Petrov and getting him back to the United States to stand trial. Seth felt that Rachel's plans on capturing Vladimir were hazy, but he liked her plans of getting Vladimir back to the United States. Once she captured Vladimir, Rachel's plan was to drive him to Den Haag in the Netherlands. Den Haag is better known as The Hague, a port city located on the North Sea in the Netherlands. She had already been in contact with a Dutch fisherman that loathed the French and owed Rachel a favor as a result of her work with Naval Intelligence. She never elaborated on what that favor was or why a Dutch fisherman would need a favor from a Naval Intelligence officer. She did indicate he was most grateful and wanted to reciprocate the favor. Rachel also contacted some American fisherman out of Gloucester, Massachusetts, who still resented the French since 9/11 and liked the idea of doing something covert to get back at them. The Dutch captain would take Rachel and her captive fishing in the Grand Banks in the northern Atlantic Ocean. The American fisherman, who would coincidentally be fishing in the Grand Banks, would meet them and bring Rachel and Vladimir back to the United States. The downside to the plan was the rocky waves and currents that Rachel and her captive would have to negotiate to transfer between the two boats. The only way they could safely make the transfer would be to go into the water. It would be a daunting task since the water is typically freezing to begin with at this time of year.

CHAPTER 103

Rachel and Seth drove to a meat butcher's store in a middle-class neighborhood on Paris's east side.

"Curious place to go after flying all night. I was hoping we might get breakfast at a nice pastry shop with a cup of coffee," commented Seth.

Rachel ignored the comment. "Come on. This is business!"

Rachel led the way into the butcher shop with Seth close behind. Rachel asked the woman for Jean Francois in French. A moment later, a tall lean man came from the back room wearing an apron covered in blood. He introduced himself as Jean Francois. "May I help?" asked Jean still in French.

"Yes," replied Rachel, continuing the French dialogue. "May we speak somewhere privately?"

Jean took a moment to eye Rachel and Seth over. He calmly nodded and motioned for them to follow him into the back room from whence he had just come. "What do you want?" asked a curt Jean. He had a good idea what they wanted, but he wanted to hear them ask.

"I know you sell guns on the black market, and we need two guns," demanded Rachel.

Jean looked back incredulously. "I don't understand." It was a common game for the gun dealers to play with an unknown prospective buyer. It was, first of all, a line of defense in case he was being set up. It was also a ploy to drive up the price.

Rachel hated the act Jean was putting up. "Look, we don't have time to play games. I know you sell guns. I want two Makarovs." The Makarov is a Russian-made pistol, smaller and less powerful than its predecessor the Tokarev but effective for what Rachel and Seth needed.

Jean looked angrily back at Rachel. "It's $1,500 U.S. each!"

Rachel was not in the mood to bargain, and she did not have that kind of money. "For both, $2,000 or I turn you over to the police." Rachel flashed her Naval Intelligence badge for good measure.

Jean begrudgingly nodded. "Come back in one hour." He was angry that someone had told the authorities about him, but to sell the Americans a couple of Makarovs to keep his freedom was a cheap price to pay. Besides, he was going to still make a little money off the deal. Jean felt it odd that someone from Naval Intelligence would have to buy an illegal gun on the black market, but he had been in the illegal gun trade long enough to know not to ask questions.

"Agreed," responded Rachel.

Rachel knew Jean was going to make some money on the Makarovs, but that was fine with her. He was, after all, a businessman, and she needed guns ASAP. *Let France solve its own gun-control problems*, thought Rachel.

They left Jean to get the guns. They stepped out of the small shop and onto the sidewalk. Rachel turned to Seth, "How 'bout that breakfast you were asking about?"

Seth did not understand a thing that just transpired at the butcher shop. The only thing he understood out of the exchange in French between Rachel and the butcher was "Makarov." "Rach, I didn't understand a thing back there except I gather you asked him to get you a Makarov."

"Make that two Makarovs," replied Rachel. "Can we get the breakfast? We've got an hour."

Seth shook his head in amazement how cool Rachel could be and her command of the French language. "I'm right behind you."

Rachel and Seth found a café a few blocks away. They chose a table outside but under the awning. Soon they were joined by a French waiter. Rachel ordered coffee and pastries for the two of them. It was cool under the awning for a winter day, but it was too nice of a day to stay tuck inside. The long flight from Washington DC had them longing for some open air, and the patio was what they felt they needed.

After the waiter left, Seth asked Rachel, "How did you know about Jean Francois and his little gun business?"

Rachel enjoyed Seth's curiosity for the underworld. "He is a known gun supplier on the Paris black market. Naval Intelligence likes to keep files on known gun dealers throughout the world. You never know when you're going to have a covert op somewhere, and a few harmless underworld gun suppliers come in handy."

"Harmless gun suppliers?" asked Seth. "There is no such thing."

"Well, we consider them harmless. We keep close tabs on them and watch who their buyers are as well as their suppliers. The information we can gather often leads to some big things on the dark side. It's stuff that no one ever hears about for good reason—except for the big stuff, obviously." Rachel felt proud of herself and her inside information.

"Obviously," agreed Seth.

After they ate, Rachel and Seth returned and met with Jean. They paid Jean the $2,000 for the Makarovs. They also bought a hundred rounds of ammunition to go with the Makarovs. Rachel and Seth returned to the Renault and headed for Toulouse.

—

CHAPTER 104

As they traveled along the French country roads, they talked about what they wanted to do when they returned to the United States. Rachel was ready to get out of the navy and return to civilian life. She hadn't given a lot of thought to what she wanted to do when she got out but hoped she could use some of what she learned from her time in Naval Intelligence. She indicated that she was considering the FBI or possibly a state bureau of investigation. Seth asked her if she considered a police department, but she felt that after her time in Naval Intelligence, a police department may not have enough challenges for her unless it was in a major metropolitan area. Seth invited her to move in with him in his house in Surf City while she made up her mind. He reminded her that life was slow and quiet, which also appealed to Rachel.

They enjoyed taking in the country scenery of France. The vineyards and old small towns with men in their berets and the woman in their floral dresses made for a pleasant drive. Winter was clearly present with the trees void of their leaves. The farmers had plowed under the previous year's crops, and the soil now lay dormant waiting the spring planting.

It was still daylight when they arrived in Toulouse. They cautiously inquired about the address of Vladimir Petrov. No one had heard of a Vladimir Petrov, but there was an American named Gordon Welsh who recently bought a small farmhouse just outside of town. Rachel showed a picture of Vladimir Petrov that Sky had given her at their last meeting, the dinner that Rachel ran out on in Washington DC. The restaurant owner verified the picture as being Gordon Welsh and described the American as very wealthy but cheap. Rachel laughed to herself, "Figures!"

It was beginning to get dark when Rachel and Seth got a room at a bed-and-breakfast on the edge of town closest to Vladimir Petrov's new hometown. They opted for one room this time.

They carried their bags up to their room. Their trip to France was business and required just the one bag each.

The room at the inn was decorated simply but quaintly. Their room looked over some fallow land with rolling hills. Seth noticed the sun was nothing more than a fading memory of the day setting over the rolling hills on the horizon.

Seth turned around from enjoying the vista and saw Rachel pulling back the duvet.

"We have a few hours to kill, got any ideas?" asked Rachel.

As Seth looked across the room at Rachel, it reminded him of the first time he saw her. The first time he saw her, she was in her uniform, and she was intoxicating. He couldn't keep his eyes off her. This time was no different, minus the official-looking uniform. Rachel had on a snug-fitting blouse and a pair of jeans. She was nothing short of stunning. Seth didn't hesitate in responding to her invitation.

CHAPTER 105

They both fell asleep after an exhilarating sexual interlude. They awoke rested and showered together. At midnight, they drove to Vladimir's farmhouse. They found a dirt road that ran behind Vladimir's house and that of his distant neighbor. A two-foot-high stone fence separated Vladimir's land from another neighbor on the other side along with a paved road that brought them here. This night would be a dry run to find his house and get a feel for the neighborhood. They decided to spend the next few days planning their strategy. They decided they would go to Vladimir's farmhouse at various times in the day to watch and learn his routine and those of his neighbors. The inn was relaxing, and the countryside added to their romantic ambience. There were several small vintners in the area for Seth and Rachel to visit that helped to add cover to their reconnaissance.

The fact that they were there to accost a trained covert operative, Vladimir Petrov, was something that was a daunting task and would need careful planning. They would need an opportune moment to kidnap him and transport him to the Dutch coast in order to escape. All the details of Vladimir's abduction would need to go without any mistakes in order not to draw attention. To kill Vladimir would be easier, but that was not the reason they came to France.

CHAPTER 106

It was a cool, rainy winter Sunday evening when Rachel and Seth set out for Vladimir's farmhouse for the final visit. It was just before ten o'clock when they left the quaint restaurant where they had dined. They had checked out of the bed-and-breakfast earlier in the day. Seth drove the Renault as the rain tapped on the windshield, and the wiper blades bounced back and forth keeping pace with the rain. He found the dirt road that ran behind Vladimir's farmhouse. Seth parked the rented Renault, and they quietly exited the car, making sure not to slam the car doors. Seth and Rachel crept up from behind the house. They were wearing black leather gloves, black sweatshirts, and black pants to blend into the night. Both were holding their Makarov in their hands, ready to fire should a situation present itself. Seth carried a small backpack that had rope and duct tape to assist with the abduction.

Luckily, there were several bushes to hide behind as they made their way to the back door. Other than watching out for a few stones slick from the rain, the trek across the property went relatively smooth. They reached the back door. There were French doors that opened onto a stone patio area from the back of the house. Rachel thought how perfect it would be on a spring day with flowers in bloom to peer out the French doors onto the stone patio inundated with brightly colored flowers. The patio area that was once surrounded by flowers was now filled with empty pots or pots with plants that had gone dormant for the winter. Some rusted-out wrought-iron furniture filled out the rest of the patio area.

Their previous trip to Vladimir's farmhouse was for the purpose of determining what kind of obstacles they may encounter in the abduction. There were no visible signs of security. Rachel and Seth came to two conclusions. One premise was that Vladimir felt as though he left no trail and had completely eluded his enemies. The second thought was that the security was confined to the farmhouse itself and as such was to give Vladimir just enough time to rebuff his pursuers. Rachel and Seth felt that their second assumption was more likely since Vladimir would not want the authorities snooping around after a lifetime of clandestine affairs. They also felt that Vladimir would feel strongly enough that he could combat most any attack.

Seth used his left hand to try the door. The handle gave, and Seth gently pushed the door open. As Seth opened the door, an alarm sounded. From the lamp on the other side of the room, they both saw an image dart across the room. Rachel pushed Seth down to the floor and dove behind a couch. Seth found himself behind an old wooden trunk.

As Seth hid behind the wooden trunk, he thought about their two assumptions. Thus far he felt their second conclusion that the security system was confined to the farmhouse itself and not to the local police department was right on.

Rachel looked around the room. The single lamp on the far side of the room that illuminated the person darting as they entered was the only light blanketing the room. Rachel took aim and shot out the light on her first attempt. The only light now was filtering in from a kitchen light and the moon glowing in through the French doors they just entered.

To Rachel, the dimly lit room appeared to be a family room. The trunk Seth was hiding behind appeared to double as a side table. There were magazines piled on a coffee table made with wooden legs and a marble top.

CHAPTER 107

When the alarm sounded from the intruders, Vladimir retrieved a Glock pistol from a kitchen drawer. He checked the clip to be sure the gun was loaded. He forced the clip back in and cocked the gun. Vladimir cautiously made his way back to where the intruders made their entry. The sound of the alarm continued to fill the night. The security system had worked as he had hoped. It gave him just enough time to take cover without alerting the authorities. Vladimir kept his back flush against the wall as he made his way. He heard a shot, and the room that he had been sitting in reading went dark. He soon realized that the kitchen light behind him made a silhouette of him for the intruders. He had to dare getting shot to turn out the light to balance the tables. Vladimir ran into the kitchen throwing his hand at the light switch. The house was now dark accept for the glow of the moonlight through the farmhouse windows.

It took a minute before Rachel's and Seth's eyes adjusted to the darkened house. Rachel motioned to Seth to go to the other side of the room to search for a different passage from where Vladimir disappeared. Seth could barely see Rachel motioning in the darkened room. Rachel followed the path from another angle, hoping to box Vladimir in. Rachel guardedly made her way. The wooden floor beneath her feet creaked as she crept along. In the corner of her eye, she saw a shadowy figure taking aim. The only thought that passed through Rachel's mind was that it was too late: Vladimir had her. As she attempted to move for cover, there was a loud noise. Rachel recognized the loud noise instantly, the distinct sound of a Makarov going off. She checked herself but then heard a thump. Something or someone had collapsed onto the farmhouse wooden floor.

CHAPTER 108

Seth saw Vladimir taking aim at Rachel and shot first, hitting him in the back of the head. His stomach cramped at the realization he likely killed a man. Seth moved to where Vladimir lay on the wooden floor to check for a pulse; there was none.

Rachel looked at Seth in the darkened room. "Thanks. I thought for sure I was a goner."

Seth smiled back. "You're welcome. Well, so much for taking Mr. Petrov back to the U.S. to stand trial."

Rachel acknowledged Seth's comment and then immediately raced to flip on a few lights around the house. She started going through drawers. She worked as efficiently as she could not to take any time to replace things as she found them.

"What the hell are you doing?" shouted the incredulous Seth over the blaring siren.

"We need to locate his records for his Swiss Bank account," Rachel demanded.

Seth thought about the alarm again as they searched, but assumed that the alarm was only for the house itself and not a remote monitoring station since there were no phone calls and no sounds of approaching sirens. Seth found the connection for the alarm and ripped the cords from a box attached the wall. The alarm ceased. Seth figured Vladimir set up the alarm mostly to scare people away, figuring he would not want the local cops stopping by unnecessarily. He also figured Vladimir was arrogant enough to want to handle intruders personally.

They began turning on and off lights as they entered the various rooms of the small farmhouse and rummaged through the house methodically. They opened drawers and closets. What they couldn't see they felt for or knocked on walls and flooring listening for hollow sounds for potential hidden compartments.

Rachel focused her search in the downstairs area. Seth went upstairs and started with what appeared to him to be the master bedroom.

Seth went into the closet in the master bedroom. He pulled a cord hanging from the ceiling of the closet, and a bare bulb came to life. Seth saw a stack of shoeboxes, a valise, and a metal box containing an assortment of important papers, but not what Seth had hoped to find. Seth tapped on the old wooden walls, hoping to find a hidden compartment. As Seth searched, he noticed one of the boards beneath where he was standing was loose. Seth went back to a dresser where he remembered seeing a small pocketknife. It was in the bedroom adjacent to the closet. He returned and pried at the loose floorboard. The board came up easily. Seth looked into the small cubbyhole in the floor of the closet. *Bingo*, thought Seth. Vladimir had placed his shoes over the compartment to help conceal the hiding place. But as Seth had stumbled around the small closet, the loose board revealed itself. "Rachel!" shouted Seth. "I think I found what we're looking for." Seth held a cluster of documents reflecting the Central Intelligence Agency logo at the top and numerous passports of varying Latin American and European nations as well as the United States and Canada.

Rachel raced up the stairs and found Seth sitting on a closet floor going through a stack of papers. They began poring over the documents.

After glancing through a small stack of documents, Seth called, "I got it! The bank is Banc Lucerne, and here are the account numbers, codes—everything we need."

After glancing through several documents that Seth shared with her, Rachel gasped, "Christ!"

"What is it?" asked Seth.

"Wait a minute!" Rachel got up and walked into the bathroom. Seth followed closely behind her. She closed the bathroom door and turned on the light. Rachel did not want to have too many lights visible from outside. She closed the lid on the toilet and sat down and began to read the documents she held in her hand. Her eyes began to tear as she sat silently reading.

CHAPTER 109

Seth stood over Rachel as she read over the documents. "What is it?"

"Carlos Hernandez."

"What about him?" asked Seth.

"He is one of Fidel Castro's people."

"That can't be. He is president of the Cubans for a Free Cuba. He was there that night at the Opa-Locka Airport when they were loading up the cargo plane. He was as saddened as we were with the outcome standing in that warehouse watching it on the infrared screen." Seth stopped when he realized that the man that brought Carlos to the airport was none other than Vladimir. The man who had identified himself at the Opa-Locka Airport as Ed Logan was, in fact, Vladimir. He was the provost marshal at Camp LeJeune. It had all come out during the hearing that Vladimir was several people orchestrating his own private little op for $5 million, and now they had the final link in Miami.

Rachel handed Seth the papers she had been poring over. It had been painful for her to read about a plot put together by a Russian spy raised in the United States. The end of the Cold War had taken much of the air out of Vladimir's sails, so he turned to greed, and Hugh had gotten in the way. Tears filled in her eyes.

Seth could see the tears in her eyes as he tried rubbing her back to console her as she sat. He took the papers from Rachel and started to read them. Ed Logan, a.k.a. Vladimir, met Carlos at a dinner party in Caracas, Venezuela. The dinner party was for various visiting diplomats in Caracas. Carlos was invited because he had met with the president of Venezuela, Hugo Chavez, supposedly trying to put pressure on Cuba, none of which ever materialized. After the dinner party, Carlos and Vladimir met several times in Mexico, Costa Rica, and Panama before Vladimir had his initial meeting with Julio Chavez, Carlos's nemesis in the Cubans for a Free Cuba. After Vladimir's meeting with Julio, all subsequent meetings with Carlos were moved to a hotel in Tampa, Florida. The

—

idea was that by having the meetings in Tampa, it would draw less attention to Carlos flying in and out of the United States. Logistics also made it easier for Vladimir to play both sides of the fence.

Rachel wiped the tears from her eyes. "That bastard!" shouted Rachel. "Castro helped set Carlos up in Miami. He funded him with money passing through the Cayman Islands and the Bahamas." According to the documents, Castro helped subsidize Carlos to keep an eye on Cuban exile dissidents in Miami that may be plotting to help overthrow him. That was the main reason only political and economic pressure were every applied to Cuba and endorsed by Carlos's organization. Castro knew that the CIA would recruit Cuban exiles in Miami if any plots were ever organized. Just like the Bay of Pigs incident.

"Rachel, let's take these documents and get the hell out of here. Someone may have heard the shooting and called the cops," commented Seth. "If nothing else, they should have heard that damn alarm." Seth and Rachel gathered the documents they found and started stuffing them into a gym bag they found in the closet. "Whoa," commented Seth. "It looks like Vladimir also had an op started in Venezuela . . ."

CHAPTER 110

Bam! "What was that?" asked Rachel, cutting Seth off. The sound of car doors slamming echoed through the night.

Seth ran to the nearest upstairs bedroom window and saw men running toward the farmhouse. Rachel made her way into the bedroom, turning off the bathroom light as she exited, when Seth turned to alert her. They heard people already moving rapidly about on the first floor. Seth grabbed Rachel by the arm and motioned for her to climb out the window on the opposite side of the room. Seth helped Rachel through the window and onto the roof that was over the family room where they originally entered the farmhouse. Seth followed Rachel through the window and onto the roof. The roof was old barrel tile and wet from the evening's rain, which made the footing precarious. Seth made his way to the edge of the roof and cautiously looked around before he made his next move. He leaped down to the patio that was just outside the family room of the farmhouse. Without saying a word, Seth motioned for Rachel to jump.

As she began to jump, she heard someone shout in English from the window they just exited from, "They're on the roof!"

Rachel leaped onto the patio where Seth tried to break her jump. They heard a man trying to climb onto the roof. Seth looked and saw three men coming from the family room inside the house. He noticed each pursuer was wearing military-grade night-vision equipment. Seth thought, *Shit, these guys are pros.*

"Run, goddammit!" shouted Seth. Rachel followed Seth to the car as fast as they could go. They heard several of the men from the farmhouse close behind. When they reached the car, Seth jump into the driver's side, throwing the gym bag he was carrying onto the backseat. Rachel got in on the passenger side. Seth's hands were trembling as he put the key into the ignition and started the car.

A man reached Rachel's door as the small Renault engine turned over. Since Rachel locked the door as soon as she got in, the man pounded on her window with his fist. The man pulled his sidearm to smash the glass when Seth threw the car in reverse, knocking him to the ground. The car sped backward on the dirt road, slipping and sliding, until it reached the paved road. Once on the paved road, Seth threw the car into first gear and jerked the steering wheel to the right, causing the tires to squeal as they took hold on the slippery pavement. Seth drove the Renault as fast as he could, trying to put as much distance between them and the professionally trained men.

Rachel watched the pursuers return to the farmhouse and get into a large white van. As Seth passed the driveway that lead to Vladimir's house the van pulled onto the road behind them fishtailing at first until the driver could gain control. "Jesus . . . who are those guys!" shouted Rachel. "They don't dress like cops." Rachel was remembering the black shirt and pants of her pursuers. She also remembered them wearing black knit caps and some of the men with night-vision goggles. It finally occurred to her that the men called out in English as they climbed though the window onto the roof.

"My guess is that the way they were dressed, they're CIA. I think they were looking to tie up loose ends since the French government wasn't cooperating," answered a rattled Seth. He was staring intently at the road as he raced through the French countryside.

"Why are they chasing us?" inquired Rachel. "All we did was kill that bastard! If anything, we gave them a helping hand. What else could there be? Hell . . . we already testified against Vladimir."

Rachel was smart, thought Seth, but also sometimes a little naive. "They probably want to know what we found in the house more than anything. My guess is we may have more in that bag than we know. When we can sit down, I think we better go through what we have a little more thoroughly," commented Seth. "I have a feeling that bag on the backseat is going to shake a few people up, and that's why those pros are chasing us."

Seth looked in the rearview mirror and could see the van a quarter of a mile behind him. He had the small Renault going as fast as he could drive it on the windy French back roads. The dampness in the air and on the roads caused even more difficulty for Seth to handle the unfamiliar car. His driving instincts from his training with the Charlotte Police Department were taking over. The van was doing everything it could to keep up but was experiencing the same slippery conditions as Seth. Both were skilled at driving in adverse conditions, but both were driving in the dark on unfamiliar roads with vehicles not designed for high-speed driving.

A full moon helped Seth follow the foreign road, but was aiding his pursuers as well. Seth needed a break if he was somehow going to lose them. He knew he got his training driving police cars with the Charlotte Police Department, but he also knew his pursuer had similar training most likely with a federal agency, so the tables were balanced.

The Renault screamed through the countryside and small villages. The van kept pace, but the back roads prevented the van from coming up alongside the Renault to force it off the road. Seth couldn't understand why the pursuers didn't attempt any shots at them, but felt at the same time grateful they elected not to shoot.

"Look out!" shrilled Rachel as a farmer came out of a side road on his tractor. Seth swerved, just missing the tractor.

Seth thought, *What the hell is he doing on a tractor at this time of the night?* Seth watched the van's attempts to avoid hitting the tractor in his rearview mirror. The van tried in vain to stop and ended up careening into an old building ending their pursuit of Rachel and Seth. Seth gave one final glance in his rearview mirror as he watched the farmer rush to the aid of the accident victims.

Rachel cheered, "That's it! They're out of it. We're home free."

"I don't think so," responded Seth. "I would imagine they're calling ahead to get someone to meet us in Paris. They know we have to get there to get back home. This could just be a stay of execution. We may still need to use your original plan of meeting your fishermen friends in the North Atlantic. If we give them too much time, with their connections, they could try pinning Vladimir's death on us as murder. My goal is to get off this continent as soon as possible!"

Rachel's happiness evaporated when she realized Seth was right. The two of them sat quietly in the car thinking of what they needed to do next.

CHAPTER 111

When they arrived in Orléans, Seth pulled into the train station. "I've got an idea. We'll take the train from here. We need to find a hiding place for the car. When we get to Paris, there will be a ton of people at the train station. We can try and blend in as much as possible. I figure they're going to watch the train station, but I think they're going to put more of their resources into looking for us travelling by car. I'm sure they already have people watching the freeway video monitors looking for this car." Seth drove around some of the alleys and side roads near the train station until he found an obscure location.

The station was open with a small crew overseeing the operations. Rachel bought two tickets on the first train leaving for Paris while Seth looked around the immediate area for a restaurant. They were both starved and exhausted. Their plan to return to the United States with Vladimir in tow was a bust since they had to kill him or be killed. Their circuitous route through the Netherlands with the assistance of some fisherman was still an option since the CIA was hot on their heels. Seth found a small restaurant around the corner from the train station that was scheduled to open in a little over an hour. He returned to find Rachel exiting from the train station.

"So what's the story on the train?" inquired the weary Seth.

"I got the first train I could to Paris. It doesn't leave for a couple of hours though."

"It looks like we're going to have to wait on the restaurant too. We might as well wait in the car and take a look at what else we have in the backpack." Seth felt that the car was the best alternative since it was cold out on this February morning.

Rachel and Seth returned to the Renault. Though Seth parked the car off the beaten path, he positioned himself to keep an eye out for any unwanted company. They split the pile of documents. Seth took the bank information and set it aside. He wanted to make sure nothing happened to Vladimir's former nest egg.

They started another pile of documents related to Vladimir and Carlos's rendezvous and other sordid dealings. Seth and Rachel couldn't believe the detailed notes that Vladimir kept. They only assumed that he kept them such that if anything happened to him, he had leverage.

"I think I found out why we're being chased," announced Rachel. She handed the documents to Seth as she wiped new tears from her face. She turned her head to try and keep Seth from noticing, but it was too late. She stared out at the nearby homes as lights began to illuminate the once-darkened community, and people slowly entered the street to begin their day.

Seth sat quietly reading the information Rachel had handed him. "Shit, you're right. That son of a bitch was one busy man. If he had not been too greedy, things could be a hell of a lot worse."

"Yeah, but it looks like things have already been put into motion," answered Rachel. "If we don't intervene soon, he may have accomplished more than he could have ever dreamed."

Seth lowered the papers he had been reading when he noticed what time it was. He also saw people milling about. "Let's get something to eat, and maybe we can think a little clearer. I need coffee and to splash some water on my face."

As they entered the restaurant, they could feel the eyes of the locals upon them. Rachel and Seth gave a polite smile and nodded to the curious onlookers, who promptly returned to their own business. Rachel ordered coffee and pastries for the both of them in her best French. After she ordered, Seth excused himself so he could go to the bathroom and wash his face. He needed to wake up. Once Seth returned, Rachel did the same.

After breakfast they headed to the train station. A number of people were already gathered on the platform waiting for the express train to Paris to arrive.

It wasn't long before they heard the cacophony of the train whistle as it approached the station slowly before coming to a stop. Rachel and Seth boarded the train and sat next to each other. They hoped to take turns catching a quick catnap before the train arrived in Paris. They placed the gym bag between them for safekeeping. They both panned the room trying to determine if anyone was watching them. They were not sure if paranoia was getting the best of them or not, but once they felt no one was watching them, only then could they slightly relax. The trip into Paris from Orléans would not take long. Seth tried to plan their next moves while Rachel napped with her head resting against his shoulder.

CHAPTER 112

The train slowly crept into the station a little after nine in the morning. Shrills of steel rubbing against steel echoed throughout the train station and in the railcar Seth and Rachel were sitting. Rachel looked out the window next to where she was seated to see if anyone looked as though they were connected to a U.S. government agency. Seth was standing in the aisle taking a long hard look out the other side as he leaned across an elderly couple. "Excuse me," commented Seth to the elderly couple. "Just looking for some friends that are to meet us." He was lying, but he needed some excuse for the visibly disturbed couple. Seth thought that they probably only spoke French, so his excuse was wasted, if nothing else he felt it sounded polite.

Seth smiled at Rachel. "Good . . . the station is nice and crowded with morning commuters. Let's try and blend in."

As the train stopped, Seth grabbed hold of the bag in one hand and Rachel's elbow with his other for a quick exit from the train. They moved calmly yet quickly with the other passengers to avoid drawing attention to themselves. They made their way through the gate and into the main station. They were almost to the front doors of the station when they noticed two men staring at them. One of the men pointed at them for the benefit of the other, and the two men began moving quickly toward Seth and Rachel.

"Those men over there are coming after us," commented Rachel as calmly as she could muster under the circumstance. She used her head to show Seth the direction of the two men.

"Yeah . . . I saw 'em too." Seth was calm and as he looked around the station for alternative exits. "Run!" shouted Seth. Seth was holding Rachel's hand as they exited the station to the right side of the main entrance and headed to the nearest cab.

As they jumped into the cab, Rachel shouted to the driver in her best French, "Drive!"

The cabdriver was startled by the sudden intrusion and asked where they wanted to go in French. Seth understood nothing the man was saying. "Just go!" shouted Seth.

Rachel could see the man wasn't responding as urgently as they hoped. So she asked the driver to take them to the Eiffel Tower in French.

Seth did not understand anything Rachel said but did catch the words "Eiffel Tower." "Are we going to the Eiffel Tower?"

"There are usually lots of people there," commented Rachel. "Besides, this driver seemed annoyed by your reaction. We need him to not remember us when we get out, and more importantly, we needed him to just start moving."

Seth liked Rachel's quick thinking. He looked out the back window of the cab and saw the two men that chased them out of the train station getting into a dark sedan driven by a third man. There was plenty of traffic to inhibit being tailed, but Seth didn't want to let his guard down for a second. Seth motioned with his head to get Rachel to notice the men getting into the sedan behind them. He asked Rachel, "Can you ask this guy to step on it?"

Rachel politely leaned forward and asked the cabdriver in French if he could drive a little faster. She indicated that they were late meeting some friends and would he mind. Seth soon felt the car moving faster.

They arrived at the Eiffel Tower. As Rachel promised, there were lots of people with tour groups and a number of people milling about on their own. A number of the people were schoolchildren dressed in their respective school uniforms with varying colors. Rachel and Seth entered a small café with a view of the great structure. They sat just inside the café out of sight of passersby but were able to see most of the area surrounding the café. They ordered coffee and a pastry. As Rachel and Seth ate their pastries and drank their coffee, they used the time to strategize. Rachel was anxious to call Sky to get him ready for their next move. She found a telephone booth in the back of the café next to the restrooms. Seth stayed at the table and kept a wary eye out for the men from the train station.

CHAPTER 113

"Sky, it's me."

"Okay, I'll call you back," responded Sky. Sky wrote down the number off his caller ID connected to his phone, compliments of the FBI.

Rachel hung up the phone and waited. It seemed to her like an eternity, but after fifteen minutes the phone rang.

"It's me," sounded the voice. Sky left his office and drove to a nearby hotel where he found a telephone booth in the lobby to call Rachel. He remembered it from his drives to and from the office. He did not want to talk to her on his phone at his desk or even at home for fear someone would be monitoring his telephone calls.

Rachel recognized the voice as Sky and gave him the bank name, account numbers and the password for Vladimir's Swiss bank account. It was the information she and Seth found in Vladimir's closet hiding place. "Look, I think there is around $5 million in the account," continued Rachel. "I want you to keep a million, my mother and sister get a million each, and the rest in an account for Seth and me." She wasn't doing all this for the money she said to herself. This was to help her and her family after her brother was murdered.

"I got it," replied Sky. "The buzz around here is that the CIA is after your respective asses."

"Yeah, we noticed," answered Rachel. "I've got more for you," continued Rachel. "I'm gonna e-mail it to you."

Sky gave her a separate e-mail address that he and the old gang maintained for illegal hacks into corporations and their other nefarious activities. Even after beginning work with the FBI, he felt he should always have a backup account for times just like this.

"I've gotta get it scanned before I can send it to you. Just keep an eye out for it."

"Got it," replied Sky. "Good luck!"

"Thanks . . . we could use some luck!"

They both hung up, and Rachel found Seth still calmly seated in the café. "Everything go all right?" asked Seth.

"A-okay!"

"Good, then you need to get a move on," commented Seth, referring to their plan they just cooked up in the small café. Seth already had requested the bill and left some money on the table as a tip. Seth wanted Rachel to leave first.

Rachel left through a back door only for employees that she noticed when she went to call Sky. She took the bag of information they found at Vladimir Petrov's farmhouse. Rachel walked several blocks, ducking periodically in to various shops along the way to check behind her to see if anyone was following her. Rachel found a subway station once she felt that she was alone. Once inside the subway, Rachel found a map and located the Université de Paris-Sorbonne (Paris IV). She bought a ticket and waited for the next train to take her to the Université de Paris á Sorbonne-Paris IV.

—

CHAPTER 114

Seth moved to a table toward the front of the café. He figured that the CIA used every resource available to them to find out where the cabdriver had driven Rachel and Seth. By moving to a table just in sight of those outside, he was hoping to be noticed by the CIA pursuers. Seth periodically would look inside the restaurant to give the appearance that he was waiting on Rachel to return. It wasn't long before Seth noticed two of the men from the train station staring sporadically in his direction. He could tell from the expressions on their faces they were angry. Seth could only assume it was because he and Rachel ditched them at the train station. Seth deliberately gulped down the rest of his coffee and made his departure from the restaurant. Before he walked out of the restaurant, he made one last deliberate gesture toward the back of the restaurant as if somehow communicating with Rachel.

Seth wandered in the opposite direction that he knew Rachel headed. He found himself wandering along the Seine River near the Notre Dame. Eventually Seth meandered into the Sheraton Hotel lobby. He called the CIA office in Langley, Virginia, and told them who he was and that he wanted to speak with someone in the Paris office. He waited, and before he knew it, the two men he spotted at the train station were outside the telephone booth where he was sitting.

One of the men politely knocked on the glass partition and indicated with his hand for Seth to step outside. Seth calmly obliged the request. Both men stood on either side of Seth. The one who motioned for Seth to exit the phone booth whispered in Seth's ear, "We want you to come with us. You can either come willingly or not. It really doesn't matter, but you are coming with us." The men standing on either side of Seth firmly took hold of his arms and led him out to the sedan that Seth had seen earlier in the day. The same driver was behind the wheel that he saw when they left the train station.

CHAPTER 115

It took Rachel no time at all to make it by subway to the Université de Paris á Sorbonne-Paris IV. Once she found the Université de Paris á Sorbonne-Paris IV, she found an informational map of the university near what appeared to be a student union. Rachel enjoyed wandering through the great Sorbonne University. She could tell from the aged buildings that it was rich in tradition without even having to know its history. She noticed the various disciplines inscribed in the facade of the respective buildings as she made her way through the campus. Rachel couldn't help but notice bicycles so inundated that they almost obstructed the entrances to the various buildings. She noticed that most of the flowerbeds were dormant for the winter. She wandered around a little more before becoming frustrated.

In her best French, Rachel asked several of the students the directions to the library. They were eager to help her. The last person she asked for directions as she made her way to the library was Will Thompson, an exchange student from the University of Missouri. Originally from Shrewsbury, Missouri, he decided to take a semester off to hone his French language skills. He had hoped once that he graduated from the University of Missouri, he might pursue a career in international business. Will was of average height and slightly overweight. His best asset was that he was well polished.

"Excuse me, are you an American?" asked Will.

"Yes," replied Rachel. "Is my French really that bad?"

Will wanted to say yes, but he was too polite. "No. I can just tell who is an American when I see them here in Paris. After a while you can't help but notice."

"Signs?" asked Rachel.

"You know . . . clothes, hairstyles . . . the look," replied Will. He felt embarrassed as he tried not to hurt Rachel's feelings.

Rachel knew it was because of her poor French. It had been sometime since she needed to speak it regularly. She appreciated Will being as polite as he was. "Look, I need to get to the library. I have some documents that I need to scan and e-mail to a friend of mine back in the States. I was hoping to use the library's resources." Rachel and Seth decided that Rachel could use the Internet access at the Université de Paris á Sorbonne-Paris IV. They would undoubtedly have scanning equipment and anything else she would need to send Sky the information they acquired at Vladimir's farmhouse. She could speak enough French to get by. Most people would never give a young woman a second glance making use of the university's resources. It would be the best place for her to go to send Sky the information. Seth, on the other hand, would lead the CIA away from her. He would be the decoy.

"Can I make a better suggestion?" offered Will. "The equipment in the library isn't bad, but you can use the computer equipment in my room. It has a lot more muscle than what they have here in the library. My place isn't far."

Rachel wasn't sure if Will was on the level or if he was hitting on her. "Thanks but . . ."

Will could see Rachel's reluctance. "Look, I'm not hitting on you. It would be my pleasure, you know, one American to another, both a long way from home."

Rachel could see that Will was just being nice. She didn't really see him as the kind of guy that would have an easy time meeting women. "Well, if you don't mind," answered Rachel.

"Come on then." Will was almost giddy. "My next class isn't for a couple hours, and I wasn't going to do anything but study for a test I have next week."

Rachel followed Will to a small studio apartment just off campus overlooking the campus. When she entered the room, she notice the bed was unmade. There were some breakfast dishes still in the sink. There was a small rickety table in the kitchen area covered in books with two chairs on each side. Off to one side of the room, she noticed a computer, a scanner, a fax machine, a printer, and piles of books. It all sat on a rectangular portable folding table. There were posters covering the walls, mostly of the traditional sights in Paris and what appeared to Rachel to be a group picture of the past season Saint Louis Cardinals baseball team. *Men!* Rachel thought sarcastically.

Will dropped his book bag onto the bed and moved in front of the computer. He turned everything on. "Whenever you're ready to begin. Do you need some help?"

"This is very nice of you," commented Rachel. "No . . . I think I can manage." Rachel worked several computers in her Naval Intelligence office and during college. She also had one in her apartment in Alexandria, Virginia.

"Coffee?" asked Will eager to please.

"Yes. Thanks. That would get great," replied a distracted Rachel. She was still worn-out from the past couple of days, and a little more caffeine would be just what the doctor ordered.

Will went over and lit the gas burner on the stove. He didn't have an electric coffee machine, so he brewed it on the stove. Will found some pastries in the refrigerator and warmed them in the oven. He put them on a plate once they were warm. He brought the coffee and pastries to where Rachel was hard at work.

She thanked Will for the pastries and coffee. He plopped down on the cluttered bed and began reading from one of his textbooks, making notes and highlighting certain text as he went along.

CHAPTER 116

Seth's head was covered with a black satin bag, and his hands were handcuffed behind his back for his ride over to the CIA's Paris headquarters for the more covert operations. He surmised that he was being driven to an old hotel near the Notre Dame because he recognized the three o'clock chimes from the Notre Dame bell tower. He recognized them from when they stopped off at the Jean Francois's to buy the Makarovs on their way to Vladimir's farmhouse near Toulouse. The two men that caught up with Seth at the Sheraton led him forcefully into the old hotel. Seth could hear them passing through a series of doors before they removed the black bag covering his head. Seth realized that once the bag was removed, he was in a full-blown CIA operation center in Paris. The men had led Seth into a back room where he was greeted by two other men he had never seen before. The room was barren except for a metal table surrounded by four metal chairs. It reminded Seth of his days as a police officer with the Charlotte Police Department except this room was a lot older.

"Mr. Seth Jarret, or do you prefer 'Chief'?" asked one of the men who seemed to be in charge.

"Seth is fine or Chief Jarret, of course." Seth was feeling cocky since he knew the CIA was somewhat behind the eight ball once Rachel sent the information to Sky.

"You have been one son of a bitch to keep up with," commented one of the men remaining in the room. The other men that escorted Seth to the location left after placing him in one of the chairs in the room. They left his hands still handcuffed behind his back.

"Thank you . . . I guess," replied a confused Seth.

The man half-smiled at Seth's reply. "We want to know what you found at Vladimir's farmhouse," stated the man.

"Who's asking?" replied Seth. He had a good idea of who was asking, but he wanted confirmation.

The man became a little annoyed. "If you don't mind, we'll ask the questions."

"Actually I do mind!" countered Seth.

"Maybe we should turn you over to the local authorities for murder," responded the annoyed man.

"Murder! I don't think so," answered Seth. "He was shooting at us. I believe that is called self-defense, even here in France."

"After you broke into his house, I don't think so. Besides, it won't matter. We'll give 'em whatever they need to convict." The man was clearly annoyed and indicated he had the political muscle to do so.

Seth knew the man was right. He decided to ease up on his sarcasm. If the CIA wanted to, they could manufacture whatever was necessary to put Rachel and him behind French prison bars for a very long time. "We found some papers," responded Seth. "Papers indicating that your man was behind the whole thing at Camp LeJeune and in Cuba. That he recruited people in Miami and helped orchestrate the whole operation wherever he needed to. It also indicated that it was CIA money behind the whole operation."

Seth was making statements he knew that had already damaged the CIA during congressional hearings. He was holding back on Vladimir's plans to kill the Venezuelan president Hugo Chavez in order to cause unrest in Latin America and South America. Vladimir had already contracted the assassination plot by recruiting a CIA operative in Panama and dispatching him to Venezuela. The plan was not the CIA's intent, but part of Vladimir's plan. He wanted to further spread anti-American sentiment throughout the region. Though President Chavez was a friend to Cuba, killing him would effectively make him a martyr and strengthen Raul Castro's power throughout the region. Seth had no intention of informing the CIA where Vladimir hid the money that Cuba had paid him to draw Tito Mendoza out so the Cuban interior ministry's men could gun him down in the warm water of a Cuban bay. This was the information Rachel was sending to Sky. Once Sky had the documents, he would direct them to the right officials in the FBI and, as a precaution, release the information to the media. Once the documents were made public, the CIA would have no choice but to back off on Seth and Rachel. Seth was buying as much time as he could for Rachel.

"Where are the papers now?" asked the man who had been conducting Seth's interrogation.

"They're in our car in Orléans," answered Seth.

The man ignored Seth's response because he knew Seth was lying. "Where's Ms. Dugen, or should I say Ensign Rachel Dugen?" asked the irritated man.

"Shopping, I suppose," responded Seth. His sarcasm was starting to creep back as time marched on. Seth noted that the interrogation had gone less confrontational than he had anticipated. He wondered if the CIA had a backup plan or if they already knew where Rachel was and was just stringing him along. He wondered if the CIA was holding Sky somewhere in Washington DC and were just waiting for Rachel to send the information they acquired from Vladimir's farmhouse. Seth realized that he just didn't care anymore. He was tired. He didn't think the CIA would turn Rachel and him over to the French authorities because of the potential political fallout. He would just play things out and see where it went.

The men continued to interrogate Seth, becoming more frustrated from his sarcasm with each question. Periodically the men would take turns leaving the interrogation room to blow off steam.

Chapter 117

Rachel e-mailed all the scanned documents to Sky and waited for a confirmation from him. When she received his confirmation, she felt a moment of relief. Sky was just the right maverick for the job. Rachel looked over at Will, who was still lying on his bed reading his school textbooks. "That's everything," announced Rachel.

Will looked at his watch. "And with time to spare to make my next class. Cool!" Will jumped up from his bed. "Can I get you anything?"

Rachel smiled at Will like a mother at her own children. "No. You have done plenty. Thanks . . . you've been a sweetheart." Rachel gathered up her things and headed for the door. Will gathered his book bag and few other items. They exited his apartment and headed out onto the street.

Rachel looked at Will. "Do you mind if I ask why you have been so helpful?

Will paused and smiled politely at Rachel. "When I saw you, you looked like a person that needed some friendly, old-fashioned American help. Your French needs a lot of work, and I was afraid that if you went to the library, the locals would have eaten you alive."

Rachel leaned forward and gave Will a big hug. "You have been wonderful. Let me pay you."

"No. You will ruin my good deed for the day," replied Will.

"Well, take the money and spend it on your girlfriend or your friends. Tell them that you saved a lonely American girl from heartache." Rachel handed Will a hundred dollars.

Will stared at the crisp hundred-dollar bill. "Now that you put it that way." Will reluctantly took the money. Rachel hailed a cab and asked to be taken to the airport. She and Seth agreed that once she sent the e-mail, she would head immediately for the airport. He told her to take the next flight to Washington DC with him or without him.

—

CHAPTER 118

A man Seth had not seen before entered the interrogation room where Seth had been undergoing four hours of questioning. The man approached the gentleman leading the interrogation of Seth and whispered into his ear. The man who had led the interrogation looked at Seth. He stood up and exited the interrogation room. As the man exited, two burly men entered and stood directly behind Seth.

The new man who was now sitting opposite Seth introduced himself. "I'm Purnell Marks." Purnell looked at the two men standing behind Seth, "You can uncuff him." One of the men pulled out some keys and removed the handcuffs from Seth.

Seth rubbed his wrists. They were sore from being restrained for the several hours he was in the interrogation room. "It's about fucking time," commented Seth.

Purnell pulled a pack of cigarettes from his pocket. "Care for a smoke?" he asked Seth as he held the pack of cigarettes out toward him.

"No, thanks," replied Seth. Seth was cautious. He knew enough about interrogations to know when he was being played.

Purnell looked at Seth. "Relax! I know you think we're playing the good-cop bad-cop routine!" He put the cigarette onto his lips and lit it with a lighter he found in his pocket.

Seth looked incredulously at Purnell. "Am I free to go?"

"Sure are," answered Purnell.

Seth cautiously stood when he realized no one was impeding his exit. As he reached the door, he stopped and looked back at Purnell. "She got the information to the FBI and press, didn't she?"

Purnell stood and methodically walked to where Seth was standing. He took a long drag of his cigarette and exhaled. "Yes." Purnell started to walk away before turning back to look at Seth. The two men moved next to Seth. "You and Rachel were pretty clever. Clever can be a bad thing, you know." Purnell moved in front of Seth and got close to his face. "I guess you probably realize by now my name isn't really Purnell Marks. I get called in when things get out of control. I . . . clean things up." Purnell turned his back and walked a few feet away from where Seth was standing while the other two men moved even closer to where Seth was standing. One of the men placed his hand across the door letting Seth know that if he wanted to leave, things were going to get physical. Purnell looked sternly at Seth. "I'm guessing that with Rachel's friend, Sky, you've probably recovered some or most of Vladimir's money."

Seth started to object with Purnell regarding the money, but Purnell cut him off.

"Please don't try and bullshit me! We know what's going on. This whole goddamn thing got out of control because Vladimir's direct supervisors dropped the fucking ball. I don't." Purnell moved in close toward Seth once again. "I assured my direct boss that once you got Vladimir's money, we would never hear from you, Rachel, or Sky again." He paused long enough for Seth to absorb what he had just heard. "Am I right?"

Seth knew the time for sarcasm was over. He also knew that Purnell, or whatever his name really was, was sent to tie up loose ends willingly or unwillingly. He was the part of the CIA no one ever talked about. Seth looked into Purnell's face. "I know you're right!"

Purnell looked at Seth with a triumphant approval. "One more thing, that whole goddamn mess in Venezuela can be forgotten as well. We know you leaked what you knew, and that we will have to fix it. As far as us wanting to knock off President Chavez, that is bullshit. That was all Vladimir trying to pump up Castro or Raul now. The Cuban government was behind all of that, but Vladimir got greedy and wanted his money too soon." He looked over at the men standing on the other side of Seth. "Take him to the airport." The man approached Seth and started to place the black bag over Seth's head. "He won't need that. I'm sure Chief Jarret will have forgotten just about everything about his trip to France by the time he reaches Orly." Purnell looked at Seth waiting for some kind of confirmation.

Seth stared intently at Purnell. "What trip to France?"

CHAPTER 119

Rachel was at the airport sitting in a bar drinking a glass of Merlot when she saw Seth walking through the terminal. "How did it go?" asked Rachel.

"It went better than I expected. The fact that I am here right now must mean that you sent everything to Sky," replied Seth. "When do we leave?"

"Two hours!" Rachel motioned to the waitress for two more glasses of Merlot. They sat and drank their wine until it was time for their flight.

"Are you sure you're all right?" asked Rachel.

Seth looked tired. "Yeah." He took a slow, deliberate swallow of Merlot. "I don't think we had better discuss this whole thing with Vladimir again. And that includes Sky!" Seth looked across the terminal and saw the two men that brought him to the airport looking back. He nodded, letting them know he had seen them.

Rachel could see Seth was a little edgy and changed the conversation.

CHAPTER 120

Rachel and Seth took an Air France flight back to Reagan International in Washington DC. Just before they boarded, Rachel called Sky and asked him to meet them at the airport. On the plane, Seth and Rachel truly relaxed for the first time. Once the plane was airborne, Seth eased his chair back and fell asleep. Rachel eased her chair back and rested her head on Seth's chest and fell asleep.

They both awoke when they heard the pilot announce for everyone to prepare for landing. "Hey, Rachel, do you think you'd like to come back and live with me on a small island in North Carolina?" inquired Seth.

"I'd love to," responded Rachel. "I don't think Naval Intelligence will try and hold me to my military contract. When can I move in?"

Seth gave Rachel a big smile. She responded by walking into his open arms and gave him a big kiss on his mouth as they stood waiting to exit the plane.

"Is this something I can expect regularly?" asked Seth in a playful manner.

"Only if you're good," replied Rachel as she slowly slipped from Seth's embrace.

CHAPTER 121

Rachel and Seth's plane arrived in the late afternoon. Sky was waiting for them as they came out of customs. Sky started to update Rachel when she cut him off. "Let's wait until we get to your car. I don't want this for everyone's ears."

Sky knew Rachel was right. What they were about to talk about was much too sensitive for just anyone to hear.

They loaded their bags into Sky's car. Rachel sat in the passenger's seat, and Seth sat in the back. Sky started the old car that took a few chugs before the engine revved up. Sky headed for Rachel's townhouse in Alexandria, Virginia. Rachel turned the car radio on rather loud. She hoped that if somehow Sky's car was bugged or someone had supersensitive listening equipment, it may drown them out.

Seth understood what Rachel was doing, but thought she had seen too many spy movies for her own good.

Sky smiled at Rachel. He loved the cloak-and-dagger stuff. Unknowingly Sky agreed with Seth that Rachel had seen too many spy movies and she had gotten too caught up in her own cloak-and-dagger.

Sky started in, "I accessed the account numbers at Banc Lucerne. What a piece of cake. Did you know Vladimir had almost a full ten million dollars in his account?"

Rachel chimed in, "You mean $5 million, don't you?"

"No, I mean $10 million. That cheap bastard spent only about a hundred thousand dollars. Most of that money came from the proceeds when he sold his house in Bethesda. I think he cashed everything in and booked to France. He was definitely going to stiff the IRS from selling his parents' business." Sky laughed to himself and then continued, "I'm sure that was the least of his concerns. Look, I opened four accounts: one for the both of you, one for your mother, one for me, and one for your sister-in-law. I transferred a million to an account for your sister-in-law. One million dollars I put into an account for me,

---

339

per your instructions. I put one million in an account for your mother. The rest I put into an account for the both of you. They're all at Banc Swiss. I was scared to leave it at Banc Lucerne but wanted to keep the money in Swiss accounts to stay out of reach of the feds, at least for a little while." Sky handed Rachel three of the four bank confirmations for her account, her mother's, and her sister-in-law. "I'm pretty sure that the CIA and FBI know we stole the money. They're not sure how much was there because the only money they really know about is from the sale of his parents' business. I routed the money all over the place so for them to trace it would be a monumental task. Besides, I don't think they really give a shit. You whacked that SOB Vladimir and both the CIA and FBI figures, you did them a favor. Ya know, tying up their loose ends."

Seth ignored what the CIA did or didn't know. He felt it would be best for all concerned to just let the whole CIA and FBI drama to end. "Sky . . . after this conversation, I think it best if none of us ever discusses what happened with Vladimir, Cuba, etc., again."

Sky looked at Rachel for a reaction.

"Sky, Seth is right. We're going to have to let it end."

"Okay," replied a disappointed Sky. "Let me just finish though."

Rachel and Seth looked at each other trying to figure out a way to take some of the wind out of Sky, but it would be best if they let him finish. They could see Sky was in his element when it came to computer spy games, so they let him continue.

"The French, on the other hand, want to know who killed Vladimir. It's all over the news that Interpol is looking into who killed that son of a bitch. I hacked into their system, and it appears that they don't have squat, so they're hoping to find a snitch or at least someone that saw something. I wouldn't recommend that either of you make a trip to France anytime soon. Both the FBI and CIA are not talking about Vladimir. It only makes them look foolish. The CIA just wants to see this whole mess blow over. So you need to keep your mouths shut, which, it appears, you are already doing. They both are smarting from the black eyes this whole thing brought about."

CHAPTER 122

Rachel waited for Sky to wrap up his harangue. She could see he was loving life. From his computer-hacker days as a corporate parasite and now with a million bucks in the bank and he an icon to his FBI computer peers, he was feeling pretty damn good. "Excellent," replied Rachel. Rachel knew Seth was right about the CIA wanting retaliation, but after listening to Sky's harangue, she knew that the CIA would hold Vladimir's death over their heads. "There is more though. We need to contact Jack. Jack Cooper. There is more to what went down last year in Cuba. I would like to see if we can right a wrong. Do you know how to find him?"

Seth couldn't believe what he was hearing. "Rachel," spout Seth. "You're not serious about pursuing this, are you?"

Rachel looked sternly into Seth's eye. "If we don't bring this whole thing out into the open, the CIA will hold it over us forever. Hell, they may bring it out just to make sure that we can't talk as we spend the rest of our days locked in some French shit-hole prison where no one would give a damn what we had to say."

Seth knew Rachel was right. The CIA could nab them in the middle of the night and in a few short hours find out that they were turned over to the French police. Seth looked back at Rachel and nodded his agreement.

Rachel smiled approvingly at Seth. "Okay, Sky . . . can you help us find Jack Cooper?" Jack was the only glimmering light of honor that Rachel could think of who was associated with the federal government. Everyone in the CIA that Rachel and Seth dealt with was more concerned about covering up the Vladimir issue than seeking the truth.

"Rachel, who do you think you are talking to?" Sky retorted. Sky changed direction and headed for his new condominium in Georgetown.

Rachel looked around Sky's abode. She would never have expected someone who was a perennial nonconformist to live in a trendy condominium. His taste in furnishings was equal to the task with a leather sofa with coordinating chairs and a marble coffee table. He had the latest in flat-screen television and stereo system. Rachel glanced into his bedroom to find a matching bedroom suit with a king-size bed. The kitchen had granite countertops with all new stainless steel appliances.

"Sky," asked Rachel, "how much are they paying you at the bureau to afford all this? By God, this is Georgetown! I'm looking around and seeing high-end of everything."

Sky immediately had gone to his computer and began booting up. He looked sheepishly at Rachel. "My folks were so thrilled that I was working with the bureau, ya know . . . a respectable job and everything that they raced up here and helped me get settled in. I, of course, added a few highlights—"

"Sky! You're not telling me that you did a little of your computer magic to get some things that don't belong to you!"

"Well . . . maybe a few things. I just couldn't help myself."

"Sky, you're with the FBI now. You can't keep doing that shit."

Sky shook his head. "Yeah, I know." He got on his computer and started hitting the keys on the keyboard. In a matter of minutes, he called out, "I got it. Jack's living in Orlando. According to what I'm seeing, it looks as though he got a transfer from the Charlotte office and a promotion. It looks like he's movin' up in the world."

"You're scaring me," commented Seth after watching Sky track down an FBI agent in another state. "You found all that in that short of a time?"

"They don't call it the information highway for nothing," responded Sky.

"Okay, boys," Rachel called out. "Let's get him on the phone."

CHAPTER 123

"Hello."

"Is this Jack Cooper?" asked Rachel.

"Yes," replied Jack.

"This is Rachel Dugen."

"Lieutenant Dugen!" replied Jack in a cordial and inviting manner. "How are you?"

Rachel was happy for the friendly greeting. She knew it would make things easier for her since she was asking a favor. "I'm doing well. And yourself?" inquired Rachel.

"Fine." Jack knew Rachel wasn't calling for free tickets for a trip to Disney. He knew she was probably about to drive the CIA and FBI crazy with her stubborn demeanor. "What can I do for you?" asked Jack.

"I need for you to meet me in Miami."

"Miami? What's this all about?" inquired Jack. Jack knew this trip to Miami wasn't going to be fun in the sun. "Please tell me you don't have more information regarding this whole Vladimir fiasco." With as much recognition as Jack got from the Vladimir fiasco, including his promotion, he wanted it behind him. Too much butting heads with the CIA wasn't the wisest career move for a federal agent. It was a steady diet that Jack was not interested in pursuing.

"I'd rather not discuss what I have to say over the phone. I'll explain when I see you." They made plans when and where to meet the next day in Miami.

"Now we need to get hold of Julio Chavez," commented Rachel. She called Julio from information provided by Sky and asked him to meet her at the same place. Julio was still in mourning from the failed coup attempt in Cuba. His fellow Cubans for Free Cuba sympathizers in Miami were thrilled that he had made such a bold move. Julio, however, took a leave of absence from the organization to grieve.

Seth and Rachel asked Sky to stay in Washington in case they needed his computer talents and to limit his further involvement. If the FBI knew what he had done thus far, he would surely have been charged with using FBI resources illegally and a host of other charges. To fire him would put a notorious hacker back into circulation, and the FBI was not about to let that happen. But some kind of disciplinary action would be warranted if they found out what he had done. Little did they know that Sky had his own plans. He was planning on taking the million dollars that he got from Vladimir's account and starting his own company. He was making plans with his old cronies back in Atlanta and using his million dollars as seed money to start his own computer-consulting firm.

CHAPTER 124

Rachel and Seth arrived at Miami International Airport and took a cab to Bayside on Biscayne Bay in downtown Miami. They went to the small amphitheater overlooking the bay. A small band was playing calypso music. The steel drums echoed in the tiny amphitheater. A group of tourists were gathered in front of the stage area. Some took seats in the small arena. The sun was shining brightly over the venue. When they arrived, Julio and Jack were already there. They moved to an outdoor café so they could watch the people at the amphitheater and listen to the band. The café was sparsely populated, so seating was a formality, and the occasional eavesdropper was a nonissue. Rachel and Seth enjoyed the peacefulness of their surroundings. They ordered coffee. Once the waitress left, Rachel started going over what she was eager to tell Jack and Julio. She showed Julio and Jack the documents she and Seth retrieved from Vladimir's house in Toulouse. For the most part, it was information with which they were already familiar since the fallout of Vladimir's death.

Rachel watched as Julio's eyes hurriedly scanned the documents he was holding. His eyes suddenly widened, and he assumed a more rigid posture as he read. "Where did you get this?" inquired Julio.

"From Vladimir's house in Toulouse," responded Rachel. "They're valid documents. Proof that Carlos and Vladimir conspired with the Cuban interior minister and set those people up in Cuba for a massacre."

Jack spoke up. "Does the CIA know this?"

Seth jumped in, "My guess is that they know all this by now. We forwarded all the information we found at Vladimir's farmhouse to the FBI and the media. The information went to the FBI because we needed leverage with the CIA. We forwarded the information to the media for leverage against the FBI and the CIA in case they both wanted to hang us out to dry. We have a feeling the reason the media never made it public was because both the CIA and FBI squashed it. It would have caused too much fallout in the Latin American community. We can only guess that the FBI and CIA are leaving Carlos alone because he knows what really went on, and if he were to be arrested, it would become public. You were the only person we knew at the fed level that we could trust. We wanted Julio here so he could see the documents firsthand and know some government department didn't fabricate this information. He is also well respected within the Cuban community, so we figured between the two of you, you could figure out how best to deal with Carlos."

Julio smiled at Seth, nodding his acceptance of the compliment.

Jack jumped in once he saw that Seth was through. "The FBI and CIA can't take him down. If we do, the Cubans here in Miami will think we're trying to shut down the organization. Even worse, they may accuse us of manufacturing this stuff to cause discord among the Cubans and the Cubans for a Free Cuba. Maybe Julio has some suggestions. Emotions down here are already on edge with the feds after that whole goddamn Ilian Gonzalez bullshit from awhile back! They'll never accept the documents from a federal agency."

"You're right," commented Julio. Julio sat in silence for a few minutes pondering viable options. "Seth and Rachel, I want to thank you for bringing this to my attention. If you would excuse us, Jack and I need to talk."

Seth and Rachel sat at the table. They both found themselves looking at Jack for some kind of affirmation.

Jack took his cue. "It's okay. We appreciate what you have done and the care you took in bringing it to our attention. I think Julio's right. Let us take it from here."

Seth gulped down his coffee and said, "Good-bye."

Rachel graciously followed suit saying good-bye to Jack and Julio.

As Seth and Rachel left the two men in the café, they knew it would probably be the last time their paths would cross. They left the documents they acquired from Vladimir with Jack and Julio.

Jack waved to a FBI agent to take Seth and Rachel back to Miami International Airport. The agent motioned his acknowledgment and promptly pulled a black sedan around for Seth and Rachel to get in. Jack gave the driver instructions to return and then watched as the sedan drove off. He watched them wave their appreciation. Jack knew he too would never see them again.

CHAPTER 125

Seth and Rachel got into the back of the black FBI cruiser. "What do you think is going to happen?" inquired Rachel.

"I think I have a pretty good idea," responded Seth.

The FBI agent pulled in front of the C concourse at Miami International Airport. The traffic was prolific with horns blasting indiscriminately. The FBI agent jumped out of the sedan and thanked them for their contribution to the FBI.

Seth wondered how much the young agent knew. He figured that the FBI agent was just being polite since he seemed uncertain of his roll.

Seth entered the bustling airport and made his way to the US Air ticket counter. Rachel stood immediately behind Seth. "One ticket for Wilmington, North Carolina," asked Seth.

Rachel interceded, "That will be two tickets."

The confused clerk stopped and looked for some indication from Seth.

"I thought you had to go to Washington," asked Seth.

"Yes . . . just not right now."

Seth blushed as he turned back to the clerk. "Make that two tickets to Wilmington."

The clerk smiled at Seth and Rachel. "Two tickets for Wilmington, North Carolina."

"Don't you need to get discharged?" asked Seth, holding the two tickets in his hand as they walked away.

"Yes. I already requested a discharge from my commanding officer, and within a few weeks, it should be coming through. With everything that has happened, they were all too eager to release me from my military contract. And I will be granted an honorable discharge. I've got a little time before I have to return. Besides, I thought you would want to drive up to DC to help me bring my stuff back."

Their plane took them to Charlotte where they changed flights to Wilmington. Seth called Ned to meet them at the airport. It wasn't long before they found themselves sitting on the deck of Seth's house watching the waves and drinking a bottle of Merlot.

CHAPTER 126

Two months later, Seth received a copy of the *Miami Herald* in a large envelope with no return address. On the front page the headlines read "President of Cubans for a Free Cuba Found Dead." The reporter went on to write, "Carlos Hernandez, president of the Cubans for a Free Cuba, was found dead in his home of a massive heart attack. Julio Chavez assumes the organization's presidency." A small note was attached to the newspaper: "Thought you might be interested." It was signed, "Your friend from Paris." Seth stood at the kitchen counter as he read the next several lines of the article. He stopped and looked back at the attached note. *Purnell Marks!* he thought. *He wrapped up loose ends.* Seth left the newspaper on the kitchen counter and walked out onto the deck where Rachel lay in the sun sipping a margarita with Argo lying at her side.